THE CANNIBAL SPIRIT

●●●

HARRY WHITEHEAD

HAMISH HAMILTON
CANADA

HAMISH HAMILTON CANADA

Published by the Penguin Group

Penguin Group (Canada), 90 Eglinton Avenue East, Suite 700,
Toronto, Ontario, Canada M4P 2Y3 (a division of Pearson Canada Inc.)

Penguin Group (USA) Inc., 375 Hudson Street, New York, New York 10014, U.S.A.
Penguin Books Ltd, 80 Strand, London WC2R 0RL, England
Penguin Ireland, 25 St Stephen's Green,
Dublin 2, Ireland (a division of Penguin Books Ltd)
Penguin Group (Australia), 250 Camberwell Road, Camberwell, Victoria 3124, Australia
(a division of Pearson Australia Group Pty Ltd)
Penguin Books India Pvt Ltd, 11 Community Centre,
Panchsheel Park, New Delhi–110 017, India
Penguin Group (NZ), 67 Apollo Drive, Rosedale,
Auckland 0632, New Zealand (a division of Pearson New Zealand Ltd)
Penguin Books (South Africa) (Pty) Ltd, 24 Sturdee Avenue, Rosebank,
Johannesburg 2196, South Africa

Penguin Books Ltd, Registered Offices: 80 Strand, London WC2R 0RL, England

1 2 3 4 5 6 7 8 9 10 (RRD)

Copyright © Harry Whitehead, 2011

*Publisher's note: This book is a work of fiction. Names, characters, places and incidents either
are the product of the author's imagination or are used fictitiously, and any resemblance to
actual persons living or dead, events, or locales is entirely coincidental.*

Manufactured in the U.S.A.

Library and Archives Canada Cataloguing in Publication

Whitehead, Harry, 1967-
The cannibal spirit / Harry Whitehead.

ISBN 978-0-670-06580-6

1. Hunt, George, 1854-1933—Fiction. I. Title.

PR6123.H578C36 2011   823'.92   C2011-903927-3

Visit the Penguin Group (Canada) website at **www.penguin.ca**

Special and corporate bulk purchase rates available;
please see **www.penguin.ca/corporatesales** or call 1-800-810-3104, ext. 2477 or 2474

FOR ANITA SIVAKUMARAN

CONTENTS

NEW YORK CITY
AND
BRITISH COLUMBIA

SPRING OF THE YEAR 1900

PART I · GRAVEBOX

AND I AM GUILTY. Disgusting Orgies? I am guilty of it all. Blood dripping off my godless fangs, black in the flame-light roaring in the centre of the great-house. Cavorting heathens. Me: legs kicking up, naked member swinging, masks of bear and wolf and raven turning all about, carved wood mouths clack-clacking. My fingers clutching at some poor waif, his blue eyes wide-open-terrified, fed on blood and liver till he was fattened up sufficient for the pot. A blow from a blade, and the fair-haired little wretch's organs spill out on the ground for my appreciation. Me—with all them naked savages about me, screeching and hollering—here's me scrabbling in the dirt to raise up a steaming kidney, a liver, a heart.

My name is George Hunt: Indian Man-Eater, Mutilator of Corpses, Cannibal—and Man of Reason. There's the rub.

Ten days have passed now, since the trial finished back in Vancouver, and I am come here to the city of New York. A whole continent traversed in a week! And after all those days on the train, I arrived late last night, creeping in like some errant husband what's been out rousting longer than he ought. The wind slapped rain at the window of my hotel room as if it were the middle of winter instead of April. I saw long avenues of stone, lights winking on and off in windows, the odd lone soul rushing between the street lamps to be somewhere, the passing of a carriage, hood drawn up tight against the weather. I thought it strange to see this city near to sleeping, as if such a place—the very heart of the world!—could ever sleep.

Now I am here in the American Museum of Natural History, amidst the dusty beams of sunlight what break the shadows to sharp angles. A long gallery stretches off to either side of me, filled up with rows of glass cases. I stand before this mannequin, with its eyes glassy balls of black, a fat mop of what looks a horse's mane perched up on its crown as hair, a moustache to match, and its face painted in the deepest brown—a face what might seem a demon's, if the sheen of its skin was not so matte, so completely barren of all life.

It has been dressed in an antique suit of body armour, arduously carven out of cedarwood and painted black. This suit of armour what is the cause of all my troubles these past weeks. It has come on ahead across this land. And now it is here.

I reach out and run my fingers along the body of the Sisiutl, the double-headed snake carved on its chest, the two mouths joining tongues at the sternum. The Sisiutl, what's coils lie twined beneath the earth. The world, and all there is in it, rests upon those coils and is subject to their movements. I see again the chieftain, Big Mountain, standing proud above the carcass of the deer, saluting the initiation of his son into the society of the cannibal dancers, and wearing this suit his ancestors had also worn for all the long generations before him.

I have been brung here to the museum as an expert—an authority on the Indians, no less. I have the book I wrote with Professor Boas in my hand (with the rumpled newspaper clippings tucked away inside). And all the past days of travelling, I have been studying its detail. *The Social Organization and Secret Societies of the Kwakiutl Indians*, by Franz Boas. My name is there, in the acknowledgments. *I am indebted to … without whose assistance …* Truth is, I know the book as a priest knows his cursèd bible. I have been reading it over and over like some schoolboy learning his dates in history, till I am so filled up with clans and family relations, with stories—myths, as Boas calls them—manners, ways of cooking, hunting, the powers of chieftains, men of medicine, and the rest, that I am ripe enough to be rotten with facts. I am to aid in cataloguing the Indian artefacts here—most of which I have collected for them myself, these past fifteen years or more, and many of which do fill up the glass cases, the walls and columns of this place.

How did this black armour come to be at the centre of my troubles? It is what Professor Boas will want to hear about. He will demand every detail. His own assistant, tried as a cannibal, no less! *Disgusting Orgies!* as it was written in the newspapers. *George Hunt accused of assisting at savage hamatsa cannibal dances where human bodies were consumed!* I imagine Boas crowing with glee when first he did hear of it. He'll poke me, like a boy with a stick at a clam, till he has drawn all nourishment from its telling. He'll glory in it, so he will. He will dissect me, measure me up like one of his skulls.

Yet the events what led up to the trial are still so scrambled in my head. David's death coming at the same time as the charges laid against me. The ritual they did accuse me of and the rituals of David's funeral all tangled together. David's death the beginning of it all. Big Mountain's suit of armour at the heart of those charges what was laid against me. A mess. A tangle indeed.

When I think on that, and on all my failings, and as I look to find some gleam of something—life? mercy? spirit?—in those black glass eyes, I realize it all does begin with yet an older tale.

It was full forty years ago and more, back when I was still a young man. At eighteen, I had come into my own by getting married. My wife was an Indian of high Kwagiulth stock—Kwakiutl, as Boas always writes the word—from one of the noble families back then in my village of Fort Rupert, at the north end of Vancouver Island, and I became a noble Indian myself by marrying her. My mother was of a tribe from further north, but my father was a white man. He was factor for the Hudson's Bay Company at Fort Rupert when I was growing up, before the company pulled out, bringing poverty on the people thereabouts. All of which is to say I am a half of each race, white and brown and maybe neither for being both. Growing up with such a mash of languages, I hardly know at times what dialect I am speaking in.

I had a friend whose name was Making-Alive. Some time after I was married, Making-Alive says to me, "Get up here to my village and we will teach you the ways of being a man of medicine, now that you is become a chieftain among the people, though you still be but a breed."

I did not believe in the ways of the men of medicine. Shamans, as Boas calls them. The word's from out of Siberia or some such, and the Indians on our coast the same as the peoples of that far continent. It is all too strange.

Anyhow, I thought here is the perfect chance for me to learn their tricks and fraudery, and, after, to expose them for the liars and the cheats they are—me being half-bred to reason, as I might put it. So up I goes to

Making-Alive's village and learned all these tricks and words and games of making medicine.

Some months after I had finished my learning, I was away in my canoe trading for the Hudson's Bay Company. It was night and I had thrown my anchor stone. I lay in the bottom of the boat and sleep was close on me, or else it had come. Now perhaps I slept and dreamt, or else it was in truth that a killer whale come up then right by my canoe. It lifted up out of the water, and hung over me, the ocean falling off its body like a waterfall. All those tons of its flanks in black silhouette against the stars, fins as wide as my canoe was long.

It spoke then, saying its name was Lagoyewilé—which means Rolling Over in Mid-Ocean. Then it changed itself into a huge man with great long arms and slick black skin like that of a seal in the ocean at night, and after that it turned to a killer whale again. So are the ways of spirits.

Its voice sounded like a wave breaking inside a cave. It told me that I would do my first healing the day after. Then it told me all the rituals I would need. I calls them rituals now, but I did not know that word then, long before the anthropologists came up the coast calling them such. Back then, they was just things as must be done.

The next day, I paddled the waters to Teguxste village, which I came to late in the day. I pulled up my canoe upon the pebbles and an old chieftain was waiting there to greet me. "Walas gigamé," says he. "You have come." The chief tells me how his sick grandson had dreamt, that very night past, that I was the only man who might save him. And now here I was upon the village shore, like as if the spirits theirselves had sent me.

Now up until I saw that killer whale, I had learned the medicine tricks but had not thought ever to put practice to them, and especially not in treating a youngster gasping on its sickbed. I thought I was white man enough to know the quackery I'd learned, and to put my faith in the ways of modern science when it came to maladies of the body.

But there I was, and now all the village was out and looking on me. I suppose the memory of the killer whale, and then the tale of the child's dream, had throwed me enough that I said I'd do whatever I could.

I stayed the day in the old chieftain's home. I didn't eat nor drink nor go out, except to wash myself in the waters of the ocean. The people steered clear of me and I did the sorts of mysterious mumblings and whisperings of preparation that was expected, those I had been taught by the medicine men of Making-Alive's village.

In the evening, they came to bring me to the greathouse. I passed along the shore in front of the buildings. All the painted totems of the village, eagle and fox, beaver and wolf, stared down upon me, till I might have run straight to my canoe and paddled off, if I'd but had the chance.

I arrived outside the entrance to the greathouse. Up to that moment I had been making arguments in my head for when the child would still be sick the next morning. But now it seemed like I was being pushed at and kept from entering inside that wide door, shaped like it were the mouth of a wolf, canines of blackened timber spiking down as if they'd gobble you up should you came close enough.

A voice came whispering in my mind. It told me I had need of cedar bark. So I spoke out and the old chieftain brung me a neckring, wristlets, and anklets of red cedar. I covered them in eagle down.

But the eagle down did something to me when it touched my skin. Later, the people said I ran away into the woods, and when they did bring me back, I was singing a sacred song.

Inside the greathouse, my senses came back to me. The village's men of medicine were sitting in a line, blankets wrapped about their waists, bare chested and daubed in black paint, eagle down upon them and red cedar rings. Their eyes glared in challenge. I knew they had not been able to save the sick boy theirselves; that I was a threat to them should I succeed. Their hard eyes did put the fear to me quite powerful. I felt myself then very much the boy I still was.

The sick child was lying between the shamans and the huge fire what roared at the centre of the room. Its flames burned to the ceiling, till a man must be sent into the rafters to douse the steaming timbers there. All the people of the village was gathered, lining the walls, and all of them silent, the only sound being that of the fire. My sweat poured down me and I was fearing even for my life if I should fail. Fearing perhaps that my white blood might betray my brown.

I followed the instructions Lagoyewilé, the Killer Whale Spirit, had given me the night before. I lifted up the boy and carried him four times round the fire. Then I sat down with the child on my lap, and the fire raging before my face.

I put my mouth to the boy's chest, where the killer whale had told me I should. I sucked, hard enough for the skin to bruise. Something came into my mouth and I spat it out into my palm. It lay there, black in the firelight, a bloody ball of sickness, a clinging, greasy worm.

I held it up for the people to see, and there was sighings and murmurings then all about. That moment when all their night terrors was made evident before them. All the proof of devilry. All of it was there in that bloody mess in my palm. So I rolled it in cedar bark and chucked it into the fire.

Then I stood the child on his feet, and fed a ring of white cedar bark down across his body and had him step out from it. I put the ring on a stick and carried it round the fire, then set it to the flame as well. I watched it burn to dust.

When I woke the next morning the boy was healed.

What was it in my hand? What was it? Well, I says it was the sickness.

Or do I say that? Making-Alive pleaded with me—when he was dying, when he knew I was writing stories of the people for the anthropologists—Making-Alive says, "Please don't tell our secrets to the white men." But there ain't nothing set in stone these days, and all secrets come out in the end.

So there I was, young muttonhead, before the people, with the sick child at my feet. The sickness what was resting in my hand: the sickness what I had earlier made it up in the forest, when I fled in the condition of my trance, with the men following behind. All right, I do confess it: my false trance! For truth is, I was but making pretense of my disposition then. Already, the lies come sloping in like wolverines to a carcass.

I had the sickness stored away in my pocket, tufts of it, given me by the shamans—tufts of eagle down. The secret sickness: eagle down! I put those tufts in my mouth in the forest, between gum and cheek. Later, with the boy in my arms, I bit hard at my tongue. Then I sucked on the child's body, and at my tongue as well, until I tasted my blood. I rolled the eagle down about my teeth, soaking up the blood until it did become a globulous mess; and it was that which I spat out into my hand.

But the truth of it—and no lies now—the truth is that the child was cured. He'd been afire with fever the night before, and me thinking influenza, what has killed so many. But the next morning, there he was, walking and eating and laughing, and me the hero. Well, I didn't hang about to soak up the praise. I got in my canoe and paddled off quick as I could, the fright of it outweighing the triumph I might have felt, the glory I might have wallowed in, there in the village.

And always since, I have had this question I can't answer: how did it work? How did I save him with such lies? I do not know.

But what stays with me—what I cannot cease from thinking on—are the dreams. First: the dream of the killer whale: Lagoyewilé, what is Rolling Over in Mid-Ocean. Too many years have gone by now. Did I truly dream it? Or was it no more than things I had been told by the shamans what taught me—things that, in the intervening years, have become the stuff of dream, of fantasy? I don't know. Many things are said of memory: how time builds our truths until they become what it is we *want*, instead of what it is we *know*.

But, more than that: what is the only truly mystifying feature—what cannot be explained at any level by dint of rational thinking—the child's dream. For it did occur the day *before* I came to the village. Of that, there just ain't no explanation I can find.

I have had the memory of that ignorance-wrought success to plague me in the years what followed, as so many I knew and loved did slip through my failing fingers into death. As the skills I learned from the men of medicine, and the skills I learned thereafter from science: as all those skills did fail me, and as everyone died, one after another after another.

Right up till the last. Till Harry.

HARRY CADWALLADER had just climbed up onto the jetty from the deck of the *Hesperus* when he heard the steamer's whistle blow. Out there in the darkness, it would be coming round Beaver Point and pointing its nose shoreward. Before long he saw its lanterns bobbing and reflecting on the black water. He smelled rain in the air.

He sat on an empty fifty-gallon can to wait. The three electric lamps along the jetty cast dim sodium pools, the generator coughing behind the village. He took off his hat, put it down beside him, and rubbed his fingers over his forehead, then rubbed his fingertips together. The calluses were going soft. He leaned forward, hawked, and spat down between the wooden planks. He was turning into a landsman.

That same tune in his mind. Round and over and over and round. He hummed quietly to himself. *Where I am going, well, you won't never know …* It was his mother used to sing that. But he put such black thoughts away.

He looked down on his boat. *Hesperus*, read the name on the prow, as he had repainted it in black and gold a week before. Most of the day he had spent on his knees, polishing the decks and all the timber, from rudder to prow—thirty-six feet, and ten more to the tip of her bowsprit. The deck had a central hatch leading down to the hold, steel-hinged and always locked. There were canned foodstuffs, a tough-sealed sack of rice, and three cases of his trade in there. He had spent a long hour polishing the locks and other metal on the *Hesperus* with whale grease, till they had fair burned in the late-afternoon sunlight.

The pilothouse, forward of the stern, was near high enough to stand erect inside, windows to side and front. He'd buffed those windows till they glittered like crystal. He had taken out and polished the pans and plates and cutlery, then he had re-stowed them, piece by piece, in their cupboards and drawers. The machete over the doorway was honed till a leaf would part if dropped on its cutting edge.

The boom stretched back above the deck almost to the pilothouse. If the mainsail had been patched more than once, but always neatly, now he had it furled clean and tight, as were the jib and spinnaker. She'd been schooner-rigged when he'd purchased her, though with masts of equal length. He'd straightway had the mizzen out and re-rigged her as a sloop. Then he'd placed in an engine where the mizzen base had been, and a damned fine thing it was, rare too, especially this far north along the coast. He'd been down there earlier, but even he, rat-nose keen for muck wherever it might be, could find no stain on her.

She was quite perfectly prepared for travel. "Mr. Scrub-scrub!" Grace would say. "You a man at the curtain, ready to leave." It was true. Yes, it was true.

There was a small wooden plaque above the pilothouse door that was there when he'd purchased the *Hesperus* in San Francisco, two years before. It read, "For I can weather the roughest gale, that ever wind did blow." He liked that, though he did not know its origin.

He looked to shoreward. The fires flickering through the heavily curtained doorways were the only visible light in the village of Fort Rupert. It got deathly dark once the sun was down, excepting when a family had one of their pagan jamborees on the beach. Then some preposterous bonfire would threaten to rain down burning embers upon the whole village, and even the forest—some hundreds of yards away, as, over time, the trees had been felled for their timber—even the forest got filled up with sly-darting shadows.

He hummed, *Fixing to leave … Fixing to go … Where I am going … Well you won't never know.* Ashore till dead? Well, he'd been ashore this whole winter through, and that was long enough. Best slip quietly away and be done with it. Gone. Away. An ocean away. The whole-wide-world-beyond-the-ocean away. That was how it was. How it was going to be. They could have believed nothing else of him. Surely they could not? And wouldn't it just hand his father-in-law the opportunity to shake his fat head and spout on about how he'd always known it, how he hadn't never trusted the man, shouldn't never have given him those privileges he had and so on and so forth and so on and on, as Harry knew old George would. And he'd be right, so he would. Proven right, and properly self-righteous with it, no doubt.

Whatever George's rantings and ragings might come to, Harry would be off with a pre-dawn spring tide—in the coming day or two—and there'd be the end of it.

A woman's voice called out from the direction of the sea. He rose up from his seat, staring out through the murk as it wailed in the Indian tongue, sounding some ritual lament, before falling away once more into silence.

Now he could make out the steamer's bulk as it approached the jetty. He heard the clank-grind of its paddles as they slowed. There were voices behind him and, turning, he saw that people were gathering, some to take the produce that would be coming from the steamer. But there were others as well, men and women who were his family now that he had married into them.

George Hunt came plodding down the jetty, the people parting to make way for him, his huge, grey-bristled head hunched low into his shoulders. When he glanced Harry's way, however, his eyes lacked utterly the rancour of the dispute that had arisen between them earlier. Instead, those eyes were empty now, black pits sucked dry of sentiment. Harry stepped nearer to the gunnels anyway, away from harm, humming quietly all the while.

Steam exploded, men called out, and the steamer docked. There beside the rail was a youngish Indian woman, her fat moon face ruddy from the sea, tears streaking the sea salt on her cheeks into broken rivulets. George stepped forward. He mumbled a greeting to her, and she bowed her head, her hands clenched upon the worn wooden handrail.

George crossed the gangway to the boat. Harry waited, uncertain whether he had a part to play in this drama. The woman's hands reached out. The old man took them in his. The two of them stood, heads close together, as the men worked around them to unload the goods from deck to shore.

Harry was jostled by those who had come to heft from off the steamer the blanket bundles and boxes of fish oil, dried fruits and meat, letters and parcels, tins of salmon, vegetables, cooking oil, and fifty-gallon cans of gasoline for the generators. He had himself been waiting on stock for the Hunt family's trading store, of which he was manager, playing out the role he had been given by his Indian family. A man called to him from the deck of the steamer. Harry stepped up the gangway.

"There's seven cans, when I ordered thirteen," he said, after nosing briefly through the paperwork. He spat and cursed. Yet, all the time, he watched as well his father-in-law and the young woman. What was occurring? What should be done?

Then Harry saw the roughwood coffin lying on the deck near by the woman's feet and he understood.

The steamer blew two short whistles to tell that it would shortly leave. Charley Seaweed appeared at Harry's side and took hold of his arm. "Fat Harry," he said, "now help we take David home." Charley called two of the village men over. The four of them put themselves each to one corner and hefted the coffin. They lifted it high to their shoulders and eased it down the gangway toward the jetty.

As they did so, George Hunt reached out and placed his hand on the wooden box that held the remains of his son, David. The great, scar-stippled fingers, just a few inches from Harry's eyes, pressed down upon the lid a moment.

The rain came down now through the almost windless air, heavy and straight and no one taking notice. Harry blinked, the coffin heavy on his shoulder. The orange lamplight reflected in the drops that clung to his eyelashes. He'd left his hat on the fifty-gallon can where he'd sat to wait on the steamer's arrival.

People lined the jetty. Word must have gone out in that swift, silent way Harry did not understand. The village had come to see the body of one of their chieftains returned. Now, blanket-shrouded men and women moved toward him, tattered stovepipe hats and frowning faces, the jetty boards creaking beneath their presence. The weight of the coffin lightened as others put their shoulders to it.

Through his water-hazy vision, Harry saw George helping David's wife, whose name was Abayah, from the boat.

The work of the jetty had stilled and all stood solemn now as the body was carried past. Women took to wailing and one man called from far back along the jetty, "Hap hap hap!": the cry of the cannibal dancers. He'd heard

12

it often enough during the past winter months, when all their heathen rituals carried on through endless, rain-drenched days and nights.

They carried the coffin through the crowd and onto the wooden plankway that ran along the bank above the beach. They passed before the cedarplank house fronts, the people following in a column. Firelight flickered from entranceways. Ancestor poles rose into the darkness: silhouettes of beak and claw and wing and fin. It seemed to Harry as if the images of thunderbird and whale, of raven, eagle, and of bear, gazed down on him as on some charlatan hawking false oils and charms. He whistled his tune softly to himself. *Ready to leave ... Ready to go.*

Someone stumbled behind them on the planking. A swift-hushed laugh fell flat, and now they were outside the family greathouse. Harry placed one hand on the tall pole that rose in front of the building. Behind him, he heard the shuffling of the people through the hiss of the rain. The doorway was painted as if it were the yawning jaws of a killer whale. Harry's mother-in-law, Francine, was standing there, stout against the light behind.

Harry and the other men manoeuvred the coffin down until they held it in their hands. Then they edged through the entrance as Francine stepped aside. Tears glistened like amber on her elsewise expressionless face.

The bonfire in the centre of the house was lit, its flames flashing toward the timbers. Rain fizzled faintly as it fell through the smoke vent and onto the burning wood. The men walked round the fire to the far end. They placed the body on the low platform there.

Harry stood straight and cricked his neck to left and right until the tension gave with a crack. The massive house posts rose up beside him, carved to look like gross, lumbering figures with outsize heads, their mouths open as if voicing surprise. All about the room were the masks and blankets, the giant carven boxes and eating troughs that were the heirlooms of the Hunt family. The fire was the only light in the room, and he squinted to see who might be lurking in the twisting shadows.

George stood just inside the doorway, his bulk wrapped, shapeless, in a blanket, so that he seemed some dark spirit himself, come down off a pole to brood among the people. Abayah and Francine stood to one side; and now Harry's wife, Grace, appeared and walked over to join the women. She placed her forehead against Abayah's. The two of them rested their arms on each other's shoulders. Their bodies shook.

Four women shuffled in and passed to either side of George. They made their way to the fire and squatted on the hard-packed earthen floor, cocooned in their blankets so that only their round faces beneath their wide basket hats were visible. They were all of them old, their eyes sunk deep into tough skin. One of them was Charley Seaweed's dwarfish wife, near as bowed and twisted as was he. One mumbled and then another wailed. The others took up the sound.

Abayah and Francine came forward now to sit side by side before David's body. The other men who had helped carry the coffin filed out. Harry made to do the same, but Charley stopped him. "Stay put," he said. "You only son George now."

The words made Harry breathe harder; but he walked across the room to stand beside his father-in-law. Ravines cut through the leather of the old man's half-paralyzed face, so animate on one side, the flesh hanging limp off the other. It told the tale perfectly of the two men locked inside that heavy body, the one so quick to laughter, the other to black humours and rage.

The women finished their wailings at last. Francine now spoke throaty, singsong words in the Indian language. Her voice caught at times, and she would cry out, leaning forward where she was sitting and placing her hand upon the coffin. As she spoke, George's blue eyes flared in his brown face, staring off into the darkness, though there was nothing there.

After Francine was done, she rested with her hands upon the coffin, her head bowed over it. The other women rose to their feet and shuffled out, with Charley following. The only people now remaining were George and Abayah, Harry and Grace. As she came close, Grace gripped Harry's upper arm, as if to keep from collapsing, and then they sank down to rest, all of them, upon the ground in front of David's coffin.

14

"A CHIEFTAIN COMES HOME. He has been called by the owl. He is looking for his ancestors, in the ocean, up among the trees, in among the stars. Dead-broken now." That was how Abayah called to us from the steamer that night.

I woke before the dawn, the morning of my son David's final coming home. My wife, Francine, was grunting and snorting in her sleep beside me. I laid a palm on her fat haunch and it shivered some, but she soon quietened into proper restfulness.

I rolled over and put my feet down off the platform. The tamped earth was cold. My toes searched out my boots and slipped inside. The last embers from the fire threw up vague shadows from the beaks and maws of the masks of our ancestors on the walls. I thought on those ogres and other demons of the forest which such shadows did paint for me when I was still a child.

I drew my ragged number four mark blanket about me. My joints creaked and cracked as I paced across the floor and through the heavy curtain outside.

The black was just coming greyer off east. The air was clear enough so that I saw the silhouettes of the mainland mountains starting to show theirselves, if yet the breath streamed out of my mouth in foggy billows at the cold.

I was up at an old man's hour, early enough to even beat the others of the village. A dried-out stump I'd hacked into a stool was parked up by the painted timbers of our greathouse. I sat to watch the village rouse itself.

There weren't stars, so I knew the day would come grey and flat, but without rain, the clouds being higher than the mainland peaks. The air smelled of salt and rotting fish from the beach, the rank stench of the middens behind the houses blown off inland by the fair breeze coming from the sea.

The tide was at ebb and, soon enough, the first of the women came out from the other greathouses what stretch off round the curving shore to either side of ours. Shona-ha, Chief Owadi's wife, raised her old crow-claw hand, and I nodded back with respect enough to keep her happy. She stepped down the steep bank to the pebbles, waddled away with the others toward the ebb, their baskets like snail shells at their backs, and then they bent to the task of gathering cockles.

Dawn was brighter in the air, and the high clouds raced over the sky, heavy from the east and north. After all there might be rain, if late in the day.

The first curses, farts, and hawking started from the houses. Henry Omxid stepped out from the building next to mine—cousin, clan-relative, like almost all the people are to me what is left now—naked and wrinkled like an antique toad, his fat belly sagging down over his stick legs. He flapped his arms and beat his hands at his shoulders. He grunted toward me and I told him just how he looked.

"You can go bugger a walrus," says he by way of reply, cheered no end at his own fine words. He looked to the sky. "Cold," he says, in English to make it a curse. "Rain come slow. But come." Then he turned back inside.

Others were moving on the beach now. Two men—Pax'alu and his son—was working a net back into a ball where it had laid spread the night through, drying. A few fires was being kindled outside doorways, but mostly smoke belched out the smoke holes up top of the high-sloping timber roofs of the greathouses.

I could hear Francine rustling about inside now. She'd be making up a cooking fire in the back with the last glowing coals from the night before, cursing me for taking my ease whilst she, unhappy woman, laboured at my coffee.

Chief Owadi came down the plankboards toward me, stamping warmth into his old legs. The planks groaned as he stepped off their end onto the pressed earth, his black-bear fur hat sliding sideways down his long face, him pushing it back up, then hitching his best blanket tighter about hisself. He greeted me gravely enough as he passed by, though his eyes was elsewhere as he did so. Likes his promenade up and down the beach each morning, so he does, puffed old goose.

A few of the children—and there is only a few left any more—was scuttling about, most of them naked now that it was March and spring, whatever the cold in the air. Two boys chased by, one with a stick of thin cedar by which he poked at the other, screeching out his triumph in spearing the great whale.

Francine stepped through the curtain. I took the tin cup what steamed with the fine morning brew from her hands.

Filled up with all those good things about me, I took hold of her ankle. "Whale woman," says I, shaking her so her calf wobbled. "Plenty of meat for all." She just kicked out with her other sealskin-wrapped foot so I near lost my coffee, spoke a few words on the foul sight of my balls cooling in the morning air for all to see from under my blanket, and went back inside.

I gulped a scalding mouthful of coffee. Out along the far end of the jetty, where the water was deep enough still for it to float, my son-in-law Harry Cadwallader's boat, the *Hesperus*, was bobbing. Harry. It was my first jarring thought of the day, for Harry and me didn't see exactly eye to eye, nor never rightly had since he married my Grace.

Charley would say, "The thing with Fat Harry is he's a better man than he thinks he is." But there was darkness in him, I could see it. Something terrible out of his past murking up his mind, like a still pond in which a hooked fish thrashes at the bottom till it has clouded all the water with silt.

But I had work to be doing today, and I meant to get it done. Francine called me inside. We ate a hot slab of dry salmon with a bowl of eulachon oil, the rotting black paste reeking sweetly in my nostrils. The early fire smoked, the faggots wet still from the night and from the hard rain the day before. It fogged the air till I felt for a time outside of things, the sharp lines of the timber walls, the masks and pillars and platforms twisting and curling, losing all sense of the solid.

So I shook myself to my feet and says, "I must be to it."

The family store is down the far end of the village. I gave all I saw a fair good morning. Most was on the beach now, working the boats—carved canoes, with a few of the white man's plankboard hulls as well—or they was standing about gossiping.

At the store, where Harry and Grace did most of their living, I called to them my presence and sat in the rocker on the porch. Harry came out and leaned on the porch-post to stare at the water. Grace was tra-la-la-ing out back, the first songbird of spring.

The account book was on the table there, where someone must have been working at it earlier. I picked it up and had a poke through. "You've not been keeping these as you might," I says to him, after a time.

"I've followed the methods as were used previous," says he. He folded his arms tight about him.

"Well then, you've put the numbers in wrong." He hadn't though. Winter's when the people are at their poorest and trade comes down almost to nothing. I was seeking for a fight.

Harry paced up and down some. That boy's like an ember on the air sometimes, spinning about, glowing hot, but scarce a sound to be heard. Shouldn't call him boy, I suppose, him in his forties. But too old for Grace, so I was thinking.

Shortly, he turned to me. "I've done all the books as clear and true as is. If you've a problem elsewise, then let's have it." Found some spunk at last, he had, though at the time it just brought me to anger.

Well, we swapped a few hot words. Harry says I never did trust him, and what reason was there for that? And I says, why should I, coming in off the sea out of the blue yonder? Did he think I didn't know what his hold was filled with? Well, it was you gave your assent to the marriage, says he. Maybe I was a fool, says I.

It was only Grace who came out front and broke it up. "You two idiots don't know better than to fight among yourselves, whilst the world's out there with teeth just waiting to bite you," says she, or words like them. Harry went away down the beach, whistling some tune over and over to hisself, and I collected the bundle I had come for and slunk off back home. She has the fury of her mother, and they's the only ones ever could shut me up.

They was small-minded things we spoke to each other, Harry and me, but they set me in a different mood, so that, by the time I perched myself

18

down at my desk in the corner of the greathouse, nearby the door with the curtain thrown back for light and a candle burning, I had to put away two sheets of paper as I sprayed the ink or lost my track of thinking. But, shortly, I got to settled. My old desk, she's a fine item. I built her myself some years before, fine-planed a single, fat plank of aged and knotted red cedarwood to smoothness, carved old designs what I have seen from caves and rocks, primitive and ancient, about its edges.

The bundle was by my side, wrapped secure in hide. In it was the very suit of armour what stands before me now, here in the museum. I had a letter and the story of it to finish writing for Professor Boas, to go with the bundle by post across the country and on down to New York. I sat industrious for some hours describing details—Boas do love the details—till, at last, I felt a tug at my shirt sleeve. Henry Omxid's granddaughter, four years old, buckteeth, black eyes always filled up with surprise, was at me to come out and play. It was already past our usual time. So I stretched up my arms, and groaned some. I put the writing I had done with the letter into its envelope and sealed it. I checked that the bundle was secure under my desk. It would go on the steamer due that evening.

Then up and out into the late-afternoon light, and we was away down to the stones on the beach, me to hurl them out beyond the tide, and her bouncing in delight or sulking when each of her own great, serious hurls fetched a pebble but an arm's length forward, or once, glorious, into the water as it broke so gentle on the shore that afternoon.

When she was called in for supper, I sat on a boulder, watching the weighty clouds to the north as they did gather, ready for the dark to fall so that they might roll down to fall upon us.

Then I heard the steamer's whistle, and Abayah's words came floating cross the water. My old ankles twisting on the pebbles after, as I dashed for the jetty. It is terrible waiting so long the waiting turns ordinary, but then quite suddenly it's happened. He was three years dying, my son.

We brung David's body to the greathouse, the people following. Francine piped up, voicing the old words a mother speaks to her dead child. "What is the reason that you have done this to me?" she says. "I have tried hard to treat you well since you came to me. What is the reason that you desert me, child? Did I treat you wrong? Maybe I did something to you in the way I treated you. I will try better if you come back to me. Please become well once more in the place you are going. And when you are well come back to me, child. Do not stay away there. Please have mercy on me, your mother."

She spoke them as a real mother should to a dead child. A blessing poor Lucy was not there to face that grief herself. Lucy: my first wife. Still, Francine loved David as her own, and Grace loved him as a full brother.

But when Francine spoke, the years did fall away to nothing. I felt again my love for poor, dead Lucy as a torment almost more than I could bear. I confess I hardly was thinking about David at that moment at all. The faces of all my dead rose up before me in the firelight: my two babies what died young, my father and my mother, my brother and my sister, and all those others I have knowed; all dead of some disease or other.

We did sit together all the night through beside my David's body. My poor boy, what I could not save. Not him, nor any of the others I have loved. I was a man of medicine; so called, but not in fact, by all my failures what followed.

That night beside David's body I don't know where my head did travel. Black places. Places populated by the spirits of my grief and of my powerlessness, fuelled as well with rage at the scheming of those against me. I did not think the day would ever come again.

THE DAWN CAME TRICKLING through the doorway to the greathouse. Harry was sitting beside the embers of the fire, poking at them with a half-burned stick and wondering what was to follow. Funerals happened quickly among the Indians, usually the day after death. There had been several in the months he had been among them in Rupert. They died so easily, victim to ailments a white man would snuffle with and, like as not, shrug off in time.

The real question was what kind of burial George had in mind: Christian or heathen? The old man was huddled before the coffin, his blanket wrapped about him, his head down on his chest. Abayah and Francine dozed on a platform to one side. Harry's wife had slipped off somewhere before dawn as he slept.

"Mr. Hunt," Harry spoke, at last, to the old man's back. "Should we not be making plans for the day?"

His father-in-law's head drew up and turned a little, showing the outline of his sharp nose, his thick, grey moustache. "We'll have the gravebox," he said. "Tell the people. He'll go to the island."

Harry fought down the ire he felt at the man's curt manner. He had just lost his son. It wasn't the time for such thinking. It was a time to help. He pushed himself to his feet and walked out into the morning.

Outside, he raised both arms and stretched, then took stock of the day. Mist floated low on the ocean. There was no wind. The sun was still behind the mountains of the mainland to the east. It was cold. The tide was in, and the jetty stretched out into the faintly lapping waters, the pebble beach a narrow line at the bottom of the steep bank. The *Hesperus* bobbed at its mooring out at the jetty's end. To left and right, the wooden roofs of the village arced away around the shore. The world smelled of seaweed, salt, and rotting fish.

His eyes followed the great ancestral pole by the doorway up along its length. The Bakwas—the wild man of the forest—then wolf, frog, human, thunderbird, killer whale, and, forty feet above, the great beak of Raven. If he knew by now to name them, still he could not have described their meaning. He placed his hand against the pole's wood. Rough grain and cold dew. Then he pulled his greatcoat about himself more closely and turned along the beach toward the trading store, at the far end of the village.

Here and there, men and women were already out, a few wrapped in the thick grey or filthy white blankets of the Hudson's Bay Company. Others wore faded shirts or shabby sweaters and pants. Men were folding the nets, left out the night before like always in the faint expectation they might ever dry. Women sat outside the houses, speaking to each other in low tones as they prepared food.

"Yoh," he greeted them as he passed, feeling the idiot using the Kwagiulth word, but knowing they liked him for it. They nodded, but without their usual humour, sombre to the relative of a dead chieftain, even if Harry was no more than a white man.

He stepped off the plankway at its end and onto the path that ran along above the beach. Two dogs, mange and insect ravaged, nipped and snarled around the rotten head of a halibut. Harry aimed a stone with a well-practised foot. A yelp brought him some faint satisfaction after the hardships of the night.

"Yoh," a voice called from a shadowed doorway. "Fat Harry." He stopped. A face appeared, a foot lower than Harry's own, black close-set eyes in weather-beaten skin, a smile, long on humour, short on teeth.

"Charley," Harry said.

"What news today?"

"He goes to the island."

"Walas gigamé!" said Charley, lifting both his hands into the air, the deformity of his back becoming visible as he stepped through the doorway. "David was man of people. Good for George remember."

"Will you help me pass the word?"

"Em," Charley nodded. "You don't worry. I tell people." He stepped back inside, his oversize head retreating into darkness.

Harry breathed relief. Charley Seaweed might be a cripple and a buffoon, but he would let the village know, and spare Harry his blunders. Fat Harry the American. Kwagiulth by marriage only and, if he understood it right, even then never more than a guardian of the crests and chiefly seats for his future sons, if they should come. And he'd never manage the language, so longwinded was it. He couldn't even separate the words from the throaty, singsong gibberish they spouted. If he spoke some of the Chinook jargon of exchange, still that made him but a trader in their eyes. And as to their propriety, it was a treacherous maze: he'd been scorned more times than he could think on for some paltry blunder of convention.

It was all inside out and back to front. "Fat" Harry for being so scrawny, when he was master of the *Hesperus* and ran the store with all its riches. Slim like a wolverine, so Grace would say. More like a weasel, he thought, if he caught sight of himself in a mirror: the sharp angles of his cheeks behind his moustache, the black wells of his eyes. Eyes like an Indian's, Grace said.

The first shoots were showing on the trees at the edge of the forest. Yes, spring was on them. *Fixing to leave* ... And now David, the brother-in-law he'd never met, was to be buried in the pagan style, heathens whooping and leaping and him caught up in all their depravations. He'd have to delay his departure a few days yet. He couldn't hardly duck out at such a time. It would be, well, unseemly, however George had riled him with his accusations. It didn't make a pile of difference, anyhow, when all was said and done. He'd be away on a spring tide and that was that. A few days here or there made no difference.

He thought on the first day he'd come to Rupert. Late October last. He'd borne in with a nor'wester chewing at his cracked face, barely conscious with exhaustion from days spent tacking, without a chart, in waters he'd never sailed, his fuel long finished.

He tied off and, hardly able to lift his legs, climbed up onto the jetty. He had learned from previous stops along the coast that ignoring the newcomer was the peoples' way, at least until he'd shown the reason for his visit, or if he might have some usefulness to them.

"Just fool be on sea in storm," a voice said; and there, slouched on the planking, bundled up crooked in a blanket, so that Harry had mistaken him for some shapeless stack of trade goods left forgotten at the jetty's end, was Charley.

"You got that right," said Harry.

"Have baccy?" Charley said, and "Mmm!" his lips wobbling, "Nice box!" when Harry handed across his ornate tobacco tin. Charley rolled and lit, passed back the tin, not without reluctance, and then directed Harry toward the trading store at the far end of the village.

He stumbled along past the buildings. There was no one to be seen on that cold day. Outside the store, his future wife was perched in an ancient rocking chair, smoking a long reed pipe. She wore a blue cotton dress that rode up, showing enough of her strong legs to draw his attention. She seemed insensible to the weather. On her head was a wide basket hat, her round face and sharp-slanting eyes imperious beneath.

"You need engine for you boat, Mr. Whiteman," she said. "Then you face not look like dry halibut now." She leaned far back in the rocker, until Harry thought she had to topple, and roared, beating her thigh with her palm. Harry laughed along with her.

"I've an engine," he said, which impressed her right enough, "just nothing to fuel it."

But there was no spare fuel to be had in Rupert. So he'd sent an order south with the next steamer, and waited.

Now, outside the store, Harry stood to take a breath. So overdue a paint was the building's facade that the exposed planking was grey and cracked and warped. Above, the steep roof grumbled its reminder of repairs. He liked things ordered, but the winter weather had kept him from doing much about the building's exterior.

He mounted the steps. He fumbled in his greatcoat pocket for the key, but the door was already on its latch. Inside were soft movements. He peered in through the grime on the window to see his wife peering back, her treacle skin darker still in the store's gloomy light.

"Ya, Caddie," she said and pulled open the door. "I make food."

"David's to be buried on the island."

"Ah," she said, nodding slowly, seemingly to herself.

She stepped into the daylight. They stood for a long moment staring into each other's eyes. Then her mouth fell, her cheeks took to quivering, and she walked two small steps to rest against him. He put his arms about her waist, thinking how her body always reminded him of a seal, the layer of fat and the elastic vigour beneath.

"Caddie," she wept into his chest. "My great brother is dead."

He found that he was stroking her hair, and was surprised by his tenderness. Over her shoulder the forest was a scant hundred yards away. He wanted to run away into the woods to hide. *You'll never know ...*

"I have come to ask that I may take your daughter in marriage." The day he'd gone to speak with George. Nervous like some junior tar sent up before the captain; but near feverish for her—black-eyed coquette always in his vision, whichever way he looked.

She'd be on the jetty each morning when he lifted the door to his boat's hold—wherein he slept—and emerged on deck. There'd be nothing but a blanket wrapped about her, her hair drawn tightly back so that she looked stern, yet girlish too. "Still here, Mr. White Man?" she'd say, or "Scratching balls and yawning, new day is dawning!" or "You dreaming 'bout me down in there, Mr. Caduwudduder?," tapping on the hull as she said it. She never could speak his surname, even now she was married to him. And she did plague his thoughts each night, as he lay alone in the hammock, if yet his dreams were always darker.

He'd walk the shore and she'd be always nearby when he turned about, until the people took to sniggering, and Charley piped up one day, "Best see to her, or people say you a white man have no cock."

He would have made advances, but that he'd already met her father.

"What have you in the hold?" George Hunt glared down from the jetty, his frame looming like a grizzly's in silhouette against the bright sky. It was a few days after Harry had first arrived. "More liquor for those already lost?" He was right, of course. The hold was loaded with cases and kegs of New Westminster whisky. It was his third trip up the coast, though he'd not come this far north before.

"I trade what I am able," Harry said.

"My family's traders also," said Hunt. Harry said he did not seek to impose himself upon the man's market; that he was grateful for the help afforded him by the people of the village; that he'd take receipt of his fuel when it should arrive, and be on his way.

"See that's all you take," said Hunt, and stamped away along the jetty toward the shore. Harry'd not risk the wrath of such a man by dallying with his daughter, maddening though she was to the balance of his mind.

When his gasoline arrived, however, he found the days passed and still he did not leave. He'd stop by the trading store. They would make pretense of discussing the price of various produce, the state of the clouds that day and what it might mean, the passing of a steamer visible out on the ocean. She was shy herself by now, and her humour had quite faded, until they barely looked at each other and could only stutter absurdities, before one or the other would scurry off. Harry felt himself a boy just out of puberty again.

Then one night there came a tapping on the deck above his head, and when he pushed up the trap door, she slipped inside, all chance of sailing without mischance from this landing was lost, and, soon after, he found himself asking a man he feared for the thing that man would be least willing, as he thought, to give.

So Harry spoke the words, but George Hunt said nothing, his huge body squeezed into his chair before the cedarwood desk in a corner of the greathouse, a sheaf of close-written paper laid neatly out before him, his hard eyes on Harry. So Harry squirmed and his feet shuffled like he had no control of them, until he found himself speaking words he would never otherwise have spoken.

"I know I ain't much," he said. "Indeed, I don't say I'm much of anything at all. But I have my boat and the things I know and, such as I am, I'd promise to do right by her." He resented George for drawing this from him as soon as it had been said. And was it not about as far from the truth as could be, just waiting as he was for his moment to escape?

But what made him even ask, when he'd had his taste of her already?

Oh, he wanted more, of course he did. The fine tilt of her eyelids, each alien twist of her thinking, her skin beneath his fingers, her tomfoolish jokes: he wanted more and more. And she was a good, strong woman:

26

raucous, but honest. A decent wife for any man. Still, he'd hardly been seeking such permanence. All the years at sea, gathering what fortune he could. And now he had his treasure, the *Hesperus,* and the world spread before him. He flew before the winds of his fate. He didn't tack against it, as someone had once put it to him.

In any case, the winter storms came howling down the island's coast-line off the Pacific, until it was not hard to persuade himself he had to stay. If only till the spring. So he'd promise to do right by her, he told Hunt, in the gloomy month of December, and then he said it again. But still the old man was silent, until Harry shivered at the duplicity of his own tongue, and some deeper shame came upon him. There was something, after all, when he thought on it. Something he sensed in himself that day before his future father-in-law. It felt like what? Respite? The thought of setting out upon the ocean suddenly felt too much to cope with. Running before a wind. Always running. And now to have an end to it! To feel peace. He thought on Grace until he was certain that his words were true. He would do right by her. Yes. He'd support her—and, yes, he'd do right by all these people here.

So he stood fast under the eagle gaze of George Hunt. He did his utmost not to jitter, remembering Grace's words to him: "My father is a big man, but not a bad man. Don't shake like fish in a boat. Look him right back."

At last, Hunt spoke up. "You've heard of my labours here?" He gestured down at the papers on his desk.

"You write about the Indians."

Hunt glared up through the thorny twists of his eyebrows. Then he reached and brought down a book from off the shelf above the desk. He held it up to Harry, made almost as if to hand it to him. But then he threw it down on top of the papers. The candle spluttered, showing a rough leather binding, black in the flickering light.

"Written of them?" Hunt said. His voice was like a gathering wind, blowing up toward a squall. "Whole books. On us, mind! For what is my family if it ain't Indian?"

Harry said nothing. He had heard plenty from Grace already about the man's book that he had penned with some famous scientist out of New

York. It puffed up his bride-to-be like a cock turkey when she spoke on it. He'd even had a leaf through, though he hadn't taken a whole lot of sense from it. The Indians' ways and doings, rituals and clothing, how they built their canoes and the like. Truth was, it made Harry all the more nervous in his presence. Six and a half feet of trader, Indian chieftain, writer of books ... even scientist.

"Our skin is brown," said Hunt, "and we are a family of substance."

"I don't have no prejudice like that," Harry said, and carefully.

Hunt leaned forward, his chair groaning, to better look at him. Harry directed his eyes floorwards. The silence dragged. It took an effort of will to remain still.

"There ain't much choice of men hereabouts," Hunt said at last. "Most of them dead." He was silent again. Then he said, "Well, if you'll squarely face the seriousness of what you is asking. And if she herself is willing."

Harry floundered through the rituals, feeling the fool in his Indian finery, a button blanket wrapped about him, a bear-fur hat upon his head. Afterwards, they went to the Reverend Crosby at the mission as well, and he gave a blessing, if sourly, to their union. The priest didn't rightly approve of mixed-race weddings and, especially, as the man said quite openly, ones that had their inception in damned heathen idolatry.

Grace's joy, the goodwill of the people toward him, then George handing him the management of the family store: all brought him almost to believe that this small place on the edge of nowhere might become a home.

But it did not answer. Grace was all things she should be, if she had a voice sometimes to scare a whale from the water. Still, he felt as if he dreamed his way about the village, as if he was living in some in-between place, as if—were he to shake himself hard enough—in that shaking he would wake suddenly to find himself alone, the *Hesperus* heeling far over, a moment from broaching in massive seas.

And what did these people want with him? Truly? Taciturn white man no one knew from whatever Adam they believed in. No member of any of the lineages they so obsessed over. It was as George said: there weren't men enough left no more. He was new stock, and George didn't think much of that stock anyhow. Harry had seen that well enough the morning before, when they'd had their disagreement.

Now, standing together outside the store, Grace sniffed and then, taking hold of his shirt, blew her nose in it. "Must get ready the funeral," she said.

He took away his arms from around her. "Yes," he said. "There ain't much time."

It was noon and the people were gathered in front of the Hunt family greathouse. Most squatted on the beach in family clusters, their formal blankets wrapped closely about them, sewn with buttons in designs of animals and ancestors. They wore hats made of the fur of black bear, or else white man's billycocks or shovels, and the women in wide-brimmed hats of woven basketry.

Harry stood in the doorway of the greathouse. With their wrinkled faces and their straight backs, the people looked like the bands of monkeys he'd seen once when he'd docked in Madras, aboard a steamship trading out of Hong Kong. They'd been hunkered in similar fashion, their knees drawn up, perched on the walls around the port, picking in each other's sandy fur. Weren't we all from monkeys, far back in the past? He'd heard it said, though it sounded fantastical to him, and he knew the Church would not want such slanders spoken. Anyhow, what did these people know of the spread of civilization? Of the great cities of the world, such as Harry had seen? Of the politics of empires and the powers of the great companies that were the blood flow in their veins? He'd sailed the merchantmen all across the Pacific. History had no role to play in such a benighted place as this.

He whistled to himself, softly through his clenched teeth.

Behind him, the fire thundered inside the house, its flames almost to the roof. He had ducked outside to escape the heat though he knew he'd suffer taunts for his weakness later, soft white man. They threw the fire up high and sat close about it, no expressions on their faces even as the leathery cocksuckers were being fried alive. His wife said it was for pride. Pagan ignorance, more like.

He'd been with his father-in-law through the morning, helping prepare for the funeral. There'd been food to bring in and prepare, blankets to come from the store for handing out during the dinner that evening, dancers to speak with, costumes to dig out of the wooden chests in the greathouse, masks to be taken from the walls and dusted down. The Indians did most of it, and Harry spent much of the morning, in fact, standing around watching. He had been tasked to bring the family women to the island on the *Hesperus*, so he'd been out and run her engine for a short time.

Now the men were going about the rituals prior to placing David's body in its gravebox. He heard the beaters strike time inside. He looked at the day. The sun had burned away the mist, but now clouds swept down the coast from the Pacific, low enough for rain, yet soaring miles into the sky in grey and violet and yellow whorls. He turned back inside.

The women of the family stood bunched together on the left side of the house, dressed as those outside. The men sat to the right behind the beaters, who were kneeling before a hollow log, hammering rhythm with long wooden staves. Five dancers moved around the fire, stooping low, their bodies cloaked in blankets woven of red cedar bark, masks on their heads of raven and of killer whale. The flames threw shadows, huge and dissolute, across the timber beams and uprights, and these carven images, all claw and beak and tooth, seemed to coil and quiver in the flickering light.

Harry's skin sheened, and not only with the heat. His indifferent Christianity still flinched when faced with such barbarism. Yet he found himself stepping farther inside, despite the heat and the darkness; and now his eyes were fastened on his father-in-law.

George Hunt was standing on the dais behind the fire, wearing the button blanket his mother had made for him years before and was evidently famous up and down the coast for its intricacies. It was black with red braiding, woven in design of the killer whale, the major spirit of Hunt's mother's family ancestry. In one hand he held a long staff of black wood, shaped as a double-headed serpent. His eyes were closed.

In front of the old man was the empty gravebox. Earlier, Harry had helped carry it in with Charley. It was a square box, just less than four feet along each side. All about it were carved David's crests: the wolf, frog, thunderbird, killer whale, and raven. Charley said George carved it himself more than a year ago, and David hardy enough to refuse its call all this time, though not forever.

Now one of the elder men placed a hand on George's shoulder. He nodded, his eyes still closed, and the beaters stopped. The dancers were still. An air pocket in a burning log squealed for a moment, and then it was only the roar and crackle of the fire.

Charley, always Charley, was standing close by. Now he beckoned Harry over, and two others as well. Harry hesitated. Pagan idolatry. But the other men were already on the platform and all seemed paused, waiting on him. So he crossed the floor, self-conscious, to join them. George seemed insensible to all about him.

Charley had a claw hammer to hand with which he now drew out the nails of the roughwood coffin in which David's body lay. At last, Charley pushed off the lid.

The corpse was naked. Its skin glowed pink in the firelight, but lucid and hollow, the thin lips black, the skin stretched already from the face so that the teeth were visible, brown and broken from the long dissolution of his illness. The shrunken ribs showed up acute, the pelvis sharp, and the man's genitals near disappeared as the body's juices had dried away. There was little to show of the man who had once inhabited this husk.

Together, they lifted the body into a sitting position, Harry with his arms under the corpse's armpits. It had been dead for several days already, and the rigor mortis must have come and gone. It reeked of putrefaction. He closed his eyes a moment as they hefted the body into the air. Then they shuffled across toward the gravebox. They bent its knees up to its chest and lowered it down into the box. Harry's elbows were still beneath the armpits, so now he lifted his own arms up and out, and the corpse's shoulders slumped and its arms fell forward, until just its head showed above the box's edge.

Now one of the dancers stepped forward and shouted, "Hap hap hap!" He wore a mask like a raven, but with the beak nearly six feet long, painted black and red and snapping open and closed. Harry moved away into the darkness and stood watching, his back against the far wall.

George lifted his head and opened his eyes. They were laced with vivid veins. The old man moved around to stand directly behind the head of his son. He knelt a moment on one knee and carefully lay the serpent staff upon the ground. Then he stood once more. He placed his hands on the corpse's skull. There was no sound at all in the greathouse.

As they moved across the cranium, shadows played on those stone claws that were the old man's fingers—fingers that would lift burning coals from fires as if they were pebbles on a beach. He had the hands of a sailor, though he was a man of the land.

Now George tensed his shoulders. He gripped his son's skull harder, the thumbs sliding down so they rested at its base. He stood up on his toes and pressed all his weight down through his arms. David's head bent forward toward his chest. His chin rested there, but still the old man pushed. And then the neck snapped, loud—a gunshot—through the greathouse.

The head flopped forward further so that now it was beneath the height of the box's lid, the chin resting impossibly against the lower sternum. George drew back his hands and they fell to his sides. Quickly Charley lifted the gravebox's lid from the back of the platform and carried it forward. He placed it upon the box, lifted the hammer from the ground, and drove in four long nails to seal it down.

The beaters drummed again, drowning the hammer's sound. The dancers spun slow circles round the fire, the hamatsa calling "Hap hap hap!" and the women wailing in unison their real and ritual sorrow.

The heat and noise beat down upon Harry. He tried to breathe away his nausea. Fucking barbarism! He had to get out. Onto the *Hesperus* and away. Right now. Cut from these black savages that he'd been fool enough to marry into.

Charley Seaweed was beside him, gesturing toward the gravebox. Charley tugged at his arm, but Harry pulled away.

"You white head have pain, eh?" Charley shouted into his ear, against the cacophony of the women's and the dancers' cries. "Nasty business. Oh yes." He pointed to the gravebox. "But you help now." His grip was merciless, so, instead of running, Harry followed the old Indian's bent back along the platform.

"Put hand far side," Charley said. Harry eased past George, almost cringing to avoid him. He noticed now the old man's cheeks were wet, though there was nothing of expression in his face. Harry knelt at one corner of David's gravebox. Charley and the two men each took another corner. Charley nodded. Together they heaved and raised the box to the height of their hips, hunchback Charley deformed but hugely strong, his arms bulging, as though he'd been thirty years aloft in the rigging of a sailing ship.

They eased forward, Harry and Charley stepping first from the platform. The other men in the room came forward now. Bodies bunched in and Harry felt the load lighten as they walked the box around the fire and toward the entrance.

Without ceremony they fumbled and bustled the box through the doorway. "Aaah," went up the murmur from the people outside, and "Hap hap hap!" as they rose to their feet. Harry glanced toward the beach, eight feet below down a steep bank. Canoes were waiting at the water's edge.

Some of the men slid nimbly down the bank and stood at the bottom looking up, their hands raised, almost supplicatory, in support of the gravebox's descent, and of its carriers.

Amidst the elbowing crowd, Harry took his first tentative step onto the steep and sodden incline. His second slipped from under him. His feet flew forward. His hands let go the box. His backside hit the ground and he slid down, his greatcoat risen up about his head, to roll across the pebbles and come at last to rest at the feet of the men on the beach.

As he pulled his mud-caked coat from round his neck, a cheer went up and laughter. "Hah! Fat Harry, you a seal go back to water in a hurry!" "You been drinking you own whisky again, Fat Harry!" "All that fire in house too hot for Harry!" "Fat Harry need gravebox soon!"

Hands reached down, lifted him to his feet, beat upon his back, tugged his coat back into place, until a smile forced its way onto his face.

"All right, all right, damn you all for heathen bastards," he said. When he'd gathered himself, he looked to see what had become of the gravebox. It was halfway to the beach, the men in a double line passing it down the slope, their feet firmly planted. At least he hadn't brought the whole lot with him. The other people were sliding and jumping toward the pebbles.

Along the plankway, then, came waddling the short, plump form of the missionary Reverend Crosby, with an Indian acolyte in priestly costume and a bowl-shaped haircut following close behind him. Crosby approached George Hunt, who was standing now close by the family's ancestral pole.

"You get back up there," whispered Henry Omxid behind him. "Help stop trouble." Harry sighed. He was only surprised Crosby hadn't shown up sooner; and his father-in-law would be in no mood for conciliation. To jeers and taunts, Harry scrambled back up the bank, hands helping even as a boot connected with his backside to more guffaws and cheery profanities.

Charley was at the top. "I get box in canoe," he said. "You go stop George make crazy with Rev'n Crosby. I wait people beach. Keep 'em quiet."

"Mr. Hunt," said the missionary as he halted in front of George, "I thought better of you than this." He was more than a foot shorter than Hunt, and was forced to tilt backward, his hands at his waist, to better look up at him. "Of course, I am sorry for your loss. And I understand your son was a breed and honour needs showing to that side of his blood." He came forward now, so that only George and Harry could hear him. His fat, crimson face crumpled with passion. "But you consign your son to torment in eternity by burying him in this way. We've our differences, George. I know it. But in this you must hear me." He reached out as if to take hold of George's arm, then stopped himself. "You must," he said.

He turned to Harry. "And you, Mr. Cadwallader! What do you here? Are there no words that you could speak to your father-in-law? Is there nothing you want to say? Are you in sympathy with what goes on? You and I are the only white men in this place, whatever your line of business might be."

Harry could think of nothing to say by way of a response.

Crosby turned back to Hunt. "You are a leader in the Indian community. It's for you to set examples. You've made trouble enough, going among the villages, gathering their pagan falsehoods for that book of yours."

He paused then and looked expectant, but Hunt just stared at the ground. The priest waved a hand in the direction of the boats. "You make a mockery of all we do here. Help me, George. In God's name, set an example, man! Half your blood is white."

"Today it is brown," said Hunt, with such a tone that Harry wondered if Crosby knew his peril.

Crosby grunted in vexation. "Once you helped us," he said. "You learned to read and write with us! Translated for us at the pulpit. You spoke with faith once."

"And I've since seen the price of it." Hunt looked up now at the priest. "Your sermon's at an end, Crosby. I've my son to bury."

Crosby's mouth thinned. "You risk a lot," he said. "You risk much in this."

"That is a threat?"

"Please. Save David's soul, and make a statement to the people here. Embracing the Lord is their only hope of survival, George."

Hunt had in one hand the staff with the double-headed serpent. Now he jabbed it up at the ancestral pole above them. "You see this? My son raised it. You know its story?" The old man raised his voice so that all the people could hear. "These are the totems of my grandmother. She was a daughter of the chieftains of the northern tribe. My grandmother died drowned, and my mother it was first raised a pole like to this one in her home village. She gave these totems to me. I gave them to my son. My son was a chieftain of the Kwagiulth. As you all do know."

He lowered the staff, and moved forward until his face was inches from Crosby's. Harry hesitated, thinking he ought to be intervening now, but instead held back. "You have heard, perhaps, what happened to that first pole?" George said, his voice low. "White men stole it. They ripped it from the earth of her village while the people was away at their summer hunting grounds. Took it to Seattle. Thieved it from us! So my son made these totems again and he did raise them up. Now you tell me he'd not want burying in the manner of the people?"

"I know the story, George," Crosby said. "We all know the story. Men are filled with avarice: white and brown. But it changes nothing. The Indians' future lies in the arms of Christ. There is no other way."

Hunt turned his head away and spat, then wiped his mouth with his forearm. His eyes took on that intensity which Harry had come to recognize and fear. "You'll not tell me how to bury my son," he said, his voice low through closed teeth.

Crosby had known George longer than had he, and would surely see the warning signs. The paralyzed side of the old man's face began to sag further, his sallow canine becoming exposed as the lower lip fell away. His breath came shorter now, and his right eyelid started to flicker in the manner that foretold the onset of the old man's dreadful rage.

But George had no right to be threatening a minister of God this way. Crosby might be foolish in his way, but he represented—didn't he?— higher truths than beating drums and pagan dancing, and breaking up the bones of corpses.

"Mr. Hunt," Harry said then. "Mayhap the Reverend Crosby ain't entirely wrong. How about giving David a part of a Christian burial, at least. You've had your first ceremonies already. What harm in giving your son both options for his afterlife?"

George seemed hardly to have heard. He tipped his great head forward toward the priest, the breath coming through his nose, like a snorting ox. Crosby took a small step back. "You risk your son's soul, Mr. Hunt," he said, "and the wrath of the authorities as well." Hunt raised a colossal fist before the priest's face. But, after a moment, he opened his fingers, and instead he pushed Crosby away. The man flew backward to sprawl on the plankway.

There were gasps, but also a few low cheers from the drunk among the people on the beach. Harry knelt to help Crosby up, but the priest's acolyte was there before him. The Indian's face was writ with a fury that seemed entirely out of keeping with his position. The man helped Crosby scramble up, ungainly, to his feet. His cassock caught on the rough plankboard, and a section at its base tore loudly. He clutched it into his hands, and then he was rolling back along the plankway in the direction of the mission, with his attendant following.

Crosby turned, once he had put some distance between them. "Don't any of you think that such offences go unpunished," he said, his voice a bird's squawk. Some men on the beach jeered, but others swiftly hushed them.

"You've took the souls from us already, you rat bastard!" George Hunt shouted, his spittle flying. Harry knew better than to seek to calm him now. "I'll eat my son's flesh before I'd see him consumed in your fucking purgatories!" But the priest was away along the beach and gone.

George span and stamped, his fists clenched so his knuckles shone pink against the grey pallor of his skin. Pale froth formed at the corners of his mouth and he groaned and growled, inarticulate and feral.

"Maxu," Hunt's wife spoke softly from the darkness of the doorway. Harry wondered if her intervention would but increase his fury. Yet the old man squatted down on his haunches, both hands clutching the staff, his head hanging forward to rest against it, great stuttering breaths coming from him, and his hands trembling against the planks beneath him. At intervals, he let forth low moans, midway between grief and fury, until finally his breathing began to slow. At last, he looked up at his son-in-law.

"And you!" he said. He rose slowly to his feet. He spoke coldly now, and slow, if loud enough for all to hear. "You think yourself a part of this family? You turncoating, weaselous fuck. You're no more of a Christian than am I! And your sham marriage rites with that limpdick priest? You think I respect them? You think I trust you with what is mine?"

Now Francine stepped in front of her husband. She spoke hard, low words to him, until his face unscrewed some of its tension. There were sniggers down on the beach, and Harry's name was spoken. He felt as if the morning mists slunk in through his ears to roil inside his head, until he could not see, did not know what he should do, what he should think.

Then a hand touched his face. A voice said, "Come take us the island." It was Grace. He blinked and she was there before him. George was gone, and Francine, and everyone else. He turned and looked at the beach.

George was making his way through the people toward the waiting canoe in which David's gravebox was now placed. "Hamatsa," said one, and another chanted, "Hap hap hap!" Then many others took it up. They gathered in around the old man, until only his head was visible above them. A few looked back toward him. Harry knew himself a stranger.

His wife smiled a little, and whether it was in reassurance, or in that mocking Indian humour, he could not now be certain.

THERE WAS SHADOWS ON MY HANDS as they rested upon David's skull, like ghosts come crawling. I had a task to perform and it was terrible to me. My child dead, and perhaps ritual is all that holds a man from the darkest pits of torment in such times. It was the great test of me, which skin I chose to wear. White son of a Christian father buried back of the family store in ground hallowed by the mission. Or Indian son of a mother what raised him heir to her crests and to her ancestors.

Well I chose her blood that day, and I done so since David chose that path as well. But also since I took my mother's crests and those of my own first wife's clan as well, rather than join the church congregation every Sunday, as so many did. And now as many must.

I stood there thinking this: I am George Hunt, and I am Kixitasu, and Maxulagilis, and Yagwis too, and No-oqoela, and Laqoagila; and in the Winter Dances I am Qomogwe, for the king beneath the sea, and many names more beside. I spoke them all to myself and then I pressed down until I felt my son's skull begin to quiver, and then it did collapse under the pressure of my fingers. Even as his skull broke, so his neck snapped and his whole head slumped forward to rest against his chest.

Do you wonder that I let tears fall even now? Indians put the dead to their boxes quick as possible. The neck is broke to be sure they are dead, for tales get told of voices from the graveyards, weeping in the night, and of men showing up what none know if they is living or they is ghosts. So do we make certain the dead remain dead.

I guess it's the white blood in me what meant that, once the deed was done, my mind churned and I did not know where I was or even, maybe, who. Next thing, I was standing outside the greathouse with the sun on my face, and the Reverend Crosby—that shit-faced, limberdick cocksucker— was about me.

I had heard that there was rumours being spoke against me in the village. When that man showed his face, I put two and two together and made a sum of which he was part. So, from the outset, I was not minded to hear what he might say. Then he comes to lecturing on David, and I heard also the threat behind his words. My rage came out and then fool Harry pipes up supporting Crosby!

Well, all things in good order. I did harangue Harry, even as that black-robed blackheart streak of piss To-Cop was dragging Crosby from off the ground. I do regret that now. I know Harry was but shaken from witnessing what I done to David. It must have raised the wind up him something serious. Godless savagery. Barbarian practices. All true enough, no doubt. Still, I don't suppose Harry saw my actions as more than the rage of the moment, and did forgive me after. Ain't we all monsters in our darkest hours?

After Crosby had been sent off, I got to the canoes and Charley was there to silence those drunks what was guffawing their support overloud.

Charley whispered to me, "We's with you all the way, but you make it right again with Fat Harry when you've a chance. He's your last son. Don't you forget it." Then he says, "But that bastard priest carries a shitsack of trouble with him. You best take care with him." And he was not wrong.

Anyhow, I sat up in the prow of the canoe beside the gravebox. Shortly, we were out in that motley flotilla what was making its way across to the Island of Graves. I remember one drunk fool in a sailboat raising a sheet dead against the wind and jeers to follow as he swung about and was near swamped. But all the time I was simmering still and wishing I had been at that shit-eater Crosby's throat, him representing all those limberdick teachers, doctors, Indian agents, administrators, and condescending do-gooders who would drag the people to their obliteration. That, at least, was as I saw it in that moment.

"My son, he was Indian," I muttered out loud. Old Henry Omxid, paddling in front of me, says, "But now he a dead man Indian, George. Like all of them. And that be that. Amen." And then he looked embarrassed for saying the Christian word.

So I thought on all the dead, and my rage baked so I could feel the nails of my hand dig into the hard wood of my rod of the Sisiutl, great double-headed serpent coiled under us, and Henry Omxid looked away, studious suddenly in his concentration on his work. I felt again the snapping of my son's neck beneath my fingers. I was near to roaring aloud.

Three-quarters of the people have I watched die. Dead of consumption, like David, of grippe, pneumonia, smallpox. Dead of the loss of their land and family and all the old ways of living they have knowed. Dead of disease, whisky, and despair. And David, proud believer, Indian by choice as well as blood, lungs gone hacking, rasping to his ruin. Me lingering on with my rages, though they was never enough to kill me, even as my own son's soul skeltered off into oblivion.

I watched the canoe's wake. I tried to keep my focus. But when I looked up again, Henry's face swelled up, then twisted into shapes past all sanity, beaked and fanged and clacking open and shut, snapping, then curling back inside itself, round and down, like to some sucking whirlpool of eyes and teeth and tongue.

I closed my eyes and heard my own groans. I knew I held by a fingernail from fading and being taken hold of by my rage. On this day when it must not happen! When my son must be honoured. Honoured by me. So I reached down into the flume and threw water up into my face, again and again. The world came drifting back and I looked along the boat, almost dreading what I'd see. But all the faces was human now, watching me close, knowing me, nervous. That almost brung me to laughter. These, my people: they know what a crazed specimen they harbour.

So I pulled it back. But I cannot say that I was full sane again. As I suppose events what later transpired would show.

HARRY SAT WITH HIS BACKSIDE on the port quarter gunnels of the *Hesperus*. His boot rested on the long-armed rudder, as he watched his way in among the canoes and other small boats toward the Island of Graves.

The women were gathered forward of the deckhouse and the mast. There were ten of them sitting there, their basket hats bobbing almost comically as they keened and wailed in unison.

The island was four hundred yards across and a hundred deep, low and forested, shaped as a shallow horseshoe with a beach at its concave centre. Thatched ceremonial houses lined the shore and there were graveboxes in the trees, where the people were sometimes in the custom of placing their dead. A desiccated body, half devoured by eagles, spilled from one broken box. Clouds had drawn down the light; the wind was growing and rain was imminent.

Harry stood up so that he could see over the pilothouse roof to the shore, now fifty yards away. He ran the engine faster for a moment and the boat made a run for the beach. He flicked off the engine switch a moment before there came the crunch of pebbles beneath the prow. He ran, sprightly, along the port gunnels, leapt over the side and into the shallows with a line in his hand. He tied off to a mooring stake that was driven deep into the beach some twenty yards from the water's edge. A man came forward to help the women down.

David's gravebox was lifted from the prow of the canoe, George standing close by. The lines of the old man's face seemed deeper even than before, until he looked another carved totem of some long-dead ancestor among the others lining the forest's edge.

Harry had once seen a man pitched overboard in a winter sea who, by a miracle of good fortune, had been holding a line, and clung to it long enough to be dragged close by the hull and hooked back on deck. The man lay there, saturated, as they pounded at his limbs to waken them, but his innards were frozen and Harry watched him drift away, without emotion, as it seemed, into death. Frozen: maybe that was how Harry might describe himself now. His mind was frozen.

Well, be fucked with George Hunt and his barbarous ways. And be fucked with his precious family as well, and with all these savages who sneered at him. He'd be away to sea before any of them could foment more trouble. He could almost turn around right now, while the ceremonies were taking place, and be gone before anyone had noticed.

He thought on Crosby's angry words. The man had passed comment on Harry's presence here as well, which might mean ill for his immortal soul. But there was too much already written up against him in Heaven for him to feel truly threatened by such a threat. Things he wouldn't think on now, however they did plague his dreams. And anyhow, he had sided with Crosby about the funeral. The man would remember that, once he had calmed down some.

More, though, was he worried by Crosby's reference to his line of business. He knew it wasn't his management of the family store the priest had been talking about. Three cases of whisky were there still within the hold of the *Hesperus*. He'd sold a few to the villages nearby during the winter, when the weather allowed.

Well, be fucked with the man as well, priest or no. Be fucked with all of them. He stood for a moment looking at the *Hesperus*, resting at a shallow angle with its prow on the shingle. But then he turned and followed the procession up the beach behind the gravebox, keeping to the back.

Grace was away with the other women. The afternoon sun was now lost in cloud and the light came dreary and feeble, if yet it was humid and warm. The wind brought a light rain now, though worse threatened. Harry's worn felt hat dripped water from its narrow rim, drops bouncing off his nose to make his nostrils twitch.

They entered the forest on a narrow path. The people were silent, their clothes a soft rustle. They walked the fifty yards inland to the clearing where stood the ceremonial house.

The low building had no walls, only a rough-hewn plank roof and six thick supports. Effigies of the dead stood randomly about the clearing, seven feet high, their mouths open, their round faces as big as a man's torso. At its centre was a fire, its flames stroking the long-blackened timbers above. To either side were piled skulls and other human bones. It was truly a place of hellfire. Yet there was in him, as there had been before on visits here, a shortening of his breath, a certain inclination to an almost drunken felicity, but which also contained a craving—hunger even—so that he felt faintly sickened with himself, even as his eyes devoured every detail.

Beyond the frame house, the trees were garlanded in graveboxes. The dead had been placed at every divide where boughs grew out of the main trunks, hitched up with ropes and tied off to rest among the spirits of the forest. Or some were laid in smaller houses ten feet wide and low, somewhat akin to the mausoleums of white gentry. And there were similarities, for the Island of Graves was held over for the families of chieftains; though nowadays, so his wife said, with so many dead most everyone held some sort of chiefly seat.

The people clustered in about the fire and so many were there, even in such depleted times, that some were forced to stand outside in the mounting rain. David's gravebox was placed near the fire on a low dais. The people inside hunkered down on the tamped earth. Harry stood off to one side with his back against a house support. He took off his hat and thumped it, then shook a little rain from his coat.

George was on the dais with Charley Seaweed and several of the leading chieftains of the people, who were robed in finery, and some carried masks of raven and killer whale under their arms.

The old men lining up on the dais held themselves pompous and self-important, as ever they were at such moments. He almost snorted a laugh. Yet his humour died again as quickly as it had come. This was death, whatever the rites involved and the people performing them. There was nothing good in that, excepting maybe the ending of suffering at last. But who could wish for death? There was sin in such thinking—was there not?—to wish for death prior to the utter end of all effort to remain alive?

The rain teemed now. The people who yet remained outside huddled close together, stoic in the onslaught. He looked down on the seated figures before him. They stank of fish, foul sweat, mouldering cloth.

Now the old chieftains on the dais placed their masks upon their heads, all except the leading chief of the Fort Rupert people, Owadi, bone-thin and tall, who wore a hat made of bear's fur. Owadi spoke out in the high Kwakwala of which Harry knew nothing at all. The words came cantillating from the old man's throat, the "lah" with which each phrase was always finished—that much Harry knew, at least—beating its own rhythms against the rain. The men on the dais who were wearing masks turned slowly with the words. They made small steps forward and back, their masks' fur or feathers swaying with their movement, and one long raven-like beak on its hidden cords snapping open and shut.

The minutes passed, and still the old chieftain intoned and the fire crackled and the rain still thundered on the roof. There was only lifeless desecration on George's face. Yet, with time, there came a different emotion in his father-in-law. And more than one. It seemed some conflict seethed in him. As Owadi droned, George's eyes moved around the gathering and up across the roof, and then into the fire, where they stopped and stared, as if in trance to the revel of the blaze. His eyes squinted, the left drooping in its paralysis. His lips were thin beneath his moustache. The hand that did not hold the staff clasped and opened and clasped again.

Harry had worked the merchant marine all over the world. He'd spoken, drunk, fought, fucked among so many, that surely the world had lent him skills for reading men. Yet he could not read his father-in-law at this time, except to believe some torment or, perhaps, some terrible notion was rising to the surface. What was passing through the old man's mind with such intensity? Not simply grief, nor yet the flickerings of his lunatic rage. Harry knew him enough to understand that his emotions, powerful as they often were, followed paths direct and open, so that few who looked upon his face could doubt what he might be feeling in that moment.

Owadi intoned his final words. There was a silence, just the crackle of the fire and the odd rustle, cough, or grunt. Then George stepped forward a pace to speak.

"HERE IS MY SON," I told them as they stood about me on the Isle of Graves. "My son what is named David Hunt by the whites, and Hameselal from his mother's father, Nemogwis in the Winter Dances, Chief of the Senlem Clan of the Walas Kwagiulth, great chief of the cannibal dancers, descendant of chieftains of the northern tribes, bearer of their crests, father to children what will take those crests and carry them in all eternity. A great man he was. A Kwagiulth he was, and now he is dead."

And that was all the words I was going to speak, making my point to those present—and I suppose to myself—that my family was of the people, and would stay Kwagiulth forever. But then there was more; and perhaps I knew there would be, listening on old Owadi rattling on about how the world was fearful, all the youngsters dying, and everyone else, and speaking the proper words of the funeral as he did as well.

Bitterness welled up, wrapped about with grief, and fermented with rage at all those ranged against me, as I saw it. It seemed like it was the whole world. So I spoke on, and angry words they was. Words against the white men first. How they brung their diseases and their controlling ways, their Christianity. I know that made some nervous what was regular church-going folk. I done it deliberate, though, stoking them up, provoking, prodding and poking till I knew they'd be resenting me.

Then came words against the Indians. And there are Indians indeed who want rid of me still: for working with the scientists, for writing the secret ways of the people into the books, where there weren't no written words before, just the memories of men, for trying to hold on to the ways of the people against the world's progress, as they sees it. And for seeking out the witchcraft amongst them, for exposing it, for showing them the black heart of gossip and mal-intent.

Well, what words I spoke were not those of reason. Or how I told it they wasn't, anyhow, and how far the telling went. First, I says they are weak, letting the white men walk on them. Craven for not defending their ways.

46

Then I goes on to tell them they are stupid for not knowing what I do for them, that when I buy up their artefacts I am handing money to them from the white men that wouldn't never come elsewise. That those treasures go to the museums where they will be safe. I says the stories that go onto the pages I send Professor Boas are for future times, for future people to see what once we was.

I says it angry, and many I know were turned away by my hot temper as much as by the upside-down reasoning. For it was worse. Much worse. I made threats as well. Dare to stand against me. Dare! And if you do, says I, then I will tear you up, like to the Cannibal Spirit. I will eat you, swallow you, take all of you, flesh and bone and soul, until there ain't nothing left even for the burial.

Oh, I was resting in midst of the flames that day, all the time placing more logs beneath my feet. Things that were bad already got made worse still by that speech. And then by what followed. Well, I'll not think of it yet. All in good order. Yes. All in the right order.

GEORGE HUNT'S EYES PICKED THEIR WAY OVER THE ASSEMBLY. He looked some brimstone preacher delivering a sermon to the unenlightened on God's awful vengeance. Though he spoke in Kwakwala, Harry could tell he spoke simply, with clarity, each word a blade. Yet underneath, there was such fury and, as well, such agony as to make him seem something other than human. Not more. Less perhaps: ancient, animal, demonic, the long staff he held, seemingly forgotten in one hand, adding to the menace, the serpent's heads, teeth bared, leering at each end, almost alive as Hunt shivered in his passion. Indeed, his whole body shook, and one foot stamped incessantly on the platform, as if at the next moment he would launch himself at the people before him. The flames doused his face, his teeth, his body in scarlet. They burned like blood in his eyes. The jagged edges of his nails glittered.

The rain hammering, Hunt's voice exploding through it, the air as thick as molasses, the man's presence imposing itself into all the space of the ceremonial house, until Harry gasped, fighting for his breath.

No one spoke or moved when Hunt finally fell silent and, breathing hard himself, turned his back to them. After some time, they rose to their feet. Most began to walk away toward the beach. Still no one spoke. The old chieftains removed their masks. They kept a distance from Hunt, and none looked at him as he sat upon his son's gravebox and rubbed a hand down his face.

Harry wondered if he was really angry at him. If it was possible to be angry at something not properly human.

Two men stepped up on the dais, carrying thick ropes, and George spoke with them, quietly now. They turned and clambered down once more. He looked up at the chieftains and spoke something to them. The old men were silent, standing in a circle, and Charley Seaweed was there as well. Owadi shook his head. George spoke again, intense now, his face darkening. At last Owadi spoke a few words more and, though his face showed

48

he was unhappy, he left the dais with the other chieftains and disappeared toward the beach.

"Caddie." A voice brought Harry back into the moment. It was Grace, the other women behind, whispering amongst themselves. "Do you come?"

"What just occurred? I thought they hoisted up the body in the trees now and that was an end of it."

"Talk father. Come to the beach after. We going now on the boat." Harry saw her tear-shot eyes. He made to place a hand on her arm, but she walked away with the other women. So he went over to the fire.

"Charley," he said, and the old cripple looked up from the conference he was having with another man. "What goes on?"

"Speak George" was all Charley said.

So Harry stepped up onto the dais where his father-in-law was alone, still sitting on the box with his head down. "Mr. Hunt," Harry said.

The old man looked up, surprised. "Harry," he said at last. The veins crept like vines across the whites of his eyes and the rawness of his lids.

"I thought you ended things simple now."

George hesitated. "He was hamatsa. I'll see him fully that."

"So what's to be done?"

"Take the women to the village."

"You saw how angry you had Crosby. Are you doing what's right?"

"I shit on him!" George rose to his feet. "Would you not stop prodding at me, damn you!" Harry stepped back. "Take the women." But he spoke more quietly. He put a hand to Harry's shoulder. "No questions."

"I hear David was a civilized man," Harry said, but George did not reply, even to such deliberate goading. So Harry stepped away and through the throng of silent men who yet remained. No emotion could he read in their faces, and they were very alien to him.

Out on the beach, Harry trudged to his boat. His wife and the other women were already aboard. The canoes and other boats were leaving. As he'd planned, the tide had come in and the *Hesperus* was nearly afloat. Two men helped him heave it off the last of the pebbles and he pulled himself aboard.

The boat's engine started reliably enough to warm away his questions for the moment, if not the damp and aching in his bones. He turned the boat out toward the open water. The rain fell so hard the village was invisible across the short mile of sea.

PART II · THE WILDERNESS

HARRY CADWALLADER lounged in his weathered old rocker on the porch outside the store. The morning breeze was light and spoke of sun and humid warmth all day. Out across the bay, the trees on the Island of Graves broke the horizon. Four days had passed since the funeral, and the weather had stayed fair.

Rounding the eastern headland, he saw a steam launch coming, its prow cutting cleanly through the light swell. The ensign of the Indian Agency was at its masthead. Most likely it was William Halliday, Indian agent for this region of the coast. He was coming from the south. He'd be out from Alert Bay, passing through en route to the outer villages, part of the bimonthly trip he took to make his presence felt among the people of the coast. Harry had met him a few times. He seemed a decent enough man, as far as his task was given and his values allowed. Harry had been wary, though, knowing his trade in liquor would land him in trouble if Halliday should learn of it.

As the boat neared the jetty, the Reverend Crosby stepped out along the boards and raised his hand to hail the incoming launch. With him was the Indian who'd been there the day of David's funeral. He wore still the black cassock similar to Crosby's. One of those the missionaries took in and raised in the mission schools. Harry squirmed at the thought of such a place. He knew the origin of his unease, though by Christ's blood he would not dwell on it. Memories were best left boxed away to be forgotten over time. Now and what was to come were all that was needed by a man.

The boat drew up alongside the jetty. It was indeed Halliday, his red hair and beard bright in the sunlight. He watched the man tie off to the cleat above him, the launch low against the pillars in the ebb tide. Crosby and the Indian came up and soon the three men were engaged in conversation.

"Fat Harry." Below him on the shingle the old chieftain Owadi stood puffing. Harry spoke a greeting. "I come to talk wealth of blankets," said

Owadi. Harry sighed. He knew what that meant: some thorny exchanges ending in the extension of credit.

"Come on inside," he said. Owadi, wrapped in a dirty blanket and wearing knee-high rubber boots, stepped up to the porch, gingerly with age, but his chin high and proud.

Inside was gloom and cobwebs. The store's big front windows, on each side of the front door, were filthy as always: rain, dew, the grime of engines, oil, black smoke, grease from untanned hide, dust and sea salt caking them inside and out. He kept meaning to wash them, but always the thought that soon he'd be away had stopped him from bothering.

He sat on one of the drums of engine oil that stood browned with rust in the centre of the room. He rested a boot on a broken generator head. Other parts lay scattered on the floor. He was one of the few this far up the coast who knew the workings of an engine. It was a reason George had given Harry management of the store.

Owadi stood in the doorway and examined the room, as Harry knew was protocol for any chief when visiting and on sight of another's riches, though Owadi visited the store nearly every other day on some mischief or another.

Harry rustled in his coat and pulled forth his tobacco tin. He ran his thumb across the strutting Chinese burlesque on the narrow tin's lid. He opened it, rolled a cigarette, and struck a match against the oil drum beneath him. Smoke spiralled, lilac and grey, into the rafters.

He followed Owadi's eyes around the room. There was a table in front of one window on which lay greasy-fingered piles of paperwork, an abacus, some broken chocolate, and two small jars of boiled sweets. There were shelves to the ceiling on the two walls to either side. Soaps and salves for cuts (though the mission kept the greater measure of medications), cans of salmon, sardine, and fruit, jars of molasses, tea, coffee, hard biscuits, drums of cooking oil, jars of salt, and phials of pepper. The people still relied on hunting, fishing, and gathering for most of their food.

There were cotton and canvas trousers, overalls and thick woollen sweaters uncoloured or in dull green, skirts and dresses, long socks and woollen jackets in plain or plaid. There were long sailor's canvas coats in black, oiled and waterproof, too expensive for most, silk and cotton stockings and a handful of handkerchiefs, plimsolls for the children, the rubber boots bought under-counter from the canneries' warehousemen. Harry knew every item now, its state and price, and who might likely purchase it.

He finished his cigarette and rolled the burning ember dead between finger and thumb. He sighed and heaved himself up from the oil drum. "Owadi, great chief," he said at last. "What can I do for you?"

Owadi seemed locked in indecision. Then he said, looking furtively through the open door first, "You have furs and blankets upstairs?"

"I do." As the old man well knew.

"We look."

Harry crossed the room and motioned Owadi over. A staircase went up along the rear wall. Beneath the stairs, an opening led into the back rooms where were the private places of his marriage, such few as there could be with the constant, prying company of the people. Harry followed the old man up the stairs into the shadows above. It seemed clear Owadi had words on his mind to speak and wished them secret.

Up in the loft, Harry stood blinking as his eyes adjusted. Cobwebs hung thick across the single window to the front and there was little light, if just enough to see by. To his left a wall divided the attic in two. A locked door kept the produce of real value secure—tobacco, hats, ammunition, a couple of rifles.

To his right were scattered a few boxes, cans of aging foodstuffs, and the hides and skins from trade among the people. There were hair seal, raccoon, black bear, wolf, mountain goat, elk, marten, deer, and even two land otter skins, stacked into the canted, spider-ridden corners. And there were blankets piled everywhere, great mounds of them, slowly moulding.

"Many blankets," Harry said.

"Blankets is wealth," the old chief said.

"Though they ain't what they were, now the ceremonies have been banned. And we've more than we need already, you can see." Once they had been virtually the coin of the coast. Harry'd been offered them in exchange for his whisky many times, great rotting stacks of them, of little use to anyone nowadays.

"Old ways change. Always worse," said Owadi.

"Right enough."

Owadi lapsed into a ponderous silence.

So the old man wasn't here to trade blankets. He watched the chieftain from the corner of his eye, erect, stiff, his eyelids half-closed in thought. "The world comes always faster," Harry said, "even here on the coast."

"Killing people as it comes," said Owadi.

"Aye, and sad it is. Even for me, if I ain't more than a white man."

Owadi looked at him then, and Harry realized he rarely met the eyes of any Indian man. "What can we do against you?" the old chief said at last.

Harry chose his words and was careful in voicing them. "I'm proud being a part of the Kwagiulth through marriage. I hope I'm to be trusted by you, that I've shown myself an ally to the people." Though he looked to the floor as he spoke the words.

Owadi nodded faintly, gazing sharply at him. "Fat Harry," he said slowly, "old George family is great among us. But for many, they is not Kwagiulth. You know George father, he was white, from England. And George mother Tlingit tribe, from the north. We had three hundred years of war with them people. When George marry with first wife Lucy, Tlingit and Kwagiulth come together and that was the war's end, lah." Owadi's head bobbed in ritual acknowledgment as he spoke. "For that we grateful, though there be some might think still of glory in killing men.

"To many, George is good man to stop war, to write our stories for us, and to make our history in books for white people to see." He stopped to cough, a long phlegm-filled rasp. He said, "For them to see we is real and forever—same as them, important as they is in life. But George has took many thing of us and sold them, told secret of us, and he is enemy in some people mind." He looked up again and into Harry's eyes. "You understand?"

Harry was undone by such forthright words. He was more used to burrowing hard for meaning in the Indian's usual indirection. He said, "Something is occurring?"

"But old George gone now. Flown. Gone."

"Yes."

The night of the funeral, Harry and the women had returned through the rainstorm to the village. They had ducked toward the greathouse and his wife had made it clear that that was where they'd sleep the night. Many came to join them at dinner, but the talk was low and sparse. Harry spluttered down a little of the foul black oil of the eulachon fish they so favoured, with his salmon, and some bitter stew of berries. The sun fell and the rain ended. Eyes were kept lowered and there were none of the usual jokes and tales told around the fire. More than with ritual grief or with solemnity, the air felt pregnant that evening with reservation and with doubt.

He walked out after dinner. Across the water, fires burned on the Island of Graves, where the men who had stayed on with George were still at whatever it was they were doing. But he knew no one would tell him what was happening there. So he shrugged and spat and smoked, and went to his bed among the fifteen others who slept that night on the platforms about the greathouse's inner walls.

Late in the night he awoke. The cinders of the fire cast a wine-red glow across the timber ceiling. Soft voices muttered. He saw George at the doorway talking to someone outside, and turning then into the room. The old man stamped across to the fire and squatted before it. He was carrying a wooden box, about a foot and a half on each side, that seemed carved with intricate details, though it was impossible to make them out in the gloom, and which he placed down and rested one palm on its top, firmly, as if he must not ever lose it from his touch. He took up a half-burned faggot with his other hand and pushed at the embers, his fingers almost in the flames as they flickered lazily to life.

George huddled there, stock-still, his blanket about him, massive as a bear come in out of the forest to the fire's warmth. After a time, he lifted a hand and ran it slowly across his forehead. He pressed his thumb and forefinger to his temples. Then he closed his eyes.

Harry sat up. He reached across his sleeping wife to find his tobacco tin. He rolled and licked and placed the finished product in his mouth, then flicked alight a match and drew in the cigarette's smoke. As it curled back out he saw George's eyes upon him. They gazed at each other as Harry smoked. Nothing was said, and no emotion, nor any sign even of recognition, could Harry see in his father-in-law's eyes. They were as cold and black as those of a whale. He remembered George roaring like a furnace in his passion, hectoring and railing at the people on the Island of Graves. There was some part of the man that was distinct from ordinary human life. Something outside of reason. In that moment, Harry felt that his own anger toward him lacked any meaning in the world. As well to hurl an insult at a mountain.

The following morning George was gone. He had taken his canoe and the paraphernalia for a hunting trip, so Francine had told him.

"But gone where?" Owadi said. "Why go now?"

"I was thinking misery at the death of his son had drove him off," said Harry. "Though none seem over-willing to share their thoughts on the matter."

"Ah," said Owadi. "But very wrong go now. For four days after funeral, family must stay, mourn dead, make ceremony. And then they must make funeral pole and song to sing about the dead. And after, the ceremony for his heir as well. David heir is still a boy, so it was for George to do. Many people, they is angry he go away." He was silent for a time. "And there was what happen on the island too. Many's not happy for that."

"What happened, Chief?" He'd had no luck in gleaning anything from the people in the days since. He knew something wasn't right, just by the silence with which his questions had been met, even by his wife.

"Some people think George and the man, Doctor Boas, make their book and put words inside to say we all cannibal men for real. That we eat people, and is savage all through. They is angry for that."

"There ain't no such words. I read enough of it to see it shows you in a favourable light enough."

The old man did not speak for a while. Then he drew his hand in a line across in front of him. He said, "You have many blankets. You a wealthy man, Fat Harry." Then he stepped away down the stairs.

Harry sat upon a pile of those blankets. The first shafts of the sun broke through the soiled window, throwing light across his family's petty fortune. He had lived forty-two years, and had travelled the world and come to be here. A brown-skinned savage chief had told him he was wealthy for the decomposing blankets in his attic. Yet this battered store and all its contents would scarce bring half the value of the *Hesperus*.

There'd been warning in Owadi's words. George had enemies. But that was no news at all; everyone knew it to be true. There must be more to it. Something specific. Yet what that might be, Harry could not know. He'd speak with his wife, though she was away gathering salmonberries, and would not be back till the sun set. Even then, she was more often lip-sealed on matters pertaining to the people. He was and would always remain a white man, whether he pitched his body black and leapt naked with them round the fires in a mask. More reason still to be gone.

Grace. Her brother was dead, her father fled who knows where or why or what he was doing. Yet there was no denying it, her grief terrified him. At night she was fanatical in her passions, tearing at him with her nails, biting his shoulders until he bled. She clung to him when she slept, as if she knew his thoughts, knew that if she let him go, she'd wake the morning after to find her husband gone as well. Harry lay awake half of each night, fighting a panic he could not understand, groggy and stupid in the morning, terse with her, his irritation growing by the day. There'd been strong words more than once already, always on petty subjects—what food was for lunch, what washing had not been done, why his clothes were not folded as they should be—a sailor's whining. Issues domestic and ridiculous that made him despise himself. But for the strength of her arms about him, he might have upped and run already.

All experience is an arch wherethro' gleams that untravell'd world, whose margin fades for ever and for ever when I move. How dull it is to pause, to make an end, to rust unburnished, not to shine with use. As though to breathe were life!

He'd read that in a book of poems he'd found in the hold of the *Hesperus* when first he'd purchased her. He had learned it by heart. And he'd not stay here to rust, or to be set upon by a bile-filled cocksucker hell-bent on dominion over all those close to him.

But he could not leave as yet. Not with her brother dead and her father gone. To lose her husband as well would be too cruel. He'd do what was proper. He'd see her good and safe with her father returned. Then he'd slip away, and she'd be free to find a man more fitting than was he. The Kwagiulth had no issue with remarriage. It even brought prestige to the chiefly among them, as he'd heard it, the women and the men.

He rolled tobacco and watched the dust dance in the attic's fractured sunlight.

Later, Harry rocked on his porch. There were none who'd come to buy that day, though that was not unusual in itself. There were barely a hundred and twenty Kwagiulths left in the village now. Once there'd been more than two thousand.

The humid air was heavy and everything quiet. Out on the ocean to the north and west, dark clouds were festering and a storm would blow through the night.

The tide was out and a few women picked cockles farther down the beach, their fat bodies bent forward, their conical hats reminding him of the paddy fields that ranged along the shores beneath the peaks of Hong Kong. It was a sight he'd seen many times aboard ship as they'd made their way toward the dockyards of that vast bay, with all its cacophonies and promises drifting across the water, intoxicants to the men who manned the ships.

Now Harry saw Halliday and Crosby striding down the beach, along with the priest's Indian acolyte. Harry realized he was to be their destination.

"Mr. Cadwallader, a word with you," said the Reverend Crosby, red-faced and puffing piety.

"How might you be, Harry?" Halliday smiled. He was dressed in thick broadcloth and cravat, smartly turned out, for all his itinerant vocation.

"Well, thank you, Mr. Halliday. Reverend Crosby." He nodded, and to the Indian as well. "Can I invite you in back for some coffee?"

"There's not time for that," Crosby began.

But Halliday said, "That would be fine," and they followed Harry inside and through the store.

Harry reheated the coffee that sat on the small stove in the back room. He was introduced to the unspeaking Indian, whose name was To-Cop.

He exchanged a few pleasantries with Halliday, yet Harry sensed the strain in the three men.

They took their brews outside into the backyard and sat about the rough-plank table. A low wooden fence separated the private from the common land, which stretched a hundred and fifty yards to the tree line. Just before the trees there was a tended plot with an iron fence about it, and there was laid, in land hallowed by the mission, Robert Hunt, George's father, in a mausoleum of stone.

"A good man was Robert," said Crosby, "and a fine Christian man as well."

"I've heard that, though he died before I turned up," said Harry.

"Of course," said Halliday. "Though I think on you as a permanent fixture already. There are so few of us in this far reach of the world."

"Robert helped in founding the first mission in Rupert, you know," said Crosby. "Back in '77."

"Harry," said Halliday, "you'll guess, I'm sure, that we are not here to pay a social call."

"What, then?"

"It's of George we'd speak," said Halliday.

"Ah, well you'll know he's away."

"Reverend Crosby informed me such. But you see, Harry, we have a problem." Halliday drummed his forefinger on the table. At last he said, "There's charges been made against him, Harry. Charges that need answering."

"Heinous charges," said Crosby.

Harry saw something almost feral in To-Cop's eyes, and the priest looked exultant. "What charges?"

"He is accused under section 114 of the Indian Act," said Halliday. "Under the 1895 amendment, and under the section of that statute which deals with the mutilation of a dead human body."

Harry said nothing. Then he said, knowing himself stupid as he spoke, "Mutilation ... a body?"

"Harry," said Halliday, "it's claimed he participated in a ritual of the so-called hamatsa society, which is banned under the act." His finger drummed louder. "And, whilst participating in the ritual, it is also claimed that Mr. Hunt did devour the flesh of a human corpse."

"Hell and damnation!" Harry leapt up. His hands shook and heat came to his face. "Who has said this?"

"I'll ask you to hold your blaspheming tongue a little better, Mr. Cadwallader," said Crosby. "The claims are made by persons who need not be named at this time. But believe me, the claims are there and are written down. Mr. Halliday has those statements in his possession. Statements from actual witnesses as well. Damaging statements, Mr. Cadwallader. Damaging to George Hunt and to all his family."

Harry remembered Crosby pushed to the ground the day of the funeral. He wondered what part the priest had to play in this. "But this is lunacy," he said, aiming his words at Halliday. "You all know George has those biased against him. These is false charges. And he away and not able to refute them."

"Which is why we are here, Harry," said Halliday. "Please, sit." He did so, his face still hot, indignation in his heart. There was a sneer on the face of To-Cop that he would dearly have loved to wipe away. "He needs finding and bringing back," said Halliday, "and I'm asking you to do it."

"Were easy to say and hard to do." Harry coughed. He slowed his breathing down. "I heard he goes months sometimes in the forests of the mainland."

"You will need help. I know that. But you're a white man and we'd trust you to do so, as we could not an Indian."

"No!" Harry slammed his hand upon the tabletop. "You're asking me? Are you fucking insane? I'll not do it, by Christ." Crosby made to speak, but Harry stared him down. "I'll not be party to this lunacy." Yet nausea cramped his stomach now, and his ire wavered.

Halliday had his hands up, both palms toward Harry. "I'd hoped you might see the necessity of it, Harry," he said. "I might hope, at least, you'd keep your temper with me and with the Reverend. You are the only right man for this task. I'd have you realize that. You're his son-in-law, you've a boat—and a fine boat she is." There was that in Halliday's voice when he said this that Harry did not enjoy hearing. "But know this. I can depute you as a special constable and insist. I have the right in law."

"You'd force me to track down and arrest my own father-in-law?"

"There'll be no need for such dramatic behaviour. Just find him, tell him what has happened. He'll come back. George is not a man to shirk an issue. And I will cover your expenses."

"So when was this crime meant to have happened?"

"Six weeks ago, at Big Mountain's village."

"And black doings it was," said Crosby.

"George must answer," Halliday said.

"For all his many crimes." Spittle flecked Crosby's moustache. "And those committed upon the body of his son not least."

Harry stared at him. "What's that?"

"Reverend Crosby forgets himself," said Halliday.

"Am I the only man in Rupert that has not heard these rumours?"

"We must concentrate on what needs doing now, Harry," said Halliday.

He thought on Owadi's words, which seemed prescient, what with Crosby foaming and Halliday obfuscating on the facts. But Harry could not but see the truth of Halliday's thinking. There was no one to send but him. Halliday was the agent in these parts, and he'd have tasks enough he needed to perform. There was Woolacott, the only constable hereabouts, down at Alert Bay. But sending him would do nothing but stoke further trouble. Woolacott and George had never seen eye to eye. Harry'd watched them at each other's throats on more than one occasion already. And was he not waiting for George to return before he could be gone? Finding him would expedite his plan.

Yet he despised these bilge bastards, giving out their orders to him as though he was still aboard a merchantman.

Harry looked at To-Cop, his black hair with its bowl cut. He wondered what his role was in this. He stepped round to sit on the table near to the Indian. "I see what you're saying," Harry said, all the while staring down at To-Cop, "though I'd like to know what limpdick gossiping bastard served up these fantasies." To-Cop returned his stare and did not flinch from it. The man was not the weak Christian sop he might be expected to be, wearing that garb. He turned to Halliday. "You'll pay my fuel, and for my time, you say?"

"We will."

"Then I'll go, though I don't believe a word of it."

"Good, good. Just bring him back and let him answer for himself, Harry," said Halliday. "I am grateful. Have you thoughts on where you'll go?"

"I've not. I'll go speak with Francine. And with Charley Seaweed. He's known George longest. He'd know, if anyone will tell me."

"Indeed, I have a suggestion there. I believe Charley Seaweed might accompany you on this mission. He knows the coast as well as any man."

"No." He needed no spy aboard. "I'll find George myself."

Halliday looked at him, his face without expression. Harry kept the gaze a while, but in the end he had to look away.

"Harry, I think it's better all round that Charley goes with you. In fact, I insist."

"Damnation, man. I'm no child needs cosseting."

"Just do it for my sense of well-being, Mr. Cadwallader. Charley knows everyone hereabouts. I'm sure you'll find him and be back in a few days." Halliday stood. "You'll leave immediately?"

Harry gazed out toward the ocean. The storm was nearer now, indigo and black, vast against the late-afternoon sky. "I won't till that's passed by," he said. "I'll go in the morning. Who have you told of this?"

"None as yet, outside yourself. But the village knows, you can be sure. Gossip runs swifter even than the wireless. I saw many of them in conference earlier, outside Owadi's."

"Then you'll excuse me," said Harry, "I'm away to see Charley Seaweed." And he took his fury and his doubt away toward the village.

The rain beat at the leaking roof, water dripped, and Harry tossed and wriggled until even Grace muttered and turned away from him. So he rose, wrapped in his blanket like a true Indian, and wandered through the store to stare out the window at the raging sky. The panes clattered in the wind. Lightning lit the beach repeatedly, and the pale pebbles shone incandescent in the electric air.

He fumbled on the table beneath the window and found his tobacco tin. He sat on the edge of the table and smoked. He wondered where George might be, and whether he was subject to the storm, crouched beneath the forest leaves, or hiding in a cave, or in an Indian's home. He could in truth be anywhere: up or down the coast, or inland among the mountains, lakes and rivers, even lost at sea and swamped in his canoe, though Harry doubted that, so wily a man he was, and weather-wise.

He was in a pretty situation: sent to track his father-in-law and bring him back to justice. Sent as a white man, yet husband to an Indian. And now, as his wife told him, some of the people whispered he was a stooge to the authorities. Halliday, meanwhile, threatened to depute him, even as he and foul Crosby spoke of trusting him for the only white man able for the task.

He couldn't even up and run once he was at sea, now that damned idiot of a cripple, Charley, was in tow. Unless he pitched him over the side—and he wasn't quite prepared for that, however infuriating was the man.

In truth, Harry *was* angry at the charges against George. Yet that anger was less than when first he'd heard the charge. Now he wondered somewhat. He knew that George did attend the banned rituals of the people. And, though it wasn't part of the charge itself, something had occurred out there on the Island of Graves so bad that none would speak of it, at least to him. Owadi had whispered his quiet warnings. That was unusual enough and, in the circumstances, ominous. Crosby had referred to it as well.

After he'd left Crosby and Halliday in his yard, Harry had walked into the village to find Charley Seaweed. Charley was already apprised of the charges levelled against his cousin. Harry told him of his conversation with Halliday, and how the Indian agent had suggested Charley should come. "Him pay?" Charley asked, and grudgingly Harry told him yes. He had half hoped Charley might decide he wanted nothing of the venture. But the old man just nodded.

"Have you thoughts on where he went?" Harry asked him.

"Don't know. Leave after storm. Have plan then."

"Well think quick. I'll not wait on your ponderings."

Francine was away with Grace gathering the berries. When they got back and Harry told them what had occurred, they didn't seem surprised either, though there was much shaking of heads and whistling through teeth and muttered Indian words. But they had little to say to Harry. Francine nodded when she heard Charley was involved and said to speak to him. Grace just shrugged, though she looked troubled, and even, the first time he'd seen her that way, frail. Harry had given up trying to pry things from his wife. She spoke or she didn't.

He stood by the window, watching the storm. Well, he'd learned to soak up the people's taciturnity. But it showed he wouldn't ever be a real part of their world. If he could have fled this very night, he might well have done it, and none would ever know where he had gone. But the storm made such a deed impossible. Anyhow, it would mean he'd have to go far away, since Halliday could put the word all up and down the coast that he was a wanted man. Then he'd have every damned government boat scouring for him.

Once they were away, Charley would effectively be guardian over him for Halliday. Not that Charley would be doing it deliberately. He was certain Charley had no loyalty to Halliday, beyond the pay he'd receive. Harry was bound up for now in the fate of the Hunt family. What that might mean should George fail to be found, or refuse to return, Harry did not know. For now, though, there was nothing more to be done. All he could do was try to find George, and lay it all out before him.

So he pressed the tobacco dead in his fingers, and returned to bed. His wife snored softly, and with the storm still battering at the wooden building, he lay on his side and watched the gentle rise and fall of her shoulders, until she sighed and her hand came up and held tight to his shoulder, and he drifted at last into sleep.

Harry stood on his porch in his shabby long johns, yawning and surveying the world. The dawn came clear with a light wind out of the west. The air was fresh, the usual smells of the village washed for once away. A dog barked, half-hearted. Some cocks crowed. A few of the people were up and around, down on the beach.

He sipped coffee. In the back, his wife prepared a breakfast of stewed salmonberries, mackerel, and rice, a staple for Harry after his many years in the Orient. He threw out the dregs from his cup, hawked as loud as any Chinaman, and spat a great black gobbet down onto the beach. He felt calm, resolute even. He had his role to play, and he'd perform it effectively. One thing leading to another.

He saw Charley coming toward him. "Yoh," Harry called.

Charley trudged his way up the shingle to the store. "I make food for trip," he said, stepping onto the porch. "Dry salmon. Berry, enough some box. Grease from eulachon." He cackled. "You learn like grease on boat many day, huh? You have coffee, sugar, thing, right?"

"I'll bring rice and coffee and the like, and I'll have some things to trade as we go."

"We make business together. Half profit me."

"Always a nose for the fast penny, eh, Charley?"

"Raven."

"I reckon it better to look like we're trading than for all to know our real business."

"Ek." Charley nodded.

"Let's eat. But where are we headed after?"

"Talk at sea. Ear everywhere. Give old George time think, not other bastard follow behind, not story go Hal'day ear too."

Harry shrugged. There was no one within four hundred yards except his wife, and she in the back cooking, but he knew the futility of argument.

Several of the people came to watch them at the jetty as they made ready to leave. Harry's wife was there, and George's, and Charley's missus sitting farther up the beach, shaking her head and pontificating raucously, until her husband threw hard words at her, and some of the Indians already drunk jeered him.

Halliday came down the jetty, earnest and rigid against the muttering of the people round him. "You're well today, Harry?" he said.

"Well as might be."

"Have you a strategy as to where you'll be headed?" Halliday looked to Charley. The old cripple took no visible notice as he stacked blanket bales on the deck of the *Hesperus*.

"We've some thoughts," said Harry slowly, "but none are firm. We'll get to sea and make our plans then."

"Taking some trading goods with you as well. Good, good. No harm in that." He moved closer to Harry, who was leaning against a gasoline drum. "But you'll be focusing on the job in hand, I take it?"

"I will. Trade goods may be useful in drawing information from some tightlip chieftain."

"Of course you're right. But Harry, I'd have you certain in your quest. I want to see George back in ten days. If not, I plan to confiscate the Hunt family masks and treasures, to be held against his handing himself in."

"That's a damned insult, Halliday."

"And I know, Mr. Cadwallader, that not all you trade is smiled on by the law. Still, you don't sell the rotten brews, and you're particular who you sell to. Oh, don't think I don't know you. But there are worse along the coast. Nevertheless, there are some would have had me bring you to the assiers before now."

Harry began to speak, but Halliday held up his hand. "I've kept my counsel till now, and mostly for your family and for your place as white man here. I'd hoped running the Hunt family store might put such trade behind you. There's only you and Crosby in Rupert that is pure white. But know this. You fail in finding George, or do anything else untoward, and I'll be bringing down all force upon the Hunt family. And on you, Harry. You may see your boat impounded, and you will spend time in jail."

"Damnation!" Harry said. "There ain't need for this."

But Halliday stepped back and spoke loudly so that all might hear him. "Good, good," he said. "I'll be wishing you well." And then quietly once more, "You bring him back to me, Harry. Whatever it takes. I'll have no excuses." He pulled at his jacket. "I'll see you in ten days. I know Charley here will have an inkling as to his whereabouts."

Harry had no words to say. Instead, he turned and hefted the gasoline drum up onto the gunnels of his boat, and Charley came over and helped him.

"A fair voyage," said Halliday, and walked away along the jetty. Harry stared after him.

"You find him, Caddie," said Francine, coming to stand close by.

"He's threatened to take the family's valuables if George don't come back."

"You tell George," she said. "He know what to do."

Grace came forward and stood beside him. He touched her hand a moment and she drew away, embarrassed probably at such public display. So he leapt across to the deck.

He went aft and twisted the small handle of the make-or-break ignition until the engine's single cylinder caught and chuttered. The dry-exhaust pipe rising behind him spat clouds of black smoke that grew paler as the seconds progressed. Charley untied and pushed out the prow from the jetty. Harry engaged the flywheel. He held the rudder hard to port and the *Hesperus* swung away from the jetty. They arced out past the headland, north and east of the Island of Graves. When he looked back, he saw Chief Owadi was standing on the plankway above the jetty with Crosby, Halliday, and the Indian, To-Cop, watching after them.

"So, Charley," Harry said, once the village was finally obscured by the headland. The open ocean stood to port, and the mountains and the fjords of the mainland's coastline to starboard, a scant few miles away. "Which way? Or are you still fucking pondering?"

Charley came aft from his perch among the bales. "I think all night," he said, "and no place other good. Go Ba'as. Blunden Harbour, you say." And he pointed north and a little east. "You know?"

"I do. Why there?"

"Have baccy?" Harry reached in his pocket and threw over his tobacco tin. Charley turned it in his hands a while and opened it at last. "Good box," he said. "Where from?"

Harry ignored the question. "Why're we going to Blunden?"

"George learn many thing of Nakwakto people when he young. He close many people there. George heart in them woods. Hunt for animal there many time. Maybe people see him. Maybe he there in village." He struck a match and lit his rolled cigarette.

"And Francine's Nakwakto, is she not? I wonder he wouldn't have mentioned it to her."

"He just go. Not speak first. Old George close her brother many year from when he boy. Brother die now. Same everyone. But maybe George go back there remember." Charley blew a long draft of smoke. "You know old George he paxala?"

Harry shook his head and shrugged, not knowing what the old man meant.

"Man have medicine. Shaman, Mr. Boas call. George become paxala with Nakwakto. Think George now in land Nakwakto."

"Why?"

"Know George. He like have power over thing. But cannot have power over death. He not save son, David. Before he try with paxala medicine. Maybe now go think thing from past. Have problem in head about what can or cannot do. Nakwakto—that where George become real Indian first time. Lose white blood. Now go back think about be Indian again."

Harry had never thought of Charley having much awareness of the workings of the mind. "You've more to you than you show, haven't you, Charley Seaweed?" he said.

Charley shrugged. "Or else George go die on sea." He leaned over the gunnels and spat. "Killing self big thing, now you white fuck men come."

Harry angled the *Hesperus* north toward the thirty miles or so of sea that separated them from Blunden Harbour. He tied off the rudder and stood. "Pull to it," he said. "We're as well to raise sail, with the wind so fair on our quarter. You're not just here as guide. You can labour too. And I'll be pleased if you'll throw me back my baccy."

Charley pulled it from his pocket. He smiled. "Nice box," he said and tossed it back.

The sky stayed clear and the wind still in the south and west. They made the deep inlet, at the entrance of which lay Blunden Harbour, in five hours, much of it with the tide. Harry had been here some six weeks before, trading.

Twelve houses stood against the forest's looming spruce and cedar. Several were the newer, smaller framed houses of the white man's design. There was evidence of the modern world in the milled lumber and the glass windows of many of the houses, even here in one of the more remote Kwagiulth villages. With the tide in, there was no beach. The houses were stilted, built out over the shingle itself where it sloped so steeply into the water. A plankway ran along in front of the houses, and here and there along it, steps led down to the water.

As they drew closer, Harry watched to see if he could make out George's canoe among the many others tied against the steps. But all the designs along their sides were of wolf and bear and seal, and nowhere could he see the killer whale.

"Not have George canoe," said Charley.

"We'll tie off before the house of Chief Walewid," Harry said.

"Black-soul," Charley muttered. He walked forward to get the mooring rope. "Better we speak Cousin Yagis."

"No trade this time," shouted Chief Walewid from his doorway as Harry leapt from the *Hesperus* to the steps in front of the chieftain's house. The young man emerged into the light, black squinting eyes and jagged yellow teeth. He leaned against the totem pole out front, bare but for the wolf's head high at its apex. "Too much trade already with you, Fat Harry. Go fuck off. Come back few months."

"Can we moor here the evening then, Chief? Visit with the people of our clan?"

"No white man clan here." He spat down into the water, insolently close past Harry's feet.

"Yoh," said Charley from the boat's prow. He spoke a few words in Kwakwala. Walewid glowered some, but he flicked his hand behind his head in dismissal and then his bulky, violent form vanished back inside. No other people were there to be seen. A thin dog, missing clumps of its fur, barked at them from farther along the plankway. "Them all away fish, and berry gather season start now," said Charley. "Back tonight."

"Well Walewid's not gone anywheres. And deep drunk as well," Harry said.

"Bad fucking man," said Charley.

"He ain't usually so savage." Harry thought on the liquor in the hold. Alcohol had been a mainstay of his income since he'd come north from San Francisco. It had its ill effects on some, right enough. Still, he was hardly its only source for the Indians. Many of the traders made a profit quietly from its sale to the brown men. Harry wasn't a missionary, nor any sort of do-gooder, to be changing the world, ugly though that world might very well be.

"Maybe he know already," said Charley, pointing his nose toward Walewid's home.

"What? About George? He was only charged yesterday. The storm would have stopped anyone on the water till now, and we the first out from Rupert that I saw."

"Not about white man charge. About funeral."

"Christ almighty!" Harry had pestered Charley for answers already, but he'd only shake his head, mumble "Just thing," and shrug. "Something went on out there, and none of you black bastards will tell me what." Harry stood on the plankway glaring down at Charley. "Even though it's I looking for George, and it don't help me nothing at all that I don't know."

"Not important what happen. Important what people say happen."

"So what the fuck are people saying happened?"

Charley just looked away. Harry sighed. As likely pry an oyster open with a baby's fingernail as draw information from this cocksucker. "So the gossip's passed already up this way, has it? I've not seen anyone out from the village, nor heard of it. The fishermen don't usually travel out this far, nor in this direction. They sail oceanward."

Charley sat on the gunnels, and he seemed deep in his thinking. "Dream people tell," he said at last.

Harry pondered this. "Walewid dreamed it?"

"No. Them come and go."

71

"Who is them?"

"Dream people."

"They come and go—dream people—whispering gossip?"

"Ek."

"Spare me your hocus-pocus, man," he said. "You know me more than that." But Charley said nothing more. Harry gazed away down the steeply mountained inlet, the tidal waters swirling slowly, green, violet, and steel. He wanted to smash something. Pick up a paddle and go after that chicken-bred savage, Walewid. Teach him a few manners before his betters.

An old woman, short and obese, shuffled away along the plankway. She disappeared into a house at the far end of the village. Harry thought of going after her. But it was the building the Temperance Society of the Anglican Mission had built for those seeking shelter from the wicked ways of drink and heathenism. Not a place in which he'd likely be welcomed.

He shook himself and jumped back on deck. "We'll cook up some food on board," he said. "Wait for Yagis."

The sun was low on the Pacific's horizon and the fishermen of Blunden Harbour came paddling home from the ocean in its pinkish-orange glow.

Harry and Charley sat at their ease on the deckhouse, smoking.

"Good luck take fish, this sun," said Charley. "Same colour salmon."

Already the women had ambled out of the forest, their baskets filled with the first wild strawberries of that season, the salmonberries that looked like raspberries, and with blue huckleberries.

When at last he could make out Yagis and his two sons in their canoe, Harry slid down from the deckhouse. He waited until they were turning in toward the steps in front of their house, three along from Walewid's, and then he called "Yoh" to them. Yagis merely raised a hand without looking, intent as he was on the business of landing. His younger son leapt, agile, from the canoe's prow and tied off against a thick support.

Yagis stepped forward along the canoe, carrying his sixty years and more carefully. He was wiry and short and with a scar he carried proudly from his childhood, livid, jagged and deep, running diagonally across his face so that his nose seemed split in two. He'd taken it resisting the Haida

72

slave raiders from the north who'd ranged along the coast in earlier times. So, at least, went the tale he had spun to Harry, when last they'd met.

The old man wore rubber boots, high trousers with braces, and a ragged collarless shirt. On his head was a stovepipe hat, its crown high, as if he were some brown Abe Lincoln of the fjords. Harry smiled as Yagis shrugged away a hand from his younger son and hopped, ungainly, across onto the steps.

He climbed to the plankway, where one of his two wives was waiting with a dirty white blanket. He stood staring into the distance as she draped it around him, so that now he seemed a Caesar being dressed into his toga by a slave.

When she was done he turned to Harry. His face broke into a smile, the scar a squirming snake across his face. "Hah!" he said and came toward him. "These stupid family jump like I am lord of all men." Harry grinned. "Fat Harry, yoh." They shook hands in the white man style. "Eat with me and talk and tell me what happen in the world." This last he said without a smile.

There were few formalities for dinner. Harry and Charley sat to either side of Yagis, and the old man's two sons nearby. Both of Yagis's wives were aged and ample in blankets, great hoops of cedar bark in their ears, so that to Harry they looked a matching pair, seated there across the fire.

Yagis's one surviving daughter was not young herself, married twice and both husbands dead, one of disease and the other fallen drunk from a steam freighter in heavy seas and drowned. She shuffled in the firelight and silently brought mackerel and dried salmon, a small wooden trough of eulachon oil, the pasted roots of plants, and salmonberries stewed into a syrup to be slurped as loudly as was possible from the hand-sized wooden spoons they all were wielding.

"Thank you," said Harry as she laid a small wooden plate before him on the ground.

"You want marry her, she yours," said Yagis, waving a spoon his daughter's way. "No more chieftains rich enough for she to marry. All dead. No ceremony to give her proper. Least no ceremony we can tell the white man, eh?" and he slapped his spoon against Harry's thigh. "And I never send her be prostitute," he said, and proudly.

"I've a wife already," said Harry, "and her as much as I can handle."

"Old days all the chiefs have many wives. Marry to give crests and dances. Then marry again. And the wife as well. Four times marry and then she a famous chief woman herself. Not just for sale no more."

"Everything's changing in the world."

"No, I not sell my woman. Understand the white man ways. Slaves are finish now forever, and good, I say, to that. Some good things, but not enough, have come. We are less people every year and dead more and more. This one village is all the Nakwakto together now. Before we have villages all through the inlets. So many people before, Fat Harry. Now just two children who are less than ten year old in this village. Just two. A few more marry people and children other tribe and village. But we die and go and that be that. The end." He shook his head a moment. Then he scooped a great spoonful of fish grease and supped it down and farted. "You have liquor on you boat?"

"I do."

"Then we drink tonight." One of his wives spoke a few throaty sylla-bles and he replied. "She say I a mad old man and drinking make me so." He giggled, high-pitched, sounding like a young girl. "She don't know we drink at end of world, so no problem if we mad or not."

"Ek," said Charley. They talked together and both of them laughed. Yagis's sons laughed as well, who before had eaten in silence, only throw-ing occasional looks Harry's way, so that more and more he'd come to think they knew something, and were but waiting for the subject to be addressed.

"What's funny?" Harry said.

"You the white man come with drink," said Yagis. "You one of the kill-ers. Like the Devil heself, eh? But you the good man white man too. Who to say what make sense any more? About anything? This make us laugh."

"Make weep too," said Charley, and Yagis giggled again at that.

"So all the Nakwakto villages are gone?" said Harry.

"Gone dead," said Yagis. "I from village Teguxste, up past the rapids," and he waved his arm vaguely toward the east and north. "But we move from there what fifteen year ago or more. All people gather here at Ba'as. First, for trade with white man. This place on edge of ocean to catch they ships. Later we say stupid be separate any more when we so few."

"George said once, before last I came up here, that you'd not had so much contact with the white man. Least not so much as others."

"True before. But sickness come anyway. Once people make war for slave and fur, and for sadness at dead of chieftains. And drink come the last thing. So we go slow into nothing." They ate in silence for a while. Then Yagis said, "George he come to Teguxste when he young. Many times. You know he friend to my cousin, name Make-Alive, brother to George wife before he die. But they friend long time before that too."

"Charley said something of it."

"Much fire in that bugger, Make-Alive," said Yagis. "Always shouting about something. Not enough food for people. About have medicine and things. But good for chieftain be shouting. I sorry when he die. And now this rat-prick fuck man Walewid chief, and him too many crest and name and dance he have and too young to have them. And he only shout when he in drink and about nothing of import neither." He spat into the fire.

"So George been coming here for years, has he?"

Yagis glanced from the corner of his eye in Harry's direction, and seemed to judge him for a moment. "Teguxste where George first be paxala. Long year past."

Harry wondered how to broach the subject of their search. Could he trust Yagis and his family with the truth? They had known George most of his life, were bonded by clan and family ties and had played it true with Harry in his trading, the last time he was here. Yagis was prone to drink though, and he liked a story. Could he keep his mouth to himself?

He caught Charley's eyes upon him. Charley twitched his head, just faintly, but enough for Harry to keep his counsel for the meantime.

Yagis pushed the trough of rank fish oil his way. "Eat," he said. Harry made his customary refusal, and suffered the usual derision to follow. But he saw that both the old women only watched him across the fire, their features reticent and still.

Later Harry and Charley sat outside on the steps and smoked. Clouds covered the heavens. It was dark. Fire glow wavered through the village doorways, lighting the water for fifty yards or so. From some of the houses came raucous laughter and voices raised in drink. Farther down the plankway three old men were sitting quietly, a bottle before them.

"Why not ask Yagis direct?" Harry said.

"Good man but big mouth."

"But what is it we're hiding?"

"Many men not love George. Now maybe have reason do more than be angry. Come after him maybe. Better stay quiet."

"So how then do we learn anything, in God's name?"

"Go back inside. Talk, drink, think."

Harry cursed, suddenly infuriated by the man, by the village, by everything. "You go. I can't take no more." He stood. "I'm aboard the *Hesperus* awhile." He left Charley and walked along the plankway to his boat. From inside Chief Walewid's greathouse came the sounds of intoxication. There were loud voices and he heard scuffles and shouts from the women, and also laughter. Quietly, he stepped aboard the *Hesperus*. The tide was out and the boat was partly grounded, so that the deck listed maybe twenty degrees.

Harry needed solitude. Every word he spoke felt tested. Ridicule could cover threat, and threat might mean no more than sarcasm. A smile could be a warning, and a grimace acknowledgment of friendship. Words were rarely honest or solely as they seemed, even from such an affable man as Yagis. He felt drawn taut with fury, like a cable pulled so tight it whined.

He walked aft around the pilothouse and ducked through the doorway. Not bothering to light a lamp, he opened a small cupboard by his feet. He felt for a saucepan. He'd brew up some coffee and clear his head.

After dinner, he had brought in two bottles of liquor. Harry did not personally favour drink, except when duty and respect demanded it of him. Not any more. But this night he had partaken of more than he had in some years.

They'd talked of trade and hunting, fishing and trapping. Yagis said he was reluctant to go this year and join the other men at the canneries.

"Making cash is one thing, and good maybe. But on what do we spend it if we here on reserve and only you few white men come past now and then? In summer we find food for winter. That is what we do. If we in the factory, still we must find food for winter." Yagis slugged at the bottle, his Adam's apple furious. "Who take time to catch and trap and gather? We try, but not time enough before men go to work again."

He passed the bottle to his son. "Last time, I buy fish grease from *you*, Fat Harry! Indian buy grease from white man!" Charley grunted at this. "And now salmon are less each year, and big fishing boat from Japan, America, and England even, God save Queen, make it so."

"Tell me what it is you want," Harry said, surprised by his own question.

But Yagis said only, "I want much, Fat Harry," and after that he was silent for a time.

Crouching in the deckhouse, Harry took the saucepan, opened another low cupboard door, and his fingers felt for the coffee jar. He heard a sound outside, like a brush swept lightly across a surface. He listened but heard nothing more. He brought the coffee from its hiding place and then he heard a footfall close outside, and another. Someone was on board. He made to call, but instead stayed quiet. There were further sounds then, and terse whispers in Kwakwala.

He heard a rattle and realized it was the chain that held the latch to the forward hold, which was not locked, just tied about itself, from where he'd visited it earlier. Harry stood slowly, without a sound, just enough to see through the glass to the forward deck. Against the firelight ashore, two silhouettes were visible, one stooping, the other standing. The one standing held a whalebone killing club, more than three feet long and curved into a thick knot at its end.

Fury pressed at Harry's stomach, so that he almost gagged. He took down the machete from above the door, still watching the men on deck. Quietly then, he stepped out through the doorway, keeping low. The men had swung open the door to the hold, and now one began to lower himself inside. Harry watched over the roof of the pilothouse as he moved silently around it, his left hand resting on its wall, supporting him against the sloping deck. In his right hand was the long blade.

From the hold there came an exclamation. The man inside appeared. He was holding two bottles of liquor. He placed them on the deck and disappeared again. The other laughed, stooped down and lifted one bottle up. Harry heard a voice back on the plankway, and he understood there were at least three men intent on burglary. He stopped in indecision. Then the man on deck spoke, slurring in his speech. In amongst the garbled language, he heard his own name, spoken with a sneer.

Harry stepped out from behind the deckhouse, but the other man heard him. He spun more swiftly than Harry would have imagined possible, thinking the man too far gone in drink to be so sharp-witted. He swung his club and Harry shied sideways. The club hit him on his left shoulder.

The agony of it near made him pass out, but he jabbed upward with the machete. The blade went into the underside of the man's upper arm and jagged against the bone before it carried on into his armpit. Harry's reach gave out and he pulled the blade back. The pain in his own shoulder made him go down to his knees.

The man's club fell to the ground and he fell after it, screaming. Harry could see the blood spilling from the wound and the man trying to stem it, and now the whites of the man's eyes were visible in his shock. There was a shout from the shore, then a thud on deck, even as Harry saw the head of the man in the hold emerge. He stood again and kicked out, but the man ducked back inside.

Harry spun round and saw a squat figure coming aft, crazily angled against the slanting deck, holding a short knife before him. The tears of pain in Harry's eyes made the figure blur and double. His balance seemed a thing both vague and complex, but he raised the machete and the figure stopped. Harry made to thrust at him. As he did so, his foot slipped in the blood on the deck. He toppled sideways even as the other man rushed at him. He rolled as he fell, trying to protect his damaged shoulder, and the machete dropped from his grasp as he struck the deck. He turned over onto his back, his legs coming up protectively before him.

The man was on him immediately. Harry felt the knife slide along his shinbone. He kicked with both feet and one found a target in the darkness. He heard a grunt. The other man was still screaming. Harry flailed his hands around beside him, feeling for the machete, his vision still hazed. He saw the shadow of the third man, bent double from Harry's kick.

The fingers of his right hand touched the damp grain of the war club. They closed around it. He felt by its weight that he held it at its handle grip. The man was nearly on him again. Harry swung the club, clumsy, at the man's legs and felt it smash into flesh. The man shouted, stepped back and waited, wary, a few feet away.

Harry dragged himself backward until his spine rested against the gunnels. The man came down the slope and feinted to Harry's wounded left side. He weaved, though, and seemed unsteady himself. Sitting as he now was, his equilibrium improved, Harry brought the club in an arc around his body. The man dodged away but lost balance on the sloping deck. His leg hit the gunnels. He flipped over the side and Harry heard him go into the water.

He looked toward the hold, but the man inside had not yet reappeared. There was shouting now and uproar on shore. Lamps were moving on the plankway. The injured man had stopped his screaming, and now he was moaning more softly. Harry gasped air. He looked to his own injuries. His shirt was torn off his shoulder, and blood flowed down his arm. He saw that his shoulder was in a position outside of all sensibility. As seasoned in serious injuries as he was from years at sea, still he had to look away. The agony of it brought flashes of lightning across his vision. His lower leg was soaked with blood, though he felt nothing there. He rested his head back on the top of the gunnels. He tried not to scream himself.

Again the deck shuddered as someone, and another, and then more, jumped aboard.

"Fat Harry?" Charley came into his vision, Yagis's eldest son beside him. He heard shouts and curses and Charley's face disappeared again. Yagis was calling out, loud above the clamour from the shore. There was movement now all around him, voices raised in Kwakwala, Charley's chief among them. He tried to focus. Men were standing on the deck, a couple of them holding lanterns. Some were crouched about the bleeding man. These men were close to violence, it seemed, making angry noises at Charley, who stood in front of Harry with Yagis's son beside him.

In the water behind his head something was splashing. There was laughter then, from those ashore, and jeering. Harry could see that on the plankway now the entire village had turned out. The men aboard stopped their arguing. They moved over and looked out.

The sounds told Harry the man who had gone overboard was thrashing in the thigh-deep water, caught in the deep mud beneath. Even the men on deck were laughing now. Charley knelt beside him.

"Okay, Fat Harry?"

Harry grunted. "Thief," he managed.

"Them try steal liquor. You fight."

"Who?"

"Wal'wid brother, him you cut. Wal'wid in water now." He put his hands to Harry's shoulder. Harry groaned and cursed. "Shoulder come out," Charley said. "Bad bleed. Big split. Not think broke. Club hit you?"

"Leg too," Harry whispered. He closed his eyes. Charley took hold of his right foot and turned the shin against the light. "Bleed much here too. Make bandage quick. Not bad same shoulder."

"Walewid's brother?"

"Him bad. Maybe die."

"Bandages, disinfectant, sewing needles in the pilothouse. Right top cupboard."

"First, shoulder go back in." Charley rested his hands on him. "You ready?" Before Harry could speak, Charley shucked his shoulder back into its joint. He cried out and lost consciousness.

All was nausea and pain. Harry opened his eyes. Blurs of orange flame and shadows. Then movement. Charley squatted before him, doing something to his shin. The old man looked up when he felt Harry shift.

"Not move," he said.

"How long?" said Harry, his memory returning. Phlegm was thick in the back of his throat, so that he croaked and was almost unintelligible.

Charley seemed to understand. "Sleep maybe five minute only," he said.

"What happened?"

"Them take Poodlas, Wal'wid brother, in house. Him bad. Take Wal'wid from water. Him great shame. Very funny for people. Not funny for us. Him angry try come back on boat kill you. Yagis and sons stop him, and other people stop him. Now them wait, watch." He pointed shoreward. Harry saw figures standing silhouetted against the light coming from the open entrance of Walewid's house.

Harry swore softly and tried to prop himself higher against the gunnels. He groaned as his shoulder howled protest. Charley helped him, then said, "Now not move," and went back to sewing up the long, ragged wound in his shin. Harry hawked, turned his head and spat back into the water. Charley tied the thread and cut it away with the machete, unwieldy in such a delicate operation. He poured iodine down the injury from the bottle beside him. Harry snorted. Then Charley wrapped a bandage about his calf.

A voice raised a question from shore. Charley answered, "Ek." A man came aboard and in the light of a lantern, which now hung from the mast, Harry saw it was Yagis.

"No good what happen," the old man said. He sat beside Harry on the sloping deck. "We take you back my house now. Better look after you. More safe from Walewid as well."

"I'll stay aboard," said Harry. "I'd not risk my boat by not being here to protect it."

Charley grunted in agreement. He finished the bandaging on Harry's leg and moved now to his shoulder.

"Right," said Yagis. "We move boat down by my house better." He looked overboard. "When tide back in. Maybe half-hour." Already the *Hesperus* was listing less, trembling in the placid waves.

"Maybe better go leave when tide come back," said Charley. Harry kept silent as Charley washed his shoulder in iodine, then dipped the needle in the bottle before threading it once more. "Bruise here very big and big open cut on top. Much pain for sew back." Then he pushed the needle in through Harry's skin and across and out again and tugged, and the broken edges of the wound were drawn together.

Yagis watched Harry, who just breathed heavily through his nose, knowing he was even now being judged on his strength of character. After a moment, Yagis seemed satisfied and nodded his head. "Better you go," he said. "You give Walewid much shame. All know he wrong. He try steal from you and you fight and you win. Shame on him and family that he do wrong thing, and white man beat him in fight. And look stupid in water." Yagis laughed, but with little humour. "Very funny. But if brother die, then more trouble."

Charley finished his sewing. He took another bandage, tied it into a sling, wrapped it about Harry, and secured his arm tight against his chest. Harry rolled sideways, leaned out over the gunnels and threw up. Then he sent Charley down into the hold to bring up a bottle. He guzzled and passed it to Yagis. Together, they listened to the murmur of the people ashore, each staring at the deck and deep in their thoughts, waiting for what would come with the tide.

On shore there was a larger hubbub then. Harry saw a form in the doorway to Walewid's house that seemed some shapeless, writhing darkness, turning about, blocking sometimes half the firelight inside the house behind, as if it shrunk down to drift low upon the ground, then rearing up until only a sliver of light was visible. It twisted again, and now Harry could see that it had a head, and the profile was that of a wolf. The jaws snapped open and shut, the sound a sharp clack-clack that echoed against the darkness. Then it spoke in the throaty singsong of high Kwakwala. All fell silent to listen. The voice was Walewid's.

"What's he saying?" Harry asked Yagis, but the old man only motioned him to silence.

Charley leaned in and whispered along with the narration. "Talk about clan and ancestor. Make list of he names and dance and crest. Same way chief always start talk." Now Walewid began to speak with greater passion. Charley was silent listening. Then he said, "Say you attack. Them come boat fight back. Fat Harry and he family sell whisky, make Indian man poor and crazy. He say Killer Whale, meaning you and me people, soon get dead in belly of Wolf, mean him."

He was silent again listening, and Harry heard notes of agreement muttered from the people on the shore. Charley shook his head. "Talk about George, he book, and about funeral. Say that not how Indian do. Shame to us." He listened again. "Say him know old George out in forest somewhere in land of Nakwakto. Say you and George same family. So all same bad and must make punish from Indian. If him brother Poodlas die, then you, me, old George go be skull in Wal'wid house."

Walewid finished speaking. Now he leapt forward into a crouch, the huge wolf mask shaking from side to side, the jaws snapping at the people nearby. He stood again and made threatening steps toward the *Hesperus*. He jumped back, then leapt forward again, howling out now, his voice almost a shriek at the end of its breath. Then he spun about and disappeared back inside.

"He speak enough true for men think too much now," said Yagis. "All know he a fool and too much angry. But people also angry about George. Yes," he said, as Harry, groggy now from pain, looked across to him. "This we all hear. Everyone hear all up and down coast for sure. George do bad things at he son funeral. If white man hear then more shame for us, they think we savages. And there be bad words to speak." He spoke in Kwakwala to Charley, who shrugged and muttered something terse in reply. "Best you go quick," Yagis said.

The *Hesperus* was floating now, although Harry could feel its bottom clipping the mud beneath on every ripple of the incoming tide. He reached behind him and tried to pull himself up with his good arm on the gunnels, but he gasped and slumped back to the deck.

"Not move," said Charley. "I do."

"Put me forward so I can help see the way at least."

Yagis and Charley put their arms behind him. He groaned as they lifted him to his feet. He might have lost consciousness if his shoulder was not so shrill inside his head. Instead he was propped against the front of the pilothouse. Yagis raised his voice and one of his sons came aboard. Charley pointed. The son took a bucket and leaned over the side. He threw several bucketloads of water across the deck, and it carried much of the blood away with it.

Yagis and his son stepped back ashore. They unmoored the *Hesperus* and pushed her back as Charley fired the engine. She chugged away from the village in reverse. Harry breathed as slowly as he was able. He watched the people on the plankway, who all were staring silently their way. He could not make out their expressions, standing with their backs to the shore-light, almost in silhouette. They did not move nor make a sound, and Yagis and his sons there with them, until the boat swung about and Harry could not see them any more.

"Go Alert Bay," said Charley, when they had travelled a mile or so out into the waters of the inlet. "See doctor."

Harry lay propped against the pilothouse. Charley had laid some sailcloth behind him and Harry's greatcoat over him. His head rolled with the swell. His mind drifted with blood loss and with whisky. He wanted nothing more than sleep.

He bent his right knee and pushed a little weight down through his leg. The wound on his shin smarted, but he could walk on it. His shoulder was worse, and the damage there would take far longer to repair.

Two things needed consideration. Firstly, his injuries. The one on his leg was near eight inches long, but not deep. The knife had merely slid along his shinbone and the wound should heal in time. The ragged, zigzag gash that ran down across his shoulder, resembling the broken skin of some dropped fruit, was not so good. It was a deep wound, and all around it heavily bruised from the impact of the war club. He'd seen dislocations before. It took many weeks to gain use again, and always discomfort to follow. Yet he had been fortunate: if it had connected directly, rather than just that glancing blow, it would surely have shattered the bones. Well, he'd broken bones before, his body was scarred in numerous places already, and of aches and grumbling joints he was possessed of plenty. A couple more were neither here nor there in the grander scheme.

With his good hand he drew the tattered edges of his shirt together until he felt more confident there were no parts missing that might have been buried in the wound, threatening infection. Still, with such gaping holes in him, the risk of contamination was there. He had sufficient iodine to bathe his injuries for many days as yet, however, and he'd weathered similar or worse before.

The second consideration was how quickly his strength would return. Well, he would eat something now, despite the nausea in his stomach, and he would drink water in quantity. Then sleep and, in the morning, he would know more about his condition.

"Charley," he said, "let's lay up somewhere safe for the night. Then we'd best be finding George, and quickly, now that we know so many are against him everywhere."

"You sick."

"I ain't dying yet. We'll lay some miles between us and Walewid, then hove to. See if I'm in better form with the light of day."

"Think Poodlas die tonight." Harry heard him spit.

"Well, I am sorry for that." He *was* sorry. The man was a thief, it was true, but there was something not entirely right with the night's events. Something he couldn't think through at this moment. Something that made him feel all the sicker somehow.

"All be sorry soon," said Charley.

Harry chewed on some dried salmon and hard bread. He nearly threw it straight back up, but he fought the nausea with drafts of water. Charley had pointed the *Hesperus* south at first. Now he turned west and, keeping the dim black outline of the mainland to starboard, a mile off, he followed the coast west then northwest.

"Stop by Gwax-laelaa," he said, pointing ahead. "Stuart Point." But Harry heard him only distantly. He shivered as he felt again through his hand the machete blade impact against Poodlas's bone, the flesh-impeded slither up along the arm and into the armpit. Blood was warm again across his fingers. Then he slept.

He woke in the early dawn. His gummed eyelids held together for a moment, and then snapped open. He moaned, fuddled by alcohol, images from black dreams, and the slow awakening of his senses to the injuries on his body. He levered himself up against the pilothouse. With his good arm, he brushed at the dew on his greatcoat.

He could hear Charley snoring from the open latch to the forward hold. There was a jar of water beside him. He lifted it and guzzled. His tobacco tin was also there. He cursed when he had to use the hand on the side of his damaged shoulder—the whole arm numb and riddled with pins and needles from the tightness of the strapping—to roll the cigarette. He flipped the match alight with his thumbnail, and took stock.

They were anchored a hundred yards from shore in a small cove indented in a headland that arced, low and forested, from northeast to southwest, sheltering them from the ocean proper. The day was clear and cold with a light wind from the north, and clouds far off in that direction threatening rain.

He pushed himself up. He felt as if he had been beaten over the whole of his body. The pain in his leg wound was intense now, yet he could put enough weight on it to limp. His shoulder was near the limit of what he could bear, but that was to be expected for now. The shock was gone and he did not think there was infection in him. He was not sweating, nor did he feel in any way feverish. Indeed, he felt clear in his mind. Clearer than he remembered feeling in he couldn't say how long, in fact. How was that? Something was missing.

He realized then that it was the absence of anger. There was no trace of the relentless vitriol with which these past days had been filled. Nearly getting killed and maybe murdering another would do that, he supposed.

He heard Charley grumble and swear and shift about, and knew that he was awake. So he shuffled around the pilothouse and inside.

He brewed coffee on the small gas stove. He brought two cups out on deck and handed one to Charley, who stood blinking and scowling, and helping himself to Harry's tobacco.

"How you?" Charley said, once he had a cigarette glowing.

"I'm thinking we keep going till we find him," Harry said, "though where we go I don't got no idea."

Charley looked him up and down. "Big mess," he said. "Good idea change clothe." Harry eyed himself. His shirt was black and flaking dried blood. On the side where it had been torn, it was held together only by its collar. His trousers had been ripped to the knee. The bandages on both shoulder and leg were caked in blood as well. "You face too," said Charley, "not blood you. Blood him." Harry felt across his face and spots of blood came off as dust. He ran his fingers up through his hair. It was clammy, and not just with the morning's dew. The decking was stained almost black all about.

So he stripped off his clothes with Charley's knife, and Charley went below to fetch a change. Harry had soap in the pilothouse. When Charley came back up on deck, he drew buckets of water from the sea. They removed the strapping from his arm. He scrubbed himself as best he could with salt water, and Charley helped as well, pouring fresh water from their rain keg over him at the last until he shivered against it.

When he was dry, Charley unpeeled the bandages, which tugged at the wounds beneath as they came away. They inspected Charley's handiwork of the night before. There was no invidious purple in the frayed edges of skin where they were drawn together with sail twine. Charley poured iodine upon them. Harry drew short breaths and looked up at the sky. Then Charley re-bandaged the wounds. He said, "Not know you fighting man."

"Not so great a one, though, is I?" said Harry.

"Tell story last night now."

So Harry related what had occurred. He was honest enough to say that it was he who first stepped forward to do injury to the thieves. At the end of the recounting, Charley merely nodded and pondered for a while in silence. Then he said, staring out toward the ocean as he spoke, "Kill man before?"

Harry thought on this. He had kept his history to himself before now. "I have," he said at last.

Charley nodded again. "You win fight. Many people think good you fight you property. All know Walewid fool. Know he drink. But you white. Some also think same he. Hear he lies. Be anger you." He shrugged. "Maybe Poodlas live."

"Where should we be heading?"

"Know now where go."

Harry waited. Eventually, he said, "And where is that?"

"He go Teguxste," said Charley, "where he make be paxala before, like Yagis say."

"And how come you to be so certain?"

"Just know. George cannot save son. George like ocean. Go deep. Now he go back for memory." Harry wondered again at the insights of old Charley Seaweed. "You know the way?" he said.

"No and yes."

"No and yes?"

"Not go there. Hear what people say before. Know many story. Go up past Nakwakto rapid. After, look."

Harry pushed himself up. "Then let's find him before some other fucker does," he said.

● ● ●

The *Hesperus* rode the growing swell, her prow to the westerly wind, engine sputtering enough to hold her stationary. Harry and Charley sat on the gunnels to either side of the rudder. They watched the vast storm front fermenting on the horizon.

"Three hour come," said Charley, and Harry grunted agreement.

A day and a night and half of a morning had passed. From Blunden Harbour they had headed north and a little west, following the coast. The wind had come hard and cold from the north, though the weather stayed clear. They'd had so tough a time beating into it, as close-hauled as the *Hesperus* could sail, both of them needed to work the boat, with Harry propped at the tiller barking orders to Charley—crying "Watch for the boom, you damned idiot!" on every tack—that he was soon exhausted, and they'd used the engine more than Harry would've liked with limited stocks of gasoline aboard. But, at last, the wind had turned westerly, an hour before.

Now, they were holding a few cables off an archipelago of small islets, each no more than a hundred yards across, with sparse trees and brush, and seabirds thick on each of them. Behind these islets, Branham Island was visible, dense with evergreen and curving away to the west and north. A narrow waterway, which Harry knew as Schooner Channel, ran north between it and the mainland.

"Tide change maybe two three hour more," Charley said, following Harry's gaze toward the waters streaming down Schooner Channel to collide with the ocean waves in flume and turmoil, a maelstrom from which they were protected by the archipelago. "Tide still go out, but storm wave get big make water crazy."

Up the channel at its end, as yet invisible, there was a narrow break between two headlands. On the far side lay tens of miles of inlets, and all the waters of their ebb and flood passing through a gap no more than two hundred yards across, with only ten minutes of slack water between the tides. These were the Nakwakto Rapids. To the people, Charley had told him, they were the Cannibal's Teeth, and you darted through them fast and silent, or be torn and swallowed.

Charley had been inside before as a boy, but only travelling by canoe, he'd said. They had discussed as many details as Charley could remember. Beyond were old villages, now dead. As Yagis had said, what people had survived the spread of diseases and the wars that followed had moved to be nearer the sea and the trade that plied its way along the coast.

"First gunboat of English, now Royal Canada Gov'ment come stop war party of other tribes," as Charley put it. "After, people don't need hide in waterway same before. Now Nakwakto sell skin, work the cannery and ship." Harry had met some as had seen Japan, and one Indian he'd spoken to had been as far as England.

There was some spirit left in the buggers, sure enough. Harry shrugged his shoulders and felt a dart of pain. "We'll go in closer and lay anchor till the rapids are ready for us," he said. He rolled himself a cigarette and passed the tin across.

Charley said, "Cannot go against tide. Too strong. Must wait turn. Then run with tide all way up channel and through." They smoked in silence for a while. Then Charley said, "How long you have *Hep'rus*?"

"Three years now, it is," said Harry.

"Do what before come Rupert?"

"I was selling liquor up and down the coast, as far as Fort William."

Charley was silent for a time. Then he said, "Where you from?"

"San Francisco." All this time and only now did Charley show some interest in Harry's life. A little knife work and he was become a somebody. "Leastways, it was there I spent my first years. Enough time at sea and your roots get pulled in the end." What roots of any kind there'd been. "I'm as much from Rupert as I'm from anywheres else, I guess."

"Why come here?"

Harry shrugged.

"Why not go south? Same go north go south."

Harry rubbed his palms together slowly. "The sloop's big enough for cargo and I heard there was trade growing in Canada. I might've gone on past and all the way to Russia if I'd not stopped off at Rupert."

"You bring whisky," said Charley.

Harry finished his cigarette and flicked it out onto the water. "I did bring whisky," he said. "I've a deal with my man down south. I'd take it up and down the coast. This trip I had sold the most of it already by the time I landed at Rupert."

"Find more than trade," said Charley. "Find wife. Family too."

"Aye, and I'm blessed." He wondered that such words poured out from him so easily.

Charley was quiet beside him. Then he said, "You not drink whisky more than polite. Drink more before?"

Harry pressed his fingertips against each other. "There was a time I did," he said.

"Before, I not know man you are," Charley said. "Now see you fighting man. Maybe know better now. Good Christian white man say whisky bad for Indian. Hal'day, Crosby. But most man cannot choose do what good what bad." He looked over at Harry. "You life a long story, maybe."

Harry squeezed the calluses of his palms together. "Long, maybe," he said. "But without much of meaning to it, far as I see. As is true for most men, I think."

Charley lifted a hand to shield his eyes. "Look," he said, pointing. "*Comox* come." The Union Steamship Company's SS *Comox* was rounding the headland to the south and bearing north. "Go Queen Charlotte Islands," Charley said.

"Aye, and she'll be turning round and heading back past Alert Bay soon enough. We'll hail her and send a message to Halliday."

"About what, send message?"

"About Blunden Harbour. They'd as best know there's more than white men's legal issues afoot."

"About you stab Poodlas?"

"They were thieving from my boat. I was in my rights to go at them."

"Walewid say different."

"There's plenty and wise enough who saw what happened, and you and Yagis among them. I'll not fear for myself for that. And if George is returned home while we're away, then it's best he and the others know the sentiments of the people."

"He know by now," said Charley quietly, but Harry was already running the engine higher and bringing the sloop about.

In fact, the *Comox* turned their way before they'd moved more than a hundred yards. So they lay off and waited. Harry watched the figures on the upper deck of the old steamship out front of the pilothouse. He could see Captain Eddlestone, old vulture, his stick arms directing his crew, as he took stock of the flood before him. He'd met Eddlestone once before, when the *Comox* had stopped off at Rupert.

Under the awning behind the pilothouse, various passengers were standing, though none Harry recognized.

"No good tell Hal'day 'bout Blunden Harbour," said Charley.

"It's better I do," Harry said.

91

"No good."

"Well, if you'd persuade me otherwise, you've to do better than that."

"Maybe Hal'day think George problem make Indian anger more. He give George more problem. Only make more trouble."

"But this is about me, man, and what happened. I'll have myself in trouble if he don't hear it from me first."

"Hal'day not do right thing."

The *Comox*, through the torrent now and into the calmer seas of the archipelago, slowed and stopped five hundred yards away. He saw the forward anchor slide into the water.

"They'll be riding out the storm here," Harry said. He engaged the engine and took the *Hesperus* over toward her.

A couple of lumbermen in heavy woollen jackets leaned on the lower deck rail, smoking and spitting over the side, watching their approach.

As they pulled alongside, Harry called, "Captain Eddlestone, hello to you!" Eddlestone was looking down at them. Harry saw his enormous Adam's apple wander seemingly at random across his scrawny throat.

"Aye, greetings to you," the captain said. "Mr. Cadwallader, ain't it? And what the fuck do you be wanting? Hoping to wait out this god-fucking storm with us, are ye?"

"I'm not. We're going through the rapids when they turn," Harry said. "Can you take a message south for me, to Indian Agent Halliday at Alert Bay?"

"Well I'm heading north, you mole-eyed prick. Do you lack sight as well as reason?"

Harry was accustomed, as were all along the coast, to Eddlestone's foul mouth, knowing it for his manner more than his intent. "I was thinking you might be stopping there on your way back south thereafter."

"Come aboard, then, and do what you need to do. We'll share a shot before you and your black lackey drown in them fucking rapids."

Harry killed the engine. Charley tied off and then stepped up and over the lower deck rail. He leaned an arm over and Harry put his bandaged leg onto the gunnels. He reached up his good hand. Charley took his weight and the bad shoulder shifted so that he groaned as he stepped up, threw his leg over the railing, and came on deck. The lumbermen nodded to him.

"Are ye coming up then, damnation?" Eddlestone was in drink, which was his usual state. They climbed the stairwell to the upper deck.

Of the passengers, there were three Chinamen, no doubt heading for the canneries, huddled in a circle, gaming, with two Indians watching behind them. There were a number of white men who looked to be farmers back from trading in Vancouver or Victoria. There was a priest, diminutive in black, and two men in battered wide-brimmed hats, ragged clothes, and with heavy sacks beside them, who looked to be gold prospectors. They had that bitterness of mouth and rancorous expression, which told Harry they had never flourished nor were ever likely to.

Two Indian hands were leaning on the rail. One Harry vaguely recognized, and he raised an eyebrow to him but received no response. Charley walked across to stand near them.

Eddlestone's bulbous nose, sitting strangely on a concave face, was festooned with broken veins, which ran down and over his cheeks. He held out a hand. Harry shook it. They stepped into the pilothouse. The captain ordered a greybeard steersman to fuck off, and the man shuffled out. Then he picked a stone jar from the jury-rigged iron frame in which it rested, took two filthy glasses and poured.

"You is a sorry fucking sight and no mistake," said Eddlestone, looking him up and down. "You look like Satan hisself been buggering you. What happened then, eh? Out with it."

"I fell on board and slipped my shoulder. Damn fool I am. How've been your travels?" He took a sip of whisky and placed the glass back on the table. Eddlestone threw his down and eyed Harry's drink. Then he poured himself another.

"Fucking terrible, and every limpdick retard whining over fares and stowage, every nigger Indian drunk, and the ignorant fucking white men worse." The phlegm rattled in him as he laughed. "Nothing from the usual. And what brings you to risk death at the rapids, in a sloop too large to have a pinched arsehole's hope of making it through?" He stared at Harry and seemed less in drink for a moment than he'd been before.

"I've a shallow draft and I hear there's ten feet clearance in surge. I'm trading."

"Trading your sanity to the Devil. Every red cunt's come outta them fee-jords years back now, that weren't already dead."

"Well, and you'll forgive me, I'm on private business."

"And you'll forgive me, but I'm wondering if it be anything to do with events among them shite-worshipping savages back at Blunden?"

Harry looked stupidly at him a moment. "What do you mean?"

"I been plying this coast for fifty fucking years, and my father captain of the *Beaver* before me. I seen the way things are among the Indians. I know they's as likely slice you as fuck you, and good luck to them. If I was red, I'd not be near as kind as they's been with us, with all we done. Still, I knows they's murdering, headhunting fucking savages as well, when they's like to be. And I seen it before."

He drank down the shot he had in his hands and placed the glass down. "In '66 it was, when they was up in arms against each other at Rupert, all for trade with the white man and who had the access to it. My father kept me aboard, but I see all them red man bodies floating in the water along the shore, and most with no heads, and the white men hiding scared in the fort."

He poured himself another shot but rolled the glass in his fingers. "Aye, they'll fuck with you or anyone if they's holding grudges, and shit-faced enough."

"But what of Blunden Harbour?"

"Seen that godless fuck the chief there. Wool-shit?"

"Walewid."

"Shouting abuse, warning us off, half of them all clothed up in their heathen fancies, feathers and skins and skulls and assorted other horribles, and a canoe being made a-ready. Tell you I seen it before. They's planning to fuck with someone, and proper." He drank down his glass and looked Harry up and down again. "Still, to them as has it coming, they's probably owed it."

"When was this?" Harry said.

"Hah! Late in yesterday. I fucking knewed you had a part in it." Eddlestone leered at him. "Been trading hooch and lacing it with poison, have ye? Nitric acid burned some old doxy's stomach out through her cunt, and her boy's on the warpath?"

"Not that, nor nothing like it. I'm no more than interested, since I'm sailing in the region."

"Aye, well, you'll do well to sail clear a them goat-prick bastards for a while, whatever your tale may be." He looked out the window toward the west. "That fucking storm'll slow them, wherever they be going. And you'll wait it out too, if you've still some sense left in you. I'd not risk the surge through Schooner Channel that's coming."

Harry stepped around the table. "With your permission," he said, and took a sheet of paper from a stack.

"Go ahead, scrawl out your will whilst you're at it. You're a fucking deadman ghost a-walking already, by my thinking."

Harry wrote, *Mr. Halliday, I am up near Blunden Harbour. Not found Gorge yet. I here Indians got rumors goin bout Gorge and are not happy bout him and may be war party even. Just thort you shood know it. I am still looking most diligente. We have a good idea where he is, so I ask you most humbly to not take the tresures of the family til we come back. Yours most sincerly, Harry C.*

He folded the paper and said, "You've envelopes?" Eddlestone pointed absently toward a drawer, still watching westward. Harry sealed the letter and addressed it. "Here," he said, stepping up to stand beside the captain. "And my thanks."

"Well if you will be going through the rapids, you'd best be in a fucking hurry about it," said Eddlestone. Harry looked out the window.

He had felt the swell beneath the *Comox* growing in the minutes previously and the gusting hammer of the wind, but now the waves were steepling in and straggled at their tops with flume. The wind was heavier, and the first broken clouds were covering the late-morning sun. Behind them came a cloudscape of indigo violence, banked miles uncountable into the sky. Shadows clawed on the ocean and darkness raced behind those shadows.

Harry stepped outside. He shivered, feeling chill. His shoulder ached, and he wondered if there might yet be infection in his injuries after all.

Charley was there waiting. "Go now," he said.

"Perhaps we'd better wait this out."

"Think Poodlas dead, Walewid come."

"You heard about Blunden, then."

"Crew tell me. Better go. Hurry. After maybe them come."

"They'll not be coming through this."

"Canoe can stay close land. But when them leave? Don't know. Them come after us? Maybe them think. Maybe go Teguxste. Go small river in canoe. Walewid bastard. Not stupid bastard. Go now."

Harry looked toward the entrance to Schooner Channel. The pace of the outgoing tide seemed less, and the incoming waves were beginning to make some headway into the channel.

"We're going then," Harry said through the pilothouse door to Eddlestone, raising his voice against the wind.

"I'll see you next chasing apes in Hell, you shit-for-brains fool." But he put out his hand, and Harry shook it.

"I'd give a lot to know when the ebb'll turn," said Harry. They were making their way through the flat water between two islets toward the mouth of Schooner Channel. Ahead, perhaps a hundred yards, out beyond where the small archipelago protected them, the retreating tide still roared down the channel from the direction of the Nakwakto Rapids and thundered out toward the ocean proper. But it was less intense than it had been half an hour before. "We need to travel in on its end, against the water's flow, as it weakens. Then we drop through the rapids just as it turns to flood."

"Think too late maybe now go right through all way. Look."

Harry eyed the storm front rushing down the world toward them. "Then best we get on. We'll be hard pushed stopping once we're in waters driven by that," he said. "Take the front."

With Charley at the prow, Harry with both hands to the rudder arm, his sling flapping loose where he'd slipped his injured arm out from it, and with the engine set at three-quarter full, they moved out into the churning waters of the channel.

The hull jittered. They heeled and dragged until Harry brought the sloop round. And now it scythed the tide so that the water leapt and spat. Standing waves reared above squat Charley to soak him. They broke against the pilothouse, and Harry's eyes were stung so that he had to slit his eyelids thin to see. He drove for the centre of the channel, and the waves in the deeper water became less violent, though the volumes beneath them greater, as if they surged and bobbed upon the blubber of some vast whale in its death throes.

Harry took a sight against the islet off his port bow. Almost immeasurably slowly, but it seemed they made some progress, which meant the ebb was indeed lessening. He leaned forward and set the engine full, and now they were travelling at maybe four knots, Charley up front wiping at his face and shaking his head so that his lank hair threw droplet patterns about him.

They held to the centre of the channel for the next hour, the tide's strength diminishing and the day darkening around them. Along the shore, not fifty yards away on either side, the waters formed whirlpools, overfalls, and back eddies, roiling and curling in charcoals and steel blues. They watched for tendrils of kelp that warned of rocks in shallow water.

And then the tide that held them back at last was gone beneath the hull.

"Too soon!" called Charley. "We too far. Ten minute slack between tide at rapid only."

The first rain began to fall, splatters of heavy drops in intermittent gusts. Harry looked back. The storm hung impossibly vast above them, black beneath. The flood came now in spume and scudding wavetops toward them, and was no more than a minute away. He eyed the shore but there were only rocks and brush. Nowhere that might prove a haven. "Take hold of something, Charley!" he shouted.

"Look!" Charley was pointing. Harry saw the tip of Branham Island and, coming round it, huge waves from out of Slingsby Channel to the north. Ahead and to starboard were the rapids. The storm-fed tidal flood from Slingsby battered through the narrow gap, throwing spindrift in tornado curls above the tiny islet that lay directly at the rapids' centre, and around which it seemed not possible to plot a course. There was a small bay just to the south of the entrance.

"Jesus!" Harry shouted. "We'll make for the bay and try to anchor ourselves there."

"No. Look!" And Charley thrust his finger vigorously ahead. Harry peered. Now he could make out what seemed a carven figure standing on the end of the headland between the bay and the rapids. The rain came now in sheets and he lost sight of it. Then, as the wind blew harder and it cleared for a moment, he saw the figure was human in shape and naked. It held what looked a long war club, though he could not be sure. Its long hair blew against the gale, and then its head turned toward them and Harry knew it was no statue placed to guard the entrance to some Indian holy place, as he had seen them before.

"Who is it?" he called.

"Dreamer," said Charley.

"What?"

"It come see and know. We must go quick. No stop." And Harry would have asked more, but the waves were now upon them. The stern rose up and they were heaved forward. The boat began to slew sideways, until he leaned hard against the rudder and brought her round. They fled before the surge.

"We make for the bay!" he shouted forward.

But Charley pulled himself along the deck and, clinging to the pilot-house roof, called back, "No! Dreamer tell Walewid we come. Them wait us. We stop now, them ready other side. Go now or not go at all."

"What in all the fucking heavens is a dreamer?"

"Them come go. Know secret. Tell secret." But now the sloop listed and threatened to swamp as it hit the tide from out of Slingsby Channel. Waves rushed across the deck from the port side. Charley was thrown sideways and into the starboard gunnels. He slid forward and out of sight behind the pilothouse. Harry turned down the engine and heaved against the rudder, water washing over him.

"Charley!" he shouted. He cursed when there was no reply. The storm was now fully upon them. It was not possible to see ahead through the rain. The two tidal flows were united and the *Hesperus* was caught. It shuddered and pulled and flew forward. Harry could not now have directed his boat into the bay or anywhere else, whatever his decision might have been.

Ahead then, for a moment, he saw again the small island that sat directly in the middle of the rapids. It came at him so fast it could not be avoided, the waters swelling up in spate along its sides. At the last moment, the *Hesperus* lurched and followed the tide hard around the island, so close that Harry could have plucked a leaf from one of the few sparse evergreens. He felt the hull grind against rock and then come free.

He looked south toward the low headland he knew must be close upon his starboard bow. The rain lifted for a second. The dreamer was squatting on its haunches on the shore no more than twenty yards away. Its face was black and its hair hung down about it. Harry could see the wild whites of its eyes and the sallow snarl. Its naked body, pitch-black and filthy, bobbed up and down, as if it longed to throw itself forward. It reached out one hand, or what seemed a claw, its talons angling out toward Harry, before the flood drew him on and the rain obscured it.

I WAS AWAY BEFORE DAWN the morning after David's funeral. I took my hunting gear and off I goes north and west across the water. I did not flee in the madness of grief, as some have said it. I had a mission, though I couldn't say for certain if I understood it full clearly at that time. Whether my actions was those of a rational man, I don't know.

So I paddled north and west. I passed near to Blunden Harbour, though I did not stop there. Then on through narrow ways towards the waters of Belize Inlet, ways as don't require me braving the Nakwakto Rapids, as did those foolhardy idiots what followed me. And theirs was a grand tale, but it weren't mine. Least, not yet it weren't.

In two days, I was paddling on that inlet, and I had not eaten all that time. I'd not consciously decided on it. Still, something in me had resolved that I would fast. Four days is the period the Indian usually does it. It was six before I would partake of food again. In that fevered state, strange things does one see indeed.

That afternoon, a mist lay upon the ocean—me passing through it like I was some phantom. Just the faint splash from my paddle the only sound. I could not see much further than to the eyes painted at my prow.

I noticed a swell forming beside me. Glancing down into the dull, silvery water, I saw something black, gigantic, rising up beneath me. It broke the surface, water running off it like oil, not a foot away. Black nose and white jaw and belly, and those teeth what look like files of razor-armoured soldier crabs. The pool of its eye stared black, not two feet away, then rolled up into its socket, turning to white. The dorsal fin come up, tall as a man and broken at its tip, product I suppose of underwater combat, of great tearing teeth out in the cold waters of the Pacific.

Perhaps I get carried away in the telling, but it was the state I was in: grief and hunger addling me, and now this. I ran my fingers down the killer whale's flank. Old orca, rough-edge scars upon its skin. Then it spouted and arched up to dive. Its flukes reared from the water to hang above the canoe, like some massive totem statue of flesh, before it slid back under the surface. Spume drifted over me, rank fish and brine, the full, foul sweetness of its lungs. I watched the white of the whale flicker in the darkness. Then it was gone.

Well, I might have wept then—as I might almost now—seeing that great hulk rise up beside me, with all the images it called up out of my past. But the cold of the world, and of David's death, was deep inside my bones, so I just paddled on, my face set hard. No tears had I shed for David. There seemed nothing of them in me.

Night was coming. I heard the swoosh of a shoreline, and shortly, a pebbled shore showed itself. I was exactly where I had planned on being, almost to the yard, despite the mist and tides. There was comfort in that.

Up the beach a fallen totem pole lay buried in moss, the carved face of an owl still faintly showing. Behind, the forest dripped shadows. I dragged the canoe out of the water, the canoe I made with David, when he was still a boy. And it was he what painted the eyes of the whale at its prow.

The mist had risen by then, a raw wind coming off the mountains to the east. I stood for a time looking out over that great inlet. The moisture in the air caught the light and everything was crimson. Then the sun touched the water and it was dusk.

Why do I relate all this in such detail? After that killer whale paid its visit on me, every act and thought became like crystal. I felt like I was at a distance to myself, but watching, bearing witness. I was outside of things, all emotions leeched out of me, like a deer that's been hung to bleed.

And I was back at Teguxste. Teguxste: where my current wife, old Francine, was born, sister to Making-Alive, what first got me into being a healer. I was back at that place where I healed the boy of his affliction— when I was but a young man, and Francine then still a child. There, beside the waters where that memory, or that vision, or that dream of the Killer Whale Spirit had come to me. Lagoyewilé was its name. Rolling Over in Mid-Ocean. Now I had come here again, and a whale had lifted up its flukes above me once again. What did that signify? Something. Surely something.

Anyhow, I took out my pack and my gun—the '92 Winchester carbine what Professor Boas gave me some years before, gift for acting as guide and translator, whilst he was conducting his researches among the people those years past.

I made my camp beside the old totem pole. I walked into the gloom of the forest, to cut bark from the cedars for a roof. I saw the old scars upon the trunks from the past peoples what had gone about the same task. I stripped cedar bark from the trees, muttering the litanies as was appropriate.

I gathered up driftwood. I was averse for some reason to using the matches I had on me. Perhaps they represented too much the world I had left behind. So instead I took out my old fire drill and drove and spun that long splint at the shreds of bark inside, until I'd sparks enough to place in the hearth. By time I looked up again, night had fallen.

I sat with my face toward the fire, an old man in a primitive shelter on a beach, with the ruined totems of a dead village all about, the forest looming black and silent, alone in the dark with the stars falling down the heavens above me.

I was thinking about the killer whale. I was thinking I should have followed it down into the deep waters of the ocean. And further down to the bottom of the world, to the palace of the Qomogwe, the king under the water. I'd float through the gates guarded by killer whales into the palace proper, passing seals and the spirits of the eulachon and salmon, of the sea otter whose fur was the wealth and the destruction of my mother's people.

I would enter into the throne room and there he would be: Qomogwe, transforming himself from octopus to whale to man and thence back again. I'd hang in the water before him, voicing threats, swaggering and boasting, laying out the totems of my house. I'd claim his daughter in marriage, and I'd win her with my arrogance, watching as she changed then from a seal into a girl. I'd bring her back up through the cold ocean and we'd scramble onto the shore, shivering and creeping like sodden ghosts up the shingle and into a darkened house, its door frames heavy over us. I'd have sons with her and daughters, till at last she'd hear a call one night, like a loon but out on the ocean, wailing, singing out like to a great whale, perhaps. And she would slip away back to the sea.

On the pebbles I stand, night after night, and call her name and call her name and she won't never come back, but I call her name and call her name. I call: Lucy! Lucy! She is gone though, into the deeps forever. But I will have the totems of her house for my sons to dance, and the husbands of my daughters. And I will stand in the cedar houses by the huge fires with the masks of seal and whale, and show my stories and my ancestry, and be a chief, and so will my sons be chiefs of the whale and the seal and the raven, and of the Qomogwe himself, forever. Lah.

So do the stories go.

I stared into the fire, these mind imaginings and travellings flowing in amongst the flames as they crawled on and tore at the logs there. After a time, I stood and took up my hatchet. I went down to the canoe and I hacked holes through its eyes, and, after, all along its hull, till it was beyond any hope of repair. Then I went back up to the shelter. I sat again by the fire and I stared into its hot heart.

The next morning I came awake in the early dawn. First thing I did was tear off my clothes and pace naked down the pebbles to the water, what was rippled by the bitter breeze coming still off the mountains in the east, behind which the sun still was hid.

I stood waist deep in the ocean, the cold setting my muscles to shaking. I looked back toward the shore and the old village. I saw the silhouettes of the ruined houses against the forest. The timber frames was like the skeletons of those gigantic, ancient creatures what I have heard walked the earth before ever man did exist.

I plunged my head down into the ocean and plunged again, and twice more. On the last, I held my head beneath with my eyes closed. I sank down to my knees.

I remembered the shamans of the village washing me thus before I could be showed their secrets. Four times must I be dunked beneath the waves. Then, them leading me back into the cold air, and we was away into the forest, away to learn what they did have to teach.

I opened my eyes under the water. My breath, and the eddies from my body as it moved, bubbled past. I guess I half fancied seeing the whale staring back at me. But all I saw was murk, the colour of the deep woods at twilight.

After, I dressed and then I walked along the pebbled beach toward the steep hill what stands guard at the centre of the village. The distance I had felt from myself the evening before—even whilst I was hacking away at my canoe—was gone, though still the world did appear almost disgracefully clear in its every detail. But now my mind was laced with torment, the faces of my dead so vivid that almost I felt they walked beside me, lamenting. It wasn't David, though, I saw. It was my mother, not three years dead herself of consumption. Then my brother and my sister what had died. I saw the little one who died in her first year, her pale little face, choked up with coughing. And Lucy. Her soft voice, and we married out of love, however useful was the marriage to me: her a princess, no less, of the old families, of the sun and seal and raven, and of the people what dance the ways of the King of the Ocean.

I sat on a fallen house post. Carved into it was the face of the Dzonokwa, just as they are in our greathouse in Rupert, her mouth open, round in surprise. Foolish old ogress that she is, with her sack of stolen children.

When I did misbehave as a child, my mother'd tell me the Dzonokwa would come for me. In the night, she'd sneak through the rear of the house and drag me out by the foot into the forest. She'd throw me in her sack to squirm and whimper with the other wicked children. I would lie in my bed in the darkness thinking of those bouncing limbs all about me, tangling, bruising, airless, panicked, going deep through the woods to her cave. There, the sack would be hung up on a great hook, and we'd be plucked one by one out into that terrible cave. The Dzonokwa father and child are there, huge, and their shoulders hunched up so they don't have no necks, and thundering around, bent brown teeth, leers and slobber and grunting like huge pigs at a trough. A sharp spike of wood gets held up to rumbles of satisfaction, and then, as I squeal and squirm, it is slid neatly up under my tailbone, and on bumping against vertebrae along behind the spine, coming out at the base of my skull. After, I hang, bouncing some with my own weight, over the fire, arms tied tight to my body, legs doubled back, ankles strapped to thighs, heels on buttocks, my flesh cooking, stinking, the vision fading as my eyes come to the boil, and the sizzle of skin before my eardrums split and I hear no more, and I don't scream, locked as I am in silence. I feel the belly of my skin crack open, and the spill of my intestines down into the flames. Then there ain't but the vague feeling of the Dzonokwa child prodding, poking with a stick inside me, until all feeling ends.

A boy's imaginings, and darker than pitch. Yet more vivid even than such fantasies were the true dyings of the people what I did witness. The plagues swept through us during the sixties. Rasp and wrack, black phlegm and bloody, flowing shit, sores and sunken eyes, the hair in clumps from women's heads, bones showing clear through skin. Always some new sweet stench at which to nauseate and shiver—gist for a child in the night, staring up at the shadows of the masks creeping on the walls and high among the timbers of the roof.

I walked on down the beach until I came to that place what was my destination: the greathouse where I had first healed the boy.

All that was left now was ruins, the ground thick with grass, the timbers heaped about, rotten, bled dry of memory.

I stood in the centre of that ruin. I watched seals roll in the water offshore. Now the clouds split apart and the late-afternoon sun flooded over the ocean onto me. I shut my eyes. The light was pink against my eyelids. The whole day had drifted away without me noticing. I opened my eyes again and walked back along the beach to my camp.

I went through my pack. At the bottom lay a wooden box with killer whale carvings on it. But I did not take it out, as I had meant to. I did not walk back along the shore to the greathouse, to perform the ritual for which I was come.

I thought on those shamans bathing me in the water. I remembered the excitement of that time. The emptiness of the world as now it was. I knew that there was something else I must do instead.

The box went back into the pack and some few of my necessaries for the wilderness went with it. I made my way along the beach, as far as the clear-water stream what was the reason surely for the village first being settled there, whatever the old myths might tell of thunderbirds and other fierce creatures of the sky coming down and transforming into human beings to settle on that lonely stretch of sand.

A storm was rearing its ugliness away to the south and west. I squatted down and splashed water on my face. Then I followed the stream's path into the forest.

●●●

I feel like I have been standing here, before this museum mannequin and its suit of armour, for ten thousand years. I must move my eyes off it and go among the other exhibits. The light washes in through the high windows across the floor and the glass cases. The very few people in here, what wander between the masks and poles, the great carven boxes, the old high-prow canoes, like they is half somewhere else, they give the dust to swirl like convoluting whirlpool eddies in a low tide. I am awash with ghosts, with shadows, with the fermenting juices of my own history.

I had gone to Teguxste to atone. That's a Christian word, but there it is. I had broken my canoe, and so made my decision not to go back to the world. Was it death then I was seeking for? Maybe it was. I wonder on it still.

Yet when I stood in the ruined greathouse of the old chief whose grand-son had been sick and I had healed, all those years before, it did not seem that I had come to the origin of my sorrow after all. I don't know if that ain't just the sentiment of hindsight. Who can know in the retelling of events? *Now* and *then* are but random pointers in this creation. They mould theirselves together into that which we may recount to others, and so dream that we do comprehend this elsewise senseless, pitiless place of our being.

As I was moving forward, so was I travelling backwards. Back to where? Some origin, I imagine it to be. The heartland. The first place from which all else did follow. I see it in the researches of those scientists what come along the coast. They seek for a world from which they dream their own grand civilization, what hums and whirs and broods, sprung up. A world out of the past. As if the Indian ain't lived the same number of years of the world's history as have they. Years of unrelenting change. Years of history, as they use the word. Yet have we all lived the same number of years on this Earth. Where do they think the Indians had gone off to for all that time between? Have they been frozen, like as to statues in the wilderness, just waiting for the white man to arrive—to pour electricity through them, perhaps, and so draw them once more into motion for their researches?

Still, I do aid the scientists in this whole splendid undertaking. They come to me as the expert. The native expert, with his brown blood for studying and his white blood for trusting. All the languages he speaks. And his skills with a pen—such as they are. I write the stories. I write the ways of the people and send my missives off. As to what constitutes savagery, and what does not, well on that I have my own beliefs.

It is a questionable business being an ethnographer, as my appellation has been given, but one I've come at last to feel I have resolved in myself, though I'd not get ahead of myself by so saying. Yet, even now, I believe the resolution of those questions is at the heart of this story of mine.

Anyhow, out of Teguxste and into the forest I went, following the stream uphill. Undergrowth covered the old path, huckleberry and skunk cabbage. I hadn't trod that path in more than forty years, and my memory of it was hazy at best. Still, it was along the stream that I remember following those shamans as had bathed me first in the ocean, following behind them filled up with excitement at what might happen, at what I was about to learn.

As the evening set in, so the storm I had seen earlier did arrive. I flensed a few branches and put fronds over them against the rain. I had brung dry tinder enough to get a fire going, though I weren't averse this time around to using matches. The fasting made my stomach churn and cramp.

I sat beneath my shelter, getting dripped on as the rain wound itself up into a frenzy, and staring out at the woods. The forest was strung by shadows, the trees great lumbering beasts come to rest, shabby in their rags of vine and moss. I was among swordfern, wild lilies and elderberries, vicious-spiking devil's club and dogwood. White man's names. I could name them all, as well, in Kwakwala, and list the people's uses for them. Swordfern. Sakuam: the fronds line steampits and storage boxes, cover floors, and is lain out for fish to dry. Scientists call it *Polystichum munitum*, in that dead man's tongue, Latin.

I sat there feeling alien to it all. Me, who used to speak to the trees, hold discourse with them. Used to sing ritual songs when the jays buzzed past, nervy and neat. I had led the scientists in, and they had pasted labels through the forest. Every bract and catkin, stamen, spike, and rhizome probed till it all weren't more than the engine parts on the floor of Harry's workshop. What is left of wonder in the world?

The next morning I was soaked through. I drunk a little water, then upped and walked—trudging always uphill. But my mind was far from clear by then, even as to where I was headed. I just knew to place my boots one after the other, and always uphill. Answers would come, just so long as those boots kept plodding.

Soon enough the stream was gone. The undergrowth clung and twined about everything. Blood veins, I was thinking. Whipcord muscles of a body cut open. A twig gouged my cheek—the side as is paralyzed. I touched my face and my fingers came away bloody. I have to be careful of such things. The ship's surgeon told me I had broken the nerves of my face. That I couldn't never feel anything again on that side of my head.

I wander in my narrative like I am still now bumbling in the wilds. What ship's surgeon? Well: tell a tale out of the past and it might help some in understanding all this. It is a story I was recounting to myself there in the forest—reliving, feverish with grief and fasting as I was.

Four canoes is approaching the beach at Rupert. Young George Hunt, nine years old, waiting on the shore for them to come in. He is beside his mother, Anaîn—her beautiful name. And all the people gathered on the shore as well to watch the arrival of the great Chief Shaiks of the Northern Tlingit, come south out of Alaska.

He was my great-uncle. He carried the crests and dances, masks and privilege of our ancestry, to which I was entitled, since, among the Tlingit, it all comes down through the mother's line.

Shaiks was at the prow of a war canoe full sixty feet in length, twenty warriors at the oars, painted in design of the Killer Whale, blood daubed at its mouth for all those it had eaten in war. Three other canoes followed behind. Slabs of black hardwood covered every part of Shaiks's body, all strapped with leather tight against him, and with dense carvings across them. On his head was a helmet with curling earflaps.

Shaiks's speaker was standing just behind him in the prow of the canoe, low and wide with a blanket about him, bear-skin hat on his head. He drew himself up, self-important, and called out across the water in some bastard version of Kwakwala.

"You Kwagiulth! Listen," he says. "Here great chieftain Shaiks. He the Raven. He the Ganaxadi Clan of Tantakwan people of the north. He have from ancestor crest of Killer Whale and Raven, and other many he win from killing and from marry."

I felt the excitement foaming in me, knowing him for my relative, seeing the nervous ways the people next to me was shifting and mumbling to each other. My mother had told them he was coming, peaceable, to visit. But seeing the warrior of an enemy tribe, this legend, plying in towards them with a hundred men or more: well it made for quite the fearsome spectacle. There weren't but a few men in Rupert then. Not enough to defend theirselves, and hardly a white man in the fort, away along the beach, barring my father, a few traders, and the missionary.

The shoreline comes up sharp and shallow at Rupert when the tide is high. Now the chief's canoe crashed into it, and still at speed. My greatuncle was thrown forward, hardly holding himself against the prow's high peak. The speaker was not so fortunate. He flew out, doing a tidy somersault and crashing on his back into the surf.

There he was, spluttering and gasping, being dragged and drawn by the tide, and the people guffawing and shouting their ridicule. A grand sight. They still talk of it even now. But the northern men put down their paddles, and some of them took up war clubs. A few had old muskets. They started to shouting back in anger at the people's mockery, and there was danger then of fighting.

My mother pulled me backwards and away up the pebbles. Those sharp nails on my arm. Not out of fear, though. She was but protecting her son. She was arrogant and fearless. An aristocrat.

Nakapankam came forward, him not one to roll about like some tomfool in laughter. He was chieftain then of the Kwagiulth. I called him father, so kind a man he was to me. Still call him father now in memory, though he is long dead. He was uncle to old Charley Seaweed.

Nakapankam was a tall man, bigger even than I grew to be, and in his middle years at that time. He called out, and his people came quiet to hear him. "Shaiks. Great northern chief. Chief of those we have had war with for many lifetimes. Come down from your canoe. We respect our enemies. We will not fight. We will not attack you. Come down from your canoe. We will feed you with our own food. Come down from your canoe."

Shaiks was an old man, I saw then, long hair, lank and thin and grey from out of his helmet. His face was made of cracked leather, and a fat scar ran from before his right ear down below the neckline of his armour; but his body was brawny still. He leapt down into the surf, the whoosh of the water up around him, and he didn't stagger when he landed.

The speaker was still on his hands and knees. Shaiks took him by his scruff and dragged him upright. Then he laughed, booming, holding the sorry fucker there like a drowning dog. Shook him so the water droplets flew out in arcs. Those on shore they laughed as well, and they on the canoes joined in, beating their clubs against the boats' hulls.

The beating clubs sounded like a storm looming. It quieted many of the Kwagiulth, recalling the threat that was posed by all these men of an enemy tribe. But Nakapankam walked straight into the water and put out his hand in the manner of the white man. Shaiks looked down at the hand. Everyone looking at that hand. Nakapankam's fingers callused and broken, the grime etched in every crevice. The black nails.

Shaiks let go his speaker and took the hand. They moved their arms up and down, not knowing truly how it was done. Proud chiefs but smiling. Just a little.

So brave a gesture from Nakapankam. Chieftains didn't never touch each other, nor was they ever touched theirselves. Many things it was, and maybe memory makes it more. A reference to the whites, to old Nakapankam's influence with them, and so to the protection the white man's fort along the beach did afford the people, should Shaiks be planning trouble. And, by that argument, I suppose, it did tell of the white men's place like gods, protective of the people.

And it spoke of the world as it had turned as well. The new world that was upon us all, the old ways of violence over—some things good, and some less so. And perhaps it was a sign of conniving between them two chieftains as well. Knowing they were subject, both of them, to the world and to its changing.

My mother and my father did first meet on that same beach at Rupert. It was back in the days what followed the building of the fort. I wonder was their meeting much the same? The canoes coming in. Anaîn sitting proud among the men of the north, her people. They was on their way to trade in the young cities of the south.

My father was newly come from England, and was working in the fort. Those days, of course, it was still run by the Hudson's Bay Company what founded it. He'd been smart enough for the factor to take notice of him. Back then the Company tried to marry off their traders to the Indian aristocracy. How it all changed in the years what followed. The Indians is considered like children now, since the missionaries wound their interfering ways among the people and the new administrators from the East come sneering at the savages.

Anaîn was fifteen and my father thirty when they was married. The plans had been made right there and then, maybe in a circle on the beach like the peoples of Shaiks and Nakapankam made, once all was on shore.

My mother was dead before David, thankfully, though she saw plenty of death herself: two of her own children—one drowned like her mother, my grandmother, was—and most of her friends taken before their right age. Illness, and the liquor-driven ugliness what stole her brother in a knife fight twenty years ago. She'd seen much of death, and so had I. Even at that tender age.

The smallpox had raged through the village earlier that year of Shaiks's visit. There was bodies all along the beach where they'd been thrown into the sea and floated back with the tide. The stench swathed the shore. How is it humans do smell so much worse than animals in decay? The honey rot. Perhaps it's knowing it to be the canker from such flesh as clothes one's own body? It smelled then like the most bitter end of things. And such it was.

Outside the fort, the Indians died of pox. Inside, I was locked up safe with the other whites. But I would lie up on a ledge above the gate, watching as the sharks came threshing in the surf, their fins rolling sideways as they tore at the bodies, till the foam ran black, the gulls screaming above, and hawks and eagles dropping down to feast.

There were killer whales even, further out, a whole pod of them, rolling and rowdy. I saw one limp corpse thrown up into the air, fantastical, twisting like some broken puppet. Such sights flood straight to a boy's deepest insides, with no obstacles of age and of experience to check their torrent.

Those of the Indian men as weren't dead found solace in drink. Pitching down the shore, naked and screeching, they fought each other, and sang drinking songs. They called curses to the fort, threw things, even tried to lay a fire at the wall one time. I heard the men dousing water down upon it. Damned heathen fucks, they said, and other such. Me and my siblings was banned from coming out. My eldest sister, Annie, was already in blood, chatting up the sailors when she got the chance. All the youngsters whispering slurs against the Kwagiulths. Brown-skin savages. Barbarous dogs. Spoken from inside their own breed skins. Even back then I felt more kinship with the Indians than I did with my father's stock.

I have heard it said there was upwards of two thousand Kwagiulths camped about Fort Rupert after it was built. And if that number sounds high, it was anyhow true no more than a hundred stood awaiting Shaiks that day. And hardly more back in the village. Scarce twenty years it took to so break a people.

Anyhow, Shaiks was now on the beach. He called over my mother, and me following behind. He took me by my shoulders, fingers—great talons they seemed—bruising. He stared down at me. I stood firm though, firm as I was able, and met his gaze, his eyes half-hidden by their folds, beading black like a raven's. It was the first time I felt what it might be like to be a man—more even than when I first landed a harpoon, and the blood what foamed out the dolphin's back.

"My heir," said Shaiks to my mother. His voice was like the draw of pebbles in a soft tide.

My heir!

Then the speeches that came after, interminable to a boy as young as was I, my back creaking, sitting straight as I could next to this enemy chieftain, this killer, this warrior, my great-uncle. Where were the other boys? I was thinking, hoping they were watching somewhere. Watching me in my glory.

And now I saw my father, Robert Hunt, coming from the fort with his deliberate stride. My mother had been secretive earlier, ushering me from the fort gates when the calls first went out that canoes was sighted.

What a temper that man had. All the years trading did nothing to ease it. Ranting on the people's ignorance and savagery to the ships' officers, the British, French, and the Americans—even the Russians that sometimes landed still, back then—who came buying up the fur or timber, drawing water or purchasing supplies, though less and less of any of them as the years marched by. My father raved at them all on the many ills of the dark races, even if he had married among them.

Shaiks's speaker was telling of the war with the Tsimshian tribe, the war that won their ancestors the Killer Whale canoe, and with it the great name Shaiks: Splasher of the Whale. It was a proud tale the speaker told, and the heavy little man was proud in the telling. And I guess that story is the reason I am remembering this one now, though I go about it in a roundabout way.

This, then, is the manner by which my Tlingit ancestors won the name of Shaiks from the Tsimshian tribe.

A Tlingit chieftain of the Wolf Clan died. They burned his body, but dried and kept his head, and put it in a carved box. But the Tsimshian tribe stole the box in a raid, and afterwards they throwed out the chieftain's head, just keeping hold on the box. When the Wolf Clan learned what had occurred to the chieftain's head, there followed years of raids and skirmishes between them.

At last, the Tsimshian made up their minds to destroy the Tlingit Wolf Clan, who was far fewer in number than was they. So they gathered up a war party from many of their villages, until they so far outnumbered their enemy as to be guaranteed of success.

But a shaman of the Wolf Clan did predict their coming. In his vision, he said that during the battle they would see a killer whale floundering in the slough and trying to escape.

The Tsimshian rode in on the tide. Their canoes advanced side by side so that they seemed to the people of the Wolf Clan to stretch for miles across the ocean. So many were they that they came straight at the village for an open fight. The Tsimshian chief, whose name was Yakwek, was at their head in his canoe.

"Run away to the woods and hide," shouted Yakwek to Chief Gooksin of the Wolf Clan.

"I challenge you," said Gooksin. "We two will fight alone." And Yakwek laughed at that.

The Tsimshian landed. Instead of fighting, they spread their mats and played a gambling game. "Wait until we finish the game," they called to the Wolf Clan, to show their scorn, "then we will come and slaughter you."

The Wolf Clan men stood further up the beach, tense and fearful in the face of so many of their enemies.

At first the battle went badly for the Wolf Clan. However, when they first had heard the shaman's vision, they had gone and called upon their Tlingit brothers from the Raven Clan to help them. These men were now hiding in the houses in the village, waiting to come out and surprise the enemy.

When the time came, the Ravens leapt out from the houses and attacked the Tsimshian from the rear. This was too much for the Tsimshian. They began to be slaughtered. Chief Gooksin, seeing this, shouted to his enemy Yakwek, "Will you gamble now with me?"

Yakwek, seeing defeat was upon him, fled for his great canoe, what's name was Killer Whale. But the Wolves saw this and chased him. They captured him, the canoe, and all his men as they floundered in the surf, and the shaman's vision was seen to have been true.

The Wolves decided they would honour the enemy dead by burning them. Those who are burned in death spend their days in heaven close to a fire. Those that are not will wander always trying to find warmth.

Yakwek was happy when they told him this. To him, it was as if they had paid the blood-price for all of the dead. He agreed there would be peace and no more war.

So they performed the peace ceremony. They gave speeches and they danced. The Tsimshian gave Gooksin the great name Shaiks, and as well many songs and dances with masks and mourning songs, and also they gave them the canoe named Killer Whale.

And they gave back into the hands of Gooksin the box in which that chieftain's head had been kept. The box that started the war between them. Gooksin, first of the Tlingit chiefs to be named Shaiks, kept the box and the canoe for himself.

There it is. My great-uncle had come paddling down to Rupert in that very canoe.

Shaiks's speaker was telling that story to the crowd gathered on the beach. Afterwards, he pointed to my great-uncle. "Here is Shaiks number five since the name was won," he said. "And he is most great of them."

Now all this time my father, Robert Hunt, was standing behind the Kwagiulth, my mother shifting nervous, and all the people holding their-selves tense by his presence. He was a tall man—I took that from him—but bulkier, swelling at the waist in his later years. He was fearsome in his black clothes, his thick black hair drawn into a knot at the crown, like he were a Chinaman, and beneath his low forehead, the puckered-up features of his angry countenance.

Nakapankam pulled himself upright. He addressed the Tlingit. "Here is Robert Hunt," he said. "Senior factor of Fort Rupert. Most senior white man in the fort. Blood father to George Hunt who sits beside the great chief Shaiks, and husband to his noble mother, Shaiks's niece, and so he is family to the great chief."

Then he spoke to Robert Hunt. "Mis'r Hunt," he said, his English just about as bad as old Charley's. "Come visit chief from north, important family you."

Shaiks spoke, and I didn't expect him, somehow, to have any English. "I am Shaiks," he says. "Chief of Ravens of Tantakwan Tlingit."

"Aye, I know of ye a course, Chief," says my father, in that outmoded way of speaking he had, "and I call ye father." He had skill with Indian politics, whatever his feelings might've been. But he did not put out his hand. Instead he stared over towards my mother. He looked how a volcano must be before it blows. "I'm surprised not to have heard ye was coming. I would've organized a welcome proper to yer station."

Shaiks told him he was going to Victoria to trade. "I just stop meet boy who take my place when I am dead," he says.

"I see," says my father, and only after he'd been silent for a time, glaring round at all those gathered. He bade Shaiks come to the fort to visit with him once he was done on the beach. Then he was off and away along the beach.

Some hours of talk and eating, and even a little trading, later—when promises of goodwill had been made, and of grievances forgotten, and I was fit to screaming from the boredom of it, from the excitement of having Shaiks there sat beside me, and from the fear my father's rumbling temper had put into me—those hours later, when the sun was low over the island, five of the older Tlingits went with Shaiks and his speaker along the beach towards the fort, me and my mother pacing, nervous, alongside. We passed through the fort's high wooden gate—all gone now, since the fire, ten years back. Various few white men traders were stood about the small square watching us. The home and office to the Company man was but a single-storey building back then, of plank-work structure, just inside the gate.

But the Company man was not to be seen outside. Shaiks and the speaker came in with us, the others waiting outside. He was like to some rat spirit, that speaker, with his tusk teeth and his darting eyes.

Robert Hunt was at the table inside. He had a whisky bottle by his hand, and deep enough in drink and thinking that he seemed not to hear us coming in.

Shaiks had left his helmet at the boats, but still he looked too giant in his armour and his lineage and his history to be bound by that or any room. He loomed over my father in his seat, who looked up, face filled for a bare second with what I might now call loathing. Then that grim smile of his to follow.

He sent his wife off to fetch glasses, and me to the far end of the table. I scuttled away to perch like some duck chick with ravens overhead.

Shaiks was stiff on his chair, his speaker behind him, standing, and Shaiks's eyes following after his niece, royal woman, as she was sent to serve and carry.

Soon she was back with the glasses. Father slopped whisky into them and over the wood. He pushed the glasses forward. Lifted his own.

"To progress, and to Jesus Christ" was how he put the toast, drinking, and they following him. Slammed the glass down. Poured more. They drank those down as well.

He poured again, but turned his glass in his fingers. "So, Chief," he says at last, "ye are here, you say, to take my boy for heir?"

"Not be my heir for many years, I hope," says Shaiks, snorting.

"That may be," says Robert Hunt, "but you are under a misapprehension, for my son is a white man. And no killer nor slave taker is he."

Shaiks showed nothing of emotion, just asks what more my father wants from the family. He has Anaîn and all the treasures she brung south with her for the marriage.

"I need none of yer damned trinkets," my father says, and he leapt up and marched round the table. Then he had me by my collar. It tore loose in his hand. My heart thumping in me.

He took hold of my face and twisted it toward the chief. "Boy's Christian white," he says. "No headhunting fucking cannibal savage."

Shaiks stood. He drew the long dagger at his waist. Going to kill him. Finish him. Then I'd be Indian and nothing else. Shaiks the Sixth of the great northern Tlingit. Maybe I am ashamed to admit it now, and maybe I ain't, but I was full of excitement in that moment. I wished my own father dead.

Shaiks came towards us, smaller than my father on his feet, but so single-minded in his manner that none might doubt who'd have the upper hand in combat. He held the blade for a moment before my father's eyes, and the edge was very sharp. Then he slammed it into the table instead, where it quivered, deep buried in the wood.

The speaker stood close behind, spinning his war club in his hand. "White fuck," the speaker says, softly, through his bared teeth.

Father let go my collar and straightways I tried to get away.

I wonder now how my life might have been if I had not made that attempt. For back steps my father at that same moment I am trying to pass behind him. Both of us go down, tangling in each other's limbs. The spittle from my father's fury sprays across my face. His arm goes back. His fist is above me.

It was four days before I woke, feeling first the weight of my body against the bunk bed's edge. All of it fog and pain. The lantern swinging above me, enough to make me giddy. Pressure in my head so strong that I wailed out.

I was on an American schooner. The *President Lincoln*. The ship's surgeon hovered over me. Breath like a still, he had, voice like mist.

"A miracle you've woken at all," says he. I had broken my skull. The ship had moored just hours after I had fallen, so "regrettably," as the surgeon called it. I had tumbled from a window, so he tells me, so very "regrettably."

He'd let out the blood what was clotting between my skull and my brain. The rest had been down to my spirit, says he, what had showed much fortitude. And I did take comfort in that, broken boy, creaking in a bunk.

There were wires wrapped tight about my head, which were to stay, and I was not to move. He could not give me ought for the pain as yet. I was to stay awake till he was certain I'd not slip back into the coma from which I had just arisen.

Pain. The creak of wood and rope. The shudder of lantern light. Nausea. My mother then, come aboard to be with me. Seeing her, that fortitude of mine came clattering down swift enough, to show the weepy boy beneath.

Weeks followed at the hospital down in Comox, a fat Scottish doctor there and his fat nurses, Makah women from the south, and none too soft in their manners.

When finally we did return, Shaiks of course was long away, and George Hunt was to stay a white man. So said Robert Hunt, though my father was lucky to be alive as well. It was the very seriousness of the injury he had exacted on his son what most likely saved him. The rush to help the lifeless child. But, later, Shaiks had my father against a wall, the knife at his throat. Quiet words spoken. So Annie told me. She had been watching the events as they did occur, from some secret vantage.

Thus did I come to my crippled face and, I reckon, to the problem in my head what is the cause of my rages.

All the time I had been pondering on things past, my feet had been leading me further from Teguxste and deeper into the forest. Now the undergrowth was near impassable. Underfoot was branches that came directly out from the bases of the tree trunks, and vines also, and no more bracken. I could not make sense of it.

Now there was some brightness ahead. I hacked with my machete a few more times and grey light trickled through. I was near to exhaustion. I leaned, gasping, against a trunk, then I stepped ahead. My foot went straight down through the forest floor. I fell forward, dropping my machete as I made a grab for a branch.

The machete fell away into the depths. In front of me a tree had collapsed to make a clearing in the forest. But there weren't nothing of reason in it. I was hanging out above a drop of thirty foot or more, down to the great tree's ruin.

I had been climbing up—all that while dreaming of faraway times and the greatness that might have been mine—climbing up and away from the ground into the canopy, my feet perched on the sturdiness of the forest's flora. I have heard tell of it, though never from one what is meant to have such wilderness skills as me. I was like some white prospector, so gone astray he can no longer see his up from his down.

And now the rain arrived. The wind gusted heavier. I swayed there on the brink of the void, and I crowed with laughter. I called out to my great-uncle and to my mother and to Nakapankam. Here is a fool what knows nothing! The rain beating upon me. A fool in the forest. Meal for a bear, or some deserving forest rat.

Yet it was like something broke in me with the laughing. I recalled what it was that I was doing there: the weight of my pack and what was inside it. I thought about those men and women what are my history, and where my ancestry was come from. I knew again why I was in the forest. I knew where I was going. So I drew myself together some and spoke on how I had a task and I must follow it to its end, be it bitter or no.

Back on the forest floor, after some scrambling, slipping, and sliding, I saw in which direction was the incline and followed it. Up is forward, I says to myself. Up is forward.

Some time later, I was wrapped all about in rhododendron vines, sweat burning at my eyes, feeling like I was never getting free of them. Trussed up good and proper, deep in the wilds and night coming. But I hacked some more and then I was, quite sudden, at the edge of the forest.

The lake. Some forty years or more since last I seen it. There was bulrushes fifteen feet high down by its margins, swamp hay and cattail. No one had been there in years to cut it back. The lake is a mile long and half that wide, the steep hills behind. That day, there was geese and mallard, shovellers and canvasback ducks out on the water, what made my stomach cramp and my saliva run just seeing them.

Now the rain stopped. Birds sang in the evening air. I pushed my way through the reed grass round toward the north side of the lake. There was no path now at all. Eaten by the land. Fitting that all should return with time to its original state.

Through the high reeds and tule, I spied some distance off a pole rising thirty foot into the air and, at its top, the killer whale. The weather had been cruel to it, the features all worn and bird shit smothering much of what was left. The dorsal fin was still there, anyhow, rising sharp against the sky, and the mouth still grinned, if all its paint was long gone. Wooden planks mouldered in the clearing beneath the pole. Where once there was carven figures standing all about, now I saw only mounds of undergrowth.

I had come back, at last, to the House of Shamans.

It was there that I did first become a man of medicine. My friend, Making-Alive, brung me there. He who first suggested I become a shaman.

He was the brother of Francine, and it was for that reason I did marry her after I lost old Lucy. Poor old bugger, Making-Alive, dead not two years since of the grippe, coughing and retching his life away.

I once told Making-Alive that I did not believe in such powers. Conjurors and tricksters, says I, liars who cheat the people of their money, brewing up evil, but helpless to save a man from real illness. Making-Alive just laughed. "Many ways to heal a man," he said. "More than you know, stupid white boy."

When at last I followed him up to the House of Shamans, I don't know what I believed. Did I want to expose their lies? Perhaps it was that I wanted to believe. Or I wanted power, young man as I was. Shamans is chieftains in their own right, all of it tied up together in the peoples' ways. Thinking through these memories now, here in the museum hall, I reckon I was seeking for my own brown blood—seeking to belong.

Walking inside the House of Shamans and seeing all those old farts sitting about in the dimness within, I understood that now I'd truly know if their magic was real or not. Making-Alive had told me they'd kill me if my tongue come loose and I spoke of it to others. They'd come in the night to rip out that tongue, or bleed me quiet in the forest. Well, in the days what followed, they did teach me all their tricks, and I thenceforth did keep quiet on it.

Anyways, standing there in front of that high pole among the ruins, I took off my pack and laid it down on the grass. I barely knew what I should do next. Make a camp. So I got long strips of bark and bracken fronds, scythed the grass short, cut lengths of cattail from along the shore, shaved away their leaves, and I was weaving the stems in lattices, and using cedar string to draw their ends together into mats, before I realized it seemed I was planning a proper stay.

When I looked up next, the evening was fair and the night would be the same. The storm had blown out the rain, for a day or two at least.

By twilight I had a fire rustling. The firmament bore heavy down upon me without no clouds to hide it. There was just too many alternatives, among the stars, for them to loom so present whilst I was so split myself. I hunched my shoulders against them.

The Indian says the stars is the dead. Was David there among them? And Lucy? My lost babies? All those others I have knowed and lost? Are there stars for the white dead too? Must one people's story be everyone's? How can it be otherwise? Can all souls, when their bodies shrug them off at last, know to travel to the right places their peoples have constructed for them? Can it be so convoluted? If so, then all the differing tribes and races of man are surely different species as well, if such profoundly different endings be their ultimate lot.

I have also heard it said that stars are other suns, and maybe worlds spinning round them very like this one. And that from science! It's odd to me that so fantastical a story could be born out of the very heart of Reason. Surely a wilder myth than any savage people could imagine?

I pulled the contents of my pack out onto the cattail mat. At the bottom was the small wooden box. The wood was worn with age, yet it had been cared for, polished with whale fat so that it reflected the fire's flush by that lonely lakeshore.

I placed my forehead down on the box. I do not know how long I rested there. I thought that I might cease breathing altogether, and that might be the most beautiful blessing I would ever receive.

A tuft of down, what looked like it come off the breast of a duck, blew up to rest against the side of the box. I rolled it between my fingers. Blood and down. The shamans' trick. My heart pounded in my ears, my stomach heaved so that I did actually retch, though there weren't naught to bring up. I could hardly hold sense of the world around me. So I drew myself up and stamped away outside the circle of the fire's light to the lakeshore. The lake was black, but the stars threw diamonds across its surface.

"Lagoyewilé!" I shouted. But there weren't no great spirit of the killer whale out there to help me. I wondered what the boy's dream about me had truly been, all those years ago, before I did heal him. Eagle down. The sickness coming into my mouth from out the body of the boy. The healing of him. Magic. Believing in it, if that is what I did back then.

But that great deception! Sucking the sickness from the body of the boy. His limp body in my arms. My lips upon his chest. Fever and rank sweat, and the child properly unwell, eyes rolling in his head, his skin burning.

Then me spitting out into my palm that bloody ball of illness. The sighs from the people when I hold it up to show them.

David. Lucy. My baby boy and girl. I tried it on all of them. And on none did it work.

Back by the fire, I knelt beside the box. The very same box what caused the war between the Tsimshian and the Tlingit. That once contained the chieftain's head. The box Shaiks gave my mother. That she gave me. That I did give to David at the time he danced his first hamatsa. I prised up the lid. Then my rage came over me and I shut my eyes against the horror of it all.

HARRY DRIFTED IN AND OUT OF DREAM. He saw again the blade sliding
through Poodlas's upper arm and into the armpit. He went back further in
his memories, to that first blade. That first time.

The Mormon orphanage stood high on Telegraph Hill above San
Francisco, with the stink and poverty of Sydney Town all about. He'd
spent much of his childhood confined there, once his mother died. It was
a big clapboard house with high plank walls surrounding it. There weren't
so many wooden houses of its size left, especially since the fires of 1850.
Sometimes, when no one was watching to chastise him for it, he would
scramble up through the attic and onto the red adobe tiles of its roof. There
he could gaze out to the hovels and patchwork tents where the Australians,
come over for the gold rush, made their homes, along with the other poor
immigrants out of the Latin Americas, Ireland, and old Europe.

His father had been one of those last. He was a Welshman, with one
gleaming find to his name, sifted from a river in the mountains, with
which he'd won his bawdy-singer bride. "He come in that night, first time
I seed him, great wad a greasy money in his paws, stinking high as a dead
beast. But filled up so full with hisself as I couldn't resist his twinkling." So
Harry's mother told it. Women were rare enough in the city back then, she
said, that even whores had the men doffing their caps and paying them fat
compliments. She was desperate—in those last days of her life—desperate
for him to know the details of his origins, pitiful though they might be. His
father had taken a knife in his guts before Harry had even come squawking
out into the world. So she told it. But he'd heard other stories as well: how
he hadn't died at all, how he'd upped and gone as soon as he'd heard she
was bearing his child. As soon as the money was gone.

Harry sat beside her in the wood shack out back of the other harlots'
cribs, where her employers had put her to die. Rank odours came off her,
choked by the grippe, sweat pouring down her body, grunting, coughing
to her soon-forgotten end. "I weren't no soiled dove," she said, over and

again. "You don't forget it, Harry. I sang for my keeps. I sang." But it was lies. She spent her days on her back, just like all of them, however sweetly she could croon. She wasn't evil in her lies, though. She dreamed. She had her stories. She spun them to him. She spun them to herself. But always with a soft hand on his face and a kiss to his forehead. He was nine years old when she shut her eyes and left him.

He was in the orphanage for five years—his mother's madam saying how she'd do him right, fetching him straight up the hill from her death-bed and in through its gates. Some agreement she must have kept with the men there. He never heard what was done with his mother's body. The only time the boys were let out was in groups on Sundays for the trip to church, the two men who ran the place, decked out in black, both of them thin like strutting scarecrows, following their boys, close-eyed, out and back. Otherwise the boys played—or, as often, fought—in the yard, or they studied the scriptures, once they had learned to read, a rider's crop across their neck if they should dawdle.

One day there came to the orphanage a kind and Christian soul with a puppet show he'd brought back across the Pacific from Java. The old sailor, face burnt nearly black with the sun, promised Harry the freedom of the oceans, now he was come of age, if he but made his way to find him at the docks. The Jolly Waterman was the place.

So that night Harry went up the wall, fingers tight on the nailheads that held it together. He perched there a moment on top. Below, the two Mormon men had spied him. They hurled black vengeance if he wasn't back on the ground that instant, even as one of them worked, frantic, at the locks on the gate. A song his mother used to sing came in his mind. He sang it down to them. "I am fixing to leave, yes I am fixing to go. But where I am going, I just don't know."

He dropped to the far side and ran down the hill through Sydney Town's tenements, sucking splinters from his palms where they had spiked him as he went over the wall. Chileno whores called out from their rough-board shanties to him, some cackling, showing their brown-tan buttocks as he went by, cooing and blowing him kisses—"Sweet boy," "Beautiful boy."

He scuttled past the doorways of the cheap groggeries—the Bobby Burns, the Tam O'Shanter, the Bird in Hand—hunching his shoulders, remembering the catcalls and violent, clutching paws the men inside had had for his mother. Vagabonds in slouch felt hats, smoking pipes. Australians with the shuffling gait of men who'd spent too long in irons. Maudlin prospectors belching away the paltry earnings they'd drawn from the hills. Those who had made more plied the salons and gambling houses round Portsmouth Square, down in the rich heart of the city.

He came out at the bottom of the hill and raced along Montgomery Street. There were no street lamps; what light there was came beaming out from the hotels and businesses—the Nianto Hotel, Bubb Grubb and Company, Frenchies' Irons and Hardware. He passed dogs fighting for dropped morsels in the thick mud, passed drunks rolling and squealing on the ground, passed Chinamen with big barrels of rank-smelling dried fish for sale. Men in tall hats and long beards stalked the streets as well, up on the plankboard walking ways. Page boys his own age hurled insults, jeering at his tattered clothing, and a flag on a pole proclaimed the city for the United States of America.

He turned on California Street toward the front. The corner of Battery Street, and the brick warehouses, many-windowed and five storeys tall. Then down the wharf until there, halfway along, a swinging wooden sign showed a red-faced, smiling jaunty: The Jolly Waterman.

The kind and Christian soul was inside, hanging off the bar by one arm, liquor-crazed amid the crowd of cursing, jostling stevedores and sailors at their drink. Harry stood at the doorway, half in, half out, until a clout at his ear threw him forward inside. Fearful, lacking option, Harry stood before the man. Remember me?

The man squinted at him, then took hold of Harry by his hair. He dragged him through the crowd, and a few cheered him on, and most ignored them. Then up the stairs at the back. Harry had learned enough from those who worked the orphanage to know what was coming. So he hung limp in the drunkard's grip, until it loosened as the man fumbled outside a door in the upstairs hallway, the sounds of the bar still loud around them.

126

Harry twisted suddenly loose. He slipped the knife from the man's belt, where he had seen it earlier. The man cursed and stumbled, rickety with alcohol. The boy drove the blade up into his face, both hands about the handle. It jarred along the cheekbone and slid in through the man's left eye. The eyeball split and darkened. The lens and the mucus inside slid down the blade, and the blood following. The two of them slumped against the unlocked door. It fell open under their weight. The boy lay halfway inside the dark room, atop the man's body, until at last it ceased its shuddering.

Afterwards, he walked among the men downstairs. The knife was stowed in his belt, the dead man's money in his pocket, the corpse hidden in the locked room, no one taking notice of the blood upon his face and on his thin body. He was not the only one stained in gore that night, or any night, from the fighting that did not cease along the wharf each evening, once the drinking was begun.

He walked outside and stood by the quayside. The still waters mirrored the brilliant firmament. The vast forest of ships' masts broke the horizons about him. He knew then the call of the world's oceans indeed, just as he understood the horror that lurked around every corner of a boy's life.

A day had passed since their passage through the Nakwakto Rapids. Harry had brought the *Hesperus* through the heavy water on the far side. He'd lain up in a cove he'd come upon by fortune in the blinding rain. He had dropped anchor and staggered forward to see what had become of Charley.

The old Indian was on his hands and knees in the prow, the lump of his back raised up like a whale's, and shaking his head from side to side. Where he had been thrown from his feet in the storm surge, he had cracked his temple against the railing, before sliding away forward out of Harry's sight. Blood flowed still from the wound at his head.

Meanwhile, the *Hesperus* was beginning to list.

"We took a bang to the hull," said Harry, squatting beside Charley. "I'm going below. See what's there. You all right?"

Charley waved him off. "I live," he said.

In the hold, some bales of blankets had spilled across the floor, but mostly all was still tightly stowed. A section of the hull about a foot long had been forced inward, low on the port side. Water spurted in through the broken planking. The corners of the spilled blankets twitched in the several inches of water they had already shipped.

He was half an hour hammering it right, retching with the pain from his shoulder, the sling Charley had fashioned for him hanging loose about his neck, groggy and stupid as well with exhaustion, so that more than once he drove the hammer on to his own fingers. By the time he came back on deck, gasping and seeing ghost images all about him, the storm had diminished and Charley was up and moving about in the pilothouse.

"No good," said Charley from the door. "All gone break." Inside, most of the cupboards and shelves had opened or fallen, throwing out their contents of jars and bottles, boxes and crockery. These had rolled and smashed until the floor was little more than a midden.

Charley held up a length of filthy bandage. "All gone bad." He pointed. Amongst the detritus were the shattered remains of the jar of iodine.

"Christ almighty," said Harry.

Charley nodded. "All gone bad," he said.

They set fresh water to boil on the stove. Then they washed Charley's head. The wound was ugly and did not want to stop bleeding, but it was also shallow. His fat skull, at least, was still intact. Harry sewed it closed with canvas twine. The old man sat without comment through the operation.

"Not get sick," he said. "Blood same raven."

Harry was in a worse state. The wounds in his shoulder and his leg had both reopened from his efforts at the helm and in the hold. His bandages were soaked with blood, and there were no more clean for him to replace them with.

"Sea water best," said Charley. "Keep bandage for now, go in ocean. Go on—all you in water." So he lowered Harry into the water on a rope. He swung in the tide and the salt water ground at his wounds until he could bear no more. After, Charley took off the bandages, washed them in the ocean, placed them to boil in the water on the stove, and then hung them to dry in the sharp breeze, now the rain had finally stopped.

They brewed coffee and chewed dry salmon. Charley put back the bandages. Then they slept.

Harry woke shivering in the dawn. He felt chilled, though the day did not seem cold. Charley prepared a breakfast of canned fish boiled in water to a stew, with a little of the bread that had not been soaked during the storm. They sat, side by side against the front of the pilothouse, drinking coffee.

Harry's body shook. His mind kept threatening to stray into daydream. So he wrapped his arms tight about himself and stood. He looked out. The inlet stretched away to either side, northwest and southeast, a mile wide. The rapids were still visible on the far side, the foaming waters almost benign from this distance. He was so tired still. He slumped back down beside Charley. "Where now?" he said at last.

"Teguxste south," he said, pointing. "But you shake and sick. Go back is better. Find medicine." Charley put a rolled cigarette into Harry's mouth. He struck a match, his gnarled fingers shielding the flame from the wind. Then he leaned back and looked intently at Harry. He put his hand to Harry's forehead. The skin on Charley's palm was like bark. The old Indian's nostrils twitched. "You sick," he said again, his gloomy face more grim than ever. "Maybe die sick. What we do?"

Harry leaned his head back against the railing. "Find George," he said. "Maybe he'll have medicine. Maybe he'll have a plan. He's a fucking medicine man, ain't he?" He hunched his knees up close to his chest. "And if that fey black fucker—demon, dreamer, whatever you call it—and don't think I've forgot you ain't told me one chunk of the truth of things—if it's off whispering to Walewid about where we are, then he'll be on his way for certain, now his brother's dead. If we are yet ahead of them, we ought to press on." He squeezed his palms together. "I've but a chill. It'll fade through the morning. See if it don't."

Charley muttered something in Kwakwala. Then he nodded. "South," he said.

So Harry turned the *Hesperus* south and followed the mainland. But he did not improve through the morning, and his fever did not fade. In the end, Charley took the helm. Harry dragged out some canvas and lay down to rest.

And now there came a faint aroma from the bandage on his shoulder. He knew it all too well. That smell like molasses left too long on a stove.

Damnation, but he was in the grip of trouble now. Jammed between one bad choice and another. Turn about, brave the rapids once more, and make the passage home. In what: three days? Perhaps hope to sight another vessel on the way, one with a surgeon aboard, or at least with some disinfecting agent to delay the rot's hold upon him.

Or go on and find his father-in-law. And what then? George was skilled in healing, though it was of the Indian sort. Maybe he had iodine with him. As likely not. If it all weren't too late already.

To turn back risked leaving his father-in-law to his fate, whatever that might be, should Walewid track him down. Though Walewid was first and foremost after him and Charley, was he not? But he had said he'd take the skulls of Harry and Charley, and of George as well. The dreamer had seen them come through the rapids, so he'd report that back to Walewid. He'd surely work it out, where George might be. If he had even cottoned to their mission. Though what other fool mission could they be on to take them through the rapids anyhow?

So they went on and hoped to find George, and the rot might take him, unless George had the salves and skill to save him. Or they turned back, and hoped they got lucky and made it to safety. If he went back without George, then that cocksucker Halliday would confiscate the family's treasures—Christ only knew what kinds of chaos that would be the starting of—and probably the *Hesperus* as well. If that happened—well then all his plans would have come to nothing.

All this thinking exhausted him. Soon enough, he drifted into sleep.

"Fat Harry." Charley's voice drew him back to consciousness. "Fat Harry, look starbud." Harry was still propped against the gunnels of the *Hesperus*, a nest of sail canvas beneath him, a waterskin by his side. The air was filled with sea spume from the boat's passage through the water. It caught in his hair and on his brows and lashes, stinging at his eyes. Yet the breeze and the water were cool against the heat of his fever. He pulled himself up with his good arm and looked out over the side.

A killer whale rolled up out of the water not twenty yards away. Its tail rose up to hang for a moment, black against the water, the mountains and the forest behind, before it slid away beneath the ocean.

"Sign!" called out Charley. "Maqenoq, him speak loud! Shout for us hear. Why come inside rapid? Should be he only out on ocean."

The killer whale rose again farther ahead. The explosion of its breath threw spume into the air, which drifted above the water until the boat passed through it. Harry smelled fish and brine and something else, sharp but nameless, the very essence of the whale.

Harry found that tears were pouring down his face. He could not remember when last he had wept, or indeed if he had ever done so before. "Must have got caught up in the tidal surge," he shouted back to Charley, when he finally found his voice again. "Got drawn through."

"Sign," said Charley again. Then he went back to singing some Indian dirge, a rough-throated jumble of monotonous sound from which Harry could not even pick out the individual words. But in that instant, Harry felt hope come into him, where he had not realized there had been none before. It was such a surprise that he should feel so that he rose up on his feet and went to sit forward. He wasn't even sure what the nature of that hope might be, what it was he hoped for.

A half-hour later, they came near a headland. Charley shouted, "See?" Harry looked back and saw the old Indian was pointing toward a small island just beyond the headland's tip. "Dead man island. Same like Rupert grave island."

It came off the port bow, ten cables away, an islet no more than fifty yards across. There were broken statues of men, small rotting shelters, and mouldering boxes in the trees. At its far side, another great branch of the inlet forked away east, as wide as the one in which they currently travelled. The high, grey cloud was breaking up. Sunlight and shadow rolled in fractured segments over the forested hillsides, which fell steeply into the waters of the inlet. Far off he saw the sheer granite mountain ranges of the Interior.

"Where dead man island," Charley said, "there village too."

Twenty minutes later, they floated some yards off the ruin of an Indian village. A pebble beach ran down to the water, and behind, thick and tall and filled with shadow, the forest loomed over the broken timber frames of long-abandoned houses.

Then he saw the upended canoe with the killer whale design along its flanks. He saw the hull staved in so badly it would never be of use again.

"George canoe," said Charley quietly.

"Walewid found him," said Harry.

"Hmm," said Charley.

"Look at his fucking boat."

"Hmm."

"What if they're here, waiting in the forest?"

"Where them boat?"

"They could've hid the boats so we'd not see them."

"Hmm."

"What fucking hmm?"

"Think they no here. Maybe come go. Maybe something else."

Harry looked at Charley, the old man's gnarled fingers scraping at his stubble. "So what're you suggesting?" he said.

"I go see." Charley looked Harry up and down. "You wait boat."

They steered in close with Harry at the tiller again, his body shaking now with fever, but clinging to his rifle with his free hand. Charley hopped over the side and waded in. He stood for a while beside the canoe, examining the damage that had been done to it. Then he clambered up the pebbles to a collapsed totem pole about which the canoe had been secured. He squatted down, looking at something. Then he stood and came back down the beach.

"Think safe," he said.

"How come?"

"George thing here. No one take thing."

"So what about the canoe?"

"Think safe."

Harry watched the old Indian on the shore. Then he said, "All right."

The day was ending and the tide was near its fullest ebb. They beached the *Hesperus* beside the canoe, yet near enough to the waterline so that, with a heave, it would float when next the tide was in.

"I got to see to the outside of the hull first," said Harry. He put his feet over the gunnels and dropped onto the beach, but his legs had no strength in them and he pitched forward on the pebbles.

Charley helped him to his feet. He led him up to the remains of George's camp. "See," he said. George's belongings were wrapped in a tarpaulin, which Charley had opened. They lay neatly ordered inside. "George take some thing go forest. Leave thing here. If someone come, then this not be here. Be stole or move about."

"Don't explain the canoe, though, do it?"

"Hmm," said Charley. Harry slumped down on the tarpaulin, thinking Charley could wrap "hmm" in nettles and poke it up his crippled ass. The old Indian sat down beside him and drew out Harry's tobacco tin from his own pocket. He rolled two cigarettes in silence and handed one across. They drew smoke together.

Nodding toward the canoe, Charley said, "Think George do."

"How you figure that?"

"Know George many year."

"But he'd strand himself."

"Ek."

Harry smoked for a while. "You're saying he came here to stay. Or to die."

Charley just shrugged.

After they finished smoking, it was Charley who worked on the boat's hull, Charley who gathered wood and made up the fire, Charley who brewed coffee and cooked food, Charley who fetched a bottle of whisky from the hold and poured part of its contents over Harry's bandaged wounds, which were black and, at his shoulder, dirty yellow with pus.

Harry lay propped against the fallen totem pole. He did his best to ignore the stench of decay from his shoulder. He ran his fingers across the worn carving of the owl. Charley sat opposite, watching him and drinking from the whisky bottle. Then he said, "I go look sign George. You stay. Sleep." Charley hefted the rifle and trudged away along the beach, bent low, his head ranging left and right like a mangy tracker dog snuffling for a trail.

Out on the quiet waters, mist curled in the breeze like slow-dancing ghosts. It was still only mid-morning, but soon enough Harry was asleep.

"Fat Harry!" He opened his eyes. Charley was kneeling beside the embers of the fire, a pot bubbling over it. "You father-law not here," he said. "Track go forest. When come back? Maybe never." He leaned in closer to look down on Harry's face. He shook his head and muttered to himself. "Sick bad." He handed Harry a cup of coffee.

He felt as if he had been unconscious for days, but he saw by the sun that it was only noon, the light thin through the heavy, broken cloud. He sat up, leaning against the broken totem pole, and sipped. His sleep had been filled with nightmares. Raven-headed men, bloody eyes in the darkness of thickets, great fanged maws snapping. Well, he deserved them. "Short life bringers," the Indians called the white man. Here among the heathens, here on this wild coastline, whisky smuggler as he was, murderer of men, bringer of ruin—yes, he deserved his nightmares.

He had killed three people in his life. The first was the night of his escape from the orphanage in San Francisco, and he had made his peace with that. The last was Poodlas, and none could deny that he had been protecting his own. Yet the truth was he'd been quick to vent his anger and the darker places of his soul on that poor drunken idiot. There'd been many ways he might have played that scene, but he chose violence. Perhaps he'd pay with his own life now.

The truth of it was that he felt wrung with shame. And it was not so hard to fathom why. Shame for his anger back at Blunden Harbour. And shame for that other murder of which he was culpable. The second killing. Hong Kong. The door with the Chinese sign that meant Joy. Though he would not dwell on that. He would not step inside those memories. There was death enough already. Death surrounding him here and now—

134

Poodlas, this village, the people gone, the imminence of his own death, as seemed likely now. It was enough for any man to bear.

He coughed hard and long, leaning on his one good arm, spitting black phlegm into the embers. His head spun until he nearly fell forward into the fire. Charley reached across to hold on to him.

There weren't many had looked on him with favour down the years. But Grace had. And, he supposed, in his grim way, so George had as well— at least, in sanctioning his marriage, if he'd not been exactly welcoming thereafter. But even then, George was only reacting to the truth, as he had spied it: that Harry had been planning to run with the spring tide.

He was here on this dead beach, near dead himself, sent on some fool errand he'd never wanted that had brought him near his own death. Yet there was something still to be done. Some part in the spin of things for him. He had to find George. For Grace. For Francine. For this family that had been straight with him. Across the fire, Charley watched him, his head seeming to emerge directly from his chest in his deformity. Even for cripple Charley. Now he had come this far, Harry would not have these people undone—broken by the likes of Halliday and Crosby.

"White fuck," he said, not meaning to speak aloud. When he heard his own voice, sounding as if it came from deep inside a cave, he realized how far his mind had been ranging.

Charley nodded slowly, as if deep in contemplation of Harry's statement. He handed Harry the waterskin. "What come next?" he said.

"My faith were placed in George," said Harry, lying back and gasping at the air. "Too late to turn back now."

Charley shrugged. "George go up in forest," he said. "I know where."

"Then we get after him," said Harry. "Soon is better, I'd say." Charley looked at him for a time, and Harry knew the old Indian was sizing up the chances of his making it much farther. "Damn your pig eyes," Harry said. "Help me get this bandage off. Let's have a see of what I've got left in me."

Charley unpeeled the bandage from his shoulder. Harry could not keep from moaning as the scabs came away with the blood- and pus-soaked cloth. A thin yellow liquid seeped from the wound. A crust of dried pus lay beneath the skin, bulging the ragged edges taut against the twine holding them together. The skin was mostly black, and the festering stench made even Charley blink and pull away.

"Yellow not so bad. Black not good," Charley said. "Die soon."

"You've a soft manner," Harry said. The corners of Charley's mouth twitched a little. Harry sighed. "But I know it." He picked up the whisky bottle and poured a quantity down across the wound. He breathed slowly through his nose for a while, then put the bottle to his mouth and drank. "Seems I'm reacquiring the habit," he said.

"Good time for start again," said Charley.

They looked at the wound on his leg, which somehow had escaped infection. Then Charley washed the bandages in the sea. He put them in a pan upon the fire to boil. The *Hesperus* was beached at such an angle that its stove could not be used. They reapplied the bandages and then Charley said, "Best go now."

So they checked the *Hesperus* was secure, took a little food in a bag, which Charley carried along with the rifle, and then Harry followed him along the shore until they reached a hillock, which rose up dead square in the centre of the beach, perhaps a hundred and fifty feet high, its far edge stretching twenty yards into the water. Beside it, a small stream emerged from the forest.

"In here," Charley said. Harry could see now that a narrow path led away beside the stream into the darkness between the trees.

"How far?" he said.

"All this day. Some this night. Maybe you die before. Maybe not."

"If it ain't your idiot trap what kills me first."

To begin with, the trail was easy enough to follow, the water shining next to them in the thin light, the tangled undergrowth many feet high all around, yet low and broken still upon the path, so that it could be stepped upon, or waded through where it had grown a little higher. Harry had never walked inside these deep forests before. The massive trunks of spruce, hemlock, and cedar rose into the dim canopy. Vines crept and clutched and hung down everywhere about. Birds clacked and cawed, their voices sounding harsh and dead in the heavy air, which itself seemed tinged with a deep emerald. The foliage looked too huge to be real, swaying and lurching, as if in irritation, as they moved among it. Everything was drenched. Drops of water the size of duck eggs fell out of the canopy from time to time, exploding noisily. The whole forest clicked and rustled, spat and sighed, threatening somehow, not at rest, not at peace.

The sweat poured down his skin. He found it harder and harder to focus on anything other than Charley's humped back as it swerved and ducked and forced its way forward. His boots trudged and tripped, each pace sending dull but intense shots of pain through his shoulder. Slowly, his eyes lost focus, until he saw nothing clearly, and all became a blur of green shadows.

He came abruptly awake as he was falling, his foot trapped by a root or tangle of vines. The undergrowth caught him barely halfway to the ground. He lay still, rocking in the embrace of a giant spread of fronds.

Then Charley's hands were upon him, pulling him up. "Eye open better," he said. "Then not fall." So Harry ran his hands down his face, shook some of the water from his jacket, though he was pretty much soaked through. He razzled his fingers through his hair, trying to clear his head. Then he looked around.

The day was ended. The shadows had become black, impenetrable, the calls of birds replaced already by a greater silence. The stream could still be heard, just off to their left, though he could not see it. But the path, what little there had been, was no longer in evidence, at least not to Harry. Charley had a machete in his hand—the same one Harry had wielded in Blunden Harbour two days before. Now the old Indian turned again and hacked and thrust, beckoning Harry on into the gathering darkness.

Soon, however, the darkness became absolute. Eyes open or closed, it made no difference to Harry at all. There were only the sounds of sweep and thunk in front, as Charley kept to his work. Harry lifted each foot with caution, not sure what he was standing on or moving through, or what was immediately ahead. His breathing came more ragged. As time went on, his fever inched its way back through his thinking, until the world rocked as if he were aboard a ship on a heavy sea, and he knew that he could not go farther.

"Stop, you fucking whoreson," he said, rasping the words, reaching out, trying to grab hold of Charley's shoulder. "Just stop, won't you?" He sensed Charley turn back toward him.

"Not so far. One hour. Two, maybe."

"Are you crazy? There ain't nothing to be seen. You can't know where we are going. Wait till the light is up. It don't make a difference, do it?"

"Must go. Thing happen. I know it. Must go."

But Harry slumped down and sat, panting, near to retching, feeling the sodden earth soaking up through his trousers, too exhausted to care. "Ten minutes, then. Ten minutes."

Charley squatted beside him, their legs touching. "Okay, ten minute," he said.

"How in all the damned hells do you know where you're going, anyway? You told me you never been here before."

In his mind's eye, Harry could imagine the Indian shrugging. "Hear story. Just know."

Harry leaned his head back. He heard the burble of the stream somewhere close by. He closed his eyes against the darkness.

Hong Kong, 1885. Smallpox eats at the city as he walks the streets of Tai Ping Shan. It is night. By the wharf, the boatmen lie about on the waterside, black boils weeping on their wiry bodies. Among the overhanging buildings in that crowded quarter, prostitutes sit on the broken pavements, their cheap cheongsams or gaudy Western costumes riding up so that the seeping lesions on their thighs are visible. And Chinamen pirates, scarred savages with eyes and even limbs missing, weep with pain and hold out their blistered hands to him in supplication.

Carters, fishermen, and merchants in hats brilliantly brocaded with gold filigree fight each other amid the rotting slops in the gutters. They fight for fish heads and for shards of jade, which glimmer in the street lamps' sputtering flames. Rickshaws clatter past, piled with the dead, their faces and their bodies blackened and concave. There are food stalls, with fish balls and vats of noodles burbling, manned by stick crones with enormous cysts on their faces.

The staccato languages of the Chinese jabber agonies from windows and doorways, until he knows that he but dreams and walks some hellish enlargement of his memory.

He is immune to all sickness. His pink white man's skin shines proud and healthy. His purse is laden with the silver the Chinese so covet, and he knows himself rich. Yet also he knows where he is headed. He resists as hard as he is able, until he can feel his body move and twitch as it lies in the damp and the dark beside Charley. But his feet do not hear him and he walks the path still through Hong Kong.

He passes now into wealthier areas, with their ornately carven wooden courts, the five-storey hotels, the post offices, the city hall complexes, their windows multitudinous and brilliantly glassed—the museums and libraries bursting with the wealth of the Orient as it has been plucked by the British. On their steps, the wealthy die as well, white and yellow, collarless suits and sinuously patterned silk dresses belching black pus onto the ground.

Nausea shakes him and horror, so that he wants to find a corner somewhere and curl himself like a child into a ball to blank it all away. Yet he goes on, and now he is at the city's outskirts, staring up at the mountainsides, which rise near-vertical toward the black sky. A single lamp shines in the darkness on the hillside. He follows the path up toward it. His breath becomes short.

He is gasping when he stands at last before the door to the old wooden house, its thatch roof steep against the monsoon rains. His hand is before his eyes. He places his palm against the single Chinese sign scrawled in red upon the door. He pushes at it. The sign, as she had told him, that means Joy.

Harry came abruptly awake with Charley shaking him by his good shoulder.

"Up, Fat Harry. Move. Thing happen. Must go!" He allowed himself to be pulled to his feet. It was still pitch-black. Charley took hold of one of Harry's hands and gripped it. "Keep hold," he said as they moved off, the swish of the machete sounding again. Harry recalled the story of Hansel and Gretel, and almost choked up, giggling. Two lost children in the woods, except one was a deformed, leathery old savage, and the other—well, what was the other?

Spike-edged leaves raked his cheeks, his head and arms, until he winced before every step he took. But Charley's controlling grip drew him on. The fever burned in his body. Harry's mind filled again with the images of his dream. That same dream, always the same—always ending before the door. The sign that meant Joy in Chinese. He could not think on it. He would not.

Charley's grip never slackened. He wondered who this man was that could navigate in pitch black through the wild forest. This cripple buffoon who walked in darkness like he paraded along the central avenue of a city in midsummer. Nothing made sense.

At last it seemed as if there came a faint lightening of the darkness. Then, all at once as he took a step, the wall of foliage about him disappeared and he was in the open again. The shock of it made him stumble and he had to grab Charley's arm to stay on his feet. The moonlit clouds were so bright it seemed almost daylight. They rushed impossibly fast across the sky, yet down here there was no breeze at all. The stars behind were brilliant beads. A rough pasture stretched away for a hundred yards to a lake whose waters perfectly reflected the sky. Dark shadows of hills, mountains even, far off, were faintly visible beyond the lake.

But Harry still saw the streets of Hong Kong as well. It was as if two photographs were laid one upon the other. The pasture's thick grass rose up through the pavements, until the bodies of the dying lay upon carpets of benighted green, and the path to the door with the Chinese sign stretched away before him, across the lake.

He felt no confusion, though. He was calm. He observed himself, half-ways to mostly dead, a man who couldn't rightly tell his past from his present, so full of fever and suppuration was he. And if now was now, or now was then, it didn't make much difference. He might have died that year in Hong Kong. The smallpox took so many. Why it had not taken him back then, rotting him into death—as his body was doing now—he could not say.

"Look," said Charley.

Hong Kong curled from his vision like dust in an eddy from a closing door. He turned in the direction of the Indian's gaze. He saw the orange glow of a fire, halfway around the lake. Something straight and tall rose up beside it, but he could not make out what it was from this far away. His pupils adjusted to the fire's greater brightness, until it was the only thing he could see, and all that vast wilderness surrounding them dissolved away into black.

"George?" Harry said. It didn't seem possible, somehow, that they were actually to find him. That there was some end to all this movement through the world, and that it would be George they would come upon inhabiting that final space.

Charley took hold of Harry's arm and started out in the direction of the fire. Harry stumbled along beside him.

They crossed the stream that they had followed all the way from the village. Here it was twenty feet wide and knee deep, but the cold barely registered. His eyes were on the fire, which dipped in and out of sight as the trees and plants between first obscured, then cleared his line of vision.

As they came closer, they heard a voice call out.

"It's him," Harry said and pressed forward. But now Charley had stopped. Harry turned to him. "What? Come on. It's him."

"Think not good time go," said Charley.

"Are you fucking mad? We found him. Let's go." He pulled at Charley's arm, but the old man stood firm.

"Not sure good," he said. "George … " He waved one hand in the air in vague circles. "Think George not here."

"Fuck." Harry wanted to beat at Charley's head, but he stopped and thought about this a moment, trying to understand what Charley might mean in his twisted Indian way. He tried to calm his breathing, which was coming like the steam from a train engine now, so that he almost had come to gasping. "You mean he's off in a rage or the like?"

"Hamatsa go forest. Go alone."

"But you said hurry. Something was happening."

Charley stood for a moment staring up at the sky. Harry felt light in his head, as if he was about to pass out. He could feel his heart beating fast now. His shoulder throbbed with each tiny movement his body made. He tried his best to slow his breathing.

Then Charley looked again toward the fire. "Go look but stay quiet now," he said.

"All right." Harry lurched along next to him, feeling the sweat on his forehead, under his arms, pouring down his thighs out of his crotch. Yet he was cold as well, shivering as if he had the watch in an arctic gale.

Now they were no more than fifty yards from the fire. Here and there, clumps of high rushes rose above their heads, breaking their view. But Harry could see there was a tall ancestral pole with what looked a battered, weather-beaten image of a killer whale at its top, lit from below by the fire, which gave it a baleful look. Around the pole, stretching out to either side, hints of the ruins of a now long-overgrown building could just be made out, mere straight lines in the undergrowth really, but outlined by the sharp light and shadow. Mounds rose up here and there that looked suggestive of human forms, as if they were men beginning to emerge from the very earth itself.

The fire blazed before the killer whale pole. There was a small Indian shelter of reed-woven mats beside it. Other bits and pieces of campcraft were strewn about.

George was kneeling beside the fire, wearing just a pair of trousers, hunched motionless over a smallish wooden box, the one Harry had seen him with late that night of the funeral, before he had fled. The hair on his huge torso was greyed in his age, so he looked some ancient overgrown and crooked oak. As Harry watched, at last George drew the box's lid open. He shuddered, as if dry sobs were passing through his body unnoticed. He reached the fingers of one hand inside. He cried out, arching back, his hands coming up toward the sky, then down to rest across his face, as if he sought to hide his vision from the world. Then he fell forward, shaking in that way Harry had seen before when he was sinking into rage. He lay face down, then rolled, almost in spasm, on his side. One of his arms flopped over and came to rest in the embers of the fire, but he did not react. He just lay, with his eyes closed and his mouth making shapes as if he spoke, though Harry could not hear if he made any sound.

Charley was already running toward the fire. His crippled form moved at an incredible pace. He seemed to lope, as if he was more ape than human. Harry hobbled after, his breath coming in short gasps. He could not take his eyes from George's arm as it rested on the red coals of the fire.

Charley was there before him. He took hold of George and dragged him away from the flames. Harry came up to stand panting beside the fire as Charley knelt over George and surveyed the black skin of his burnt arm. George's head twisted this way and that. He bared his teeth, then both his hands swept down to cover his stomach and his knees came up as if he had been punched in the guts.

"You watch George," Charley said. He picked up what looked like George's shirt and jogged away toward the lake. Harry knelt beside George, who was lying on his back, eyes shut, and voicing soft words in the Indian tongue that Harry did not understand. His eyeballs behind the lids moved as if he was watching something. Harry could see that George's forearm was burned, but not too badly, the skin still intact, just blackened along part of its length. The foul stench of burning hair and skin lingered in the air.

Shortly, Charley was back with the shirt soaked in lake water. He wrapped this about George's forearm, and, as he did so, George jerked and swung onto his side and opened his eyes. He lay there for a moment, seeming not to focus on anything particular. Then he started to wiping at his face with his hands, his face horror-struck, like there was acid flowing down his cheeks. He grabbed at his stomach and lay curled in a ball like a baby. He cried out.

Charley had stepped away. Now Harry made to move in toward his father-in-law, but Charley shook a finger to stop him.

A moment later, George pushed himself up until he was sitting, face toward the fire. He stared at the wooden box, whose lid was still open. Harry noticed now that it was carved in many complex designs and looked to be of some antiquity. Without taking any notice of either Charley or Harry, George shuffled forward until he was sitting once more over the box. He reached his hand in again to touch what was inside, but, as he did so, noticed the shirt wrapped about his forearm. He lifted his arm up, seeming surprised. He looked to left and right, then back over his shoulder, and saw them both.

George's vision seemed to pass right through Harry, but, when they came to Charley, he leapt to his feet. He seemed astonished. He stepped backward, almost into the fire.

"Lagoyewilé?" he said. Charley said something terse in Kwakwala by way of a reply. They spoke a few words more to each other, George shaking his head, muttering constantly to himself when he wasn't otherwise speaking. Then he turned away, stepped round the fire, and paced away toward the lake. He seemed unconscious to the pain there must be in his arm.

"What's going on?" Harry said.

Charley didn't answer. Harry looked over at him. The old Indian was still down on his haunches as he'd been when first he had wrapped the wet shirt around George's arm. He looked back at Harry, his face without obvious emotion, though there was, rare though it be to see it, just in his eyes a certain sympathy.

"We go back beach now," Charley said. "George not here."

"What?" Harry stared after George. He saw him silhouetted against the lake as he stood at its edge. "Go back ... ?" He stuttered into silence. He wanted to scream at Charley, to hold him in the flames until he spoke sense again. More than with despair, the prospect of the long, almost certainly fatal, trek back through the forest to the beach filled him with something near fury.

He saw the box sitting open beside the fire. He knelt down beside it and stared inside. What he saw was George's hands wrapped about the skull of his son, that day of the funeral. He heard again the neck snapping as it broke, saw the body slump forward into the gravebox. Now, in this small box here, he saw David's putrefying face, the skin blackened in death, the eyeballs rotted away already, so that the lids were sunk into the skull, a faint movement beneath the skin as the maggots were moving.

He turned his eyes away. He thought he should feel nausea, should feel horror. But he'd seen too much already in his life. He looked over to Charley. "This?" he said, pointing into the box. "He did this?" Charley said nothing. Harry rose to his feet. He spun about one way and then another. "He cut off his fucking head?" Charley looked down at the ground.

Harry laughed, hard enough that pain shot through his shoulder. "He cut off his head, put it in a box, and brung it here in the wilderness! Jesus good Christ almighty." And now Harry felt a rage of his own flaring up, rising as if from some leprous pool deep in his guts. "Pagan fucking ... " He pointed at Charley. "I come half across the world looking for him. I'm sliced like a fucking pig carcass. You say go back? He ain't here? He's there, man!" He stamped away toward the lake.

Charley called after him. "George not here now. Gone be wild." But Harry wasn't listening to any more of their black bullshit. He came up on his father-in-law, who was standing on the narrow shingle beach.

"George!" But he did not even turn toward Harry. "Damn you. George!" He stepped round in front of him. Harry was tall, but George was near half a head taller again, though now he was hunched so that their faces were nearly level. He clutched both hands still at his stomach. In his eyes, which stared now into Harry's, there was shock, the whites showing all round the black pupils. Horror even—but nothing of recognition.

"It was me," George said, bringing his face close to Harry's, his voice a low murmur, as if secrets were being spoken, his breath foul like putrefying fruit. "The blood on my teeth."

"George," Harry said. He stepped backward, hearing his foot splash as it went into the water, his anger for the moment daunted by the pain in the man's voice, the agony in his face. "Do you not know me? It's Harry. Wake up, man." He put a hand on the man's upper arm.

But George shook him off. "I tore them out! His guts. Mine. The blood on my teeth." He stared away over Harry's head, across the lake. He called out, "Lagoyewilé!" Then he looked down at Harry again. And now he snarled, his teeth showing black. "That blue-eyed devil don't believe," he said. "He can't believe. That's what's wrong with it all. He don't believe." He whirled about and strode back toward the fire.

"You cut the head from your own dead son, you fucking barbarian!" Harry called after him, but he had no more energy to follow. He watched

George squat down beside the wooden box, glancing once toward Charley, then ignoring him completely to stare in at the box's contents.

Harry's breathing came short. His whole body felt frozen. His heart raced and now such a spate of nausea came over him that he went down on his knees and vomited bile onto the cold stones. He saw blue eyes glaring from a demon face, black tusks too fat for the mouth from which they sprang. He saw David's rotting head in its box. He had not smelled its stink only because he was grown so accustomed to the stink of his own rotting flesh. He fell sideways, his breath coming shorter and shorter, his shoulder and his brain now aflame with suffering. He longed for sleep.

But he would not give it up. Sleep was death. And he'd not die in this place of madness. He forced open his eyes. The lake lapped gently not a foot away. He stretched out a hand and felt the cold of its waters on his skin. He wiped his hand across his forehead. Then he scooped water toward him so that it splashed across his face. He crawled forward and laid his face in it. He moved his head from side to side and he thought it the most uplifting sensation he had ever felt in his life.

He pushed himself to his hands and knees, and then got his feet under him and rose slowly up to his feet. The nausea racked him again, but he refused it, gulping back the bile. He let the anger take hold of him. "I come too far for this," he whispered. Then he placed one foot in front of the other and made his way back to the fire.

Charley had not moved. He still was sitting with his head bowed. George stared into the box, muttering something to himself. He took no notice of Harry as he dropped down upon a reed mat beside the fire.

"Charley," he said, his voice not more than a ragged croak. "This man's no help to me, is he?"

Charley lifted his head. "Not man," he said. "No man here."

"We come all this way. To find this!" He threw his hand in George's direction, who was staring now into the flames, voicing something that could not be heard. "Do we wait? Ain't there a thing to be done?"

"No thing to do."

"George!" He shouted, then again. "Why don't he hear?" Charley did not respond. "All right then, but I'm fucked if I will die in such a place."

146

His body shook so hard he wondered that he remained sitting upright. "Will you lead me out from here?"

"Go back beach. Wait beach."

"I'll wait on my dying anywhere but here."

"Wait beach."

Charley got up, lifted Harry to his feet. "Walk?" he said.

"I will walk out from here, by the Christ."

Charley turned then to George. He spoke in that high tone Harry knew was reserved for ritual talk in the Indian tongue. He heard his own name mentioned. George looked up for a second from the flames, staring toward Charley as if he heard sounds from that direction but saw nothing. Then he looked across at Harry.

"He don't believe," George said, and he spoke as if he were completely sane. Then he looked away and down again into the box.

"Go now," said Charley.

Of that return through the forest, Harry remembered almost nothing. The dawn came soon and he could see Charley's hump before him or, when he faltered—as he more and more often did—Charley's arm about his torso, propping him up. He mumbled words to himself, most of which he could not comprehend. He asked Charley, "Why?" over and over. But the old cripple spoke no words at all. He had so many questions they just fell in together until there was not one clear thought he could hold to. He wanted his anger now, but it was gone. Instead, there were only George's words. Who did not believe? Why? What did he not believe? What blood?

Charley was breathing hard as well, where the added weight of a dying white man bowed him down. There were times when Harry found himself on the ground, the decomposing leaves of the forest floor sopping wet against his face. Now and then a waterskin was at his lips, liquid in his mouth. Nausea had him retching it straight back up.

He saw David's rotting head, watched it imploding slowly as the maggots finished their work, eating from the inside out, from the root of the brain to the ears. He saw a perfect, polished skull in a velvet-lined box, and all around the box, naked brown men hollered and whooped and their blades were sharpened for his own neck. He did not mind. His flesh was made corrupt. Let them choke on the poison of him.

Then he was lying on a tarpaulin and a wet rag was being wiped across his face. He shook water from his eyes and forced them to open. Before him, a pebble beach swept down to the waters of the inlet. To his left the *Hesperus* moved in the tide where it was half afloat. He blinked several times and there was Charley.

"Why did he do it?" Harry said.

"Who know? Not me. Not same what Kwagiulth do. Maybe do same he family mother from Tlingit people north," and he waved his arm away vaguely in that direction. "Maybe not. George wild man. Sad man."

The old Indian was, himself, near to exhaustion. Heavy bags ringed the underside of his eyes and his lids were red about the rims. His round shoulders seemed to slump even further forward than usual.

"Charley?"

"Ek?"

"Thank you."

Charley shrugged. "Why you not dead?"

"Be fucked with being dead." And at that, Charley smiled, the lines of his crooked face making all sorts of strange patterns. Harry shut his eyes.

"Fat Harry! Wake now." Where was this? "Must go forest, quick." Charley. Charley speaking to him. Nausea. His breathing stunted. His whole body fed to the flames, burning. "Fat Harry!"

He was pulled upright and shaken, until it felt as if a spear had passed through his shoulder and was being twisted there. He cried out. The gum gelling his lids together tore apart and his eyes came open.

Charley was kneeling over him. "Walewid come," he said. "Must go now."

Harry shook his head. Walewid? He tried to look around. "Where?" he said, but he could not focus. Sweat poured into his eyes. He coughed, hard and agonizing, but Charley pulled him to his feet.

"They come canoe. Out on water. Soon see us. We go now!"

He blinked and spluttered and did his best not to pass out. Charley slung the rifle across his shoulder, then lifted the tarpaulin on which Harry had been lying and brought its four corners together, with all that had been resting on it clattering inside. He spun it round until it resembled a sack. Then, half dragging Harry behind him, he jogged away along the beach. All Harry could do was stumble behind Charley, whose hand at his wrist drew him on.

Within a minute Harry's legs collapsed under him. He lay on the pebbles and gasped for air. His head swam until it seemed he heard the crash of waves against the base of cliffs, and him tumbling in a burning tide like molten iron. Then he felt himself heaved up. He retched, his stomach crushed somehow, and he knew he was draped across Charley's crippled shoulders.

Charley it was now whose breathing came in rasps and, very soon, as Harry heard the splash of water, he was lowered to the ground. They lay now together upon the ground, struggling for air.

After a few moments, Harry forced himself to roll to his side and open his eyes. He was lying by the stream on the beach, Charley beside him, just sitting up now himself. Harry knelt and threw up thin bile.

"We go now," said Charley.

"No." Just speaking aloud made Harry shudder and retch. "No more." He slumped down and simply tried to breathe and to stay conscious.

"Now." Charley's hands were upon him again, pulling at him. "Soon we stop hide."

"No." But Charley heaved until he came up into a low crouch. He shuffled forward like that, all the time retching, and now they were struggling up a steep hill through thick undergrowth, using hands as much as feet. Harry's eyes stayed closed now against the effort, leaves and small branches scratching at his face and body. Eventually Charley stopped, and Harry collapsed, panting.

"Look," said Charley.

Harry opened his eyes and, for a moment, they came clear. He followed Charley's pointing finger. He was seeing out through ancient, broken plankboards, from some height above the beach, as high as the tallest trees

149

along the forest's edge. Far out on the still waters of the inlet, near the headland off which the funeral island stood, a canoe was turning toward them. It was still more than a mile away, and Harry could not see who might be directing it. Then he slumped down on his side and passed out.

When next Harry came to consciousness, it was to find himself alone in some strange place, with no memory of how he came to be there. A waterskin lay by his hand and he swigged and spluttered. He was propped against a loose pile of mossy timber that might once have been part of an Indian house. Now, salal and great fronds of bracken and swordfern grew thick about him. The light was thin and it seemed twilight. He looked up toward the sky, but that brought him near to passing out once more.

A bundled tarpaulin lay near him, its corners drawn up into a bag. He came to coughing, hard, racking sounds, and then he smelled the terrible stench from his shoulder. He recalled that there was danger all around, if he could not yet remember what that danger was. So he stifled his noise as best he could until the fit calmed down again. His hands were spattered with dark droplets. He knew that it was blood from his lungs.

His body burned. His skin itched so that he thought he might go mad with its insistence. He dribbled water on those parts that suffered most, his inner arms, his crotch, his legs, the wound upon his shin. But he had no energy to move around and see more of where it was he lay.

He had been here with someone. Charley was dead. No, Poodlas was dead, stupid name and comical. Fah Wei was dead in Hong Kong, and her name stupid too. But he was not to think on that. That door stayed shut. Everyone was dying, and him as well, rotting from the outside in. Where was Charley? David was dead. George mad crazed up in the wilds—wild man. Sad man.

He saw again the slump of Poodlas's shoulders—slumping like Charley's—as the blade went in. He saw the eyeball burst in a bar in San Francisco. His body flinched with every memory. He saw the agony in George's eyes. He knew it. He understood all of it.

As the light faded, Harry fought his fever. He mumbled songs beneath his breath: songs that sailors sang when working, rhythmic and monotonous, meant to keep a mind in focus. He hummed as well the tune that was his own litany. *I am fixing to leave. I am fixing to go, and where I am going, well you won't never know.* He thought, I am fixing to go indeed, if a mite further than I was planning. And that made him smile.

Sounds came to him now, a rustling as of branches parted. He blinked and peered and saw Charley's craggy face.

"Still live, huh?" said Charley, his voice low. His words came as if from the far distance.

"Where you been?"

"Off look. Can move?"

Harry stretched. His shoulder screamed to him. "If I have to," he said.

"Good. Maybe go when dark."

"Where are we?"

"In place where people hide, on hill on beach. Very close Walewid. Come look. Not speak." Harry rolled on his front and pushed himself up. Charley held one arm. He had the rifle in his other.

The light was nearly gone but, on his feet, Harry could see they were on top of a small hillock. All around were broken timbers, though there seemed some vestige still of fortification at the hillock's rim.

"Indian in village come here if trouble from other tribe," Charley whispered. "In old days. Finish now, amen." He led Harry over to one side of the hilltop. "Not speak," he said again.

They crouched behind the remnants of a low, fallen defence, around which a young stand of canoe birch was growing, their trunks not more than eight inches across, the papery bark already peeling. Harry laid his face for a second in the cool wet moss on the fallen buttress's surface. Then, copying Charley, he raised his head up cautiously and looked over.

Through the birch trunks, in the dim twilight, he could still just about see the beach stretching away for a hundred yards or so, before it petered out and the forest came down to the water's edge. The *Hesperus* lay beached halfway along. An Indian war canoe was pulled up beside it. Two men were standing by the broken owl pole and looking down at that place where their camp had been, and George's before them.

151

The first was short but bulky, his gestures blunt, terse, so that he gave off an air of hardly suppressed fury. Even with his vision blurred, Harry could see that it was Walewid.

The other had long hair that swung about its face. It carried slackly in one hand a knuckle-ended war club. Now it crouched and moved about on all four of its thin, sinewy limbs, as if it were some giant insect. It seemed to sniff the ground about the camp. Otherwise it was naked, its body inky black. Harry remembered the sallow teeth and the long nails of the dreamer's hands, stretching out toward him as they had passed through the rapids.

"Men come go beach, look for us," Charley said, pointing down to their left.

The pebbles of the beach ran round behind the base of the hillock, leaving a gap between it and the forest of perhaps twenty yards. Eight men were walking there in the direction of the boats. They were men of Blunden Harbour, Harry recognizing a few of them, dressed for war, bare chests and faces painted black, clubs in their hands and long knives in their belts, and one with a logger's axe. Two carried rifles. A little ahead of the men, the stream wound down the beach. As they crossed it, one called out, and Walewid and the other turned toward them.

"Say not find us. Too dark make easy see track," Charley said, his voice a whisper. "Tomorrow see for sure."

"Is not here the first place they'd look?" And, even as he said this, the dreamer turned up its face until it seemed to stare directly at them. Harry could hardly keep himself from ducking back below the parapet, though in that light and through the dense canoe birch, it was impossible they could be seen.

"Come up here on hill no good in dark. Maybe we have gun. Maybe more us here. Men don't know. Tomorrow Walewid see track, make plan. We go in night."

"But where? There ain't no more than bloody wilderness, and they have my boat to ransack at their will."

Charley shrugged. "Go forest," he said.

They watched as the men, at Walewid's direction, set about George's broken canoe with axes and hatchets. With the shattered planking they made up a fire, high on the beach, since the tide was coming in.

"Big insult," said Charley. "Burn man canoe."

The dreamer spoke with Walewid. Then it took up a blanket and came forward along the beach as far as the stream. It hunkered down beside the water and laid the club before it. It drew the blanket about itself and now it seemed no more than another rock upon the shore.

The flames from the fire began to rise up against the darkness. Watching the dreamer, Harry fancied he saw a glimmer that might have been its eyes reflecting the blaze.

"Dreamer make trouble," Charley spoke quietly and laid his hand on Harry's shoulder. "Him know if we here on hill, must go down near where he sit."

"What about the other side?" Harry motioned back over his shoulder.

"Cliff and water."

"Could we come down the cliff? The water at the bottom's calm enough."

"Me maybe. You no."

"Have we rope?"

"No."

"Then we are fucked."

"Ek."

"Do we not just shoot the bastards? Pick them off. That black-skin fucker first."

"You quick for kill people now."

"They'll be quick enough in killing us, will they not?"

Charley didn't say anything.

"What in all hell's going to stop them?"

"Maybe thing change. But kill one two just make more angry. Then we die sure."

Harry put his forehead in the soaking moss once more. After a while, it seemed he was drifting between trees in a forest. It was night, though there was enough light to see other forms that were moving with him. They darted between shadows so he could not make them out. They moved toward a definite goal. Somewhere inside himself he understood what that goal might be, and it was important he should have that knowledge prior to arriving there himself. Behind him, a voice was whispering his name. Its tongue was sibilant, such that it might be a snake. He could not move his head, but now ahead of him through the forest a red light gleamed. A silhouette was forming against the bloody glow, its hair long and lank. Sharp black teeth in the darkness, the voice at his ear, and a hand drawn round his face from behind, black talons before his eyes.

"Fat Harry!" It was Charley. "Quiet." Charley's hand it was upon his mouth. "You talk you sleep. Stay wake better." Harry rolled to his side and retched, keeping as quiet as he was able. Charley knelt above him, looking out across the low parapet, one hand on the rifle resting there, the other holding him down against the earth.

The nausea receded at last. He lay curled on his side, yet shivering hard enough to magnify the pain in his head and in his shoulder. He fell once more into unconsciousness.

He woke this time wrapped in a blanket on the tarpaulin. Beside him, Charley lay, gazing out. A cloth rag was tied about Harry's head so that it covered his mouth, but kept his nose clear. It had been soaked in water, and he sucked at it desperately. He felt for a moment more clear than before, his fever less intense. He reached up with his good arm and drew down the cloth. Charley looked at him.

"How long?" Harry said, his voice a low rasp.

Charley seemed to understand. "Sleep three hour," said Charley.

Now he could hear the sounds of voices raised. "What's going on?"

"Men go on *Hesperus*."

"Fuck and damnation!" Harry dragged himself up to see.

The tide was in and the *Hesperus* was afloat once more, rolling slightly with the inlet's gentle waves. The oil lamp from the pilothouse was alight and resting on the deck. Two figures moved near the entrance to the hold, the door of which had been swung open.

On shore, the fire burned high and hard, great flames rising twenty feet into the air and throwing sparks farther still, which glowed amber and red before dispersing into the darkness. Most of the canoe wood seemed to have been burned, and two men were gathering timber from the old buildings.

Four of the men stood about the fire, their voices raised against its roar. They seemed caught up in some bragging contest, as Harry had seen many times before, chins jutting and chests inflated, two waving war clubs, and all dressed only in blankets knotted like skirts about their waists. They held bottles, and these they sucked on between their taunts and curses.

"Fucking heathens," said Harry. "Perhaps we've a chance of getting off this rock while they're busy with my liquor."

"No, look," said Charley, nodding down toward the nearer part of the beach.

There were two figures now beside the stream. The dreamer had cast off its blanket, and its black body reflected the firelight so that the skin shone like obsidian. It rested on one knee and held the war club across the thigh of its other leg. Its eyes moved over the edges of the forest, then up toward the hillock and back.

Beside it, Walewid's squat form crouched, a cloak of cedar bark about him, and on his head was the mask of the wolf. The jaws of that great carven countenance were pointed toward the forest. Of all its painted colours only the blacks and reds of its eyes and snout were plain in the firelight.

"Christ," said Harry. "Can we not shoot those two cocksuckers at least? We might sow enough confusion to make it to the forest." He wondered at his own call to action, and what point there was in any of this. They had found George and he had failed to help. Failed to be anything but another dancing, headhunting savage in the wilds. Now Harry ticked on borrowed time. He might as well die up here as anywhere else.

"Not kill dreamer," said Charley.

"Can't kill, or won't?"

"Not kill," he said.

Anger was what he had still. Anger. "Well what about those fucks on board my boat, at least?" Charley did not answer. "Maybe Walewid and that black devil will hit the liquor too."

"Not think so."

Harry stared down through the canoe birch at them. They were both motionless except for the dreamer's hawkish eyes. "No," he said, and rested his head down on his forearms. His breath came so short now.

"Even should we make it off this rock," he said, "I'd not get a hundred yards through the forest." He panted for a time to get breath enough to speak. "You got to go, Charley. Try your luck with the cliff. Go back and get hold of George. Kick the life back into him, if you have to. Maybe he's finished with his rage, medicine dance, whatever in all the black hells it was."

Charley stared at him in silence.

"I'll keep the rifle," Harry said. "Place a slug in any of them comes after you."

"You not shoot tree trunk front you, stupid man."

"I'll put the wind up them, if nothing else."

"Wait see more time yet." Charley turned back to watch the beach once more. "Maybe new thing happen."

Harry did all he might to keep his focus. But the leaping fire threw crazy, dancing shadows through the canoe birch, and the drunken chants, the rolling waves of heat and cold that coursed through him, and the growing certainty of death—all furled about him, until he seemed to spin slowly up from himself, to writhe in a vertigo like that he'd felt the first time he had gone high into the rigging in a fierce swell. A lurching, tumbling loss of control.

The cries below were the howls of wolves. Their tearing teeth might close on his body. If he had only found George, not that fool in the despair of his grief up in the forest. If he had but found the man he'd known, he'd have had answers for all this, so he would.

But Harry would be taken instead by the forest, broken down and eaten. If not by the wolves and their crude predations, then by the roots of grass and fern and tree. That was right and proper to the way of things. Perhaps he had become an Indian indeed, to think such thoughts. God might take that part of him which He desired, yet the forest could have the parts that touched and smelled and tasted, that heard the breeze-blown leaves whispering ... and now he could go. He could go. He could leave.

"Not die yet!" Shaking. Leaves and the whisper of the wind. "You not die yet!" And pain. Fire in his body. Heat. Water on his lips. Spluttering, but a hand clamped across his mouth. Charley hissing above him, "Not die yet. Something happen." Pulling him up. Pulling his head around by his hair. "Open eyes!" The beach. Yes, all of this was real, and he must understand it.

Walewid was on his feet by the stream. The dreamer crouched beside him, looking like a dog that scented quarry. Its face was pointed toward the forest. Walewid spoke something to it. It leapt up, its club swinging circles. It ran toward where the stream broke from the undergrowth.

Charley raised up the rifle. Before Harry could come to his senses enough to make a judgment of his own, Charley fired in the dreamer's direction. The rifle's bark exploded in Harry's ears. He ducked sideways, clutching at his head. Before he slid away to the ground, Harry saw the dreamer plunge into the deep woods. Just before it disappeared, its head turned back toward them, a grin of triumph on its face.

"Christ almighty," Harry said, lying back down on his side and hacking coughs, bloody spittle running out the side of his mouth and onto his hands. "I thought you weren't to kill the fucking dreamer."

"Think George come. Dreamer know," Charley said. "Now them know we here."

"You don't know it's George. It might have been a wile to flush us into the open."

"Then good wile," Charley said.

"If it is George, he'll have heard the rifle shot at least. Will he not still be too crazy to understand?"

Charley said nothing.

Harry heard shouting. "What's that now?"

"Walewid run back to fire. Men stupid drunk. Walewid shout. Now them grab thing go back hide by pole." A moment later, Harry heard a low hiss above him in the trees, and a rifle shot rang out. "Them shoot us," said Charley.

"Shoot back."

"No. Shoot again, them know place on hill we be for sure. Stay quiet now."

Harry lay on his side, curled in a ball, and tried to remain conscious. Every minute or so a rifle barked, and a bullet would thuck into the stand of trees, or hiss through.

"Stupid drunk men fire." Charley was watching the beach below. "Keep us here till day come."

All was quiet for a time. Then Harry heard something else. It sounded like an Indian chant, but far off and muffled. He would have taken it for his imagination if Charley had not tensed beside him.

"What is it?" he said, but the old Indian ignored him.

Harry tried to lift himself from the tarpaulin, but he couldn't do it. After a moment, Charley took hold of his biceps and heaved him up until he was propped once more on the wet moss.

All was consternation among the Indians on the beach. Though they sheltered behind the owl pole, Harry saw the shaking of their heads and their arms gesturing. They seemed caught up in dispute. He could not make out details, nor could he see which might be Walewid. Meanwhile, the chanting continued, more clearly now, though he could not pinpoint from where it might be coming.

"Am I hearing that?" he said. Then the voice became clear to him. "Christ!" he said. "Is that George?"

"Ek."

"What's he singing?"

"George sing hamatsa song."

"Where is he?"

"Forest."

Harry scanned the edges of the trees. "I don't see him."

"No."

Harry coughed. Blood sprayed out across his forearms. He cursed softly, and Charley looked at him.

"Die soon," he said.

"You been saying that for a while. I'm still fucking here, though, ain't I."

The singing grew louder, as if it were just within the tree line. Then it stopped. George called out in Kwakwala.

"What's that?"

"Say, what happen here for rifle shoot?"

"What about the dreamer? He's still in the forest. Warn him!"

"Ek." Charley made as if to shout down, but now Walewid leapt up from his hiding place, his wolf mask on his head still. He clambered on the fallen pole and called out at length in passion.

Charley translated. "Say George family kill Walewid family. Say revenge. Say George do bad at funeral, make bad name all Indian. Say revenge. Say George come out now, maybe not kill everyone."

George spoke again, his voice a question. This time, however, Charley called out himself. George called back. Harry watched as Walewid spun and pointed up in their direction. He saw one of the warriors aim his rifle toward them.

"What did you say?"

"Tell George we here, but say we have three rifle watch Walewid men. Say dreamer in forest. George say dreamer not problem. Now George speak Walewid, better all come talk together."

"He ain't crazed no more?"

"George back."

Walewid had climbed down again and was talking with his men. After a while, he turned and shouted. George responded.

"Walewid say not believe we three rifle. Say we shoot more if we three rifle. He not stupid Indian. But George say anyways he have rifle too. He say he see Walewid burn canoe. Big insult." There was a pause. Then, "Walewid now say talk better."

George spoke, and Charley called in response. "Ask what happen. I say same story I speak him before, by lake. Say you die soon." George's voice came from the forest, and now its tone was thick.

"George say he come out now. Tell Walewid not fire. Walewid say yes not fire." Charley pointed near the stream. "Look."

The undergrowth trembled, and then a figure emerged. It looked some part of the forest itself, as if the wilderness had taken bodily form and stepped down onto the shore. Red cedar branches were tied about it, and upon its head were strapped fern fronds. Its face was painted black and it came in a half crouch, as if it were partway between animal and man. In one hand it clutched a machete and in its other something swung like a pendulum. The figure chanted in a gruff monotone that barely sounded human to Harry's ears.

"Hamatsa come back from wild," said Charley.

"What's that he's carrying?"

But Charley didn't answer.

NO SENSE... No sense ... Blackness and lightning strikes to burst open my body, and then darkness comes again. Finally, a golden flickering at my eyelids and they come open. A roof. Flames. The burn of heat to my skin. A face. A man with his face black-painted, like he's a demon out of night. His eyes are blue. Wrong for that. Must be a breed. A man I ain't about to believe in, pretending like he is an Indian. The face comes down toward me, eyes close to mine then sweeping down along my body. A sucking at my stomach, like as if I am being drawn on by some furied whirlpool. White flame is in my guts. I would scream if I was able. But I am mute. Something coming out from my stomach, drawn through the cables of my intestines up towards the surface. The tug of teeth at my skin till I feel my stomach coming open. I can see the roof again. The breed man's face comes before me again. Blood all about his mouth. The mouth spitting. Blood, black in the firelight, blood on his mouth and chin, blood over all his teeth. My hands going now for my stomach. It is opened up, bleeding. My guts could spill across the floor were I to move. I have to hold them in. Blue eyes over me. Triumphant. If I move, I lose my entrails.

And now, behind that blue-eyed Devil's face, high above him into the roof, filling all the air, there are the magnificent, holy body of Killer Whale, of Lagoyewilé, twisting up in the smoke and flames, as if it has leapt out from the waters. It hangs, massive, above everything, and I call for it to come crashing back down and crush the Devil with his tearing teeth beneath it. But then I see only the blue eyes as the Devil hisself leans across me. His hair hangs as a curtain all about my face, till I can see nothing else. He is closer now. Closer till his lips will touch mine and I will taste the blood of my own stomach on his teeth.

Darkness.

No sense.

Then pain like a blow from a hatchet through my hand and along my arm. I jerked. I smelled the foul stench of hair and skin burning. My arm had been in the fire whilst I was in my vision.

For that is what it was: a vision. So I do absolutely believe—still now, even here, in the City of Reason that is New York, in this very Cathedral of Reason, the American Museum of Natural History, no less. This place that I have made my choice and I have come to, as might be said, in pilgrimage. This place what is testament to my decision of myself. But even here I do state that what I saw that night beside the lake was more than just the delusions of some battered lunatic, his brain all mashed from rage and loss. No. Those teeth at my stomach, the feel of the blood sliding off the canines of the Devil above me to slither hot onto my cheek, so that, even with my arm burned and half-conscious by the fire, I must wipe in horror at my face till it feels clean again, so that I must feel across the aged muscles of my stomach for a rent, and lie like a baby still inside its mother's womb for fear of the skin tearing. So immediate was that vision, and so violent its impact on me and on my actions after, that I have no choice but to call it such.

The wooden box was open by the fire. I shuffled over on my knees. The syrup-reek of corruption. The nose had sunk back into the face. The skin was black now, and the closed eyelids concave where the eyeballs was melting away beneath. I ran my burnt fingers down across David's face, lightly, for I feared he might crumble in an instant away to nothing.

But still no tears did come, as they had not since first I heard of his passing.

I woke the following morning to the dew soaking through me, and the calls of the ducks out on the lake. I made coffee, the first for many days. I sat beneath the old killer whale pole. I took up a wrap of dry salmon. The smell of it made me near to fainting. My stomach moaned as I chewed.

I see the details of that morning like they is here before me now. I was feeling how it was also such a cloudless morning after rain the night before, clear and cool and empty. Clear to think. Even my burnt forearm throbbed with a clean, pure pain that helped me in my clarity, as if in the burning there had been some sort of purging, some clearing away of the refuse what had been clogging up my soul.

Tiny pieces of salmon was caught in the calluses of my fingers. I stood and stretched till my age cracked through my shoulders. I walked on bare feet through the grasses to the shore. Away around the lake I heard wood being dragged through brush, a slap of tail on water, cubs chirruping, the industry of beavers. In the sunlight, the water ran through my fingers like streaming gold.

David's head had rotted. I should have laid it in running water till all the fat and brain and blood was washed away. That's the way of it. At least, it was the way of my mother's people for those of chiefly blood: the corpse opened at the pelvis, the entrails pulled out, then held in a fast-flowing river till clean, and after placed in the sun to dry.

The Kwagiulth ain't got no such practice. Their only mummies are those put up on the branches of trees, which by some fortune dry out in the wind, instead of putrefying. I could still see a few broken shapes of boxes, up in the trees close by the lake, where some of the old shamans had chosen to be buried in secret from the tribe, perhaps to lend mystery to their legend, or to those of their sons what might follow them, or some for belief in the power of the place, or in their own immortal souls.

Oh, I know it: the question what begs answering. What can be in a man's mind to have performed such a deed? To have chopped the head from his own son. Perhaps it is there in the story of Shaiks, in the story of the origin of the box. The Tlingit do keep such trinkets. Or once they did, at least. But there ain't no such tradition among the Kwagiulth of taking body parts of family for keepsakes. They used to go headhunting up and down the coast in times past, like many of the tribes, but for trophies and glory, or for revenge. Not like this.

I wonder if I was playing out some history I imagined to be true. Some history of which I craved to be still a part. I know the ways of the people maybe better than does anyone, with all the researching I have done. Truth be, I think now I was concocting my own ritual, piecemeal, from the scatterings of knowledge what was lying about inside my gyrating head that night of the funeral. Also, there was the needing to atone for my failure as a healer, though how separating David's head from his neck might have helped … well, there ain't much of reason in it, when all aspects is considered.

As I washed my salmon-covered hands in the lake that morning, the vision of the killer whale as it rose up above me in the greathouse of my vision was there in my mind. Of course, I had been seeing myself through the eyes of the sick boy I healed so long ago. And what a diabolical and beastish figure was I, hulking above me, my fangs those of a wolf.

How, with that whole sackful of shams, had I healed the young boy? Perhaps it was that once I did believe in the shaman's ways, as later I did not. But the boy believed that I would make him well. He was healed because he believed his dream of me. Belief, belief, belief.

I saved the boy and, after, failed to save so many. Failed to save David. I performed every ritual on him that I knew or I had ever heard of. Somewhere my faith in my own brown blood was lost. Yet surely it was my actions what mattered. Not my belief. The boy I healed was the one who needed the belief, not me. Maybe David knew I had no faith, and so he could have no faith in me. Then it was my lost faith what failed him. My lost faith in my Indian blood. How had it deserted me?

It was why I had come to the House of Shamans: in recognition of that failure of belief. I saw that then. And there was consequences to such understanding.

Lagoyewilé told me that. "One son is dead. The other is dying. There is consequence to all you do. Remember it." I leapt up, and ducks flew up off the water in surprise at me. Lagoyewilé had come to me in the night! He had been beside me by the fire. He had spoken to me. Another spirit was there with him. Some demon—beaten, ragged, savage in his intensity.

Lagoyewilé spoke to me. He said there was one as yet needed saving. What was it he said?

But I could not place all the details of the night's vision in their right order as yet. So, first things first, I says to myself. Something, at least, I knew needed doing. I went back to the camp from the lake and made free with the machete, till the base of the killer whale pole was visible all the way to the earth. My fingers tore up the turf. I burrowed like a rabbit till there was a hole two foot deep. I took up the box and put it there, in the ground. Before the soil went back in over it, however, I did lift up the lid for one last peek.

His face was lost in decrepitude. He was gone. Only the flesh remains, and that is but the rotten nothingness of the world. So I put back the lid, piled over the soil, and placed the turf back over the top.

And there was an end to it. There weren't nothing else. There weren't nothing left to think.

Boas wrote me a letter once. *Get me Indian dreams.* I wrote him one of my own. I fly upwards, as if going to the place where are the stars, for they are showing, though it be still daytime. I see all around the world: the great curve of the Earth, as it is described. Then I want to go down again, but in vain. Instead, I hang there as if from the edge of some impossible high cliff, the vertigo spoiling in me till I cry out with the terror of it.

I lay on my back on the damp grass beside the old pole. Lying there, faced with deciding what came next, I felt that same vertigo I had had in my dream. There was something, some words spoken to me in the night that had intention in them. But I could not grasp hold of them as yet.

Over me, an eagle soared in the sky. He must've been watching to see if I would ever rise again. I had no notion if I ever would.

The clouds, the eagles, ravens loafing towards their daily business, ducks come flapping in to land upon the lake. The day passed over me as I did lie there with my face pointed skywards, beside the ruins of the House of Shamans. There weren't no decisions I had come to about myself. There weren't even a plan fermenting in my mind on what I should do next. I just lay there like some blank page over which a writer sits with his pen in his mouth, head as empty as the page itself. I was done with what it was I'd come to do. Now there weren't nothing left.

But there was just something what stirred inside me. Something in the words of the vision that Lagoyewilé had spoke. One son is dead, the other is dying. On the beach a son is dying. Then I saw more clearly in my memory the face of that other demon who had been with Lagoyewilé. I recalled how

165

my shirt had been wrapped about my burnt arm, soaked in water, though I could not have done such a thing myself, lying as I was in the fire.

I dragged myself to my feet. I scanned the ground surrounding my camp. I saw that I had indeed not been alone the night before. I saw then the crooked old face of Lagoyewilé as he spoke to me. Charley Seaweed. I could almost have lost myself to rage once more, so shamed did I feel at myself in that moment of realizing. And Harry with him. Harry sick to dying.

I pulled my gear into my pack. I threw the reed mats I had made upon the fire so that they roared up in final reverence to David. I placed my hand down one last time on the turf under which my son was finally laid to rest. Then I made my way towards the forest's edge and passed inside, this time following close by the stream that emptied from the lake, knowing it for that water which eventually pours out onto the beach at Teguxste.

Down through the thick woods, during the rest of that day and on into the night, and never stopping, not for rest nor water nor food. As the dark came on, something started voicing itself to me. Did it come from out the trees? Or was it just some dreamfulness still festering in my head from the days of my fasting? It didn't have no words. Least not as I had language to understand them. Voices whispered all about me. Suggestions was proffered. Questions being asked. I tramped amongst the wild woods and just let the voices swirl about me without mind to them. And as I walked, I took my machete, cut fronds, and I drew on the forest as I would a cloak.

Now the smells and tastes of every plant and animal came clear as day to me. All of me was sense and knowing, sound and smell and rich suggestion. All the life of that black wilderness felt like it were a wind blowing through me, cleaning, scouring all in its path until I was all cleared out inside and free to sense the wilds in their fullest manner. Speaking it here in the middle of this city of machines and numbers beyond comprehension: well, it don't sound sensible even to me now. But there it is and I must stand by my experience, be it reasoned or otherwise.

So I went on through the trees, sensing all that was around me. I crunched the undergrowth under my feet, making enough noise so that I could hear the animals of the forest darting off to hide, and I could name them as they disappeared. A mule deer, two racoons, a marten, an owl above me, whooshing away.

At last, I saw in the distance the orange glimmerings of fire, and I guessed it must be on the beach at Teguxste. But then a rifle fired, and after more. Of that I could make no sense, trying to work through my memories of what I had understood to be a vision, but now was coming real, words of that gnarled old spirit, Lagoyewilé, what had passed straight through me when they should have stuck. Some threat what I should know of. I was filled with wariness then, such that I stopped and felt myself as silent as the roots of the very cedars themselves.

Then I edged forward. It weren't fear in me that made me wary, but a desire for destruction. The Cannibal Spirit from the ends of the world, come hunting men along the borders of the civilized lands. Such was I. I was like the wolf as it might pause in the stalking of its prey, silent, hardly breathing, grey snout forward, eyes not blinking, hackles coming up, planted paw, nostrils widening.

Something was moving up ahead of me, coming towards me fast, but then almost straightways slower, and then more slowly still, until it was near to silent. Now there weren't no more than a feeling of it, but I did not doubt my senses. It was come hunting too. I knew it for what it was: not quite human, not at least no longer, lost now to the wilds, and sniffing out the hiding places, knowing, listening, hearing things, taking secrets to the ears of shamans, making witchery.

Gossip's witchery in the Indian villages. I despise it. The terrors of who is making potions, plotting, talking against you among the people on which you do rely for your survival. Just knowing they is out there whispering against you is enough to kill. Small groups, they need their unity. Outside ain't nothing but the cold, and death.

It came on more definitely now, almost but not quite silent. All I could hear was a faint brushing of leaves in the darkness. An owl called out. I was not more than a tree, a bush. It cannot hear me. Upwind, it cannot smell me. I had my rifle slung at my shoulder. But instead I slid the machete from my belt and gripped the cold bone of its handle.

Some yards in front of me, faint in the dim glimmer of the fire through the trees, I saw long nails part the foliage. And then there was jutting teeth, what looked like a pig's tusks foraging. The black paint all over its face and its body, that was there to strike fear of the otherworld into those what saw it.

Come on then, find me! I am deep in the wilds. For all my half-white blood, I am more savage than even you can know.

It disappeared behind tree trunks and I couldn't no longer see it, nor hear it either. Then the undergrowth exploded next to me. It was quick-silver fast all right, and I weren't prepared for it, for all of my pretensions. I saw the club swing, and there was pain all up my arm. The machete fell from my grip. I grabbed for its throat. Then its blood-webbed eyes was right before me. Claws was at my face. We hit the earth, all tangled up in one another. Its club rolled under us and was gone, and my one arm still numb with the blow it had received. I wrapped my legs about its slithering body. I was heavier than it. It thrashed under me. Go on, thrash, you long streak of piss! I have you!

My body weight was on it, but its talons still was all about me. Then there was agony in my left eye and all down my face. But my hands caught hold of its wrists, the one at the end of my numb forearm struggling still for grip, but holding fast enough. I leaned in, bit down, tore upwards. I tasted the iron and salt of blood in my mouth, and the gristle what was the better part of its nose.

Even then it made no sound more than a grunt. The putrefying smell of the forest floor was all about us. I bit at its face again, tearing at its cheek. I felt its own teeth score across my neck. My old body didn't got much more vigour left in it. But it was weaker too. Just for a second it hung loose in my hands. My fingers let go its wrists. I took its head and drove it down, again and again in the darkness, till it was limp under me. Still I went at it, crushing its skull to broken pieces. Then the pain in my eye had me rolling away, moaning and gasping for air on the soaking earth.

I came out from the forest onto the beach swinging that brute bastard's head in my hands. I must've looked a spectacle, my face all gored up

168

where its talons had torn me, my body covered all over with leaves and branches. I was singing: "The Cannibal Spirit made me pure. Great magician, Cannibal Spirit—you taught me to devour lives. You live on nothing but blood. I give you lives to eat! I give you lives to eat! I push down your wildness. I am the life maker." Which I suppose was ironical, given how recently I had taken a life. I had started to singing as I was chopping off its head, out there in the darkness, its stoved-in skull sopping wet, loose in my hands. Maybe singing helped ease the shock of it. I do not now recall. By the time I stepped out on the beach, the singing was such a part of me that all the world felt tangled up in its rhythms.

Standing there on the beach was the chieftain Walewid, from up at Blunden Harbour. He was wearing his wolf mask, and fired up with anger and deathly purpose against me, so it seemed. We'd swapped a few words prior to my emerging on the beach already, and Charley Seaweed had been shouting down to warn me of the chieftain's dreamer being somewheres about in the forest, not knowing what had already occurred. Hearing Charley's voice confirmed what had gone on the night before at the House of Shamans was real, after all, not just product of the days of my fasting, as part of me had been suspecting. I heard Charley and it all fell clean into place, without no confusion in my head. I saw the two of them there by the fire the night before. What Harry must have made of that! I thought. He must be lying up there despairing of all us monsters.

Charley spoke some on what was happening: that I was accused by the agent Halliday, that he and Harry had come searching to bring me back to answer, that Walewid here had trouble with my son-in-law, that Harry was up there beside him dying.

Well, if Walewid now was angry, I weren't in no mood to be receptive to dialogue neither. He and I swapped more angry words and I showed him what I had done to his dreamer. I says to him, if Harry dies I'd have them all to pay for it. I says I've the spirit of the forest in me and I didn't give two shits for Walewid's men, however many of them there was. I'd took his dreamer's head. I'd take them all.

Then Charley spoke up again. "You all know me," says he. "My clan is Raven. I have the body, the bones, the blood that is made out of thorns.

I have the privilege to speak to you because I also am a chieftain of the Kwagiulth."

Then he told the men with Walewid, what was gathered further along the beach, how the dreamer of Walewid had been sent by me back to the wilderness, which was right and proper. So did I have confirmed to me, as I had guessed it, whose head it was I'd taken. He said it was wrong a dreamer should turn to a beast, as the dreamer of Walewid had done. It was wrong a dreamer should go hunting man in the forest, as if he was a Dzonokwa. It was wrong that a dreamer should go to kill another man.

"What has become of us," he says, "that we should fight here now when all are dying? What has become of us that the short-life bringers can laugh as we fight and kill each other, even as we die from their diseases? What has become of us that this should be so?"

He told them all my titles as a chieftain and a shaman. And he told them then that he, Charley, was my dreamer. "I am that spirit what is the Killer Whale," says he. "I am named Lagoyewilé." So did that secret come out into the open after all these many years.

He told them he knew I was a true shaman, which was the reason he had knowed to come here and find me in the first place. Then he says Walewid can have all Charley's secrets in payment for the loss of his own dreamer, Charley's dreaming is greater than that of the dead. "Do not think George is our enemy, men of the Nakwakto," says he. "He is one of the people. I know this."

Then he spoke to me. He tells me he can see my rage boiling, and that it weren't no good. He tells me how Walewid's brother Poodlas was dead, killed by Harry, and how Harry hisself was dying. "Many times men fight and die and there ain't nothing of use in the dying. These are days when all are dying," says he. These are days when liquor makes men fight. Poodlas was in drink, he tells me. He tried to take from Harry's boat. Harry fought him. But still, Harry is one of those white men who sells the liquor, and so has his own responsibilities to bear.

"All is in the mist," says Charley. "Nothing can be seen clearly."

He's a great one with words, old Charley, though a person mightn't imagine it to look at him. He don't hold much with speaking English, though I have noticed he understands it well enough, which I always did find a mite suspicious. Still, when he is speechifying in Kwakwala, he can be all fired up like a preacher, which is what he is, I suppose, to those of us what know him properly.

I had come back down to Teguxste fast as I could. Now I was here stuck with Walewid, when Harry was up there dying. To lose another son! As I did clearly see him to be at last. I stared at the wolf head opposite, and it twisted crazy in my eyes. This creature whose kind had set to my daughter's husband. I saw my machete hacking through the wolf head till it came to skull and brain, me tearing open its jaws and my skinning blade thrust deep inside, the blood fountain and the screaming. Terrible things.

Yet I did hear the words of my dreamer. I have always listened to Charley, old cripple, but wise. So I fought my fury hard, until at last I did become aware again that it was a man what stood before me: Walewid, the dreamer's head at his feet, the wolf mask covering his face. Now I could see, through the open jaws, the dim shape of his face. I could see there was fear in his eyes. Everything was silence, excepting for the roar and crackle of the fire.

Walewid reached up and lifted that great mask from his head. He says, "I am the shaman, the chieftain of the Nakwakto, Walewid. My dreamer is dead. My brother is dead. I am at feud with your family. Yet I hear the words of this, your dreamer. I will accept his secrets in payment for the dreaming I have lost this night." And he said to bring down Fat Harry and lay him by the fire. Then we would talk. And, after, he went off back to his men.

Charley yelled down for me to keep an eye on them drunken men by the fire, who couldn't rightly be trusted not to put a bullet in us, whatever Walewid might say. He spoke that Harry was soon to be dead. I wanted to know more of what had brung them here, of what was wrong with him, but he said, talk later. He asked if I had white medicine of any sort, which I did not.

"Well, you got to save him anyhow," says Charley.

When the two of them come from out the undergrowth at the bottom of the hill, Harry half draped across old humpback Charley's shoulders, his feet stepping one in front of the other, but his face pale enough to seem like he was dead already—well, when they showed up I wanted to tear at myself for my craziness in not seeing them for who they was the night before. Charley, what is my dreamer, my whisperer of secrets: I had called him up, the spirit of him, so I had imagined it, and Harry just some ghost following behind. Now maybe I'd done for his life by not tending to him back then. Done for him like so many before I hadn't been able to save.

We got him laid out beside the fire, and he was ranting, not making any sense, staring off ghoulish at the trees as if he was seeing spirits of his own. I kneeled down over him, but, when he sees my face, he comes over terrified, struggling as if to escape from under me. I held him, along with Charley.

"Harry," says I, and all the pain of those numberless wrongs I had inflicted on the world, as I saw it then, was in my voice. "Hear me. It's I—George. There won't be no more horrors from me, I promise you."

He seemed to run out of steam then. He lay still and looked up at me a moment. The pale of his eyes was shot with black streaks of blood veins. They seemed to float beneath milky water, like an old woman's rheum.

"I know why you done it," Harry whispers.

"I just seen too much," says I.

"I know." He looked off towards the forest, his eyes roaming like he was viewing all sorts of things that I could not. I did not know, still don't, what rivers run through Harry. But, in that moment, I knew that they run as deep as do my own.

He smiled and held on to my hand, almost like he was reassuring me. Then he lay his head back. He closed his eyes, his breathing coming in short little puffs, his skin like white wax, snot running out from his nose, blood spittle at his lips. And oh, but it was a most terrible perfume what wafted up from Harry's shoulder. It took me back to the reek of the smallpox cankers on the people's bodies, as they lay dying in my village when I was still a child.

One of Walewid's soldiers brung water from their side of the fire in a wooden bowl. I drizzled some on Harry's lips, and he gasped and licked at the moisture. I wanted to wail and shake him, to clutch him against my chest. My last surviving son. Burning up, drifting like ash away from me.

But now Walewid spoke out in the high Kwakwala. He said Charley's words had set his head to wandering, but now his head was back, and he had things to say to me. Walewid was near his men on the opposite side of the fire, but to one side, so that he was not hidden by the flames.

Walewid tells me I am a white man by what I do, telling secret stories of the people to those who should not know them, taking treasures that was our ancestors' since the beginning of the world, buying them up with the white men's money.

"I say you are a demon," he tells me, pointing across the fire. "No demon of the forest, dressed though you are as one. You are a demon of the great villages of the white men in the south." He says I am in part accountable for the diseases that they bring. What can I tell him, says he, so he will believe I ain't cursed by the bad white blood what flows so foul in my veins?

His men was growling and speaking curses across the fire, rapping their weapons upon the earth to show their approval of their chieftain's words. But I turned my eyes away and stared down at my son-in-law, as his features was squirming and clenching in torment.

"Must answer," Charley says to me, his hand upon my arm. So I set him to taking the bandage from Harry's shoulder, and I pushed myself to my feet. Now I could see them all ranged round the far side of the fire. Most of them glowered at me such that I knew our lives did hang, uncertain, in the balance.

I tell them I have been in the wilds for many days. I walked up through the forest till I came to the place where the spirit of the Killer Whale lives, the place where first I come to be a shaman. I had took my eldest son, David, there to lie in his death. I did not put him in a Christian burial ground. His body lies in the trees on the burial island at Rupert. I took his head in the ways of the northern people, the Tlingits, from which I am sprung. And now his head lies with the Killer Whale Spirit of the shamans in the famous box my great-uncle Shaiks did give to me. If that ain't properly the ways of the Kwagiulth, I do admit it. Still it does honour to the old ways of the northern people, of which I and my son was chieftains also. If that action of taking my son's head was not agreeable to the whites, then I do call damnation on them for trying to put me, to put us all, inside a cage of Christian bars. And if it shames the people, then damnation is coming to us all, I says. For all our pride is gone.

Then I spoke to them about the Killer Whale Spirit I had seen in my vision by the lake. "He hung there above me, as he has done before—and he has even spoken to me, guiding my actions. He would not show himself to me if I were only a white man.

"But Walewid," says I, "many of those words you brung back from your mind's wandering are the same words I have been asking of myself. I have taken the stories of the people and I have written them in the books of the white men. I have taken many of the treasures of the people for the white men's houses of knowledge." I do not know if my actions are good or if they are bad, says I. I am Indian by birth, as the Tlingits do trace their ancestry through their mother's line, and by my marriages am I Kwagiulth. "Does anyone here question this of me? I did not bring the white man here. But here he is. The people die. How many in Walewid's village still live? Of every four men there is now only one. But those who are dead still speak in the words what I have written, in the treasures that now are with the white men in their museums.

"But do not call me a white man," I says. "To the white man my skin will always be brown. To the white man I am always Indian. My son was a great chieftain. He was chief of the hamatsa of the Fort Rupert Kwagiulth. Now he is dead. My daughterson lies dying before me. All comes to nothing. Lah."

After, I stood there gulping at the air. Then I tore off the leaves and fronds and branches of the forest that were wrapped about me, throwing them all upon the fire. Great plumes of smoke billowed up where they burned, until we could not see each other at all for some time. I thought: Yes, all is like the mist. Charley is right.

"I have heard George Hunt and Lagoyewilé," says Walewid at last. "It is true the people die. But we are not yet dead. We are still here. We are not shadows. We are not the white man's shadows. White blood in George Hunt's veins makes him forget his strength. He must choose his blood. Yet I know how it is he forgets. The people live by fear and rage. Lagoyewilé has spoken the words that are good. White men laugh at our fighting. Every death is a victory for them. George Hunt should remember that he shows his blood only by his actions."

Walewid came up to his feet. "There will be a blood-price paid for the death of my brother," he says. "So we will sit and we will watch this white man, Fat Harry, come to his death. When he has gone, there will be an end to matters."

Once he was finished, there was hollering and wide assent from Walewid's men. But I jumped up, my machete in my hand. I kicked at the fire and a brand leapt in the air, cinders flaring, near blinding me.

"No!" I fair to screamed the word. "There's too many of my children already dead. I'll not lose another!" I would kill all of these men here if need be. I sensed Charley beside me, on one knee, the rifle he carried aimed now towards Walewid's men. One of them, gaudy in a yellow woman's lacy shirt, torn near to ribbons so that it ruffled about his torso, made to lift a gun from the ground beside him. Charley fired off a shot, and the pebbles exploded close by the gun's butt. The man flinched away, holding his face, and blood flowed through his fingers where a fragment of stone must have caught him.

The others made to rise, but Walewid yelled to his men to stay where they were. He strode over to the man in the yellow shirt and took to cuffing him about the head, cursing him for the addlepate he was, till the man scuttled off with his arms over his head to lurk and sulk at the edge of the firelight. Some of the men jeered, but Walewid spoke hard words and they shut up soon enough.

Walewid spun round then and stood squarely facing me. We met each other's eyes for a time. I know there was violence in mine, but he faced me and he looked like he was thinking pretty deep, the right side of his upper lip twitching just enough for his canine to show faintly orange beneath.

So I says to him, "One death won't count for another. Come. From what Charley says, it weren't so simple, what did happen aboard Harry's boat. There is two stories here."

We was silent for a time, me panting and sweating, even if my voice had strained to sound even-handed. Finally, Walewid sat back down, stretching out his arms to each side and beckoning for his men to do the same. There was much muttering at that. The man in the yellow shirt had smeared his own blood from the wound at his cheek across his face, in finger-lines. His eyes gleamed out, full of malice, between the stripes of drying fluid.

Walewid spoke. He says that Charley reckoned I was a true shaman. "Then go on and try to save your daughterson," he tells me. His men weren't happy with that, but he held up one hand. "Listen," he says, and he laid out my choices for me.

His choices was these: If I failed to save Harry, then that was good, because the man who killed Walewid's brother would go to his death. Yet if that happened, he would kill me as well, since then he'd know that I only pretend, and am not a true shaman. He'd know my vision of the Killer Whale story was lies, and that I was but a vile white demon who only acted a shaman.

If I did nothing and Harry died, that was good, because his enemy would still also die. Yet he'd kill me, because he'd know I was afraid to show my skills, since they was false.

If I tried to save Harry and I succeeded, then he would say that that as well was good, because I was fit to be called a Nakwakto shaman. So would he count my daughterson Nakwakto also. Harry would become like a son to Walewid. Both of us would live. He would think George Hunt was a man of proper blood, and a man with strength enough to speak on the people's behalf among the white men.

If I did nothing and Harry lived, then he would kill us both as blood-price for the death of his brother.

So he ain't all wind and piss after all, thought I. Quite the crafty wolf.

"Do you promise to keep your men from us for as long as it will take?" Charley asks him, and he says he will.

"I don't know if ever I wanted to be one who speaks on behalf of the people to the white man," I says. "Yet these are good words from this, our friend Walewid. I accept them. For I will not want my life if my daughter-son dies."

Charley spoke to me. "His men are all drunk from whisky off the *Hesperus*."

"I seen already the bottles strewn about," says I.

"Walewid ain't in drink yet, though," says Charley.

"Well, let's watch that he don't start," says I.

"Truth is, I ain't never seen him in finer form," says Charley. "He's more a chief than ever I give him credit for."

I explored Harry's rotting shoulder. Pus bubbled from it, and its edges was black. His body shook as my fingers delved inside the wound.

"He'll be dead, and soon," Charley says. "Though he has spirit to have lasted this long."

But my mind was working like quick-fire. I whispered with Charley, sending him off into the forest to search out red peat moss, chokecherry, white spruce, and devil's club. Charley whined on the ruinous state of my eye and face, but I couldn't feel nothing from it, so intent was I on the task before me. He muttered at how I didn't know owl shit from putty, but he went off anyhow into the forest to do what I had told him.

I was thinking about belief. About my own. About Harry's as well. Was there ought of belief in him that I might work with? Some belief that he might have, at least, in me? As a man? After what he had seen up at the House of Shamans, I could not believe that he did. He'd struggled to get away from me when I was over him just before. And the last time we had properly spoken, back at Rupert, it had been in anger. I had told him he was not to be trusted. But here he was: come all this way into the wilderness searching for me, and taken an injury so bad it might mean his death. Then I had spurned him in my trance up in the wilds.

That boy what I first cured when I was young: he had all the belief for both of us that day. It's the victim what must have the belief. They must have some sort of faith in the doctor. Though had not my vision been telling me the doctor hisself needed belief as well?

I looked down at Harry. His breath came light as a sparrow's. But now his eyes was open again. They looked up at me, and almost they looked a child's—innocent, like all the dark portions of his life was erased, and he was as free of the world's burdens as a newborn. He said something, but so quiet I could not make it out. I leaned close.

"What will you do to me?" he said.

I put my hand upon his cheek. "I am saving you, boy. See if I don't."

He nodded. "All right," he said, and closed his eyes.

I called for more water and placed it to boil in the fire. After some time had passed—and I thought it eternity—I heard Charley coming back from the forest. I saw he had all I had asked for, and had brought as well some bark of the red cedar. I pulled my skinning knife from out my boot and heated the blade in the coals of the fire, until its edges glowed white. Then I thrust it into the boiling water, watching the steam spiral up.

Once it had cooled some I had Charley over, holding on to Harry, though he seemed unconscious. So I started to stripping away what was rank from Harry's shoulder. I flicked the first piece of black flesh from the blade into the fire. But then Charley says, "No," and he goes off and fetches a red cedar leaf. "Put it all on here."

It was a mercy Harry was under. Even then, he writhed about till Charley had to rest his knees upon his chest and on his healthy shoulder to keep him still enough for me to work. He kept yelling about not passing through a door, how no one would know where he was gone. Soon enough, though, he fell into some deeper unconsciousness and, after, he lay still— so still, there was times I had to lean forward and listen for his breathing to be sure he weren't dead yet.

I told Charley to flense the bark off the white spruce branches he'd brung from the forest. He named me an old woman. Hadn't it been him what showed me the trick in the first place, those years ago? I just tells him to boil up the water first for it to go in.

Charley set another tin of water on the fire. He peeled and scraped out the inner bark, and tossed it in the tin as it was coming up to boil. "Take pity on him who lies before us," he sang to it.

Charley then took another pan from Walewid's side of the fire—asking with a pointed finger first, the chieftain nodding, terse, by return. He set it with water from the stream to boil as well. He tore off the fruit from the chokecherry what he'd gathered, then stripped and broke the stems and threw them all in the can, with the sharp-tooth leaves to follow. They'd have to distill for some hours before we could feed the brew to Harry, but they was the best I knew for easing fevers, and for cleaning out the blood.

I worked slow, trying to keep from slicing the tendons and longer muscles what passed through the shoulder, but I was taking much away that would stop Harry's shoulder working properly again, if he survived. I had already performed some fell surgery that night, just earlier in the darkness of the woods, with my machete. But I held firm and did not dwell on that. There was images what came to me as well from the night of David's funeral, and they was harder still to ignore.

On the other side of the fire, the men of Blunden Harbour had gathered together. They was speaking in high, bragging tones, swigging from the bottles they still had, and hurling words of scorn our way. Walewid alone sat in silence, watching us without expression. I wondered if he had the control over his men we would need, if we was to survive this night.

Eventually, I ceased my knife work. There was now a great gaping hole in Harry's shoulder. Blood welled at its bottom, but I could not see anything else that looked infected.

"Do you have the red peat moss?" says I.

But before he handed it over, Charley whispers to me, "You ain't making the proper performance of it."

"Be damned with performance," says I. "Harry's cold and won't remember none of it anyhow."

"But they," and he pointed across the fire, "they won't forget none of it. Leastwise not Walewid. Show them you's a proper man of medicine, George."

"I ain't got the tools what I need for it," says I. He just shrugged. Well I cursed the old fool, but he was right. So I stripped some of the red cedar and twisted them into a neckring for myself to wear—which was why Charley had brung it out of the forest in the first place, of course.

179

"Take the damned spruce bark off the fire and cool it," I tells him. I dredged up my old song what I used to sing when I was performing my healings as a younger man. Then up gets I and walked four times around poor Harry, all the time singing my sacred song. The men had fallen silent now, watching me. I took off the cedar ring from about my neck and ran it up and down Harry's body.

"His clothes have to come off. Burn them with the cedar ring," Charley whispers to me, like I don't know it. But first, I turned towards the ocean. The moon lit up the water. I could see out across it for miles, the mountains black menaces in the distance. I called out. "Carry away all that is bad, Supernatural One, Long-Life Maker. You Killer Whale Spirit!" I almost thought I might see that killer whale what rose beside me when I first came into the inlet. But the waters were still, and there was no other sound.

I turned back and knelt beside Harry. I took off his boots. Then I cut away his clothing with the skinning knife till he was naked. I bundled those rags together and I pushed the cedar ring around them. Then I stood and faced the fire. The men was all watching me still. "I pull out the sickness and I burn it," says I. I sang my song and I threw the bundle into the flames. They crackled and flared as they took my gift.

At my feet, Harry looked grey, sunken of chest, and already dead. I knelt by him now. Charley handed me the tin with the spruce bark mulch. I poured off what excess water there was. I pushed my hands into that larger pan of water what was bubbling away on the fire. I rubbed my fingers together in the blistering heat of it, till I reckoned they must be clean of dirt.

I took out the white spruce mulch and layered it down into Harry's wound, spreading it about the edges as well. Then I pressed some of the red peat moss across the top of the wound.

Charley ain't so stupid as he looks. He'd been winding what cedar bark string was left into thin rope. Now we tied it about Harry's shoulder to hold the moss secure upon it.

I stood up and stretched my shoulders.

"That's it?" The man in the yellow shirt was standing in the middle of the other men, pointing a finger at me. "Do we let you live for *that*? Is there no more to your medicine?" Some of the other men shouted agreement at this. Walewid said nothing.

Charley was beside me then. "Take the sickness round the fire four times, and give it to me after," he whispers.

I looked down to where the rotten slivers of flesh were sitting, rank, on their cedar leaf. So I took them up and started to singing again. The men was jeering me now, though. But I kept the leaf open on my palms, and paced about the fire. When I passed by them, two of the youngest made little leaps at me, feigning violence and whooping, waving their blades in circles over their heads. I turned towards them. I held up the leaf. "Watch that I don't blow this out upon you," says I, "making you all feel the sickness. Bringing you all to rotting." They kept off me then, though they didn't stop from marking me with scornful words. I knew we was at the edge of the razor, and surviving might need more than just the fixing-up of Harry.

I sang and I stepped about the fire four times. Charley was waiting for me at the last. Now he cried out, and his voice was that of the raven. He held up his hands and I slid the leaf onto his open palms. He kept on with his cawing, but now he hopped—like the bird as it moves about on the ground—he hopped across towards the men on the far side of the fire. Some of them laughed, but there was tension in them that I could see as well.

Charley moved until he was no more than a few feet in front of the group of men, with Walewid still sitting, stock-still, nearby. "What sickness is this?" Charley says, shouting out the words. "What sickness is this?" Now he folded his hands so that the leaf curled in half to seal up the rotting flesh inside. He pulled his palms tight together, linking up his fingers.

"What sickness is this?" says he, and he threw his hands out towards the men. They flinched, some of them. But there was nothing there. The leaf was gone.

"It is nothing!" Charley says, leering, his voice a hiss. And, as they took to jabbering, Charley came back round the fire and sat down beside Harry. I dropped my old bones down next to him. He drew out Harry's gaudy tobacco tin from his pocket and built himself a cigarette. He lit it with a coal from the fire. He blew upon his fingers where he had held the coal.

"Make they heads crazy," he says, in English, looking at me and twirling a finger round and round by his ear. He chuckled quietly. Then he drew on his cigarette and blew a long, slow stream of smoke into the air.

PART III · WHITE MEN

"BRING ME HEMLOCK BRANCHES. I will make a ring with them. With that ring I will bring back the soul. I am the life maker. I am the life maker. I am the life maker. I am the life maker." My face is daubed in red and white paint. Mud is in my hair. I am naked. I use the plants of the forest. I call down the spirit of the cannibal what dwells deep in the wilderness. The Cannibal Spirit. Red smoke rises from his house. His slaves are out gathering corpses for his dinner. His servant, the raven, devours the eyes of his master's victims. The Hoxhok bird lives also with him, tearing out the brains of men with its long beak, and the Cannibal Spirit's grizzly bear, who delights in killing with his bare paws. That is me. Old grizzly in the wilds, great massive paws grappling and tearing.

There ain't no cannibals. Put your slavering white man tongues back inside your craws. Wipe up the drool upon your chins. There ain't no savage men on the coasts above Vancouver, chewing human flesh. There is brutality enough in us already. But I ain't no more tasted human flesh than have you, choking down thin wine and wafers in the cold mausoleums what are the churches of your Christianity.

I can kill a man. Yes. It is easy. But to feast on him after? Maybe it is Christianity itself makes white men so obsessed. Perhaps parts of the bodies of enemies was ritually ate, once upon a time: that fairy tale saying we invoke when it is all too grim to have been just yesterday. The past is a forest impenetrable.

I am here in New York, before this black suit of armour what is the cause of so much, though I have not even reached it in my story yet. I have walked among the glass cases and the objects in this long hall. I knew all I saw, for it was me gathered nearly everything here: these masks of whale and dogfish, sun and seal and wolf, eagle, thunderbird, and bear. The cannibal birds, one with its long beak broken, as it was not when he had sent it off, and but poorly repaired. The great face of the raven, flared nostrils through which the man who wore it might see. I still can see whose eyes they was did once look through.

There are masks with the faces of shamans, their lids half closed as they discourse with the spirits. There is an old, old mask, one I had known most of my life and even questioned in myself, as I closed up the packing lid, if it should be sent away from its home. It was one of the first I did collect, back when I did still ask myself such things, the grim, stupid, lumbering face of the Dzonokwa. And beside it is the mask of the Qomogwe, its devilfish tentacles wrapped all about its flat whale face.

All of them seen through dusted glass, so that they seem no more than swift-dimming memories, caged here in the great granite architecture of the museum.

I have seen that some is marked with small paper signs naming them, as often wrong as they was right. Many, though, do not have tags at all. How might they be viewed by the few white people I have passed, slowly pacing the halls? I read all the tags. I have gazed in every case and tried to recall the circumstances of their collection.

There is a canoe laid out along the roof of one case. What a struggle it was to pack for shipment. Carved from one solid piece of cedar, fifteen foot long and painted all dainty in red and white and black at its prow. The owner was drunk when I bought it off him, and regretful after. I had to turn quite forceful in seeing the man away.

In one case there has been set up a scene from daily life, using three mannequins, two women and one man, the women squatting, hanging bark that has been already shredded to dry upon frames. The man works the cedar with his hands. I was before the frozen scene for I could not say how long, staring at the waxen, empty faces.

Against the walls are smaller poles and feasting dishes in design of seal and killer whale and bear, five feet long and more, carved from single blocks of cedar, filled once with steaming eulachon grease, or seal blubber, or mounds of sour-cooked fish. There's broad spoons, as wide as hands, by which the people scoop and slop and eat at ceremony. A gravebox, still so beautifully painted in black and red. It was from Rupert itself, built only for the purpose of being sold and shipped off to the East.

185

There's button blankets. One is hung upon a wall between two high windows. It has a black background and designs of the raven in red and white. I ran my fingers along its bottom edge. It is a blanket my mother made to sell to the museum. My hand rested there on those materials her fingers spent such time upon, the complicated artistry of her own fine fingers as they did weave and sew.

There's rattles the shamans shake above their patients, thick cedar bark neckrings, and all manner of utensils used by the people in their everyday lives—all laid out in the glass cases of the long gallery.

And there is a mound of skulls I took from all those islands of graves I did come upon in my travels up and down the coast. I have plundered the graves. I have shown but little respect for the holiness of such places.

I ain't never before killed a man, though, and I ain't planning to do it again. But the truth of it is that it ain't hard. I look in myself for some terror, guilt, horror at my actions. But there is none. I done what I had to. That's it. I might be the only man I know alive still what has actually taken a head in warfare. Oh, they was famous headhunters in times past, the Kwagiulth. As was many of the tribes up and down the coast. There's skulls aplenty to be found in the gravehouses of the old chieftains. And Boas is a great one for skulls. I've sent him dozens I have unearthed, at two dollars a piece, thank you very much. And I have taken him all around the villages of the people, measuring skulls, both living and dead. There's science attached to it, what asks if some men may be shown to be more primitive than others by the size of their craniums. Boas thinks it bunkum, and wants to show that we all are equal under the sky, and I ain't disagreeing.

Still, digging out a skull from a grave is one thing, killing a man and severing his head with a machete in the mud and darkness—well, ain't that just something else entire? I wonder if I will tell Boas this part of my story. He would love to hear it. But I can't be sure what he'll think of me after. Perhaps it is my own head needs measuring.

If it ain't simple killing a man, it ain't so simple neither to bring a man back from the point of death. A man what has his blood filled up with corruption. Harry lying in my arms, his breath a faint mist, the particles of his soul dispersing, my grizzly paws at his neck. "My supernatural power restores life. My supernatural power makes the sick walk. I have the strength of the Cannibal Spirit. No one can stop me." Such are the words of my shaman's song. Voicing a few choice words and hoping for the best of it. There on the beach at old Teguxste, I sat by Harry through the rest of that night, crooning my song to him, on and on, holding him up betimes and feeding him the brew we had made from the chokecherry plant. I had to stroke his neck to make him swallow, so far gone was he. Charley stripped out the green inner bark from the devil's club he had taken from the forest, and put it to boil as well. I sent him off for spruce, cedar, hemlock, and alder bark to add to the concoction too.

It is said by the people that souls have no bones, they have no blood, for they are just like smoke or shadows. They have no house besides the body in which to reside. When that house is razed, so the soul goes out and is blown away to nothing. Harry burned. I used the rest of the peat moss to soak water and bathe his body as it raged with the fever. I did battle to safeguard the house of his soul.

Those soldiers of Blunden Harbour had pretty soon drunk theirselves to unconsciousness. The fight had been took out of them by Charley's prestidigitating. They'd done no more since than grumble and gossip and throw the occasional high comment our way. So by the time the grey, clammy dawn found its way across the waters, it was just me and Charley and the unspeaking Walewid left. He had barely moved those past hours in his watch over us.

Through the night and through the day following, I passed hemlock rings over Harry, I sang the songs of the shaman, I cleaned out his wounds, and, once I'd seen there wasn't no more of rottenness in there, reapplied the dressings. I fed him the brews. I worried at him, trying to make him show some sign of wakefulness. I whispered to him that he was my son. I spoke soft words in his uncomprehending ear like I might to a child. I trawled through my memory for anything else that might serve to help him.

Charley clucked and pottered. He wouldn't let off till he had applied some of the remedies to my own face. The men of Blunden Harbour slowly came awake in ones and twos, farting, muttering, going off to take a shit. Their interest in the matter seemed muted now. Even Walewid had rolled hisself up in a blanket and snored like some bull elephant seal.

The men ignored me, wandering along the beach and in amidst the broken houses. Harry was insensible. Even Charley slept, making noises to match Walewid. But still I played out the role of shaman. Chanting, calling on the Killer Whale Spirit, the Cannibal, other spirits of the wood and water, hurling logs on the fire and calling up its flames, running hemlock and cedar up and down Harry's body and pacing about him in ritual parade. It was for me that I kept on. To shore up that failing belief what I believed had proved fatal to so many I had sought to save. I must believe for Harry to live. So was the impulse what drove me.

And then, sometime after Walewid had coughed and hawked and grumbled hisself up again, early in the afternoon of the day, as I imagined it—for the cloud had come down low above us, and all was flat and grey and seemed outside of time—at last Harry took to spluttering. I rolled him to his side. He coughed black bile, though he did not waken. After that, he breathed much heavier, drawing in great gulps of air, wheezing when he exhaled once more. I pulled blankets over him, for he came to shivering now. Sweat began to pour off him, where before his skin had been cold to the touch and dry. There was the faintest trace of blood come into his face. I cooed and whispered in his ear. He mumbled, as in a dream, but did not wake up.

When I looked up, Walewid was staring over at me. There weren't no expression on his face, but he gave me a small nod. Then he stood and called out to his men, cursing them all for idling idiots and telling them to pack up their gear into the canoe and make ready for the off.

Charley was beside me. He rested his hand on Harry's forehead. "He ain't there yet," says he.

"Oh, we'll have him back," says I. And I knew it to be true.

"There'll be a feast," says I to Walewid. "You will be my guests. I will give away much to you. We will be as family to each other."

"I got better," says Charley. He went aboard the *Hesperus*, calling the soldier in the yellow woman's blouse to come with him. This man was slow and bleary-eyed today, without the fire in him from the night before. The two of them took to unloading what was in the hold of the *Hesperus*. There was blankets and some clothing. There was tinned foodstuffs. And there was a couple of cases of whisky left as well. Others of the men came to help, and they loaded these goods across from the *Hesperus* into their war canoe.

Eventually, when all was done, they took up the last of their gear and boarded the canoe. Walewid stepped in last. As they was making ready to leave, I hurried over.

"What of that?" says I. I pointed along the beach to where the dreamer's head still lay on the shingle.

"It was taken in war," says Walewid. "He is gone. He is yours."

"There will be a feast," I says to him.

"I will come with my secrets for you," Charley says.

The men at the rear of the canoe pushed off. They paddled away. They did not look back.

"A deep swamp we have walked out from," Charley says, "and come up clean." He laughed and clumped me on the shoulder.

Five days later, we rounded Cormorant Point and came in sight of Alert Bay. It was the middle of the afternoon and the sun was bearing down so the sea could hardly be looked at. I felt such expectation, such confidence in myself, that I could but barely stop from shouting out across the water to the people in the village: "Prepare yourselves! I have much to tell you!" Like a child I am at times. For what we all had spoken—Charley and me, and even Walewid, on the beach there in Teguxste—had run round and round in my head, getting crafted further into form, until I was almost bursting to speechify.

When we snuck out through the Nakwakto Rapids—those treacherous waters for once proving kindly enough to let us pass without incident— the killer whale did follow us through. Its great dorsal fin rose up like the shadow of fatefulness against the forests behind. It must have seen our hull as alike to itself and so was led back through. Still, you might imagine the ways I chose to read that portent after, on the journey south.

189

As we came closer to Alert Bay, I gazed on those two cannery buildings, what are the lifeblood of that small town. Now they reared over us, with their high sloping roofs and all those windows in long lines, the sharp angles of the stilts holding it all up above the water, like some great caterpillar on legs what seem too gangling to bear its weight. There weren't but little activity as yet, so early in the year. The thunder of those steam engines, the hammering tin cutters, the explosions of the steam retorts that boom out across the bay all summer. I thought: here is a monster still dozing, waiting to come awake. We must feed it fish till it be satisfied. But Indians don't have to be slaves, feeding the maws of white men. Though, it is mostly Chinese and Japaners what Spencer employs nowadays.

It was Spencer what truly founded Alert Bay. And, after, he took my sister Annie for his wife and become as well my brother-in-law. It was about thirty years back now, and Reverend Hall moving his mission from Rupert some years later, once he'd come to realize the Rupert Indians was proving unpliant to his sermonizing. I used to stand there next to him each Sunday, in my best Sunday smarts, doing the translating. I'd hear the people murmuring to theirselves about how preposterous was the things I was saying, even as Reverend Hall was getting all fired up with the righteousness of his God.

We steered in towards the jetty beside the canneries. We tied off by old Dan Copperhand's fishing sloop, and everyone clustered round to witness our return. So I yelled for help in carrying Harry along to Doc Trelawney's. I could see all knew there was events afoot. The wry looks of many. None responding to my good graces. Still, it did not dint my enthusiasm. Halliday might be awaiting me with his iron cuffs, and I did know that there were those arranged against me for all the wrongs they did consider I had done upon the people, all bundled up into the charges what was arrayed against me. And I would soon come at the heart of what those charges was. Charley had laid out all he knew to me about the charges against me, whilst we was waiting on Harry to be well enough to travel from Teguxste, and I had a pretty good notion by now of what they must be constituted, if yet I did not know for sure. Arrest me, then! Let me stand up in the courthouse here in Alert Bay, in front of all of them, and speak my piece on who I was, the spokesman that I was for the people. Let them decide: the people, packed in, as I envisaged them, to hear my words. I'd make old Reverend Hall blush for lack of passion when he saw me delivering what it was I'd have to say about the great wrongs done the people, about who it is we are!

Still, Harry was yet in a ruinous state. If he had been conscious, mostly, these past days, he still didn't have the strength even to raise himself up to sit, let alone to walk. The evening after Walewid had left, Harry came round sudden, spluttering, wild-eyed, calling out as if he had woken in some new world entire—Hell, perhaps, or Purgatory, so shocked did he seem. He couldn't seem to make no sense of his surrounds. He viewed Charley and me as if we was demons summoned up to taunt his sanity. But soon enough he fell back into slumbering. His breath came easier, and I felt then, for the first time since I had buried David's head beneath the earth, that I could sleep as well. I was near collapsing with fatigue.

Charley promised to sit up, and I wrapped up my bones in a blanket and lay by the fire what we had kept roaring. I didn't wake again till the sun was risen. Charley was snoring beside me like a beast. Harry was awake, lying on his side, staring at the embers of the fire.

"So this ain't death?" he said to me.

I put my hand on his head and told him no, it weren't death. It was life. "No snoring Indians in Heaven," says I, nodding towards Charley.

We didn't talk much in the days what followed. I started a couple times to explain myself about David, but I didn't properly have the words myself as yet, and I saw that Harry didn't want to hear them anyhow. But he seemed content enough in his mind. He looked about like the world was fresh to him, and what few words he did speak was always polite. He voiced how grateful he was that I saved him more than once, till I had to tell him to shut his trap or I'd find some way to undo my methods.

We got him along the cannery jetty to the beach, and then along the plankways of the village, with many hands holding him, all bound up in a blanket like a moth in a cocoon, towards the hospital. The doctor there, Albert Trelawney, drugged him up, and Harry looked a pretty sight sinking down onto that hospital bed, a smile like he was back in his mama's

191

arms. We had a laugh at that, but I was happy to see him situated safe at last, for all that I had kept him living thus far.

Once Harry was laid abed, Trelawney ministrated some to me as well. He gave me a felt eye patch, which I still am wearing now, and what don't help to soften my appearance much. He asked me how I come to be injured so. Charley piped up, "Wolf!" which was a good one. He ain't but a young man, Trelawney, and not three years out from England, that nervous tic to his plump face. Annie tells me he hadn't never been happy here. Still, he can doctor. His training is from London itself.

I was keen straightways to present myself to Halliday. So I asked Trelawney on the whereabouts of the Indian agent, and I didn't much like it when he told me that he did not know. His eyes went all about the room, anywhere but to my own. There's white man's gossip every bit as noxious as there is Indians'. So off we went to see my sister Annie and her Mr. Spencer.

As we walked down the beach, the people were outside their homes in the early-evening sun. They did mutter at our passing, and no words of pleasantness did they offer us. "We about as popular as a face full of seal shit," says Charley.

My brother-in-law was waiting for us on his porch. He is a Scotchman, as so many was what came along the coast to make their fortunes in the time of my father. Anyways, great old lanky fella that he is, he waves us inside with no more than a gruff greeting, and not much of good humour on his skeleton face neither.

There is a blanket hung up in that hallway of Spencer's house what is famous among the Tlingit people of my mother's line, an old blanket out of history, come down the generations. My mother brung it south as a part of her dowry. She wore it all her years among the Kwagiulth. Wore it proud in her lineage. When I did look up to see it hanging there, the events of the past weeks came flooding through me of a sudden, till I was near to being overwhelmed by my emotions.

Then my sister—dear, sweet Annie with her stern dresses and her so-serious face—she came out from the drawing room. "My brother," says she, standing before me with her fingers on my arms. "What happened to you?" She put a hand to my face. I almost might have wept then, but all I says is that there was trouble what now is over.

"Was that Harry you carried in to Trelawney's?" Spencer says. I tell him yes, but that he was mending well from a knife wound what he had sustained some days before. "Gods, man, what has been happening to you all?" Spencer's voice was filled up as much with ire, so it seemed to me, as with sympathy. Charley told him I had saved Harry's life with shaman medicine, but Spencer just huffed at that and says we'll talk after dinner. I could see something was screwing him up inside, and I guessed it was me. He and I haven't often been of one mind down the years, though I like to think we have respect for each other. I know he don't much approve of my work with Boas, though he had not openly spoke it before.

We ate fresh chinook salmon, and potatoes fried, and peas from the Spencers' garden. Mighty good did they taste after days in the wilds. Once we was done, Spencer poured whisky and we sat out on the porch.

I told the story of the past few days in as few words as I could muster. Just how Charley and Harry came looking for me on Halliday's orders, how they had liquor-fuelled trouble in Blunden, but had pressed on and found me. I didn't speak on those events up by the House of Shamans, just told them how we had fixed Harry up and returned. I kept off telling him as well of the ins and outs of what did occur with Walewid. There didn't seem a point to it at the moment.

"You've placed yourself in a mire of shite, George," says Spencer, "and helped nobody in the doing." I asks him where Halliday had got to, and learned he was away two days before, and that conniving rat-bastard Constable Woolacott with him. Spencer didn't know, or wouldn't say, where.

"What's been said?" I asks, and Spencer was then quite roused.

"Christ, George, what has not been said?" says he, and wants to know if I had heard the charges laid against me.

"That I am accused of participating in a banned ritual," says I.

"Well, well," says he, "that's just the start of it."

"And I am accused of cannibalism," I says.

"You will, I trust, assure me outright that that is not correct," says he.

193

So I says, "That part ain't true." I tell him how I had been at the ritual, though I don't tell him much else. He shook his head and grumbled to hisself some.

"Now will you tell me what happened exactly at David's funeral? For there's rumours, terrible to acknowledge, all along the coast." I was reticent at first, but he pressed me. So, I told him how I had taken off David's head and been away into the wilds with it.

What a fury he flied into! He invoked the good Lord almighty more than once. He paced up and down the porch, spluttering and waving those long arms of his about, raving on the family name and savage practices, and on what kind of man I thought myself to be. In fact, on all that I have been deliberating on in the recounting of this tale.

"What will you do?" he says to me at last, once his steam had vented sufficient that he was able to talk near normal once more.

"I am Kwagiulth," I tell him.

"Perhaps you are," he says. "But how do you plan on answering the charges laid against you?" I told him I'd not hide from attending rituals of the people. "You'll not help the people by confessing," he says.

"I don't help them by lying neither," says I, and I tell him how the white man stole the ways of the people till there weren't nothing left of them to clutch to no more. I told him I had words to say on that, and not just to him.

"Well, well," says he. "Yet in court you'll do no more than propagate the stories of their savagery," he says. "But what about your family? Have you given thought for what it might mean for them, should you be thrown into the jail?"

I had been thinking on such things, of course, since we left Teguxste. What was my responsibilities? Walewid and Charley had made it clear to me that, if I was to stand by the things what I had done *before* the people, then I must stand up also *for* the Indian. Bringing Harry back from the dead had made it all the more important to me somehow, like as if the spirits of the people had truly come through my hands to heal Harry. And the killer whale following us out through the rapids. Who can ignore such portents?

If nothing else, I had a debt to pay for that gift I had been given. The gift of Harry's life. My last living son. If I had responsibility to my family, it was all tied up in that which I had toward the people as a whole.

So I told Spencer I would stand up in the court at Alert Bay and say I was not afraid that I had been at the ritual: a ritual which was part of the right ways of the Indian since the beginnings of the world. Those people of which I was a proud member. Let the heavens fall round me after.

"Though, as I hear it," says Spencer, "the people won't be minded to support you at this time."

"It is true I ain't so popular right now," says I. "Be that as it may, I must say my piece."

After that, we sat for some long time in silence.

At last, Spencer pipes up. "I see you've complex thoughts on the matter," he says, his voice cold as January. "But I tell you, George, you bring disgrace on the family by the events of David's funeral, not honour, as you seem to imagine it. And disgrace as well on the people of which you claim yourself a part. Owning up to being at a legally forbidden ritual—a ritual at which the Lord God knows what practices were carried out, however coy you might choose to play it—will not do ought but harm." He slugged whisky and gazed out from the porch, along the beach, toward the fires and the dark houses of the village. "Far as I'm concerned," says he, "you're on your own in this."

Even Annie would not look up to meet my eye.

Constable Woolacott came for me the next morning, just after dawn. I was sitting out on the porch with Charley, drinking coffee and feeling as if the whole world were rousing itself in my name. We had already seen the police boat moored alongside the *Hesperus*, where it must have come back in the night. So I was not surprised when that mean English prick came stomping up to stand before us.

"You been skulking in the jungle," says Woolacott by way of greeting. His face—what is visible behind all that grey fuzz of hair and beard—was puckered with the vile depth of his hatred of the Indian. When I did not reply, he says, "Know I have come for you. That you is arrested on charge of cannibalism and the mutilating of a corpse, and of performing heathen rituals which is banned under law."

"Well," says I. "What's to be done with me?"

Then he tells me I'd be kept till the next steamer turned up, and after taken down to Vancouver for trial.

My throat got so tight I could not form words for some time. At last I stutters out, "Vancouver? You'll not try me here?"

"We will not," says he. "Your crimes were better punished publicly, so all might know the wrongs you've done. Perhaps it will aid in purging the dirt-worshipping savagery you people live by." Charley muttered at that, low and in Kwakwala, sentiments impolitic on the man and his profession.

"I must be tried here," says I. There was panic in me. I might almost in that moment have turned tail and run for it, back to the forest, if there'd been anywheres to go on this small island.

"All's in place and Vancouver's expecting you," says he, and when I asked where Halliday might be, he wouldn't tell. "He's away on business" is all he says. "About which you'll hear more soon enough."

Charley leapt up at that and put his face close by Woolacott's. "Where Hal'day?" says he. "What he doing?"

"None a your fucking business, Charley Seaweed," says Woolacott. "I represent the law on this shit-riddled coast. Don't forget yourself. I'm like to take you in too."

I was breathing hard, trying to keep my self-possession. Where was Halliday? Charley had told me the Indian agent was threatening to take the family possessions, so I understood what must be vexing him now. But I could not imagine he could actually carry out such a conscienceless deed. I asked Woolacott, was he planning to keep me here till Halliday came back?

"I'm not," says he. "You'll be aboard the first steamer south, with me safeguarding you all the way."

I stood on the Spencers' porch with the dawn sun in my good eye, and I didn't rightly know what to do or say. Woolacott had his hand on the butt of his pistol and was threatening force if I did not come straightway with him. He had with him three Indian bully boys—three, mind you!—

toting axe handles, all hocked up on power and shilling. But there weren't nothing inside me, excepting confusion. So in the end I just followed him meekly away along the beach. Charley made to follow, but Woolacott warned him off.

"His family be obliged to feed and water him. So best you talk with his sister and get something sorted," says the constable, and his voice was glutted by triumph.

He didn't say nothing more till he had me sealed behind bars in back of the Indian Agency hut. "See how much smart talking there's left in you now, eh?" was all the words he spoke, then he left me to fester on my own.

I paced about some. I looked out the barred window onto the barren space behind the village, the trees felled long ago for timber. It looked a charnel ground to me. Later, I heard Charley's voice raised out front, and Woolacott's in answer. After, Woolacott came in and set down before the bars the iodine Trelawney had given me for my eye, though he held up the phial of laudanum, smiled, and put it in his own pocket.

I sat on the billet below the window, shut my eyes, and looked inside myself for any trace of that rage for which I imagined I'd now be subject. But none of it was there. Instead, I was near overcome by images from the past days. I saw the whale from my visions, but he seemed a thing out of some other universe entire. I saw again the blows by which I severed the dreamer's head. The butcher's feel of it. The air pumping in my lungs. I knew there was savagery indeed in me, brutal murder of which I had shown myself capable.

I saw as well a hundred trades I'd made for artefacts up and down the coast, packing them and shipping them—cheques payable to Mr. G. Hunt, Esquire. The pages of stories I had written and promises made and broken in the writing. My family connections hung before me like great spiders' webs, and all of them betrayed by every shipment, every scrape of pen on paper.

Vancouver. There'd be none there to hear the words I had to say. None as counted, or who might listen or care. What point was there in my incarceration, then? It was vainglory. In Vancouver there would only be the assizes to speak before. For the whites, I'd be an Indian guilty of his crimes by his very nature. To the Indian: a half-breed guilty of betrayals too numberless to count. And then the final insult of David's jerry-built tangle of a funeral. If it were true I weren't in court to answer charges on David's funeral, still in my confused thinking it was all becoming tied together. And if I had any chance to get hold of witnesses to help me, I'd need ones sympathetic to the man I am.

When next I opened my eyes, the shadows spoke of late afternoon, and I had passed the whole day in my thinking, without getting any nearer to a solution.

Charley came at dusk. "Fuck bastard Wol'cot," he said first in English, what at least made me smile a bit. He'd had to battle hard before Woolacott would let him in to visit. I ate the food Charley had with him—some bread, dried fish, and a paste of salmonberries—and he told me what he'd learned.

Not content with waiting on my arrest, Halliday had been busy distributing evil rumours that I had brung humiliation on the people in all the things I did. And there would indeed be many keen to speak against me, says Charley. Where he was at now, Charley had not been able to discover.

Of the white men in the village, he had learned less. Corker, headmaster at that damned boys' school, was away along the coast, gathering children like some lanky white vulture version of a Dzonokwa. All he wants for is a sack. Reverend Hall claimed he was too busy to talk to Charley, what hurt some, given the years we had spent in each other's company and, in strange point of fact, the sort of rancorous respect we had for one another. He ain't all badness, the Reverend. Not like his crony Crosby, with his spite and his scheming malice. Reverend Hall it was what taught me to read and write, as I have said. Spencer was at the cannery and only boiled his head when Charley came near. My sister was as yet too angry to talk sense.

Charley had a letter with him. I tore it open. The heading stated it came from the American Museum of Natural History, New York. It was dated March, 1900, and addressed to Mr. George Hunt, Post Office Alert Bay, Fort Rupert, B.C.

It read: *My dear George, I did receive your letter and the accompanying artefacts, for which my thanks. My schedule is as yet unfixed, and you have not yet given a date to when you will join me here in New York to work upon the museum collections. I understand that you may need to work for Mr. Spencer in the cannery in the summer months. Yet I could promise you a better wage should you say you could come immediately. Please write as soon as you are able.*

When you visit, I shall be most keen to press you into writing more of the paxala shaman myths and practices, and ideally of your own experiences therewith, of which we have so often spoken in the past. I understand that there is much that must remain a secret even until after our own deaths. Yet I do believe such material to be of the utmost importance to future generations. I, for my part, am willing to work with you in any way on this, to eschew all personal glory that might pertain to the publication of such tracts, and to bestow them somewhere appropriate for those that should come after us.

I send my kindest regards to your wife, to David, whom I do so hope is faring better, and to all your family. With kindest regards, yours very sincerely ...

It was signed, *F.R. Boas.*

Well, I have plenty to tell him on those aspects of healing what I have been conjuring with.

I told Charley to find me pen and paper when next he visited. For I had to write Boas straightways and tell him of my predicament. Then Charley and I talked some more.

"I'll not lie for being Kwagiulth," says I.

"Though what you did was Tlingit," Charley says, "if it were anything at all."

But, I pointed out, he was talking about David's funeral, not the ritual for which I was arrested.

"Well that is how it works in eyes of the people," says Charley. "You will need witnesses to support you, if you is to have any chance at escaping justice. Who'll travel as far as Vancouver to help the likes of you?" He tells me Spencer ain't necessarily wrong in wondering who I thought I was helping in admitting to the charges. I'd but propagate the view of Indian savagery to an even wider audience, which weren't any part of what he had been discussing in Teguxste.

199

But in my mind it ain't savagery, which is the very point, says I. In Vancouver they won't give two shits, says he, and at that we left it. Old mother Charley tells me I must use the medicine on my eye, and then off he went.

Well, I did barely know my left from my right by then. All the things what I had been planning on and thinking through so swiftly come undone. But the pain was brutal enough in my head and eye—had been, in truth, all these days past—that I took heed of Charley's words. I was distracted enough with my thinking, though, that I pulled off the bandage, opened up the bottle of iodine, and poured it direct over my wounded eye.

I was still cursing an hour later when I heard the sound of the steamer's whistle, as it would be rounding the headland and coming into the harbour.

I was dabbing my eye with water and feeling sorry as a salmon on a slab, when Woolacott shortly showed himself through the bars of my cage.

"Steamer's in," says he, and warned me to be ready on his return.

"Let me out. I'll go stretch my legs," I tell him.

"Shut your garret," says he, and off he went.

"George," comes a low voice then, from the window at back of the cell. Charley'd brought paper and pen, and was wanting to know if he should be along with me aboard the steamer. Lacking all funds as we was, the option didn't really arise, however.

I sucked on the pen for a bit, mind blank as to what needed saying on the page. In the end I laid out how David was dead and I was to be tried. I asked Boas if there was any funds owed me that he might send on. It was painful in the writing, letting someone know of David's passing. I reckon the letter probably sounded a bit plaintive by the end. But I was in a hurry to finish, not knowing when Woolacott would be back. So I pushed the paper back through the window soon as it was done, along with Boas's letter with the address at the top for Charley to show the telegraph office.

"I'll be needing Spencer's money," I says to Charley, "for bail and lawyers and such."

"He won't like it none," says Charley, and I knew it. But I pointed him towards Annie, once she'd calmed down, as his best way of making inroads.

Soon, Woolacott was back, with two other men alongside. One was a bully-boy from earlier. The other was a man I did know well enough. He was the man what had accompanied Crosby that day of David's funeral on the beach. The man the sight of which made me start to put twos and twos together, and to make numbers what added up rather better than any had before. His name was To-Cop.

"So it's you what's got this whole shitstorm raging, then, is it?" I says to him, as Woolacott was cuffing my hands together through the bars.

"I do my duty as a deputy," To-Cop says without emotion. But I could see in his eyes a spark what spoke of something more.

Now I did comprehend more fully the conspiracy there was against me. To-Cop worked with the missionaries, had grown up amongst them, and even wore the black apparel betimes, as he had been the day of the funeral, though I ain't convinced he is rightly a priest. More pertinent, though, was that he had been present at the ritual for what I was charged. More than present.

"We both know things about that day," says I to To-Cop. "You ain't exactly untarnished yourself." He only smiled, as Woolacott pulled me to my feet, my hands secure behind my back.

I asked Woolacott to pick up my medicine, but he would not. "The prison warden will see to what you need," he says. He took me by the arm and led me out, To-Cop and the other man following.

It was dark by then. The steamer's lamps sparkling on the water as it bobbed by the cannery jetty up the far end of the village. Nearer, firelight flushed from the doors of houses, and one bonfire on the beach threw up great amber flames, and red sparks churning, what shone then dimmed and disappeared, as if exhausted at the efforts of their brief existence. The people was lined up to watch in silence the prisoner's progress among them. I felt the spirit in me ebbing away.

When we was halfway through the village, we passed those few what had come off of the steamer.

"Father?" says one, and I strained to see in the dim light. It was Abayah. Seeing David's widow there, so unexpected, was almost too much to bear. I hung my head down without speaking, feeling such shame at my predicament that I could not bring myself to look her in the eyes.

"What is this?" she spoke up in English.

"Come on," says Woolacott, "quickly now," and he tried to pull me on. He seemed anxious.

Abayah clutched at me, and she wept. "Where do they take you?" says she.

I tell her I am to Vancouver for trial, and near was I to weeping myself.

"Have you not heard?" she says, but Woolacott sought to quiet her.

"Get away home," says he, and pushed her.

"Whatever you do to me," I says to him, "you will not ever put your hands to my daughter." I spoke quietly, but Woolacott moved back. Some spirit to resist was there still in my blood.

Then Abayah tells me what had happened in Rupert. She tells how Halliday, Woolacott, and some deputies had taken, by force, the family's treasures just the very day before, and how Halliday had gone away with them after in his boat.

Woolacott had his hand on his pistol. "Now George," he says to me, his other hand palm out, evidently catching the gist of our conversation, though he don't speak Kwakwala, even despite the years he has been resident here. "You just keep your calm," he says.

My voice low, I say to him the threat was only to have been carried out if I did not return.

"We didn't know you was back till now, did we?" says he.

I asks him where they have taken everything, but he says, "You don't need to know, George Hunt." He draws his pistol as he says it.

Then Charley was at my side. When he heard what had gone on from Abayah, he was about Woolacott as well. But the man would tell us nothing further. Instead, he had his pistol raised up and pointed square at me. To-Cop and the other was beside him, toting their billy clubs, all spunk and nerves. People was about us, gathering, and the whites of Woolacott's eyes plain visible.

Charley stepped in front of me. "Stop!" says he, forceful, to me. "Getting shot won't help nobody." He was thinking my rage would certainly come upon me. Instead, I felt nothing more than a wash of defeat.

That stayed true even when I looked into To-Cop's animal eyes at Woolacott's shoulder. Despair had unmanned me. Even in that moment I was surprised at myself that I should wilt and not give way to my rage. What was become of me? Here, when I might with such justice feel anger, that I should instead roll over and lie belly up to the world.

Now several people had their hands on me—men of the village, I saw. Abayah was there still. She clung to Charley, who pushed in among the men holding me. He whispered close in my ear, "I am your dreamer. I'll learn the truth of it." So I allowed myself to be dragged away, along toward the cannery jetty.

The steamer was the *Comox*, and old Eddlestone looked down on us from the rail alongside the pilothouse when we came near. "By the blessed tits of the holy whore of Babylon," says he. "Will you get that felon aboard, 'fore I shove off without all of you mistresses of shite." It's like that man has a condition of the brain, so foul is he in all he says.

I was pushed aboard, down stairs, and into one of the small cabins. Woolacott locked me to a pipe which rose alongside the porthole at the far end of the cabin. I saw To-Cop standing outside in the passage, his face dim in the lantern light, but his eyes aflame with triumph. Then the door was thrown shut and I was left alone.

Of the three days I spent travelling south in Eddlestone's steamer, shackled the whole time, there ain't much to say. Woolacott brung me two meals each day, and wouldn't speak nothing at all. I pissed and shat in a bucket, and there weren't no ways to wash. The cabin stank—the unemptied bucket in the corner, my unwashed body, my unchanged clothes. My eye wept pale liquid. After glooming and rankling and chewing on everything over and over, in the end my mind just turned empty, as if it waited outside of time for what would follow. There weren't nothing of scheming to do. Nothing of plans. I was chained up and on my way to the jail.

The steamer's whistle woke me, the third morning, the cuffs sharp at the chafes on my wrist. I heard sounds, some cacophony, not of the ship itself but coming, dim, through the hull.

I peered out of the tiny porthole. At first I could make little of what I saw, weary and stupid as I was. Then the shapes of the mountains, the great expanse of water ahead, and the tapering land close by, told me we was passing First Narrows and entering Burrard Inlet, that is Vancouver Bay.

Beyond those details, however, I couldn't recognize nothing. I've heard tell of the changes that had come but, when last I was there, Vancouver weren't yet established. I worked one summer season as a fireman at the Hastings Sawmill, stoking the mill's steam boiler eleven hours a day and half an hour for lunch, until my shoulders raged injustice and my hands couldn't barely grip the coal shovel.

All was very different back then. I lived with three others from the village what had travelled south with me looking for employment, one bed for all of us in a rough-board one-room shack in Gastown, as it was called back then by all what lived there. I was a drinker in those days, ranging through the town, midst the few bars' hard clientele. A big man and rageful was I—more, if such was possible, in my younger days. Still, I took some sound beatings that summer, and dealt not a few as well, late in the evenings, prompted by all manner of insult, real or otherwise. But I came home that autumn with near five hundred dollars in my pocket.

All of which is to show that, the last time I had been in that region, there had been not more than a few tens of houses lining the shore.

Now there was quite hundreds of vessels, steamers, sailing ships, and all number of smaller kinds, moving about on the waters before me. A ninety-foot sailing steamer passed close by the porthole, high white pilothouse at its centre and a black painted hull. Once it might have been filled with Klondikers. Now, who knew where all the men and women on its decks was bound?

Ahead, great swathes of buildings lined the shore like jagging teeth, smoke rising everywhere, the thundering of machines and the high whine of buzz saws from the mills, crane arms silhouetted against the sky, and the high chimneys of ocean-going liners amid the thorny angles of what seemed a million sailing masts, all viewed through thick and filthy glass, so that it seemed to me some vision of a future more terrible and strange than any I might previously have imagined.

I pulled back from the porthole, pain spearing in my head and no clarity of mind by which to embrace such a vision. So I lay back down on the bunk and only listened as we drew in towards the city's wharves.

Woolacott came shortly after I felt the steamer bump against its moorings. "Time to be out this shithole and on to the next," he says, the first words he had spoke since we left Alert Bay. There was two men with him, black tall hats with silver crests, and silver stars at their chests. "Christ almighty," says one. "Reeks like the sewer, don't he? Fucking savage."

Woolacott uncuffed me from the pipe, then sealed my hands again, this time behind my back. He led me down the corridor, the Vancouver policemen following.

At the door, sunlight snuffed out my vision for a time. Woolacott dragged me on blind, until my good eye found its balance. We were at the gangway and I stepped onto it and stumbled down.

The noise blew against me like a gale. On the wharf, stevedores were shouting, and some took to jeering at me, bound filthy Indian nigger. "Get out of it!" shouted one policeman, and too much was happening for anything to cease for long. Rusting cranes lifted bales from off the steamer, slanting, swinging, dangerous above in the brightness of the sun.

The water was surfaced with endless thousands of logs girning in the light swell, steam tugs buffeting at them, and a great sign what read *Hastings Sawmill*. Long low warehouses and sawdust eddies swirling yellow in the sky, but changed so much that no part of it did I recognize.

Then we was through the unloading and amidst all those many-windowed warehouses in brown brick and stone what line the docks. We was jostled by a hard crowd of sailing men—burned faces and squinting eyes. "I don't give two fucks for your silver star," says one to our policemen. He shouldered Woolacott as he went by, Woolacott blustering, as provincial as was his prisoner.

We were out now onto a thoroughfare of dust and horses. I tripped over a metal track. I heard a claxon bell, and bearing down upon us was a trellis-fronted steel contraption that froze me on the spot, me staring up at it like some squirrel at a diving eagle.

A policeman pushed me on, and I saw it to be a streetcar, as I'd heard of them, a single carriage and people hanging off and gawping at me. One Chinese boy I saw, plump cheeks and a pillbox hat, dressed up like some toy jack-in-the-box—then gone away past with the electric crackle from the cables above.

My eyes followed the streetcar. The road did stretch away into the distance as far as I could see through the dust. All along on either side was stone buildings, and a few still constructed of wood, glass fronts to shops, towers and turrets and flat-roofs, and spidering cables criss-crossing the street above. On the pavements: tight buttoned suits, top hats, bowlers, and women in black skirts and white shirts, high wide bonnets and flowers, turning from me with noses raised—people dressed fine as if on their way to church, though it was too busy to be Sunday.

Yet, as well, there was ill-clad boys lurking on street corners, and a coal dray dragged by two grey mares with coal-coated men aboard, faces black like forest devils. Raggedy men stared at me, grey-tangle beards to their waists and shreds on their bodies, fool's gold failure in their empty eyes. Six Indian men was huddled on iron steps which run up the side of a building, smoking, bottles in their hands, Salish men by their faces, but dressed in the uncoloured cloth trousers and collarless shirts of industry, watching me without expression.

The air was full of grit and dust as we passed by a huge building site. Rising at its centre was a building bigger than I had ever saw in life, ten storeys or more, and the hammering of steam shovels, same like I had seen them in the coal pits at Nanaimo.

Horseshit to dodge, and motor vehicles exploding noise, no more than horse-carts with engines beneath and a wheel by which to steer. Four men was perched high in one, cravats at their necks and arrogance in their chins and the waggle of their moustaches. White men what owned the world.

I've been in Victoria many times before, and seen the docks filled with ships and throngs of people moving through the town. Yet a town is all Victoria is, and that I only realized then, seeing for the first time clearly what a city is and what it does.

A crowd poured out the arching cavern-mouth of a high brown edifice what seemed, with its twin-peak turrets and steep roof taller than the greatest cedar, almost some German castle from pictures what Professor Boas showed me once of his native land. *Canadian Pacific Railways* read the sign. Here was the church of all this limitlessness then, and the whistle screams of the engines within like fiends, their voices beating down on me till we was past.

Woolacott leaned against me a moment, so that the man seemed needing of support as much as might his captive.

"Just down here a ways," says one of our policemen, me a shuffling half-breed, the taunts of frayed children on the street corners, the sun pulsing hot now on my hatless head. What was there of hope among such multitudes?

Boas told me a tale once of how he took an Indian chief, from off the central plains of America, up atop a high building to look down on New York. Boas said he hoped to show the man what it was he faced in his struggle to keep his own nation intact. The Indian asked him why the people kept walking round and round the bottom of the building. It took Boas some time to persuade the chieftain that they wasn't doing so, that they was all, in fact, different people. When he finally had convinced him, the old man fell silent and would not speak again that day.

So did I finally comprehend that old chieftain's state of mind.

When we arrived at last outside the police station, and Woolacott pushed me forward up the steps, it seemed a dark and quiet respite inside. Shadows. A cool stone floor. And then words, hollow, as if spoken in a cave.

"This him, is it?" "Big bastard." "Smells like shite." Woolacott muttering by return, his voice low and his tone uncertain. I had not heard him this way before: not chock full of his usual self-importance. All was turned by the tides of such a world, tumbled opposite and upside down, until the waves came so convoluted that they made no sense at all.

"Well, clean him up," said a voice, weary. "And get a doctor to his eye. Cannibal savage as he may be"—and these words were spoken with irony, I noted, even mazed as I was from the city—"still no reason we should act the same."

I looked up to see the man what had spoken sitting behind a table weighed down with brown files and paperwork. Plump in his face and flame-cheeked above his uniform, he'd have looked cheery were his expression not so grim.

"Mr. George Hunt?" he says, and I respond in the affirmative. He asked me if I'd had the charges laid against me clearly stated, and he cast such a look at Woolacott as to suggest such might well not have been the case.

"I'm charged with being at a banned ritual," says I, stuttering some.

"And the mutilation of a corpse," says he, and went on to read from the charge sheet what he had before him. "You're a unique case," he says after. "We've had nothing like this before that I'm aware of." And he asks me if I have a lawyer, at which I reply that I ain't. "Have you money?" says he.

"No," says I, and he asks if I was planning on mounting a defence. Well, I didn't have no answer to that. Eventually, I says, "I don't know."

He speaks on the seriousness of the charge and how I'd be locked away in the jail if convicted. Then he asks if I've anyone I could send a message to.

"My brother-in-law, maybe," says I. He says he'd get me pen and paper shortly. Then he sent me off to be scrubbed and locked up.

"What should I be doing?" pipes up Woolacott.

The captain eyed him over the pince-nez perched low on his fat nose. "You're the constable that brought him here?" says he and, when Woolacott nods, "Then you can see to his cleaning, since you are responsible for his current condition." Seeing Woolacott under the harsh eyes of scrutiny did bring to me some solace of retribution, if but for a moment.

I was led away down a hallway strung with flickering electric lanterns. I was stripped, given soap, and stood under a shower. After, they gave me thin cotton pants and shirt. Only my boots was I allowed to keep of my own few possessions. Then they led me deeper still into the building and placed me in a cell with two other Indians, drunk unconscious on the only pallets.

Woolacott looked in at me through the bars, mouth curled up, savouring. He spoke of how he'd be away back to Alert Bay. "Might not be seeing you for a time," says he before he goes off.

I sat upon the floor, my back against the windowless wall. I put my face in my hands, hoping, I reckon, to shut out that world which I knew now I had no chance, ever, of affecting. It was despair, yes, but also it was shame, embarrassment even, at my own naivety.

HARRY CAME AWAKE, crying out, his fingers splayed in the air before him. He was soaking wet, the wound at his shoulder pounding where he had rolled onto it in his disquiet. The nightmare: the streets of Hong Kong, the plague, walking to the door with the Chinese sign for Joy writ up on it. Waking as his hand reaches out to push that door open. Always the same.

He lay on his back for a while. Then he cursed and swung himself up and out of bed as if the sheets were themselves riddled with pestilence. He pulled the blanket about his body, picked up his tobacco, stole quietly out of the room and down the stairs of the Spencers' house in the darkness. He went through the dining room and out the twin doors to the porch. Outside, he gulped air until his breathing slowed. The night surged above him. Ragged cloud raced across the stars. The moon had already dropped beneath the horizon. The wind blew strong and cold from the north. He rolled a cigarette. He sat on the rocking chair, smoking, his bare legs, with the brash scar running down his left shin, propped up on the porch's railing.

It was five days since George had been taken to Vancouver. Harry had slept away the first two. On the third, the weather had been hot, and the room in the hospital baking, until he had to get out and breathe the freshness of the wind. So he'd made his promises to Trelawney to be careful, and shuffled up and down the beachfront to the cheery insults of the people.

Yesterday, he'd moved his things from the hospital to the Spencers'. Mr. Spencer was terse, but showed concern for his injuries nonetheless. And he did not ask for details on how he had come by them, which was a relief. Annie fed him new bread, butter, fruit, and enough sweet, feminine fussing to make him pine some for his own wife. They said nothing of his father-in-law. It was Charley who'd explained the events of George's arrest. Now Charley was away somewhere. "Go learn story" was all he'd say.

He watched the faint glimmer from the stars on the soft-lapping tide. His breathing had calmed. The images of his nightmare had faded enough so that they no longer plucked at his reason. He knew what lay beyond the door, knew the origin of the nightmare. The memory was terrible. As terrible as anything would ever be. It was shame. It was guilt so overwhelming it sucked him down like a turbulent sea into darkness. Yet now that he had been to the very boundaries of his own death and been saved, he would not turn away from anything before him again.

He strode through Hong Kong that day, that summer of '85—that summer of plague and human folly—strutted through the chaos of the streets, a white man made immune by liquor, opium, and ignorance, and, that day, by the rage of jade-green jealousy. Of what had been in his mind when he pushed his way through that door, he was so blind stupid drunk he wasn't sure he knew now, or even that he had known then.

Into the whorehouse he went, along the dark hallway, and through the heavy velvet curtain at the far end. The room beyond, that he knew so well—and that he would not turn back from viewing now, in his mind's eye, though the sweat sprang up again on his forehead, despite the coldness of the wind—the room beyond was strewn with red and blue silk cushions on the floor, tapestries of courtesans and their lovers on the walls—all of it cheaply rendered, threadworn, stained, tattered. A red lantern in the middle of the room swung slightly as a result of his entrance. Two Chinese girls, scrawny arms, drawn faces, the whites of their eyes made brown by opium addiction, stared up at him without interest. There was no one else there. Even the amah was not to be seen.

The curtain at the back of the room shivered, and then there she was. Fah Wei. Her face was like a ten-year-old's—smooth, a round pimple for a nose—excepting the thick rouge she applied at each cheek until she seemed some child clown. Her hair fell nearly to her waist, tied tight in a plait, a white cheongsam to her knees, her skinny arms bare.

She feigned not seeing him at first, just spoke a word to one of the girls. But, when he advanced upon her, she looked up finally and smiled, the small crinkles at her eyes that showed her disdain, the black mischief of her unconcern. "What fuck you here for now, Harry, neh?" she said.

Harry cursed her, shouted at her. Called her dog, slut, bitch. Raged at her there in the whorehouse on the hill above Hong Kong. Had she transacted a fuck with a man he knew, perhaps, who later boasted the delights of her? He couldn't remember. The imagined slights. The drunken arguments that had no real origin. She drank as much as did he, drowning out the sorrows of her life.

When first he was with her, she snuggled, fucked him with passion, as if new to the game herself. He watched her slenderness when she performed those things he knew were possible from his own childhood in the house where his mother worked. After, she would trill and wash and whistle, tell him, "I like you, not like others," sing to him lewd songs the sailors taught her. He'd laugh right along with her, but each was a reminder of those rough scum, and the rights they also had to her body. He had been years enough at sea by then to know the way of things. He'd rousted enough in port towns. Visited with whores enough. A rope rubs and rubs against a splinter, year on year, until at last it snaps.

Once they had passed their paid time together, he would stay on to drink, sitting in a corner, glowering, the red lantern casting shadows over him, tap-tapping his fingers, eyeing each new visitor with hatred, until the amah would send him away, and Fah Wei would kiss him and whisper, "Not think them, only you." Each time—as now he heard her again in memory—her tone was a little colder. He'd stamp away to some opium trader in the town, mollify the gut-twisting injury of her in the smoke and flickering candlelight, the hoarse monotones of dirt-eyed Chinamen.

He sat on the porch outside the Spencers' home and remembered the last night, saw it like a play in a music hall, him in the front seats—best in the house.

In the whorehouse, she is taunting him. She pulls that narrow blade from her ankle-boot. She points it toward him, and then at her own breast. "This love?" she says. "You, me? You stupid! You love? Buy me. Make me home. That love." She dandles the blade in his face. "Or you fuck off." She pokes his chest with the knife. He feels a button of his shirt pop, sees it fly up between their two faces, hang a moment right at the level of their eyes, like some magic bauble, before it falls away. She laughs, but not with humour—with scorn. He hears the other girls in the room laughing as well.

He pulls the knife from his own belt, that same blade he had levered up into the eye of its previous owner. He can feel again its balance in his hand—feels it still now, though it never left that room.

"Want fight me?" She swings her tiny blade in circles before his face. "Fight me! Little fuck man." Goes down into a fighter's crouch. She slaps the blade against his forearm. It leaves a small welt of blood.

So he swats it from her hand. Then he takes hold of her by the hair, pulls back her head. He thrusts the knife blade down through the side of her neck to pierce the artery. The blood explodes out.

He feels the heat of her blood on his skin, on his face as it covers him, hears the screams of the two girls in the room. Feels the panic in him swell. The instant horror at what he has done, at what it is not possible ever to take back. He cannot hold on to the light as it is fading from her eyes. Cannot keep her from death. Her head lolls now. She is gone.

The smallpox was everywhere in Hong Kong. Debauch and revelry had overtaken the city. He'd been waiting, like all of them, for the first signs of sickness to rise up on his own body. Ships weren't coming in nor going out. It felt as if he was present for the last days of the world.

And then he had run his knife through her throat and watched her life gurgle away. That was all there was. That was the man he was capable of being. She died of his madness.

There was a night, late on a watch, some months later, the months between forgotten now. He hung off the end of a spar, far out over the ocean, a cable's rough fibres under his fingers, gazing into the water as it plunged closer and yawned farther away in the swell. He imagined it sucking him down, away from the anguish of the life fading from her eyes. He willed his fingers to let go of the cable. But he didn't have even the courage for that.

And in killing Poodlas, Harry had shown his own rage still stewed inside him. For the truth was, he could have called out, spoken with the men who had come aboard the *Hesperus*—drunk men, as he had been so often in his life, and with such results. He could have talked the situation to some resolution, instead of being drawn by his anger into violence.

There was a ship's chaplain who saw him leaning out above the ocean in the time after her murder and had the courage and perseverance, where others steered clear of his dead gaze and his swift fury, to force a few words from him. "You can forgive yourself your wrongdoings," the chaplain told him, "but not till you have wholly recognized their gravity." But there was no judging such an act, except in letting his fingers slip from the rope and his body disappear into the ocean. There was only recognition.

He saw again David's rotting head in the box in the forest. He understood George's passions. He had no right to judge what George had done. Harry understood the agony of death. Of horror. "I just seen too much," George had said. This coast had black emotions laid all along it, as did the world.

He rolled the butt of his cigarette around his fingertips until the wind caught up the pieces and drew them swirling away into the night. He arched his damaged shoulder up and round. It cracked and burned. It would not be fully whole again, and there would never be the strength there had been before. But he still had his arm, still had his leg, still had his life. He knew now that there were men of miracles, and he knew his father-in-law was one. Charley had been circumspect on the details of his healing. "George use Indian way and white way," he said. "Clever bastard."

High in the rigging on lookout once, he'd seen a falcon far out over the sea where it should not have been. As it flew down to settle and shiver not ten feet from him, his eyes saw past its ochre body to the first faint shadow of land on the horizon. The falcon turned its head and seemed to follow where he gazed, its black beak a savage silhouette. It called out, harsh, rasping, then shook its feathers and took flight away toward the shadow. He had shouted down to those below, "Land!" and made his shilling for first-sighting.

He leaned forward in the rocking chair and rubbed at his knees, where they had chilled in the wind. He would not add to the list of his sins by deserting these people. By upping and running out on the girl he had taken for his wife. He did not have to keep on saying forever, "Here I am and this is the limit of me!" He did not have to stay the same. He had been dead and had been made alive once more. He could be any man he chose himself to be.

Harry paced back and forth along the cannery jetty, taking his exercise, as Trelawney had warned him that he must. He watched the village fishing boats coming in with the late-afternoon tide, the orange sun behind them. He spoke a few pleasantries to the men and women working on the dock in preparation for the opening of the cannery, in a week's time.

The night before seemed almost a dream in itself now. He'd finally returned to his bed with the first light of dawn, and had not woken again until lunchtime. But he felt rested—rested in a way he could not remember ever having felt before. His wounds ached and itched, but he could give a damn for them. He felt fresh, clean somehow, ready for whatever might come next.

Looking out at the sea, he saw the blunt snout of Indian Agent Halliday's launch coming in behind the fishing fleet. He pulled himself to his feet and hobbled away down the jetty and back along the shore. He passed the women at their labours, sewing nets and drying herring or berries on great rush mats on the beach, or building cooking fires outside their homes in the fair promise of the evening. Many smiled at him, and he raised his hand or spoke a few words by return.

He came to the Indian agent's office at last, down the far end of the village, near to the Spencers'. He levered himself down on the steps out front, and sat there, blowing from his exertions.

Harry had counted back the days since he'd stood on the jetty at Fort Rupert making ready to go find George, and Halliday had voiced his threats. Ten days he had given Harry to find his father-in-law. Ten days exactly it had been to their arrival back in Alert Bay. Yet Halliday must have left for Rupert at least a day prior to that.

He had not long to wait. Soon Halliday came striding down the plankway, a canvas pack on his shoulder and a satchel in one hand, dressed as was his custom in thick black jacket and trousers, grey flannel shirt, and broad black tie, salt stains smeared across them all from his passage on the water.

When he caught sight of who awaited him, Halliday hesitated for a moment. Then he came on in determined fashion. He lifted his hand as he approached in greeting. Harry pulled himself to his feet.

"Back, then?" Halliday said. "And what news have you for me?"

"The news that I kept my end of the bargain. I hear the same cannot be said for you."

Halliday paused at the bottom of the steps. "The men at the jetty tell me you brought George back. And he's away to Vancouver with Woolacott?"

"He is, though he'd been better tried here."

"It warranted a state trial. It was too critical a case for a local court."

"You took the family's property."

"Ten days I said, Harry."

"Aye, ten days exactly was it when we landed back here."

"And ten days exactly was it when I made my confiscation."

"You said to bring him to you."

"And I was waiting in Rupert."

"Damnation, man, I'll not believe you kept your end of things. Where have you taken them?"

"You're quick to choose yourself an Indian, Harry Cadwallader."

"I'm more of them than your damned breed, you fucking liar."

"Hold your temper, man. You will not curse like that to me."

"Cursing ain't enough for it."

"Please!" Halliday put his hand in the air, palm forward, and pointed to two wicker chairs up on the porch. "At least sit. We'll talk properly of what's to be done." Harry held to the steps' rail and felt his head light with emotion. He thought that he might fall. "I see you're far from well," Halliday said, placing his pack and satchel on the lowest step and looking up at Harry. "Tell me what has happened, won't you? I'm just back and know none of the details." He came up the steps and put his hand on Harry's forearm. Harry made to pull away but then allowed himself to be steered to one of the chairs.

"Ten days," Harry said when they were seated. "You gave no leeway."

Halliday linked his hands in front of his face, and tapped his lower lip with his thumbnails. "Unfortunate," he said at last. "I really did expect you back at Rupert. That was, after all, where we parted." He stared into the distance for a while. "There were," he paused, "certain circumstances."

"What are you saying?"

"Woolacott and I had two men with us. But we were only four. We waited a day. But our presence did not go unnoticed, the rumours going round. We'd have been in danger had we not acted when we did."

"You'll forgive my lack of sympathy."

"I'd have you understand, at least."

"So you'll return what's ours?"

Halliday worked his fingers together, as if they were tight from work. Then he ran them through his thick red hair. "You want me to be the enemy of this story. But I'm not, you know. I am most wholeheartedly *for* the Indians."

"Our property, man."

"There are procedures must be followed."

"A devil on your procedures. You're in the wrong and must make things right again."

"It will take time."

"Where, for the love of Christ, have you taken them?"

"Into safekeeping."

"Where?"

"Safe."

"Where safe?"

"Harry, how impolite must I be in saying I'll not tell you?"

"Be fucked with you, Halliday."

"Harry, you're injured, sick, and I understand your ire, but you'll cease your cussing me. I'm Indian agent here. I will have your respect."

"Your agency might be harder to police than priorly."

"Is that a threat?"

"An observation. You make no friends in doing this. Did you not receive my letter through Eddlestone?"

Halliday put his palms together as if in prayer, then placed the tips of his forefingers to his lips. He said, "I did. I confess I was more disquieted than reassured by its substance. In some ways it proved a spur to action. What was this war party to which you made reference?"

Now it was the turn of Harry to pause. The issues with Walewid were now resolved, and Halliday was the last man he wanted knowing the details of what went on out there in the wilds. "About that I was wrong," he said. "Just drunks too liberal with their words. But I wrote we were on George's trail. Could you not have trusted that?"

Halliday said nothing in response to that. Finally, he said, "There's other things we need to talk on too."

"Are there?"

"Your liquor trading, for instance."

"That's over."

"Meaning?"

"I'm through with liquor. It don't do more than serve the interests of those who seek the Indians' destruction. It keeps them slaved and beaten down, doing nothing but drink, when they should be battling to keep what's rightfully their own ways of living." He leaned back in the wicker chair, stopped for the moment by his own eloquence.

"Ways that breed indolence," Halliday said. "Ways that breed subversion to the progress sweeping over this country now. The Indian must change or perish, Harry." He pushed himself to his feet and paced about the porch. "There is great tragedy in the decay of a people's society. George resists, and there is dignity in that resistance. I see that." He turned to look down at Harry, and now his tone came flat and hard. "See it enough to fear it. When George goes visiting banned rituals, he sanctions them. If the people hold to their ways, they will sink in face of the future. They will be without hope. Will you hold back the future? Will George? It is here already, Harry. And rituals of cannibalism and savagery! Do you really think they do anything for the Indian? And what George did was not more than nihilism."

Harry was thrown by that. "What are you talking about?" he said.

"David's funeral. Of what did you think I spoke?"

"But he is arrested for participating in a ritual of the hamatsa, ain't he? What's it to do with the funeral?"

218

"Yes, yes, of course." Halliday was leaning against the porch rail, silhouetted by the low red sun behind. Harry could just about see the man's eyes upon him. "But he made more enemies in doing what he did at David's funeral than ever he did in attending a banned ritual."

"Taking his head?"

"You do not know?"

"I heard that part."

"It is said George ate his dead son's flesh."

Harry felt his face burning with his anger. "Who says this?"

"Were you not there? I thought to question you on this."

"I left. Took the women. Some stayed."

"Well, they are the rumours. All are angry. The white community is quite up in arms."

Harry sputtered. "Is all the world obsessed with cannibals? George is no evil man. He seeks to protect the people."

"Oh come, he exploits them as much as does anyone. He's been piratical in the plundering of this coast."

"The book in't like that."

"Writing for Boas. Paid a wage by Boas. And secret myths and tales he's written that, to the Indians, were not meant for public telling. Oh, I'm sympathetic to Boas, don't get me wrong. Marking down a dying people's culture for posterity. And I understand the placing of historical artefacts into the safekeeping of museums. But don't confuse Hunt's behaviour for nobility in the service of his people. He plies a trade even as do you. Or *did*, I should say, if what you say is true."

"You're wrong." Harry got slowly to his feet. "I'll not believe what you say about him. George did take the head of his son away into the wilderness. That part is true. And I know he would stand up and confess to it. He buried it there in some tradition tied to the ways of his mother's people. This other. I'll hear it from George hisself or I'll call any man what speaks it a liar. And you have taken and hid what's owned by my family. In that you're as piratical as any."

"Harry, go rest. Recover. We'll talk more on this, I promise. How did you come by your injuries?"

"Seeking my father-in-law," he said, and he limped away toward the Spencers' house.

That evening, the white men and women of the village came to dinner at the Spencers'. It was the Reverend Hall's seventieth birthday, so Annie had informed Harry when he returned to the house.

Now Harry sat in the dining room. Places were laid along the table, and a fire roared in the hearth. Halliday arrived before the other guests, and disappeared directly into Spencer's office, deep in conference with the man. When the Indian agent emerged again into the dining room, sombre, trailing the tall, grey-suited frame of Spencer, Harry greeted him with no more than a nod.

There were eleven round the table for dinner, including Harry. Woolacott was back just an hour before off the steamer from Vancouver. He sat near Harry, with the policeman's timid, unspeaking wife between. Dr. Trelawney was there, Mr. Spencer and Annie, and William Halliday, with Maud, his wife, beside him. Directly opposite was Mr. W.A. Corker, headmaster of the residential school, and himself a former missionary, his beak nose high, and never a smile to show from that wintry face. Then there was the Reverend Alfred James Hall, honoured at the far end of the table, with his wife, low and stout and dowdy beside him.

It was the first time Harry had been a part of such company in a formal way. He felt a bit like a foredeck tar invited to the captain's table. So he kept his silence as much as was polite, ate with his mouth closed, and tried not to clatter and scrape his plate with the cutlery.

Once dinner was done, the women removed themselves to the drawing room, while the men remained behind, drinking a whisky that had travelled from Scotland around Cape Horn, and then by way of Victoria to the Spencer household.

"A treat to drink the real stuff," said Albert Trelawney, his melancholy for home writ plain upon his face and in the tone of his words.

"And better than that acid-brewed shite the Indians crave," said Walter Woolacott, and he threw a glance from under his black brows in Harry's direction.

"Well," said Spencer, raising his glass and staring into the whisky's tawny depths. He stood. "A toast, then, with this precious liquid. To the Reverend Hall on his birthday. And to the continuance of his good works among the native population." There were general murmurs of assent and glasses waved. Then Halliday stood.

"Gentlemen," he said. "If you will forgive a more formal moment still. Acting as I do for the Department of Indian Affairs, and so the Dominion Government itself, I take this opportunity to offer my appreciation for, not only the good works of our dear colleague the Reverend Hall, but for those that all who are present this evening perform." Harry guessed there would be some around the table might happily exclude him from such praise. "I propose another toast," said Halliday. "To progress!" More murmurs followed, glasses were waved.

"Come then, Halliday," said Spencer. "What of our progress?"

"You'd know as well as I and better, Stanley," said Halliday.

"But your overview! I don't claim to comprehend the grander forces that are at work." There was irony in his tone. "I simply employ the Indian."

"And procreate with the fuckers too," Harry heard Woolacott mutter, who'd been drinking steadily all evening, though he was far enough along the table for Spencer not to hear.

Halliday frowned at the constable, sitting close by him as he was. He said, "The Indian owned this land before ever we were here. We absorbed his country and called it our own. And we've a promise made to the Indian—and to ourselves, mind you!—that they be treated fair and squarely, with justice. And if there is injustice still—and there is that, I make no bones about it"—he glanced Harry's way as he said it—"still do I believe the schools and the medicine and the imposition of fair laws are bringing that circumstance nearer. There'll be a time when the Indians will have their enfranchisement, and become respected British subjects of the federal dominion of Canada."

"A fair speech, William," said the Reverend Hall, "and political as well."

Halliday smiled thinly. "When they built Fort Rupert, it's said there were three thousand Indians came to live nearby, and today no more than a hundred and twenty left up there. The white man has rained destruction on them. I'm hardly astounded when they resent us."

"So it's our fault, their blasted savage ways?" said Woolacott.

"Yet that is no reason," Halliday went on, ignoring the constable, "not to aid in their improvement. Indeed, our task is only made more earnest by our culpability."

"You'd perhaps to tell my boys that," said the headmaster, "when they stick a knife to themselves and, claiming injury, beg to be returned to their families."

"Adding another to my sick list," said Trelawney, "and it so long already."

"And the girls," said Hall, "sent south to the cities to prostitute for the monies needed for their ceremonies."

"'Tis true the Indian seems to lack that fine feeling we call sentiment," said Halliday.

Harry turned a spoon in his fingers. He wondered what might Annie Spencer's sentiment be to such opinion. At the head of the table, her husband seemed barely to be listening at all.

"Ain't that a bit general?" Harry said.

"I've lived here all my life, Harry," said Halliday. "Forgive me, but your take on matters Indian is scant as yet … and, shall we say, privileged."

"Well, let us speak on a particular matter," said Reverend Hall. "George Hunt is away to Vancouver, and the good constable just returned from taking him there. What news, Mr. Woolacott?"

"He's at the police station awaiting trial."

"A very unfortunate case," said Hall. "I've known him now so many years. His father helped me open my first mission, at Rupert, back in '77." He laughed, his otherwise frail voice rich in its humour. "George was quite the good Christian back then."

"You speak lightly of a serious matter," said Halliday.

"I know he is no friend to you," said Hall. "Believe me, I have argued with him many a time on issues relating to the scriptures, and of its teaching to the red man. But he is a passionate advocate for their rights and their traditions. I respect him, even as I do not agree with what he has to say.

222

Still, I know my colleague Reverend Crosby has not such sympathy on the matter."

"He's a damnable menace," said Woolacott.

"Walter," said Halliday. "Remember in whose house you are."

"Aye," he grunted toward Spencer. "I am sorry for that."

"I'm currently in no mind to disagree," said Spencer.

"Well." The Reverend Hall gazed at nothing in particular as he spoke. "It seems he has truly brought misfortune on himself at last."

"So it's true then that there are cannibal feasts still happening here on the coast?" Trelawney said. His whole body quivered, but his eyes glittered.

"Believe it!" said Corker. "Somewhere out there even now a corpse is being most hideously butchered, and the fire is being laid."

"It seems incredible." Trelawney's bottom lip hung open slightly in his excitement. "Is it every part of the body that is consumed? Do the women and children also partake of such meals?"

"Mainly the men, as I have heard it," said Corker. "Though it would not surprise me to hear they were all participants together in sin."

"Well," said Trelawney. "Really it is remarkable in this modern era to imagine such events continuing!"

"Dirt-worshipping fucking heathens, all of them," said Woolacott.

"Enough, Constable!" said Halliday.

Harry's resentment had been rising as the conversation continued. Now he could hold on no longer, even in such company. "Seems to me it's more that George is subject to conspiracy than that any of these damned insults be true." He gazed about the table in defiance.

Halliday eyed him without expression. Hall looked down at his whisky, and Corker looked as if he was ready to burst, his face near purple. Trelawney shifted in his seat.

"What might you mean by that?" said Woolacott. "If you've accusations, make them plain."

"You're the policeman," Harry said. "It is you that is making the accusations. George a cannibal! If I accuse you of anything, it's stupidity, man."

223

Woolacott eyed him dangerously. But Harry stared right back. Only the vacant chair where Woolacott's wife had been lay between them.

"Yes, yes," said Halliday. He raised his hands to invite calm. "That's quite enough of this, I believe. From both of you—if you will forgive me, Mr. Cadwallader."

"Halliday told me what happened at Rupert with the family's property, Harry," said Spencer. "An unfortunate business. I understand you feel anger about it."

"I'm surprised you ain't feeling it yourself," Harry said, aware he was close to offending his host. "Yet it is made more so by the Indian agent's refusing to tell the whereabouts of them now."

Halliday looked uncomfortable. "If you'll give me time to organize their return," he said.

"I've a better thought," said Harry, and he stood up from his dining chair to look down the table at Halliday. Woolacott, in his place between, still glared black thunder at him. "You tell me where they are, and I'll go fetch them."

"It's not so simple, Harry."

"And why's that? Seems simple enough to me. I've a boat to do it."

"Give me time, is all I ask."

Harry blew air from his lungs and clapped the table with his palm. Trelawney jumped slightly, then half laughed in his nervousness. Harry looked to Spencer. "The two of you discussed the case against George?" he said.

"There's little enough to say," said Spencer.

"Then you'll let him rot, Mr. Spencer?" Harry said. "You'll buy the tale that George travels along the coast, stops off in the villages, chops up dead bodies, fries them up over fires, serves the body parts up for feasting like the beef we supped tonight?" He picked up, for want of other options, a coffee spoon, and threw it down in the middle of the table. "Can it only be me sees the lunacy of this?" All now looked away from him. He stood quietly for a moment. Then he said, "How is he even to make his defence, when he's locked up in Vancouver?"

"Right where he should be," said Woolacott. "Attacking a clergyman!"

"Now we come to the right of it," said Harry. "Pushing Crosby at the funeral is what truly brung all of this about, eh? Not the damned cannibal dances you are all so salivating over." Part of him wanted just to stride straight out the door—through rage, yes, but also for his own gall in standing up like this to these men of substance, in whose midst he found himself but of whom he was not an equal. Instead, he sat once more. He drummed his fingers upon the table.

Halliday sighed. "Not entirely," he said, "though it did prove something of a spur to action, I'll confess it. Assaulting a member of the priesthood in full sight of the whole village! It just could not be allowed to stand."

"So why not charge him with that?" said Harry. "Bring him up before the judge—even if that be you yourself—here in Alert Bay. Be done with it. It was his son's funeral. Crosby came rampaging in. God's truth, I'll stand in his defence and state that there was circumstances mitigating."

Harry gazed about the table, but none would meet his eyes. "Mr. Spencer!" he said, when he could bear it no longer.

Spencer tapped his fingers in uneasy rhythm on the tabletop. "I had a telegraph come from him," he said quietly.

"What? George? When?"

"Yesterday."

"What does it say?"

"That he is awaiting trial, kept in the police station cells. As Woolacott has told us."

"That's it?"

"He wants money for bail. Five hundred dollars." Spencer looked around the table, his chin high, defiant. "But not from me. If he's to play this idiot game, I'll not be a part of it."

The others remained silent.

"Mr. Spencer," Harry said at last. "Sir. With the greatest respect to you—and I apologize for my manner of a moment ago—but, sir, you are married to his sister!"

"I made my position clear to him, Harry, when you were in hospital. That's all there is."

"Mr. Spencer," said Halliday. "If I may." He coughed. "I know that I am, in Harry's eyes at least, somewhat the enemy of this piece. Yet I'd like to say something about George. I've had my battles with the man for some years now. We disagree on many, if not most, issues. If the allegations against him are proven true—and the evidence is compelling—then he must be punished to the full extent of the law."

Harry made to speak but Halliday went on. "However, I do agree with Harry when he says George cannot prepare a proper defence while he remains incarcerated in Vancouver. I do not believe George is a man to up and run. And I'd be much surprised if any round this table thought as much. In posting bail, you'd not be *giving* him money then, since it would be returned on his coming to trial. At least you'd offer him the chance for a fairer hearing."

"You'd lock him up and after support him?" Harry said.

"I'd see things done fairly. Not just for him but for all to know that this were done with due diligence to the law."

"Stanley," said Reverend Hall after a pause, "I must say I believe Mr. Halliday is right. Justice in these matters is important."

Spencer leaned back in his chair, raised his glass to his lips and drained it, then lifted his eyes toward the ceiling and sighed. "Damnation on that man!" He rapped his knuckles on the table for a time. "All right," he said, "I shall front his bail. But nothing more." He leaned back in his chair and put his hands on the top of his head. "Not one penny more. Anything else he might need, he'll have to raise himself. Or, if there be any left along this coast whom he has never wronged, then they can come to his aid. I have a cannery to run and no time nor money more to be spent on that man's foolishness."

The following morning, Harry woke late, sore in his shoulder, but refreshed. Fragments of dreams played strongly still in his mind. The usual images from those dark days in Hong Kong, but mingled with brighter impressions: a seal twisting and diving in sunlit waters, a woman's impish laughter, the fine grain of highly polished wood beneath his fingers.

Over breakfast, Spencer mentioned that this was the first day of cannery production. "You'll have to take your boat out some and moor it away from the jetty, I'm afraid. There'll be a deal of trawler traffic for the next few days."

So he strode down the beach in a brilliant morning. Up on the jetty ahead, he could see Chinamen barking and scurrying, wide-brimmed hats flopping, arms beckoning and gesturing wildly to each other. Spencer brought them in each summer from Victoria, housing them in the dormitory flophouses he'd built farther inland through the trees. Harry had heard them singing their strange tunes in the night, smelled cooking rice and frying chilies, as if the experiences of his previous life had manifested themselves through his dreams into reality.

The cannery boomed loud enough that one might hear its industry many miles away on the water. The hammer of the great log-fuelled steam engine that drove its machines, the gravelling steel slither of the overhead pulley networks trundling the pallets of cans about the building, and the multitudinous noises of two hundred and fifty men and women at their work.

A large trawler was just unloading. He stopped to watch, some yards from the stairs leading up from the beach to the jetty. The Japaner crew were spearing the fish carcasses up from the hold with long, steel-tipped poles. They hurled them down to be collected on low handcarts by the gang of Chinese labourers on the jetty. Harry saw by their taciturnity that there was little love lost between the two groups.

He sat on a boulder. He picked up a sea-smoothed piece of wood and poked absently at the stones by his feet. The previous evening, once the others had left, Annie had come to talk with him. She'd told him George would need several hundred dollars more to pay for a lawyer. Five hundred she'd said as a minimum, and she didn't see that her husband would be persuaded to help further. And she had told him that Halliday and Spencer had spoken on the family treasures. They were, she said, currently housed with a Dr. Newcombe—a friend of Professor Boas—down in Victoria. "But you must not speak of it to anyone as yet," she said. "Please. Let us see my brother's trial to its conclusion first. Then we will deal with whatever comes after." So he promised her his silence, if yet he vowed to himself that he would be down to Victoria himself, once all was settled, and bring them back himself.

"Fat Harry!" He looked up to see Charley waddling toward him on his bandy legs, the great hump on his back rolling like some top-heavy boat in a swell.

"Where've you popped up from?" Harry said.

"Go find man come to trial help George. Witness."

"And?"

Charley flopped down on the ground in front of Harry. He shrugged. "None help."

"Then he'll need a good lawyer."

Charley grunted. "No money," he said, but he looked keenly at Harry as he spoke. Harry did not meet his eyes, prodding still with his stick.

After a time, Harry said, "I know it. But I'd hoped I were done with all that."

"Help George. Not help George. For you think. You still have plan leave coast, leave wife, go away, not come back?"

Harry glanced up, startled. Charley was smiling. Harry made to speak, but stopped himself. He stared out toward the ocean. Charley shifted round to stare out with him into the freshening breeze. The cannery thundered about them.

Abruptly, Harry stood. "Get yourself ready," he said.

"Ek." Charley reached out and patted him on the leg.

Harry climbed the stairs onto the jetty. Among the workers, he spied a native man he recognized, Tom Copperhand, sober for once and working with the Chinamen. "Where's your father?" Harry called above the racket.

Tom pointed away toward the storehouse out back of the cannery.

Harry turned in that direction. Worst of all was the rotting saline stink of the gut holes beneath the jetty, storage pits where the fish butcherers threw down the skin and fins and offal to be taken out to sea and dumped. The stench lent the whole place, with the sun pouring hot upon it, a feeling of Hell itself.

Dan Copperhand was squeezed between two stacks of crates that rose fifteen feet toward the cannery storehouse's cobweb-heavy ceiling. In one hand he held a sheaf of paperwork, a pencil stub in the other. He peered short-sightedly up at a label that hung, half peeling, from a crate above. He wore high rubber boots to his thigh with suspenders over his shoulders to hold them up, but no shirt covered his aged brown torso. His sagging belly crushed up against the boxes in front.

Dust drifted down where he had disturbed the storeroom's quiet equilibrium. He sneezed and spat words in Kwakwala that Harry guessed to be curses.

"Yoh," Harry said.

Dan twisted his head to look at him. "Fat Harry." He inched his way out and stood shaking the dust from his shaggy grey hair. "Come out, let's smoke."

They sat together in the sunlight on a crate. Harry passed Dan his tobacco, and together they rolled and smoked, hawked and spat between the planks to the beach below.

"Summer's up and running, then," said Harry.

"Money for Spencer to be making."

"Oh, you'll find ways to scratch a penny or two from the season, Dan Copperhand." Harry smiled. He knew Dan from the past months running the family store. The man was always useful if something particular was needed. "Contact all over place," Grace said of him. The wealthiest Indian on the coast, as others put it, most of them grumbling, envious, as they did so.

Dan just grunted. "What about old George?" he said.

"He's to stand trial."

"He's all the white men ranged against him," Dan said. "So I hears it."

"You heard it right."

Dan nodded, slow and sombre. "Needs money for trials," he said.

"True."

"You here."

"I am."

229

"I got to do something about that damned bastard Chief Bear Killer. Pay him back for his feast somehows."

Harry had heard Dan's beef before. How Chief Bear Killer had given Dan a huge feast. How he'd shamed Dan with his largesse. How Dan now owed him by return a feast twice as grand. "I understand," Harry said.

"Need to give that man a big feast. Big whisky feast. Make him drink so much his stomach fall out on the ground."

"You need whisky."

"Good whisky."

"I can get it for you."

"Good, cheap whisky."

"Whisky's whisky. Cheap whisky's no more than bad alcohol mixed with bad things."

Dan snorted. They sat again in silence for a while. They had had this conversation before, but Harry had not the supplies to offer him.

Now he said, "I need money for George."

Dan rolled the last of his cigarette between his fingers. The ash fell to the planks and was blown softly away by the strengthening breeze.

"Got to make it now," said Harry.

"Good, cheap whisky," said Dan.

"How much you need?"

"Make his stomach fall out on the ground," said Dan.

They talked details and a rendezvous. Harry said he needed half the money up front. Dan went off and came back with three hundred and fifty dollars. "Family money we all save to make feast," he said. "Don't lose, or you see me in gravebox next time." Harry folded it and placed it in an inside pocket. Then they sat once more, smoked and watched the men at their labours. A westerly blew strong now against Harry's route out of the harbour.

"Guess you gonna need you engine," said Dan.

"Once out the harbour I'll be good."

"How long you gone?"

"If this wind holds, I should be back in six days or so."

Dan poked with his pencil stub at the crate on which they were sitting. "Fifty thousand cans to fill for shipment to England," he said. "When I was young, I didn't know there could be such a number of anything."

A great explosion of steam erupted from the outlet pipe to one side of the cannery, as a retortman released the pressure from an oven. They watched the cloud billow out and up and swiftly dissipate against the indigo sky.

"Whole different world," said Harry.

Dan leaned forward and spat. "I hears that," he said.

As Harry walked back along the shore, the Indian he had seen back at Rupert with Crosby and Halliday stepped out from behind a building. To-Cop. The man was dressed in a stiff, black jacket with a white cravat at his neck. His bowl-cut hair flapped up in the breeze. His black eyes gleamed sharp beneath.

"Heading out?" the man said.

"It may be," said Harry.

"North to Rupert?"

"Maybe."

"You're friendly with Dan Copperhand, then?"

"You've a keen nose for my business."

To-Cop just smiled. "Well," he said, "a safe trip." He walked away into the trees behind the village. Harry watched him go.

Charley threw Harry the mooring line and leapt over onto the deck. He pushed against the jetty piling and the *Hesperus* turned its nose away from the shore.

The engine made slow revolutions. Harry engaged the flywheel and felt the hull's familiar shudder and then the propeller's traction in the water. The *Hesperus* eased away from the jetty, past the Japanese fishing trawler. Harry turned and raised his hand.

Dan Copperhand was perched now on top of a piling, staring after them. He lifted a hand in return. "Don't sink, Fat Harry," he called. "Don't let them guv'ment gunboats take you."

"I'll do my damnedest."

"Come home safe."

He took the *Hesperus* out of the harbour. The day's brilliance near blinded him, so that he had to squint against it. Far off, the mountains of the mainland held still some trace of snow at their peaks, and the myriad greens of the forests streaming down into the fjords and rivers. The sun played summer dances on the rippling sea. Vancouver Island stretched away north and south a mile ahead, its own mountainous spine spearing up against the western sky. Two dolphins leapt together, some hundred yards off his port side.

Charley sat, silent, at the prow. He wondered if he ought to tell Charley what Annie had said about the family's treasures, Dr. Newcombe, and Victoria. But he had promised her his silence. So he cut the engine and together they raised sail. With the wind strong on the starboard quarter, they turned south. The *Hesperus* listed, and he ran his hand in the foam until it spat and flew up to coat his face with its cool touch. He thought he'd never felt such joy before.

EACH EVENING I DID BEAR WITNESS to the cells' passing business: drunk sailors and lumbermen mostly, bleeding, either viperous or sotted too stupid to resist. Once, they brung in a gaudy-suited white man, bright broad cravat and cummerbund, roaring bloody thunder with his three doxies in tow. One of them was an Indian girl and Kwagiulth by her face, rouged and primped, not thirteen years old. They led her on past with the other whores towards the women's cells, leaving her pimp to strut amongst us, cocklike, till at last he hunkered down on the floor with the others and grew quiet in the tedium of it.

All of them was transient visitors, excepting me. "No point sending you on to New Westminster," as the one-arm jailer, John Clough, spoke it, "only to bring you straight back again for trying."

An age or else no time at all it was in there, till my mind was froze, like I was being held in purgatory, twixt one world and the next, with nothing to do but suffer the endless seconds till fate did bring its next piece of mischief for me.

At last, one morning, John Clough came to fetch me. "There's one to see you," says he.

"Who's that?" says I, but he just flicked the keychain from off his belt, spun it expertly to the right key with his one hand, and turned it in the lock. I come out and perched on the bench along the wall opposite. Four other cells there was and men in all of them, white or Indian, and even a Chinaman, wire thin and staring at me deadpan as the others mostly snored. Clough's young mate came forward and knelt to put shackles at my ankles and my wrists. I was shuffled out the door and along the building's middle corridor beyond.

We got before another door. "Top barrister, he be," says Clough. "You'll watch your words with him. None a your fucking red man surls, d'you hear me?"

The man inside the door greeted me polite enough. He told me he was William Bowser, defence attorney. I leaned forward, heavy in chains, to take his hand. I felt powerfully the imbalance of our positions. He dismissed John Clough, who went out muttering on the need for wariness when in such dubious company as myself.

Bowser was a grand-looking gentleman, plump, red faced, in his forties as I reckoned, smart dressed in a black suit and a bowler hat that lay beside his papers on the table. "Mr. Spencer at Alert Bay has instructed me to arrange your bail," he says. "He is your brother-in-law?"

"He is," says I. "Though I'd not expected his help."

He tells me he has been reading my charges and finds hisself rightly interested. "I've not seen its like before," says he. "Indeed, I don't believe such a case has ever come before the courts." They were making of me a test case, as he saw it.

Well, I just grunted at that. They was all against me, as I already knew it.

"Which gives me some hope," he goes on. "All will depend on the quality of the witnesses."

I saw there was creases of good humour beside his eyes, which met mine without compunction. He mentioned the condition of my injured eye. It had not yet been tended to since Rupert, though I had given it little thought. It didn't seem like something to be worrying on with all else against me as it was. It had closed up, scabbed and dried, but a thin white fluid came out of it and down my face at times. Scandalous, he reckoned it, and told me he would have a physician sent for smartly. Then he asked me what I thought my defence might be.

I had been pondering precisely that, of course, this time behind the bars. But in that moment it seemed I had nothing to say, or else I had too much, and all I could do by way of reply was clasp my hands together and rock back and forth on that chair like a retard.

Bowser was watching me with his beady grey eyes. "So," he says at last, "regarding bail. I must enter a plea of not guilty, or one of guilty with mitigating circumstance. Pleading guilty would lead to your more immediate sentencing. Mr. Hunt, what will it be?"

"What plea should I make?" I asks him.

It wouldn't be professionally appropriate for him to lead me in such a fashion, however. "I suggest," he says, one eyebrow arching up, ironical, "you ask yourself if you are guilty of the charges laid against you."

"Guilty of eating the flesh of a human corpse?" says I.

"And of participating in a ceremony banned under Canadian law," says he.

"'Tis true I was there," says I. He asks if I played a role, and I tell him just by being there I played a part.

"The issue of most import will be whether you partook in the mutilation of the corpse," says he.

"It is the ways of the people at such a ceremony that a corpse be cut up," says I, leaning forward to rest my manacled fists on the desk. "Since the first days of time has it been so. I will not deny the ways of the people for no man nor white judge and jury what may be seeking my ill and those of the people."

Bowser did not speak for some while after that. Then, says he, "You are the son of a white father and a native mother?"

"I am," says I.

"And you've chosen your affiliations as being with the bloodline of your mother?" says he.

I looked for sarcasm in his face, but there weren't none to be seen. "If there's brown in your blood, then that's forever how it is," I tell him. "Don't matter what I'd choose for myself, the world will always see it so."

"But where does that leave you in relation to the charges?" he asks me.

"I'd not recognize their legality," says I, and thought that sounded nearer the truth than anything I'd yet said on the matter.

"I fear the bench won't likely be prepared to hear such an argument," says Bowser.

"That may be so," says I, "but there it is."

"I must confess to you I find the details of the ritual somewhat, ah, distasteful, as they have been written down. Such would be similar for the jury as well, I suspect. Yet," he goes on, "I have seen much of the certainties of men, and how such certainties may serve to do no more than oppress the lives of others. So it is I find myself in sympathy with you."

235

Nonetheless, as it stood I was on my way to prison. Might be six months or several years. It was an untested law, so there weren't much by way of precedent. "I question what purpose the position you are making for yourself will serve," he says, sounding much like Spencer had. "What will it change? Whose life will it change for the better? Who will listen?"

I tell him I had hoped to be tried in Alert Bay, and to have spoke my case there among the people. My people. "But if it's here I must speak my piece, then so be it," I tells him. And the truth of it is I had come to the conclusion that I was done for anyhows. That being so, I'd damn well say what I had to say to whoever was there to hear me.

"Well you have not given me much to use, Mr. Hunt," says he and suggests maybe I should plead innocent for now, whilst bail was posted. "That at least will give you an opportunity to go home and give some thought to the matter. Perhaps your family may have opinions to offer." He tells me I can change my plea at a later date, though it might result in a longer sentence.

"I've not money to pay you any further, Mr. Bowser," I tell him.

"I'll not work for nothing," says he, "but it's a case I am keen to be involved with. You must understand there are expenses that must be born in any trial." Anyhow, he says, we'd discuss it later, once I had made my bail.

Then off he goes and I was left alone. Dust swirled about in the sunlight what flowed in through the only window, high up on one wall. I found myself remembering a shoal of herring I had fished one day. They was being worried at by seals till they spun about, reflecting in the sunbeams so that they seemed a rainbow whirlpool stretching down into the deeps. I flung out my net and drew in hundreds, even as porpoises twisted now amongst them, and killer whales coming last to herd and swing about and throw their tails, so that the stunned herring was hurled up into the air. Seagulls dived and scooped them up. The sun flicked off their scales until it looked as if I was amidst a world of rainbows and diamonds, and me but a tiny part of that great, glorious massacre.

I thought on how alive and young and brim-filled with the murderous joy of it I'd been. I realized that there was patterns in the world. The dust swirling and the herring doing similar. Science it is, such thinking. But it is religion as well.

Then John Clough came to lead me, shuffling in my chains, back to the cells.

I'll not dwell on those days I spent in jail. Eventually I was up before the judge. Bowser managed to talk me out of getting up right then and there to speak my mind. So instead I held my tongue tight for the time being, and I was bailed to return in just fifteen days. I had to borrow money off Bowser for my fare home.

"He's a tough old fish, this judge," Bowser says to me outside the courthouse. "I would not trust to clemency, should you switch your plea to guilty. Get yourself home, Mr. Hunt, and talk to your family. I can't think they will want you languishing in prison over some ill-thought-through— and ill-placed—desire to make a statement."

He reckoned I'd need some hundreds of dollars for his fees, for transporting witnesses and the like. I says I wasn't likely to find such an amount. "Then you'll go to prison, Mr. Hunt," says he, grim faced like a judge hisself. And so we parted.

I stood there for some time after he'd gone. Choices must be made, but I had not the wherewithal to make them. My freedom weighed heavy after the many days of my captivity. Even to raise my head so that I might see again the huge, violet plumes of smoke away above the buildings, which showed where was the port—even such tiny motions of will felt hard beyond all measuring. Something was wrong with everything—with my thinking, with my place in things. But I was without the words I needed to give it name.

I gathered myself and crossed the road to sit upon steps leading down from a covered boardwalk.

It was late morning. The streets roared all about me. Yet I did feel cocooned, like when I was a child and we'd play in the snow, burying each other under the drifts, with only our eyes and noses showing, until the sounds came like echoes from elsewhere. All was far away, and the city no more than some but dimly recalled dream place of evil intent.

Someone spoke then, saying, "Do you need something, friend?" I turned to see a man in a tall hat and black longcoat stood before a shopfront that I saw was a undertaker's. I shook my head. "Well, there's dosshouses aplenty in Gastown," the man says, pointing away along the street.

I had washed my clothes the night before, where I'd been given them back to wear before the judge. But I still made a sorry spectacle and knew it: boots, scruff trousers, and a weathered shirt of no determinate colour, without a jacket. A mismatching tie which Bowser'd brought me to wear. Over my bad eye was a new patch the physician, what had come to examine it in the cells, had given me. He cleaned it up, but he didn't think I'd see again through it, though he said that miracles had happened in the past and, no doubt, must happen more in times before us.

I rose from the steps, and stepped out into the traffic towards the docks and home. Luck favoured me, and there was a vessel steaming north that afternoon. I'd half fancied I might finish up aboard the *Comox* once more, and old Eddlestone cursing me all the way to Alert Bay. But such was not the case. Instead, I'd ship with the *Coquitlam*.

I bought half a chicken and a hard-packed ball of rice from a skinny Chinaman with a barrow. I watched as he silently took the abuse of his race from the stevedores he served. I thought, he ain't so dissimilar to the Indian. Brownskin, second-rate human being.

I perched on an iron mooring post beside the water, pulling half-heartedly at the chicken, and fingering the rice apart, to fall into the water, the fish rolling over each other to snatch and gulp amidst the city's garbage bumping there. I watched the steam tugs out in the bay, hauling and butting the lumber towards its final end in the city's sawmills.

I saw as well the arrival of the cruise ship the *Empress of India*, its whistle reverberating around the great bay, its glittering figurehead, its long bowsprits and sloping masts, the slim bows and the overhanging stern so majestic, looming over me like a glacier, and all the people calling out from its decks, the throngs gathering on the shore in their finest costumes, till it seemed the entire city must have turned out to witness its arrival and to celebrate their success in luring such munificence off the world's oceans.

I was bustled and cursed out of the way by a stevedore, so that the huge cables could be drawn in with longshore poles and coiled about the mooring posts, one of which I had been sitting upon. I watched the new arrivals from across the Pacific as they poured down the gangplanks to fill yet more the multiplying city.

When at last it came time to board the *Coquitlam*, I lay down under the awning and was immediately asleep. I believe I curled up into a ball upon the planking like some lost cub.

I was three days aboard, the steamer stopping at all its possible ports en route. The money from Bowser was finished. I went hungry, till the lumberman berthed on deck beside me, high in drink and not put off by my silence, brought enough back for the both of us from where he'd hopped ashore at Nanaimo.

His name was Jack Crabb, out of Evansville, Indiana—"not never looking back"—short three fingers of his right hand after a chain snipped them away, hauling a redwood near Bella Coola. I ate the dried salmon and bread, but refused his offer of liquor. Crabb slapped me on the back and says, "Half my insides is tore out from this shite, spitting blood in mornings. You done right avoiding it.

"Thought myself pauce of luck, I did," he goes on, "till I sees you. Pardon me for mentioning, but you is a sorry-looking sleeping Jesus, and I ain't lying."

I had no words for him, though it didn't seem to bother him none. He burrowed in his pack and drew out a ratty Bay blanket, which he placed across my shoulders. I was near blue with cold from the night before, though I didn't realize it till after I was so cosseted.

We sat then in silence together, watching the two dolphins what danced and leapt in the steamer's wake.

"Still, there ain't much you need to get along," Crabb pipes up at last. "And as to what sort of a man you is: well I seen men say 'Yes!' to a question about theyselves and 'No!' to the selfsame question the following day— and believe both answers as if they was speaking from their very souls.

What manner of a man you is ain't more than a matter of what situation you finds yourself in, day by day by day. And that be the truth, amen."

I stepped back onto the cannery jetty at Alert Bay twelve days after I had left it in custody of Woolacott. Eyes followed me along the front till I stood before the greathouse of my dead son, David, what is halfway along the beach. Whispers must have gone ahead, for Abayah was waiting on me at the entrance. She drew me inside, holding hard to my arms.

We spoke but little. I was overcome and hardly able to walk the few steps to a bed and fall down upon it, before I was asleep. She was by my side when I awoke, her two children owl-eyed behind her. As she prepared food, I took them on my lap beside the fire and spoke a few words in answer to their queries on the speed at which the embers burned, the poor state of my beard, what was under my patch, and when their father was planning on coming back—which finality was more than yet they was able to grasp.

Later, rested up, bathed, and dressed in David's clothes, I stood outside Spencer's door. In truth I did hesitate before knocking. I'd seen my brother-in-law earlier through the open doorway at Abayah's, stopping a moment as he passed by to peer inside, grim faced. I guessed those who'd seen me on the jetty would have told him of my arrival. Of what might be in his mind, however, I did not know.

Annie answered the door. "You've a hollow look to you, brother," says she, and tells me I must eat with them.

"Better see your husband first," I says, and she nodded, sombre, directing me towards the dining room.

Spencer had his back to the fire in the grate. He was nursing a brandy glass. "Will you have one?" he says, and I tell him perhaps I will. We watched the bustle of the flames for a time. "You made bail, then," he says, and I thank him for it. "Though I was navigated into it," he goes on. "If you will believe it, you've Halliday to thank, and the Reverend Hall." At that I was greatly surprised. Strange enemies indeed! "And Harry spoke quite vehemently on your behalf, so he did. I don't mind telling you I'd not at first been minded to help."

"Anyway," I says, "my thanks."

He asks me what the lawyer said to me and what I planned on doing next. So I tell him the lawyer reckoned the case was pretty strong against me.

"Yet you pleaded not guilty?" says he.

I tell him I did, but was considering changing my plea when I came to trial. He wanted to know how long I'd be in prison then, and I says there ain't no precedent to tell me.

"You'd plead guilty to cannibalism and heathen practices?" he asks me.

"I may," says I.

"Then I'll not aid you further," he says, near boiling with his rage again. "You've brought disgrace on your family." He tramped outside, but, a moment later, he was back. "And I'll trouble you to know I expect to see my money back," he says. "You'll not run for the forest."

I assured him I wasn't planning to.

"Go see your sister," says he. "Mayhap she can talk some sense into you."

So I sat with my sister at the kitchen table, those two women as helps about the house behind us. I could feel their eyes upon me.

"Your husband's full of fury at me," I tell Annie. "Though I don't blame him for it."

"You have made a fool of yourself," she says, "and of us."

"I've not money," I says, "even should I wish to defend myself. And the family treasures taken." I told her how the lawyer had quoted several hundred dollars as the least amount I'd need.

"Stanley won't help you," she says. "Not again."

"Perhaps I'm right for prison," I says.

"Perhaps you are," says she.

I left the house before dinner was ready and walked out on the beach, slippery with seaweed in the ebb tide. The clouds were breaking in the strong northwesterly what was blowing, and the stars came and went in bursts. It was dangerous, and dark without a moon.

I heard a seal call, probably from that rock offshore that only shows itself when the tide is low. More than one boat's had its guts ripped out by that sharp granite.

Then a voice says, "Seals calling you home?" and Halliday was beside me.

"I'm of the killer whales," I tell him.

"I sometimes wonder if you're not truly of the seal folk, though. They come ashore on nights like this, do they not, to cause mischief among the people." He laughed, soft, but I didn't hear no malice in it. "Truth is," he says, "I'm glad to see you back, George."

"Oh?" says I.

"Means bail was made and you've a chance to defend yourself."

"I heard you argued my case to Spencer. I thought you'd rather have me shackled."

"I do think you're bad trouble, George, I won't deny it. But that's no reason for you not to see a fair trial."

"As long as prison's at the end of it," says I.

But he reckoned the trial was more important than the outcome, giving chance for questions to be raised in public discourse on the way of things. "But, George," he goes on, "I find, despite myself, that I like you. Always have done. You've passion for the welfare of the Indian. I admire your sentiment. It's just you are misguided in what you believe is best for their survival."

"And my going to jail will help you prove it?" says I.

But, says he, hanging to the old ways does nothing but cut off the Indian further from the fruits of progress.

"So you'd tear out the Indian soul to safeguard it?" says I.

"What you call a soul I call but society," says he. "And society must move with the times. I'm more interested in the Indian body, which must be fed, must work for its survival, must become a part of the larger body of Canada."

"I'd see Canada recognize those what was here first."

But the country has moved too far for that, says he, and I saw he was much moved. "Damnit, George, I am familiar with the injustice. But this is the reality. Old ways fall behind and are lost."

"Old they may be," says I, "but they're also who we are. They're what we have left against despair."

"You say 'we,' George, but look at you! Your sister's married to the wealthiest white man in the area. Your father was factor to the Company, and you're employed by famous scientists from the great universities of America! You are a success, man. Gods, you're also Indian aristocracy, if you'd have it that way round. You're an Indian success!" He paused to catch his breath then. I had no words to speak to him, for my mind was a-spin at what he said.

"Chieftains and medicine men and berry gathering!" Halliday goes on. "Do you think the world has time for such things? The Indian has to accept what is happening around him."

I was quiet then. I was just back from the city, after all. I had seen the future. It was true.

"I must be back to my wife," I says at last. And I realized that was about all I wanted at that moment. Old Francine beside me.

"We've convincing witnesses, George," says Halliday. "Convincing evidence. You'll not get off these charges. Yes, go home. See what's there. Look on the poverty, the loss, the misery. Ask yourself if this is what you wish for your people."

"What of my family's property?"

"They'll be returned in time," says he. I ask him where they are, but all he'll say is "Safe," even when I press him on it till I am quite irate.

"Damn you, Halliday," I tell him.

"No," says he, "damn you, Hunt! Damn you for not seeing the truth. Damn you for not being the advocate for change you might have been. You think you stand for your people. Instead you stand for their doom." And he turned away and walked off along the beach into the darkness.

I heard him stop after some yards. "One other thing," says he. "Do not think I am unaware of what it is that Charley and Harry are up to."

"What's that?" I says, baffled. But he was gone.

I spent a wretched night. Halliday's words plagued me and I didn't know that he weren't right in all he'd said. I asked Annie where Harry and Charley had gone, but she told me they were away back to Rupert.

The next morning I hitched a ride north on a fishing boat skippered by a cousin of mine, who made show of keeping busy through the voyage, without no time for conversation.

The crew were mostly Japaners, with three Kwagiulths who also kept clear of me, muttering together and one joking loud enough for me to hear the white word *cannibal*, with low laughs to follow. I sat brooding at the prow, wondering at myself, at who I was. My great plan, boosted so in my healing of Harry, to be the voice of the people. It all seemed, then, the very depths of foolishness. I'd no money to help myself even should I wish to hope. Vancouver had put paid to all such fantasies I might have had of making a defence what justified the ways of the Kwagiulth.

Anyways, the tide was full at Rupert. The boat left me right on the jetty. I stood for a time out there, taking in the details of my home. It weren't no more than a month since I had left for Teguxste. That so short a time had passed seem scarce credible.

The sun broke through the clouds and the roofs did glisten then with dew water. I smelled first the salt wind and the sweet seaweed. But, after, I smelled the reek of the middens what are strewn so casual behind the houses. I saw the dogs scrawning amongst them, sores on their bodies, bickering over fish heads. Three of the children ran naked along the plankway, their bodies soiled, their hair in cankerous braids. Old man Moody was squatting on the beach, oozing soft shit onto the stones.

Halliday's words kept at me till I wondered if I might be better just waiting for the next boat to moor up, stepping onto its deck, and never coming back.

But in the end I walked shorewards and along till I stood outside my home. I looked on my ancestry what is written on the great pole there. The paint is chipped and weathered now already, though it ain't been up so many years. It seemed then as if it didn't have no import, mouldering relict of a dead-end time, like a rabbit born with three legs that has somehow lasted to maturity, till, at last, a wolverine does bury fangs into its neck to bring about its rightful end. So the white fangs at our necks. Fangs made out of engines, great ships on the oceans, streetcars, libraries of books, museums. But even as I thought those things, they shamed me out of words, so that I hung my head as I stepped inside.

Old Francine was sitting by the fire. Her eyes came wide at the sight of me. Then she waddled over and gripped my forearms so tightly. "Devil's back," she said. Her fingers ran across the patch upon my eye. "You're no more than trouble to me," says she, and I believed it, though she gripped me harder as she spoke the words.

THE ENGINE PUTTERED SOFTLY, keeping the boat's position steady on the faint swell. Across a half mile of black water, just a few lights still showed at Alert Bay. It was late. By the height of the stars Harry reckoned it close to midnight. Soon, then. He watched the shore. Charley murmured slow litanies to himself, a monotonous dirge beyond comprehending.

They had made swift progress south and west down the Queen Charlotte Strait, past Malcolm Island and into Johnstone Strait. This was as far north as Harry had travelled in past trips trading whisky, before he'd come farther last October to land up in Rupert. They'd passed Campbell River at the south end of Discovery Passage. Charley had raised his hand and hailed those he knew so many times in the canoes they passed that Harry wondered if there was anyone at all along the coast was not acquainted with the old cripple. The wind kept strong off the starboard quarter as they sailed right down the middle of the Strait of Georgia. So strong, the *Hesperus* listed, the mast creaking, sails cracking like rifle shots at every small adjustment. The town of Comox was an orange glimmer against darkness the second night, as they travelled on, taking turns to sleep. The following morning, Nanaimo and Gabriola Island were hardly visible away to the south as they rounded Lasqueth Island and turned east.

Charley told him how he'd been to visit the village where the ritual for which George was accused had happened. But there were none there willing to speak for George. Word had come to the village that he had blackened the good name of the people with his son's funeral. Even the chief, whose name was Big Mountain, had refused point-blank to honour his long affiliation with George's family.

"I have big secret 'bout him. I say will tell all people," Charley told Harry. "Still, he don't want help."

"You've secrets on us all, have you not?" Harry said, recalling how Charley'd been on to his plan to leave Rupert and be gone.

"Not secret strong make chief come help."

246

Charley told him To-Cop had been present at the ritual as well. In what position, Charley would not say. But when Harry spoke of his encounter with the man at Alert Bay, just as they were leaving, Charley shook his head. "Bad. Watch that fuck man. Make trouble sure."

"But who is he?"

"Bad man from bad paxala family. But he go priest school. Bad twice now."

After that, they barely spoke the whole way. The westerly gusted ever stronger, if never quite turning to a gale, Harry at the tiller, Charley seeing to the sails on Harry's orders, unable as he was himself to do much with his one good arm, the other still in its sling, and likely halfway to crippled for good. But the landscape exhilarated him in a way he could not recall ever feeling before. The vast inlets of the mainland, the great snow-tipped mountains in the far distance, both on the mainland and west on Vancouver Island, the jade green of the forests plunging down the sharp hillsides to the water's edge. They saw pods of killer whales. On a granite outcrop, seals barked and bustled like dowdy madams at the market.

They made it to New Westminster in three days. Harry's man in that busy port town was a foreman with the stevedores. Through three short hours of an evening, they traded and put aboard the cargo. "Not blue vitriol, nitric acid, nor jack else evil, guaranteed as always," the man promised. Harry tasted a keg to be certain anyway.

The trip back went as smoothly, the same strong wind serving them equally well for both legs of the trip. They kept alert for signs of the government gunboats, which plied the waters all up and down the coast searching for such as they. Charley cackled to himself a few times en route. "Smuggling good business," he said. "Me you. Big future."

Harry had few thoughts of the future any more. "I'll be happy enough just to be back at Rupert," he said.

Grace. It seemed incredible to him now that all that time of his desire to be away, he'd barely given thought to her. Here was a gift the world had offered up, and him too blind to see it given.

And Charley had known all along of Harry's plans to be away. Had George?

Well, here was Harry now, bobbing on the water a mile offshore in the darkness, waiting on a sign from Dan Copperhand. Harry Cadwallader: a man full capable of standing up and doing what was right. Though it was strange, sure enough, that doing right meant doing the very thing he had decided was wrong. Fifty kegs of whisky in his hold. Halliday would drool if he knew what was floating out here at this moment.

A light came on near the cannery. It winked on and off, then twice more.

"There it is," Harry said. He uncovered his own lamp and repeated the signal. He watched the light flash twice in acknowledgment before it was extinguished.

Twenty minutes later, they lay some four hundred yards off the southeast corner of the island. Harry killed the engine and let the anchor drop down through the shallow water.

They heard the engine of Dan's swift ketch shortly after. Harry showed his lamp again, since thicker clouds had now drawn over the new moon and the night was blacker than a bucket of tar.

"Yoh," Dan called, and threw across a rope. Charley caught it, and Dan drew alongside. Harry heard his engine disengage, but remain idling. "Good trip?" Dan spoke softly now.

"No gunboats, storms, or leviathans, praise be."

Charley spoke a few quiet words in Kwakwala and Harry thought he heard the name To-Cop mentioned. Dan, who had stepped across the joined gunnels, spoke quickly in return.

"What is it you're saying?" Harry looked to them both.

"Ask if To-Cop stay Alert Bay," said Charley.

"I seen him a few times down by the jetty," Dan said. "Charley here thinks he's spy to Halliday and Woolacott."

"Let's be done with our business as soon as may be." Harry lifted the trap door to the hold and swung the lamp he held inside.

Dan peered down. "There is a sight!" he said, eyeing the kegs. "Pay back that cocksucker chief double." He fumbled in the chest pocket of his shirt and drew out a wad of money. He leered and winked as he handed it to

Harry. "Bring George home early, eh?" Harry pocketed the money and leapt down into the hold.

He hefted the kegs up through the trap door, although it was tough work with his bad arm. He had to lever them up with one hand and his knee, one keg on top of another, and Charley reaching down, lifting them and handing them across to Dan, who'd removed himself back aboard his own boat.

They'd been at this for some time, and near three-quarters of the whisky had made its journey aboard Dan's ketch, when Charley stopped, leaving Harry perched with a keg on one shoulder as his method had improved. When Harry made to complain, the old Indian raised his hand for silence. "Listen," he said.

Harry eased the keg down and raised his head outside to hear. He heard the slither of water along the hull, the wind drawing lightly at the furled sails, the drone of Dan's engine idling, the clink of the anchor chain as it moved against the cleats. Then he heard it: another engine, turning slow revolutions yet insistent, closing, not far off. A smaller vessel's engine, much like his own. There were only three small boats with engines in the area, and two of them were moored right here. The other was Halliday's.

"Sweet fuck." Harry drew himself out of the hold, in time to see Dan hack with a machete at the rope that linked their boats together, even as he was engaging his engine. It roared life beside them, larger, faster than that of the *Hesperus*.

"I go now," said Dan, as his ketch moved swiftly away from their own. "Sorry."

"Get the anchor up!" Harry pointed Charley forward. He made his own way aft. Yet even as he sought to work the engine into life, he could hear how close was Halliday's boat, not a hundred yards away. And now the traitorous clouds parted and the moonlight came through, enough for him to see the Indian agent stood at the prow of his vessel, and other figures visible behind.

"Harry Cadwallader!" Halliday called across the water. "Harry, I see you there. Don't seek to move off. I am coming over and will board you."

Harry ducked forward again, until the deckhouse hid him from view. Charley was sitting there on a keg.

The Indian looked up at him and shrugged. "Not luck today."

"Let's get these kegs over the side," said Harry and made to lift one.

"Not time," said Charley. "Keg float. Them see. Too late."

Harry swore. He was as angry at Charley's composure as he was at their situation. "Then what the fuck to do?"

"Have baccy tin?" said Charley.

"You want to fucking smoke?"

"Give tin."

Harry stood a moment fuming at him. Then he drew the tin from his pocket. He threw it over. "Choke on it, why don't you," he said.

Charley just smiled. He opened the tin and turned it upside down. The contents dropped out to the deck, where the wind made the papers separate and the tobacco drift in clumps away across the planking.

Halliday called out again. "Don't try to run for it, Harry! We have you."

"Give money. All of it," Charley said. "Quick now."

Harry stepped forward and handed the money across. Charley placed the money inside and sealed the tin. "And what do you hope to achieve by that?" Harry asked.

"Not get water in. Good box."

"What in all hell you talking about?"

"Them not see me. Me go." He pointed shoreward. "Swim. You stay."

"Me stay?" Harry struggled for a moment to think. But Charley was already up and moving to the gunnels to the far side of the direction from which Halliday was approaching.

Charley sat with his legs dangling over the water. "Good tin," he said. "Where you buy?"

"Hong Kong," he said without thinking. "Girl gave it me. Long time ago." Charley dropped quietly into the black water. Harry hurried across to look over the side. "You'll sink, won't you? That great hump on your back?"

"Not sink," said Charley. "Turn like whale in ocean." With that he disappeared beneath the surface, even as Harry felt a bump as the Indian agent's vessel drew up against the *Hesperus*.

He sat upon a keg. He ran his hand up through his hair. He thought about Grace. His wife. She'd laugh to have seen old Charley disappearing into the water like that. Lean right back, slapping at her thigh and roaring, like the first time he saw her. Well, Harry had done what he could do. For her. For her family. For his family. And it was enough, was it not? Enough for any man.

I SPENT THAT DAY OF MY RETURN TO RUPERT just sitting by the fire in the greathouse, Francine feeding me, looking on the empty walls where the treasures of my family had been took by Halliday. My wife saw there weren't words yet for speaking, and she left me alone.

Later, Grace came visiting. Don't we always talk of our sons? But she's a treasure more than all the masks and blankets I might gather along the cursèd coast. Well, I gave her to Harry, and I did it knowing there was darkness undiscovered in that man.

Grace was all concern for me, and for her husband, who had not yet returned. In Alert Bay, I'd understood from Annie that he and Charley had left six days before for Rupert. Charley'd told her they was heading home.

Where had they gone? I could not believe disaster would have come upon them, Charley the wily dreamer and Harry with all his years at sea. And there hadn't been no storm that I had seen.

Charley'd spoke of his doubts on Harry before he and Grace was married. Harry was a wanderer, "a ghost on the waters." He'd be away with the spring tides, so Charley thought. But Grace was so sure. Harry so solemn when he came to ask her hand from me. He's near twice her age, though he don't look it, with that boyish face and his sprightly bearing.

I guess I'd wanted to believe in him: white man of substance with that sleek-lined boat of his. Now my head was plagued with all sorts of black doubts. I even entertained a moment's notion of Harry pitching Charley overboard, a hand on the old man's hump and a quick shove.

Anyhow, I told Grace of her husband's injuries, making light of them, but said he and Charley was away on business for me and would shortly be back. When she asked me of the trial, I said I needed time to think. We'd all talk on it soon enough.

I watched as she and her mother sat wittering away at the back of the greathouse. I felt bound all about by shame and I did not speak another word that day.

The next morning, I was shook awake by Charley hisself. "Francine tells me you've not spoke a word on what's been happening," he says, once I've dragged myself up to sit out front in the grey light of the dawn. I was so befuddled I couldn't hardly keep my eyes open. I felt like I needed to sleep for a month. Or for eternity.

My wife and Grace was making coffee out back. I says to wait till they come join us then we'd speak more. I didn't even think to ask him where Harry might be, or where the two of them had gone off to.

That was the first question from Grace, though. "Where is my husband got to, Charley Seaweed?" says she. "Out with it."

"We hear George's story first," says he. Well Grace bridles at that and goes on some, but "You mind your uncle Charley" is all he says, waving a finger under her nose. She raised up her eyebrows and rolled her eyes about, but she held her tongue anyway.

"You're not the most popular man in Rupert," says Francine to me.

"Nor up the coast and down," says Charley.

"Crosby's been making trouble since you left," says Grace. "Speaking slurs against you, even to those few who go to his sermons on a Sunday. And Owadi has been saying things. And others too."

In short order, I told them of what had occurred since I was shipped off to Vancouver.

"You don't know how long you'd spend in jail?" says Francine. I says I don't, and when she asks what's to be done, I tells them I was minded to plead guilty and to speak my piece on the injustice being done the Indians by the banning of their rituals, even in a court so far off as Vancouver.

We sat, then, for a while, and no one speaking, with the day brightening before us, and the village coming slowly to life. I felt their eyes upon me, but I could not look up to meet them.

At last, Francine spoke up. "You are a white bastard-son madman," says she. "My father always said you were. They truly made a devil of you in that fat city."

Grace asks what in all good Christ almighty did I think I was about, and speaks a few choice words more as well. Charley just sits there, staring at the ground, humpy and brooding.

"But I was there for the hamatsa feast," says I at last. "The flesh was cut up and eaten. Whatever was the nature of that flesh, nothing but the very worst will be believed by a white jury. There is nothing better for me to do as speak my mind." I tell them Halliday says he's witnesses to prove it all, and strong ones too.

"But, Father," says Grace, "can you not try to save yourself? Fight!"

Seeing her there, her fists clenched and her thick hair vibrating about her face in her passion, I felt almost took apart then. Something just began to show itself to me. Something I had not thought. Something as yet without words. "I thought to stand up," says I, my voice a frog croak, "and say the things I had to say before the people in Alert Bay. Down there in the city I am nothing. How would you have it? What fight do you propose? Let us hear it."

She just jumped up and strode off to stand, one foot up on a boulder, hands on her raised thigh, shaking her head. She was so much like her brother at that moment. David was always stamping about, chock full of opinion.

"You daughter is right," says Francine. "Where have your guts got to?"

I stood and stalked over to Grace. I threw out my hands to take in the village about us. "Have you not seen the filth?" says I. "Don't you know the want we're in? The cesspit down which we all is falling? Most of us dead! Yes," says I, the spit flying out of my mouth like I had come on demented, "the city put the Devil in me, wife. The Devil that knows too well of things. There ain't no fight that we can make against the killing of us. Soul and body, in the killing of us."

"And this is your argument for pleading guilty?" says Grace beside me.

"There ain't nothing of hope, whatever I choose to plead."

"What are these rumours, Father, about David's funeral? You took off his head. I know that, though I found it difficult to believe." She paused, and I saw that she fought her tears. I says I was following Tlingit ways and ancient they are. "But there's other rumours, Father," says she.

"I've not anything else to tell you," I says.

"There weren't nothing else," says Charley.

Grace spun away from me. I saw her shoulders hunched and the pain it seemed I was putting into her. "I'd not believed I'd see you turn so shameful," she says, her back to me, and then she walked away along the beach.

I didn't call after her, nor speak at all. I could not even answer my own daughter's grief.

"Are you so stupid?" says Francine.

I swore at her, words I won't now repeat. "How many of your family have you lost?" I says. "You've not felt the pain of it as have I."

"I know it was Lucy bore him, but David was a son to me, as Grace is a daughter." She spoke quietly, but, after, she stood and went back inside.

"Well now you've nearly done for all of us," says Charley. "You spoke fine words to Walewid and his men," says he. "What's become of them? Perhaps you left them back at Teguxste?"

I sat on the ground and rested my back against the boulder. A few light drops of rain began to fall. "I'd thought to do so. I thought the court would be the place for it. I had not seen the city then. There ain't nothing left for us, Charley. We're spent. Were better we accepted it. Hacking up corpses, be they human or otherwise, ain't how the people will make their way in the white world. There ain't no hope of turning back from it."

"So you walked out on hope. But how does all this bear on you going to prison?" says Charley. "Is it not better to fight the charges and be free to play a part, whichever world you thinking's out there? The two don't necessarily connect."

"They do," says I. "I just don't got the words for it."

"Well best start trying to find them, before the New Westminster jail opens up its doors to you."

"Even had I the words," says I, "I have not the means to defend myself."

At that, Charley throws something across to me. I picked it from the dirt and seen it was a tin for holding tobacco. There was a bawdy Chinese dancing girl upon its lid and I remembered it as Harry's. "What's this?" says I, but Charley don't answer. I ask him, anyway where is Harry, and where they both have been. But he just pointed to the tin. So I opened it up and there inside was a great sheaf of money. Hundred of dollars there was. I was amazed. For a time I just did not have words to speak. Then I stuttered out some query, and Charley tells me how he and Harry had been away smuggling whisky to raise funds on my behalf. I'd thought, in giving Harry management of the family store, that he'd turned his back on such things. Seems I was wrong.

"Where's Harry now?" I says.

"In Halliday's jail," says Charley.

They had brung whisky up from New Westminster—which was ironical, being as how I seemed shortly destined for the same small city's prison myself. But word had got out of their adventure, and Halliday was waiting for them on their return. Still, old Dan Copperhand got away with his whisky for a feast. Charley got off with the money, and made his way straight north to Rupert, by what means I never asked: a cousin, a canoe, flying cross the water. I still wonder at how he gets about so quick. Of what fate awaited Harry in Alert Bay, he did not yet know.

"Will you squander Fat Harry's gift on your misery?" Charley says to me. Then he upped and was away as well, saying he was off to tell Grace how fared her husband.

I went back inside, holding the tin full of money. I sat beside the fire at the centre of the house. Francine had made a great blaze of it, and the flames burned at my face. She was sitting by the cooking fire at the back, drinking periodically from a roughware bottle. I heard her muttering to herself. Eventually, she rooted about in an old box, then came over bearing a bundle.

"You've a package come," she says, and dropped it in front of me. Then she headed away back to her perch at the back of the house.

It bore the postmark of New York. When I pulled it open, there was a letter inside, and another smaller packet, bound with brown paper and string.

My dear George, it read, *I am in receipt of your last letter. I am most dreadfully sorry to hear of David's death. So brave a man he was. Please do read the other paper I enclose.*

Of course, I will do all I can to help you in your present difficulty. I have written as well to Mr. Spencer. Meanwhile, I am sure you will manage your way out of these present difficulties.

I am very much disappointed that you did not mention your availability to come to New York. The collections here at the museum are in a most catastrophic disorder and would so greatly benefit from your expert eye. As I wrote in my previous letter, I am also most keen to pursue the subject of the paxala with you. I understand, of course, your worries regarding your current predicament, but would appreciate hearing some word at least of the possibilities for our collaboration. You are welcome to come immediately you are able.

Please let me hear from you at once. With best wishes,

Yours very sincerely,

Franz Boas.

There was a postscript. Indeed, there was two.

P.S. I enclose a cheque for moneys owed you.

P.P.S. I also enclose a copy of our book, should it be the case you no longer have one in your keeping. It contains, as you will recall, your name on the title page. It might prove useful.

Does the man live in some different world entire, I thought, away east in his museum? Do prisons mean nothing, and life and death but details to be nosed at, like a dog to a turd?

I held the cheque to the light and saw the amount. Thirty-three dollars and twenty-five cents. I near consigned it to the flames.

But, instead, I picked up the package, untied the string, and drew off the paper wrapping. The book looked the same, and was the same as all the others what have been distributed up and down the coast. If I had only knowed the trouble it would cause me, I might not have felt such triumph the first time I ever saw it.

I already had a copy at home. Of course I did. Another treasure to me. Thousands and thousands of pages I had scrawled. My bad script, my shaking hand, my English so weak when I set pen on paper, so much worse even than when I speak. It just closes me up like a mussel in air. Boas did advise me to write in Kwakwala, but use English words. It all jumbles. Frogspawn.

I opened up the book at random and turned the pages, not reading. So many of the stories was my own or those of my family. My life printed out on paper, bound up and placed high on a shelf in a library somewhere to be perused by scholars. I was those pages now. Perhaps I was now forever, though nowhere was my name mentioned as the subject of those stories. I was but one more Indian. Many different Indians. *Culture.* That white word. There ain't no word for it in any Indian language I know. Call it life. I was life translated. The Kwagiulth as they are in libraries had become my own life translated. So was the direction of my thoughts.

I tossed the book sideways on the ground. I lifted up the letter again and looked to the second page. It was handwritten in Boas's careful script, neat and small, in the written high Kwakwala the two of us so laboriously crafted.

I have so much regret to miss the funeral of this, the great chieftain, your son David, it read. *He was strong in life and proud. I know it must be a proud ceremony. I know that the people will give him great respect.*

Yet there is not pain to compare with such a loss. Your son will always remain alive in your heart, as my own child who died in years past remains in mine. This pain we share and many also in these days feel this pain, but it is not the less.

I give tribute to your great son.

I read his letter and after my whole body shook with the grief of it, though still I didn't have tears to spill. But I wanted to race up and down the beach screaming, to smash the world into pieces, tear out its liver with my fingers, or throw myself upon the fire and be done with it. I put my head down on my chest and barely knew that time passed.

Eventually I heard Francine return. She sat beside me and handed me a tin cup, steaming and stinking finely of coffee. "You are an idiot," says she.

"I know it," says I.

That night, I lay beside her, watching the dull glow from the fire moving lazy on the empty wall above—the wall where once had hung a mask of the killer whale what my mother did bring south with her, when first she came to marry.

I felt the faint stirrings of my rage, though not strong enough to cloak my mind. I realized it was the first time I'd felt it since the night I had killed the dreamer. There was blessing in its absence, I supposed, though in fact I felt some sustenance knowing it still lurked there inside me.

Not that rage has always led me right. It was my rage, was it not, had placed me in my current predicament? Attacking Crosby that day of the funeral, I'd brung what plot there was against me festering beneath the surface out into the open to bear fruit. Would Halliday have brung charges if he'd not heard I had assaulted the priest?

Is rage even the right word for my affliction? That is what I have always named it. Though of rage itself I'd happily see more levied against the white man's grip. Do I rage at the modern world? Like a soft tide against granite, as much use were it to do so.

What had brought us all to this—I lay on my bed thinking—this end? As if the people flowed like suds of soap into a drain, washed away by, first, the traders, then the Christians, feverish and fervent, the British, and, now, this new Canadian administration.

Where was the killer whale? Where was the great Cannibal Spirit? Was he gone forever now, deep into the forest? Or had he been snuffed out, till he did not exist in any form no more? Was belief a scene of battle what took even the history of the dead away as well, till there weren't no trace at all? As if nothing of a people, of a world of those spirits, should remain, or even seem as if it had ever been.

I drifted into a light sleep. I dreamed that I did stand high above the ocean, and the tide flowing back in ebb from the cliff beneath me. There was a beach of boulder and pebble, slimed green with algae under a dark, low sky.

And now I was there on the beach, still far from the water, my boots slip-sliding as I walked the rock pools towards the stooping, black-clad figure ahead.

The figure spat curses. I came round in front of it, and saw it was my mother, but ancient now and her face broken with pox. She was sorting among the pebbles, plucking at them, eyeing and discarding them, the thick Presbyterian dress she always wore in her last days of life muddied and soaked at its hem, lank upon her.

"What have you lost?" I asked her. She started up and looked about, but, seeing nothing, hunched down again, muttering. "Where is it?" I says, though I had no idea of what it was I spoke.

Her hand pointed vaguely away toward the ocean. I looked and now I was right by the water's edge. The surface shuddered at each tiny wave's destruction on the shore, bleak charcoal ripples that, as they fell back, drew my eyes to the horizon. Clouds hung low, heavy, threatening.

A terrible longing filled me. My chest heaved. I choked and wept. The tears ran and I tasted their salt upon my lips. And now I was beneath the waves, the dim light filtering down in freezing, emerald shimmers through the misty water. The longing was gone and now there was only peace.

My feet touched the ocean floor. All about me, long tendrils of kelp flexed and billowed, a slow-dancing forest through which small, silver-flashing fish lurked and sped and hid in their appetites and their terrors.

I reached out for one and my finger glanced along its tiny flank. Perhaps its heart stopped at the shock of my touch, for now it came to rest and floated onto its side and down towards the ocean floor.

Something like a muscular lightning bolt flew from the kelp shadows. A seal's face, nose jerking, big black smiling eyes, and its head snapping sideways, mouth snatching the dead fish, then away again into the murk.

The mourning rose again in my chest until I felt I might gag. I knew my mother sought for something she could never find, and I, here under the ocean, was her last chance if only I might learn my way.

Some presence there was then, vast, menacing in the gloom ahead. It came through the snaking kelp, the dead-smiling face of a killer whale, near broad as I am tall. But, behind it, the thick tentacles of the devilfish—the giant octopus—curled out from its flanks towards me. I knew I was in the presence of the Qomogwe, the king beneath the sea.

"Is it here?" I asked it, even as I felt the soft suckers clamping at my skin. The killer whale opened wide its mouth and turned its head to the side, so that it might take my head into its jaws and devour me.

I woke to the sting of sweat in my eyes, the fire dead and nothing to be seen. My breath came short. I felt the night terrors such as I'd not since I was a child, afraid of shadows on the walls, of teeth and monsters.

I got up, the bones in my shoulders cracking and my hips stiff, knowing myself an old man. I stepped into my boots and drew a blanket about my naked form. Then I paced across the floor to the doorway.

I drew the curtain aside and stood for a moment, shivering as a northerly gust pulled at me a moment, before it died away.

I sat on the edge of the plankway, my unlaced boots dangling above the incline to the shore. As in my dream, the tide was out and the beach scattered with boulders, though also with the rotten jetsam of the village. A narrow moon threw a pale, thin light upon the village.

Away to my left, a dog barked, then shrieked as some dozy, irate Indian might have struck it.

I lowered myself onto the slope and slid down onto the beach. I made my way, slipping on the wet pebbles, towards the water. There was now no wind, the ocean still and the air cool without being cold.

At the water's edge, I dropped my blanket and stepped out from my boots. I paced into the water, careful of my footing, till I felt the sharp incline of the drop-away—that ridge with which the war canoe of Shaiks had so ingloriously collided those many years before.

I pushed out into the deep water and swam. The cold sea plucked at me till my muscles did spasm and my body shook. So I floated, face down, my head beneath the surface. The salt water burned at my eye beneath its patch, the pain like panic as it clutched my skull.

The memory of the dead fish in my dream came back to me. I opened my eyes under the water. But all I saw was darkness. I wondered if I might sink as had the fish, down into the deeps to be eaten. I wished for it.

I remembered, as I had not since the event itself, the pouring rain what fell down upon me at my son's funeral, the hurt in Harry's eyes when I sent him to take the women home.

Before me were the expectant faces of the hamatsa society men who had stayed behind. There had been words that must needs be spoken in secret, and even rituals to perform. And though I weren't no more than a father to the dead chief of the hamatsas, which in itself meant nothing, so my authority was such that they all was awaiting me to act.

261

Charley was there still. He weren't a member of any particular group, but always present, his twisted back, a rain-soaked hummock, proof to all of his supernatural authority.

So they stood in the rain and waited for me. And I drew up my hatchet from my belt. I drove its edge under the gravebox's lid. I pushed and yanked till I was near to frenzy, the rain driving in my face. I couldn't hardly see at all.

And gradually I drew the lid up, till it fell away to the ground and my son was once again exposed.

The men was murmuring now. What is he doing? What part of ritual is this? But they still trusted me. Charley put his hand to my arm. I just shrugged him away. All I could see was the nape of my dead son's broken neck, where I had thrust it down into its coffin with my own violent hands.

I was still holding the hatchet. So now I reach in to hold the hair, to lift the skull so that the neck is better exposed. I draw it up. And then I plunge the hatchet down. Again. Twice more. The body of my son flops forward and down into the gravebox, and there are ragged tendrils of skin, far gone in putrefaction, about the rent where my son's head had recently been. The stump of the severed spine, pale spinal cord, folds away into the meat below, like a snake retreating back into a hole.

Oh God, that I am such a man! That I am capable of such acts as these! No, let me tell this tale through. For there in the blackness of the water, it was the first time I saw again what I had done.

The hatchet falls from my hand, gored and foul, and David's slack countenance, where I hold up his severed head, grey and turning already to black in places, long spent of its life.

I go down onto my knees then. A pagan missionary praying to the gods of his brown people. Or to the One True God? Pleading. Forgive me. Despising, maybe? The rain thundering on me and my arms dropping to my sides. The thud of the head as it hits the ground beside me, me falling forward so my own head knocks against the gravebox. Me choking. But shaking myself upright straight after, refusing my own dissolution.

So I pull myself up once more with my one empty hand on the grave-box's lid. I look down into the box at what I have done.

The rumours of the coast have this as well to say of me. That I did then reach for the skinning knife at my belt, drop the severed head, lean over the box. That I did draw up the torso, grip it by the shoulder. That I did slice at the meat of David's neck, cut away a strip of that rank flesh, place it then between my teeth. The smell of ripening death in my nostrils, biting down, sucking as if on dry salmon, stomach clenching, gagging bile to stream with the dead juices of my son, acids blending and burning at my mouth, swallowing down the flesh.

That is what they say of me. White men lick their chops at such thinking. But that the people theirselves have been thinking it as well! That my daughter should suspect it!

So cannibals roam our forests. Brown men consume the flesh of other men. I ain't never seen it happen. And here I am, the only man living directly accused of it. A half-breed white. A fool in his grief. Fool guilty. Fool dispossessed. Not saviour. Not hero. Not even devil. Just fool. I am guilty of all crimes. Such is the way of the man who exists between worlds. All sides may cast their crimes upon him.

Floating out there, face down on the water in the darkness, seeing again those memories, I opened my mouth and the seawater came in. I thought, I can breathe it till the weight in my lungs drags me down.

Instead, I coughed and thrashed and spun till I floated on my back, still hacking, my arms widespread, beating at the water. I spat and gagged. At last my airways cleared and my breathing slowed.

And the rage came into me. But it was a clear rage. A rage that purged. Flames, yellow and hot to burn out the petty reckonings of my despair. I called damnation on the world. I called it on all those what hindered me, on all those what spoke ill words of me—Indians and whites alike. A pox on them all! I was not subject to them. I was not victim to them. To any of these men and women who sought to brand me as their own—or as the enemy.

263

Above, the sky was clear, the stars brilliant, imposing, weakening the moon's pale claw to nothing. "There are no monsters!" I said. I shouted it over and over.

I woke beside old Francine the next morning feeling chock full of shame, but clear as to the scope and nature of my foolishness. I thought on Harry placing himself in danger for me. On all those others what looked for my welfare. It weren't justice, after all, to let them suffer so, that I might wallow in my pity.

I went straight to the store to speak with Grace. I told her of all I had in me. "My mind had left me," says I. "But jail ain't helping no one. I know it now. I'll find a ways out of it. See if I don't." She cast a pretty leery eye on me, and didn't have much to say by return. I know it would have to be by my actions that I would make her see I meant my words.

My first thoughts was to head back to the village where the ritual for which I stood accused had occurred. But Charley says to me that he has already been there and none weren't ready to stand me as witness. I suppose I ought to have knowed it already, but I was quite angered for a time.

"They don't want to be before a court saying they was also at the ceremony what is banned," as Charley says, and I suppose he was right. Still, Mr. Bowser weren't going to be overjoyed when I turned up with just myself and some doubtful-looking old cripple Indian for company.

Charley and me hopped the next boat heading south to Alert Bay, the money in my pocket. Grace came with us, refusing all appeals to stay behind. "You've near to killed him, then had him locked up in the jail, and now you'd refuse me to see him?" says she, and there was no answering that. Poor old Francine got lumbered with opening up the store each morning. Still, I knows she don't give too much time to the tricksy ways of the people in their negotiating, so I weren't overly worried on that score. "Do what is right to come back to us," says she by way of goodbye, and that was all the words she had, so angry and fretful as I guess she was.

I went first to see Halliday. He had Harry locked up for a month for his misdeeds. There weren't much to say about that. He'd caught him fair and square with a cargo of illegal liquor. The Indian agent smiled on

Charley when he saw him. "You're a strong swimmer," says he. Charley just shrugged his lumpy shoulders.

"What of the *Hesperus*?" says I.

"She is made forfeit by his actions," says Halliday. But when I started to protesting on how much of my family's property he had done from us already, he raised up his hand to quiet me. "I am not ignorant of Harry's motivations in acting as he did, George. The law tells me I must auction off all vessels that are taken during such offences. Be assured the auction will be closed and Harry will be but the sole bidder."

"And the starting price?"

"Affordable."

I humphs and spits and stomps some, but Charley saw the wisdom of things and drew me off. "He ain't all evil, that one," says he, as we went through the back of Halliday's office to go visiting with Harry.

Abayah and Annie was keeping him fed. He was resting there on the bunk under the window, right where I had so recently been myself, his head back on the wall, eyes closed and snoring. He had his shirt off, the ropes of his sailor's arms and shoulders resting loose, the one side what had been injured drooping lower than the other, the great hollow depression of his wound striped purple now with lumpy scar tissue, and none too pretty on the eye. Still, he looked a man quite perfectly at peace in that moment. Then Grace spoke out, cursing him for a flat-faced idiot getting chopped up so. His eyes came open and, seeing Grace, he rose up like a duck from the water with a pike at its ass, stood there, shuffling and with his fingers squirming as if he was up before the judge hisself. She had a few comments of her own he needed hearing. So I gave him a few words of my thanks, told him I was sure to be seeing him soon, shared a sympathetical look with him over Grace's shoulder, and we left them to it, eyeing each other, wary, through the bars.

Anyhow, there weren't much as I could say. I didn't want to speak more on my doubts about him, even to say they was gone. I had been so wrong about it all. And he seemed to have pardoned me for the horrors what he saw up there at the House of Shamans.

We stopped overnight with Abayah before the steamer was due the following morning. I went by Annie's. "I have had it told me, by such as know, that I am a fool and, quite probably, mad with it." To which she added her agreement. "Well, now I am about trying to make amends," says I. So did we part then, on good terms, though I did not go see her husband—didn't seem much point before whatever was to happen did.

So Charley and me went on down to Vancouver. My lawyer, Mr. Bowser, when he sees me and Charley, did shake his head, and made it clear my chances wouldn't be more than panning for gold in the bath.

I had other thoughts.

A few days later and there I was, waiting outside the court in a fair morning turning to hot, sitting on those steps what I had stood on two short weeks before, when Mr. Bowser made my bail for me. As the city rattled past, so the dust mounted up from off the road like smoke devils.

Charley Seaweed was beside me, ready to state to the court there hadn't been no human corpse present at the hamatsa ceremony for which I stood accused. I confess I was a mite dubious at how useful he might be to my cause: his leathery brown old Indian face, short most of its teeth, what looks more often than not as if it is leering, filthy, at some young saintly missy striding by, his hunched back, what was made all the more fantastical by being dressed up smart in a new grey shirt and black morning jacket.

As we waited on Bowser turning up, so we did watch those down at the far end of the court's stairs. There was three of them. One was a tall man and thin. His name was Copper Dancer. Beside him was a shorter man by the name of Inviter, as I might translate it. Both was well dressed enough in black suits and cravats that I knew they must be funded by others wealthier than theirselves. They paced and turned, paced and turned. I could see they was made discomforted by the city's overbearing presence. They did not look our way.

There was a third man also present, he dressed in the black gown of the priesthood, and his bowl-cut hair without a hat. To-Cop sat upon the lower step and watched us back, without expression.

It was the morning of the second day of the trial.

The first day I spent listening to those as was arranged against me. I heard tell of the wrongdoings what I had performed at that ritual, as the prosecution and, after, as To-Cop did recount them. To-Cop told how he had been present that seventeenth day of February as a spectator only at the village of the chieftain Big Mountain. He was there to watch a dance of the hamatsa, what is one—as he did describe it—who dances and eats a dead body. I learned how the corpse of a dead old woman was brung in to the greathouse by the hamatsa dancers. I learned how I was called forward by Big Mountain, how I went all about the house singing my sacred song, how I took a long blade and chopped off the corpse's legs and then its head, and did give out portions to all the hamatsa chieftains present, and then how we sat and ate up all the fleshy parts of the body. I heard as well how I stood up, at the end, and advised everyone not to say anything about it, as it was a most serious affair.

Well, it was a day of appealing storytelling, for sure. But there is another version to be told, though it was not to be the one I was to tell in court. There is guilt tied up in it, but of a different sort.

It was February. I had been a long day travelling across a cold and life-less sea, the sky a grey haze what it can't be seen where the air does finish and the clouds begin. The day was ending and my bones creaking when I pulled my canoe up the pebbled beach at the village of Klawitsis. Chief Big Mountain's village.

The people was at their preparations for a feast. As I walked up among the buildings, I says a word here or there to those I know, and I saw how the piles of blankets stacked up inside the doorways, ready for distributing at the feast, was threadbare and not of those quantities I remember from past days.

"George is here," old man Seal Singer says. "Hide everything away or he'll leave with his canoe piled up with our treasures."

"I'll take a couple of your fat daughters as well, Seal Singer," I says. "You've plenty spare."

"They're all away south to the cities now," Seal Singer says, more quiet, and I knew it was to work on their backs among the white men.

I came to the greathouse, and there was the chief inside, Big Mountain, old now, if huge in his body still. "There is witchcraft afoot," says he.

"I'll find those what are doing it," says I. "I'll take the game from them."

That night I slept out beyond the edge of the village among the dead. I lay there among the graveboxes hidden in their wooden mausoleums, and above me in silhouette against the stars was others strung up and lodged on the branches of the trees. Some of the people spied me there, and I knew I was spoken on and wondered at, feared perhaps as well, which was a good thing for my endeavours.

Next day, I strode out through the forest. After some hours, I stopped for a blow, leaning against the trunk of a red cedar, speaking a few quiet words to it: mossy, ragged master. I was wondering at how the years creep in, and me not noticing, to steal from me my vigour.

It was some ways ahead, fifty yards or an hour's hard walking, I didn't know. Lagoyewilé—what is Charley Seaweed, of course, when he's sneaking about doing his dreaming for me—had told me where to go the evening before, as we sat by a fire at the water's edge, the forest hanging over us, a day's paddle still from Klawitsis village.

"Follow the route I tells you," says he, "and blackheart fucks at the end you will find."

So I had walked for three hours from the village in the direction what he told me, and then he said I'd see the fire by its smoke.

But there was a rainstorm raging, and the forest bleeding green shadows. So no smoke could I see, nor much of ought else besides. I'd fancied putting a bullet in a deer as I went on, but no animals moved in that sodden wilderness. The only thing in my nose was the fresh-mould smell of rain. No sound was there more than hiss and drip and, dull through the miles of forest, the roar of thunder out on the ocean.

Well, the storm passed over at last and the forest steamed and sucked. I walked the rough track, quieter now, my better ear forward, sniffing for woodsmoke.

I heard them first: words chanted that I couldn't make out, but following the rhythms of a stick being beaten on a hollow log.

Now I saw smoke ahead, rolling up amidst the trees. It was blue-dark to tell me new-cut hemlock was being burned.

A yellow cedar lay across my path where it had fallen long ago. With its trunk, its branches, and the flora it did bring down in its ruin, and all of it covered now in moss and vines, it rose full fifteen feet in height before me, and the smoke billowing from the far side.

Off to my left, I spied a rope hanging down from the top. So, taking hold, I pulled myself up.

At the top, I rested on my belly on the soaking moss. I edged forward through the undergrowth, which was like a giant spider's web. At last, near trapped among the tangles, I could see down the far side.

There was a small clearing, no more than thirty foot wide, carved out by hand from the rhododendron thickets what sprawl among the fir and cedar and the hemlock trees.

The fire in the clearing's centre was hissing and crackling as it fought the damp from the storm. There was fresh-cut branches of hemlock, their leaves still on the twigs, resting close beside the fire, which threw up clouds of smoke. The smell came to my nostrils strong and bitter.

Two men was there. Both was wearing sackcloth trousers and that's it. Their bodies and their faces was daubed in charcoal till black, but for the lines of sweat which had run down their skin to show the brown beneath.

One of them, short and bandy-legged and his hair long near to his waist, was resting on a dead log, a leg to either side, beating the wood with a length of cedar. His chest was heaving so that it was clear to me he'd been about his task some time already.

The other was more than six feet tall and thin like an aspen. He strode around the fire, throwing up calls and wails into the air, and now I could make out the words.

"Big Mountain," says he. "You are suffering. Hah, hah, hah," and his arms rose up each time he spoke. "The great chief soon will be dead."

Off to one side, there was a small stream coming out from the undergrowth. It had formed into a black pond by the fallen tree trunk upon which I was hiding like a lizard. The pond rippled with the flowing-in of water, the reflections of the fire's light all shuddering and crazy in it. Beside this pond, I saw the packs of the two men. There was an ancient Hudson's Bay Company musket as well, sawn down to half its length, its stock green now with age, but its iron still oiled and clean.

The man beating time shouted out, "Make him dead! Make him dead!" The other one went over to the far side of the fire and now I saw a shape lying on the wet earth. Beside it was a blanket laid out and items resting upon it.

The tall man stooped down and lifted up a skinning knife from off the blanket. Then he took hold of the shape. I squinted harder and now I knew that what I had come to discover was true, for lying there was a human body.

Its legs was curled up against its torso and it had been dead for many years, its skin all leathered and black. The body was dried and shrunk, as they do, till it looked more a child in size than the adult it once was. Its head had been hacked off and lay in the mud some little ways off. I could see by the length of its grey, straggling hair that it was the remains of an old woman.

So the man with the skinning knife gripped one of the corpse's arms and put his knee between its legs and its body. He pulled upwards and pressed down with his knee, grunting, till there was a crunching sort of a dull explosion. The corpse's legs snapped forward to hang, still curled, but loose from the torso, and the body flopped onto the ground as the tall man dropped it.

Then he hunkered down. With the knife he did something I couldn't clearly see. Shortly, he stood once more and held up what looked a leather pouch, but was the withered tit of the dead old woman.

He rolled the body away with his foot and I saw that most of the skin from the corpse's right side had already been took off. The tall man knelt on the blanket and dropped the tit beside him. He rooted among the other paraphernalia what was there.

I spied another rope tied off nearby me that fell down toward the clearing, ending just before the edge of the black pond.

The tall man was still at work on the blanket, and the other one beating his rhythms on the hollow log. Both was facing away from me.

I eased myself around so that my feet, instead of my head, was now aimed towards the clearing. I pulled my rifle from off my shoulder into my hand, checked my machete was secure and that my knife was safe in its bootsheath. Then I took the rope in my empty hand.

Keeping watch on the two sorcerers in the clearing all the while, I lowered myself down the tree trunk till the slope was steep enough that I was hanging only by the strength of my arm. Then I let go of the rope.

I slipped on the mud at the edge of the pond and went down on one knee, even as the man beating rhythm at the hollow log swung about and spied me.

I jumped up smartly and ran round the pond, slipping and slithering, to the two men's packs on the other side. The tall man spied me now as well. The man at the log was on his feet and scuttling my way.

I got to their packs and took up the Hudson's Bay Company musket. I tossed it into the pool and raised up my own rifle. At that moment, something thumped against my chest and knocked me backwards a step.

But I held up the rifle to my shoulder and looked along its barrel at the men, who was standing still now, gazing black murder at me. I glanced down for a moment. There was the tall man's skinning knife what he had used to chop off that dead old woman's tit, lying on the ground at my feet, and that he must have throwed at me. I checked my shirt for blood but there weren't none. It had hit me handle side round.

So I smiled across at him. "Copper Dancer," says I, "your luck ain't worth a shit today."

Well, there was bad words spoke between us then. But eventually we was all sitting round the fire and my rifle still aimed at their sorcerous hearts should they be minded to try any fancy stuff.

"Go on," Copper Dancer says, "take our knowledge for your own, so that you become a powerful sorcerer like us." And it was true I wanted to know all that they had been up to, though I had other reasons than sorcery for wishing such knowledge.

The next afternoon, I arrived back into the village. By the way the people viewed me, I knew some guessed what my mission had been, and others had had it told them. So when I held up the bag in which I lugged the game, they fell back and murmured amongst theirselves, or else they turned away and spat upon the ground. A few backed through the doorways of their cabins into darkness.

"In the witchcraft place," I tell Chief Big Mountain, as we stood beside the ocean, "I beat the sorcerers and I took away the game. The game what is the cedar bark with which they caught your breath as you was sleeping, and your piss and shit, and as well a stick you used for eating. These had they buried in the ground, wrapped in a corpse's skin, beneath a fire of hemlock. I dug them up and I was careful I did not disturb the contents inside the skin. I put it in this bag and brung it here. Now take it and throw it away into the sea."

The chieftain hurled the bag out into the water. I had placed a stone inside and it disappeared under the surface. Big Mountain spat on the pebbles for fortune. "You have saved me," says he.

"And put the Devil to witchery," says I.

"Now the hamatsa can be called in from the forest."

We went back up the beach to the chieftain's greathouse. The people watched me, but I weren't certain there was much of admiration in their eyes.

Later, the fire danced high into the timbers of the roof. The leading men of the village clans and their sons sat, stolid and sweating, about it, affecting to ignore the danger to the building what the flames threatened. Each had a Bay blanket wrapped about them. Some wore bear-skin hats and others was bareheaded, but all had their faces painted black, as members of the hamatsa society are in the habit of at such occasions.

I was sitting further back in the shadows, with the women and the lesser men and children. I had my notebook open, a pencil stub in hand, and my skinning knife by my boot for its resharpening. Charley was lurking somewheres about. He had come paddling in that afternoon, visiting with his cousins, as he told the people.

Four women entered, cradling a large bowl carved with images of eagle, whale, and raven, five feet long and filled with eulachon oil. They knelt down before the fire. The men shuffled in and gathered about it, took up the wooden spoons, and with much slurping gusto, set about the meal.

Big Mountain was among them. His body was covered by armour of wooden plates, painted black. All about the middle of the armour was drawn the image of the Sisiutl, the great twin-headed snake that coils beneath the world, and on which we must walk so careful. Each plate was secured about his body with thin strips of hide, so that it followed the chieftain's every movement. He seemed almost a carven figure hisself, and I was reminded of that armour what I had seen Shaiks wearing all the long years ago, if the designs was not so much alike, they being of differing tribes.

The chieftain waved me over. "This great shaman comes and cleans the sorcery from us," he says. "He is truly of the people."

I joined with them in eating the eulachon oil. There's comfort in its acrid taste. The comfort of long winters when the food is nearly gone and only the kegs of grease remain. Or the comfort of the feast, and the rituals by which the people voice their union.

There was those around the bowl who eyed me without expression as they ate. But one, a short young man of no more than twenty, with a pudding-bowl cut to his thick hair, stared black-eyed malice. The fire gleamed bloody gold on the small cross what hung at his neck. To-Cop, as I have since come to know his name. I didn't hardly give a thought at the time to this boy and his discontent with me. There was so many didn't like me. So what if there was one more?

Now I heard a call from outside, from the forest behind the house. "Hap hap hap!" came the call, the call of the cannibal, the call of the hamatsa what was yet to be tamed.

Three men, one of them To-Cop, disappeared into the back of the house. Shortly, three figures emerged from the place where they had just gone off to, wearing masks of dog and bear. They squatted and leapt forward, the shredded bark what covered their bodies shaking and spinning out as they lunged at those watching.

The call came again from outside. The dancers raised their heads, then fled from the house through the open front door.

Outside could be heard the sounds of a struggle. In the open doorway a figure showed itself, two of the dancers holding its arms as if to keep it from the room. It was covered in fronds of undergrowth and of cedar, so

273

that it seemed as if it had been created from the forest itself. Its face was daubed thick with black paint and its mouth was held wide in an O of surprise or rage. The whites of its eyes showed vivid.

It pulled itself free and raced inside. It squatted, backside on its heels, its knees forward and arms stretched out towards us. Its face scanned the room hungrily, as the dancers filed in behind it, chanting now.

They gathered about the hamatsa. They grabbed it and it fought, pulling at them, struggling, leaves and broken twigs scattering about the floor. Then it was free again. It grabbed at a boy's arm and bit down upon it. The boy didn't draw back, nor cry out. He just let hisself be bit.

The hamatsa raced outside, disappearing into the darkness, the dancers following. Presently, they was back, this time led by the hamatsa, who spun and snapped and cried out, but was left to roam free. He was carrying something, which he lifted above his head once he was through the doorway. He came near the fire and I could see it was the dead carcass of something. It was shaped so it might have been human, but was wholly covered in evergreen leaves and fronds.

The dancers placed the figure on two boxes. Big Mountain stood up. He raised in one hand a headdress, like to a turban and made of cedar bark. In the other, he held a fat-bladed machete, its edges glimmering black reflections. He pointed it to the four corners of the house. Then he looked over at me.

"Will you?" says he, and I knew the honour being offered. I looked about the room at the faces of the people. Eyes as flat as slab-laid salmon gazed back.

I shook my head. Instead, Big Mountain placed the red turban on the head of his own son, the boy whose arm had been bit, fifteen years old and struck by awe.

"My son rips apart the bodies of dead enemies and tames the cannibal," says the chief. Then he gave his son the blade. The boy walked round the fire singing his sacred song.

After, the boy knelt before the carcass. He pulled some of the evergreen away. He hacked down, and again, and once more. Then he lifted up a thin leg, the leg of a young deer, strewn in bracken.

The hamatsa leapt in and snatched the limb from his hands. It put the bloody meat to its mouth and ripped until its black face was smeared in tattered flesh and gore.

The boy cut again at the body, severing the leaf-strewn head, the other leg, and both the upper limbs, and these he handed to the dancers, one by one. He sliced slivers from the torso and held these up to his father, who took them and distributed them amongst the men about the fire.

The hamatsa squatted, quieter now, in front of the fire, watching the others consuming the flesh. As they ate, so it rose slowly higher till, at last, it stood fully upright. Then the three cannibal dancers was once more close about it, and now they started to lift the fronds and branches from its body.

When all the evergreen lay about the figure's feet, Big Mountain wiped away the black from the hamatsa's face. Beneath, the face of a young man was now to be seen: the chieftain's eldest son. "I am back," says he. Men laughed and pounded him on the back and shoulders till he winced, smiling back at them, shy in his triumph and his new membership to their society.

The three other dancers took off their masks. One of them was To-Cop. I wondered what view the missionaries might take if they knew that this, their own young man—as I had seen from the gold cross at his neck—did partake of such Satanic spectacles.

Later, I sat with Big Mountain. He had removed the wooden armour earlier, and now he tucked his blanket tightly about his elsewise naked body. He stared into the fire for a while. At last he says to me, "Did you kill them?"

"I did not," says I. I told him how I had taken their boots and their weapons.

"They will be unhappy at you," he says, and I agree that he might have a point.

"And with me," says he.

Well, they was already a mite unhappy with him, wasn't they, says I, or had he forgot the reason I was here. "The power is with you again," I tell him. "The people are with you again."

He nodded. "They try to compete with me. I beat them. But beat them using you. They won't like it that you, a breed, should beat them. They will be shamed."

"Which was part why you brung me here, I reckon."

At which he smiled. "Your dreamer made a good argument for it," says he.

"Anyway, be damned with foul witchery. I hate it. I stamp on it wherever I do find it," says I. Then I get down to my other business. "I've heard the canneries aren't hiring so many this spring. And Seal Singer sends his daughters away south."

I saw that To-Cop was watching from across the fire. I spoke quietly now to Big Mountain. "I've money to offer you," I tell him. He says he guessed it. I am here to buy his suit of armour, says I.

"You won't!" says he. I'll give him fifty dollars. "No!" says he. I'll pay him now, before the new season begins.

"I have heard," says he, "that in your book it's written that we eat the bodies of dead people for real."

I tell him it don't say that at all.

"Many are angry," says he. "And they are ashamed. The book tells we are savage men."

I thought on the two sorcerers performing their tricks out in the forest. I thought as well about the carcass that had just been consumed and, in its consumption, how the wilds is tamed. How fear is tamed. "The book don't say that we are savage men," I says. "It tells our stories and the ways we live."

"There is nothing as beautiful as my armour," says he. "I will give it to my son." But there ain't no money in the villages. The Chinese come from Vancouver to work the canneries. Japaners work the fishing boats. Whites take the land. I tell him I'll be away before the sun comes. No one will see me go.

The chief pulled a charred stick from the edge of the fire. He drew shapes in the earth in front of him. I looked down at the shapes. I nodded.

Big Mountain threw the stick back into the fire. Then he walked away across the room and went out through the door. I swept my fingers in the earth and wiped away the numbers there.

To-Cop found me later that evening on the beach. I was making certain my canoe was tightly moored but ready for the early start.

"The great shaman cured the chief of sorcery," To-Cop says to me in English. I did not respond, but To-Cop went on. "I've not seen my uncle, but I am sure he'd want to speak with you of the secret knowledge of shamans."

"Your uncle?" says I.

"Copper Dancer," says he. "I wonder where my uncle is. Sometimes the wilderness takes a man."

"Sometimes it don't," I says. "He'll be back with time. I know it."

To-Cop walked up and down alongside my canoe. "Killer whale at your prow," he says. "Strong totem." Then he tells me he works for the mission.

"I see the cross you wear."

"But my blood is of the people," says he. I tell him how I witnessed that today at the ritual. I could see he wondered at my implication by that. He looked as if his head was fair being boiled by his anger. I wondered if he was gearing up for some physical assault on me. But instead he turned away and walked off.

"I read your book," he says over his shoulder. "I did not enjoy it."

To-Cop, Copper Dancer, and Inviter, the three of them waiting outside the courthouse to view their revenge as it will be played out upon me. The chieftain, Big Mountain, was back in his village. Him, what had refused to help me in my time of need—though in that I do not blame him. This suit of armour I had been packing and writing on the very day David did come back to me dead, and what Francine had posted onto a steamer south, after I was gone into the wilderness.

So I was alone, but for old Charley. I spoke now to him: told him to cease his spitting upon the steps. "We're in midst of the civilized," says I, but he don't look overly impressed.

To-Cop called across to me then. "I hope that is a bible you are holding, Mr. Hunt," says he. I turned the book over what I had in my hands, to look at its front cover. "And if it is, I hope you may find some solution in its pages."

To-Cop. What should I make of this man: proud, filled with the belief in his superior position? With his bowl-cut hair, still in the style it must have been when he were a boy in the mission school. Yet, as well, a willing participant in the pagan ritual for which I stood accused. Participant, and also chief prosecution witness! And now beating down on me with his Christian sermonizing. What could I comprehend of such two-facedness? Such deception? But he stood there glaring over at me and there weren't a shred of self-doubt in him, his eyes glowing fire—the bright flames of his most true belief. It didn't make no sense at all.

Well, there ain't nothing of sense to any of it, excepting when I sees his relatives what I wronged beside him—relatives what is practitioners of black arts of sorcery which the Christian church does most heavily frown upon, and which To-Cop would have been raised in the mission school to despise.

But not so. There he stands, carrying both parts inside hisself and without a faltering shadow to be seen.

So, then, did I understand that beliefs ain't more than the uses to which they is put. Circumstance is all. And what of circumstance? What drives a man whilst he is caught up in the complications of the moment? Well, it ain't no higher sanctity, of that I was certain, looking on To-Cop.

Beliefs, they mould theirselves to circumstance. And so does our character do the same—our very nature, perhaps. Like a sandbar in shallow water. Each time the tide rolls back, it is the same sand, but in different shapes, different forms. That's all there is. And it ain't about there being monsters or otherwise. It ain't the truth of monsters. It is the wilderness itself. We are the wilderness.

Could we be more than that? I wondered at it, there on the steps, my fate like a sparrow in the beak of a raven. Could belief be such that it was stronger to resist the tide of circumstance? Weren't that the ways of the great man—the man what changes worlds?

To-Cop had said he hoped I might find solution in the book I held in my hands. "I believe I have done so," I speaks over to him by return.

"Though it will not save you from the consequences of your crimes," says he.

I turned the book over and over in my hands, thinking on his words.

"It may yet," says I at last, though quietly enough that he could not have heard.

I opened the book to the title page. I ran my fingers across its text. Then I closed it up once more and waited on Bowser's arrival.

Fact is, we weren't the only ones what was stood about on those steps. For my trial had caused quite a stir, it seemed, and many had come to be in the viewers' gallery inside. Come to view a real-life cannibal, I imagine. They must have been reading the morning newspapers, for there hadn't been more than a few reporters present the day prior. I had seen the newspaper headlines that morning—"Disgusting Orgies," "Human Bodies Were Consumed," "Corpses Being Cut Up." Oh, but it was juicy material!

Inside—as we all did file in together—the court's furniture and fittings was constructed of dark wood, polished and polished till they shone in the light what come in through the many tall windows. Me and Bowser was up front with Mr. Cane the prosecutor on our right. What I was feeling—sitting there that second morning with all the eyes of the white world upon me, a sense, in the rustle and buzz of the courtroom, almost of festival, of public entertainments being performed—what I was feeling, before the judge and jury did come in, was mostly excitement. Something akin to jubilation even. Elation—that is the word for it. My pulse throbbed. My breathing came short, like I'd been a hard few hours paddling. A thin gloss of sweat was upon my skin. Let these people come to watch, I was thinking. Let them see the man I am! Let them fear the forest—the wilds—and what goes on out there. It seemed almost a disappointment to be fighting against the stories what had been told by To-Cop and the prosecution the day before, to be working to disavow these people of their most succulent fascinations.

"All rise!" came the call and we was on our feet for the judge and jury. The jury lined up to one side. They was all stiff collars, tight suits, and smartly crafted moustaches. But I could see they was caught up like everyone else there in the pure salivating grotesquery of the case.

Well, Inviter and Copper Dancer was first up to give witness. They was translated by the interpreter—a breed out of Victoria and none too certain in his comprehension. Still, there wasn't much as was new to hear. They scowled a bit at me and caused enough stirs with their grim fantasies on my hacking, chopping ways, to add to To-Cop's from the day before, as did keep the gallery gasping and amused. Then Mr. Cane made a summation of all those vile lies and so, at last, he rested the prosecution.

Now Mr. Bowser stood up and walked out into the centre of the courtroom to make his statements.

"Our case will consist of a complete refutation of those stories told by the Crown," says he, his manner so soft you might almost imagine he was discussing the planting of flowers in his garden. "We will state that Mr. Hunt was the victim of a vindictive trap set by To-Cop and these other witnesses, all of whom it will be noted are members of To-Cop's immediate family."

He stepped over and he lifted my book from off the table in front of me. "I will show," he says, and at last the volume of his voice rose some, "that Mr. Hunt, far from being the brutal, cannibal savage portrayed, is in fact a man of science. He was no more than a spectator that day and, even when called upon, did nothing more than observe the actions of the ritual. Which ritual, we also allege, was in fact a pantomime, and no human corpse was even involved."

Well, he called old Charley first to the stand. Laughter played through the crowd at this gargoyle clown as he waddled across the floor to the witness chair. The interpreter translated for him. He stated clear enough that there was nothing but the meat of a deer at the ceremony, and I didn't even go near to that. Mr. Cane don't bother with cross-examining him. "No questions," says he, but he played funny to the jury, raising his eyes up to heaven as if to say, "Look at this monster before us! Can any of you believe such a man?" At least Charley left off from leering at anyone.

So then it comes to me. Here he is at last! The real monster. The cannibal. Here before our very eyes! A real live consumer of human flesh.

Throw him a missionary. Watch him heat the pot. I didn't give two shits for any of them. I strutted cross the floor and positioned myself in the chair. I tells my name and placed my hand upon the bible to make my declarations of fidelity.

Mr. Bowser said not a word at first, just stood there, the thumb of one hand hooked in his waistcoat pocket, the other hand resting flat on our table, seeming lost in thought. That set a muttering in the gallery. But then he hefted and carried over my book. He put it in my hands.

"Mr. Hunt," says he, "would you care to open this book to the title page? Thank you. Now would you please read out to the court what is written there."

So that is what I do. "Smithsonian Institution. United States National Museum, *The Social Organization and Secret Societies of the Kwakiutl Indians*, by Franz Boas. Washington, the year eighteen hundred and ninety-seven."

"And after?" Bowser says.

"Based on personal observations and on notes made by Mr. George Hunt."

"Now please turn to the preface and read that section of the first page which is underlined."

"'The great body of facts presented here were observed and recorded by Mr. George Hunt, of Fort Rupert, British Columbia, who takes a deep interest in everything pertaining to the ethnology of the Kwakiutl Indians and to whom I am under great obligations. I am indebted to him also for explanations of ceremonials witnessed by myself, but the purport of which was difficult to understand, and for finding the Indians who were able to give explanations on certain points.'"

"Mr. Hunt," says he, "are you a cannibal?"

"I most certainly ain't."

"Are you, in fact, a man of science, an ethnographer and researcher working with other scientists, such as the famous professor Franz Boas, in the study of that people called in this book the Kwakiutl?"

"I guess I am just that," says I.

The atmosphere in the courtroom sank down with every word we spoke. I was, indeed, a most profound disappointment to all those present. I was not at all the thing. Not at all what they had come hoping to see. I was that most awful of categories: an ordinary man. Strange though it might sound to say, when Bowser did finish his examination of me, and turning to the jury, held up the book and shrugged, before walking over to place it before the judge—well, in that moment, I felt every bit as disenchanted by myself as did they.

PART IV · NEW YORK

AT EIGHT O'CLOCK THIS MORNING, Professor Boas's secretary, Miss Andrews, was waiting for me in the foyer of the hotel what they had arranged on my behalf, and where, late the night before, I had come to off the train.

She looked me up and down with a direct and a discriminating eye. "You are all I expected, Mr. Hunt," says she with a bright enough smile. She had small teeth, a wide gap between the front two. She held out her hand and I took it, a tiny bird's claw I might easily crush. Her hair was pale brown, just on the turn to grey, and drawn tight back into a bun, thin shoulders inside what looked almost a man's tan coat, with a thick ruff I saw to be the winter fur of a fox.

"How do you do?" says I, feeling a rawbone idiot, and when she asks if I did sleep well after such a trip, I tells her, "Like a babe all night," though I had not slept a wink.

"The whole continent traversed in a week!" she says. "We live in remarkable times. Still, I am become accustomed to such things, working for the professor."

I followed her through the streets. She was always a step ahead, her hands waving at some feature or other, explaining it all to me in words I couldn't hardly hear above the city's din. She shouted out for a cart to slow so that we might cross a wild street. She ordered a gang of rough, barefoot boys from our path. The tallest flipped his felt cap to her in mock salute.

The high buildings loomed to either side. All was still in shadows, though I knew the sky to be cloudless overhead after the rain in the night. Above the shop awnings, rickety old iron balconies trailed sheets and shirts and other laundry. It was as if I walked in some steep canyon what had walls all broken up by foliage.

Thick dust rose out of the many sites of construction. There was more people even than in Vancouver. From the roof of the hotel, I had seen their numbers grow in the early morning. Now they called out from the vegetable stalls they had set up along the road. Miss Andrews shook her head and laughed, undaunted, as an old woman wearing a smock out of some previous age of the world waved a cabbage in her face.

Men was smoking on the backs of carts, or rubbing down their horses with sacking, their jackets fat with grime and the sweat of their animals.

The carts was loaded with old pieces of furniture, cheap clothing, coal, lumber, basketry. Two little girls scampered past, shrieking with laughter, chasing a purple hoop as it wobbled drunken down the pavement.

Maybe it was that first experience of Vancouver which guarded my senses from the overpowering scale of this city. Such experience and the days what have followed the trial, the long hours of the past night, pacing up and down in my hotel room till I was ready to rip my way through the window to freedom, even be it five floors down to a hard end. The din and bustle of the streets seemed far away. I was rough-eyed with tiredness.

"And so we come to softer climes." We turned a corner and came into a wide thoroughfare. Motor vehicles and horse-drawn carriages of all kinds was moving down the centre of the road, the shopfronts huge, glass-fronted affairs with mannequins dressed in many fine fashions in the windows. The men and women what stared in at them wore black suits and cravats, their ladies had grand, wide-brimmed hats, white shirts, and thick, flowing skirts in different designs. "All the great and the good of our fair city," says Miss Andrews and she throws me a look what I might name as ironical.

We arrived to a heavy door at the corner of a massive building. "The back entrance," says she, "though not, I assure you, the tradesmen's."

We passed down several corridors. "A maze for swallowing the wayward," Miss Andrews says. At last we came to a small anteroom, windowless, lined with cabinets all about—"My lair!"—and then I was conducted straight-ways into the professor's office.

The room was strewed all about with paperwork, piles and piles in yellowing heaps, books stacked on shelves and on the floor. There was a mask of the bear on a wall, that I myself did pack and ship some years back. Two small funerary men with outsize oval heads was standing there on the desk. Boas himself was sifting through a sheaf of typewritten transcripts. His phone was ringing beside him, but he ignored it, jumped up, and I saw he was sprightly still in his thin frame, as he came round the table to greet me.

My first thought was that this was not the man I knew, that always-composed, always-smiling character I did recall so well from his visits to

Rupert. Now, his broad dome of a forehead was all cracked with tension, his small mouth thin-lipped under his thick, silver moustache.

"Yes, yes, welcome, my good friend," says he, and takes my hand most warmly, and he looked up at me with such affection that I was quite unable to respond. "So very pleased to see you here safe and well. And come so soon, after all! But I am about all sorts of things this morning. Forgive me if I am curt. We shall meet for lunch and after we can talk. I have set the whole afternoon aside for us. Dilly-dallying. Low-level politics. Oh, I am encumbered by nonsense." He clapped both hands to my shoulders, says, "Yes, yes," and turned back to answer his phone.

Miss Andrews escorted me out. She gave me five dollars and had me sign a paper chit. "Take a coffee in the museum and then wander round. Get some feeling for the place," says she.

"Miss Andrews, please!" Boas calls out. So I left her to scurry back into the professor's office, and I walked along the darkly wallpapered hall. I took a couple of turns at random, having no idea now where I was. Then, opening a door, I stood in a long gallery with high windows what was filled with artefacts entirely strange. They was boxed in glass, or hanging from the walls. *Peru*, I read, and *Mexico*.

I walked through them, trying to understand what stories they might represent—the carved heads of fanged men in flat-topped hats, skull faces like those drawn by children, skeleton figurines made out of wood and paper, and great tapestries in brilliant colours.

Then I came into this gallery what houses the artefacts of the people. And here I am. I look into those black eyes of the mannequin on which Big Mountain's suit of armour is hung, and I don't see anything at all. Not life, nor pity, nor mercy. Just the skin of wax and two glass beads.

"A magnificent piece." Boas is standing beside me, though I had not noticed his arrival. He runs his fingers along the Sisiutl. "He is coiled beneath the world and we walk upon him. May our feet tread lightly. Have you ever sent us such a treasure?"

"Did you finish already?" I says.

"It is early afternoon."

"I lost the time." I realize I am worn and hungry, my one good eye strained from squinting.

"Yes, yes," Boas says. "Come, then. We shall walk through Central Park, take lunch at the Pavilion, and you may tell me all your news." We go out through the vast main entrance. We cross the wide road out front towards the trees and the parkland on the far side. I look back at the red-tinged granite of the museum's front, at the twin towers and the turrets and, far above, the turrets' conical roofs.

"It has almost a martial air," says Boas, but I have no opinion to offer of such magnificence.

We sit at a table outside what is called the Mineral Springs Pavilion. "In the Moorish style and quite without taste of any sort," Boas says. All about us are men what speak mostly in a foreign tongue. "It is where the Germanic Jews gather. The *Times* has suggested it is akin to Kissingen or Carlsbad." Boas shakes his head. "The comparison lacks all foundation." He removes his hat and draws his fingers up across his high forehead and through his thinning hair. "Now," he says, "I am quite ready to hear your story. Will you tell me of your tribulations? In full, mind! I wish them in full."

So we eat together, and I tell him my story. At first I trip over my words and it is hard to keep a clear mind. But I am a storyteller. That, at least, I know myself to be. So my fervour rises till I speak out almost in defiance, and I see that there are those on tables nearby who eye me and speak of me. Boas takes pleasure all the more for the attention we bring, raising his eyebrows to those people who are watching, lifting up his own arms and exclaiming, beating his fist at times upon the table with relish. I speak lower when I relate that part where I did take the head of the dreamer—for I tell him all—and he leans forward and his eyes are afire, though his face stays solemn.

Eventually, the sun falls behind the great buildings that line the park. I pour the drinks down my gullet which Boas orders, hardly noticing them, Boas barely interrupting now. It is another hour still before I am done.

"I am a man of science, I was saying to myself. A brown man of science. Let them answer that. Let my prosecutors counter that." I draw long breaths. My sweat cools in the early-evening air. "And I was right, for they did acquit me."

I swing about and stretch out my legs. I think on the cold glass cases and the artefacts in the museum. The peoples' lives froze out of time, like swift-fading photographs, worn now at their edges and curling yellow, gleaning nothing but dust from the furious motion of the world.

I draw up my eye patch, open that bad eye and close the other, and then I do the same in reverse, and again. Sheep are grazing in the small meadow out front, ridiculous with the grand towers of the city behind. Through my bad eye, the sheep are phantoms, the light inverted so that dark is light and light dark, all colour drained. I fancy I can see other figures moving at the edge of my vision. I fold the eye patch down once more.

Boas lifts a tiny, thin-stemmed glass to his lips and sips at his brandy, then holds it up against the streetlights what is twinkling nearby. He turns it slowly in his fingers. "A long tale in the telling," he says, "but remarkable. Remarkable! And then you leapt straight on a train to be here."

"Charley took word back home for me. Truth is, Mr. Spencer will not give me work after all that has happened, and you are now my one sole employer. I ain't got two pennies worth rubbing and no way to come up with more. Grace and Francine make a better job of most of our affairs than I do anyhow, if but they'll curse me some for coming straight here as I did. And Harry will take care of things, once he is back home, which soon enough he'll be. They'll do well enough without me for these few months."

"You must write up all the rituals you have spoken of."

I remember the joke about Boas among the people. They don't mind him sitting there beside them taking notes, hour after hour. They don't mind when he follows them to bed. But they do mind when they wake the next morning and he's still right there, pen ready, watching their every move.

"You run, my friend," says Boas, "as deep as the end of vision. A real headhunter, here before me! I am gratified you chose to confess. My ethnological blood fair courses through my veins." He is quiet for a moment. "You can see a little through your injured eye now, then?"

"Each day more light comes into it."

"For that I am extremely pleased." He drinks down the last of his brandy. "Come!" He rises to his feet. "I've something to show you."

We pass around the sheep meadow and bear right beside a lake. The cold northerly of the earlier part of the day has gone, and it is a warm evening for the time of year.

As we walk, Boas speaks of all we have to do: developing the Northwest Coast Hall in the museum, the naming and describing of those things I have already seen. And there are countless others in the storerooms as well.

"There is a shipment from Dr. Newcombe in Victoria which I have hardly had time as yet to open, though I hear there are some magnificent items, a brilliantly carved staff of the Sisiutl among them. You may go through it first. See what it contains. And then we must edit the writings you have been sending me. I have so many questions from their reading." He throws his hands into the air and sighs affectedly. "With my teaching, my curatorial responsibilities, the journals I administer, the people I have in the field, the damnable administration and the oafs that I must deal with, it is almost beyond me sometimes to cope at all." Yet he strolls on at a leisurely pace.

"Have you had more news of your family's property that was taken?"

"No," says I. "Halliday still voices promises of their return. But I worry they've been sold on."

"Some stories take forever to conclude, and some never do, I fear," says Boas, rolling his cane in slow circles as he walks. "I shall trust for their return."

Two young women riding bicycles approach, all smiles and lace and easy laughter.

"What do you think of our city?" says Boas.

"It's a fair place. Though I wonder that people must live one on top of another, instead of side by side."

Boas snorts. "A reasonable point." He puts a hand to my shoulder. "You and I, we stroll here at the very heart of the modern world." He speaks with a certain mockery. But yet there is fire in his voice. "Along the aisles of the great Church of Reason itself, if you like."

"Well," I says, "seems I have joined the congregation of that church." But to that, Boas makes no answer.

We have come now to a wider thoroughfare with formal trees along its edge. Here, high-backed victorias with high-trotting horses parade up and down the lamplit promenade, their occupants bundled in fur collars and high hats against the cold.

We pass by an iron-cast bandstand around which is gathered a few old men and women, perched on the chairs what have been made available there. A poorer-looking woman with a shawl about her head smokes a pipe. Some ragged men are here and there stretched out on the grass, or sitting with their backs against the trees, chewing and spitting tobacco juice upon the ground. Two shabby boys dig dandelions in a flowerbed, until a police officer in a tall hat, swinging a billy club, shouts for them to clear off.

Further along, we wait whilst a boy of maybe twelve steers a miniature carriage pulled by a team of goats. Two well-dressed children sit within. An overweight woman, dowdy in black, follows, breathing heavy, despite the slow tread of the goats.

We come to the end of the boulevard. Here there is high wire fencing, and a sign above a turnstile reads *New York City Zoo*.

Boas says, "We must visit the chimpanzees. But some other day." He points forward. "Now, here we are."

We are standing at the edge of a small field which borders on the park. Across the wide road at its far side is a huge construction site, where a building rises up already fifteen storeys or more, clad all about in wooden scaffolding, great booms of hammer blows, men crying out, roiling clouds rising from the whole into the evening sky as if the very stone is sweating in its labours.

On the field itself is placed a marquee coloured in orange and yellow and blue, thirty feet tall, and twice that in length. A banner strung above its entrance proclaims *The Fabulous Circus of Grotesquery*, and beneath is written *The Greatest Cornucopia of Human Freaks That Ever Was Brought Together, and Other of the Strangest Oddities from All Around the World*.

A man stands upon a dais outside in a top hat and a bow tie, with a long-tailed coat. He is grizzled in appearance, as if once he might have been a prizefighter. He holds to a chain that is strung about the neck of a shaggy woman beside him.

"Step along now, friends. You never saw more hideous wonders. Worse even than the terrible wild woman I is but barely clinging to the restraints hereof." The woman takes a dutiful step away so the chain tightens. "Twenty-five cents will purchase you such primordial *awe* as you ain't never saw *before*." He holds his arm high in the air and waves his finger behind him as he speaks. "Here ... in this un-hallowed home to human horror!"

"I saw, in this regrettable place, that which may indeed make you wonder," Boas says. "If only for a time."

When first I see the shaggy woman, I cannot properly comprehend what I am looking at. She is so lofty and thick set, so completely hairy over all her body, with a long beard what sweeps down off her face, that I only know her to be female by the heavy, swinging tits inside the ragged material of her shift, and by the words the carnival talker speaks. I stare like some hayseed idiot. I see a lumbering female figure in the forests of my childhood nightmares.

Boas pays and we walk on inside the tent. I wonder then if I have fallen into some vision, or if I lie still in my hotel and all the day so far has been a dream, or the drumming of the train on its route across the continent has drawn me off into sleep again. Or, yet, if I have left my home at all to travel so far and come to this place, in the middle of this park, in this city at the very centre of the world.

The ground is covered in sawdust and straw, so it feels as if I walk on thick grass, or on a pillow, each footstep sinking a little as I follow Boas forward. Two great chandeliers hang from the roof of the tent, each of them composed of many oil lamps. They cast an unreliable light on to the platforms what run down each side of the central walkway. On some of these are cages. On others, figures stand like statues or perform their chosen exhibition. There is the smell of old sweat and of something sugary and rotten. People walk among the exhibits much as I did see them in the museum, careless, speaking, so it seems, of other things.

291

On the first platform, a white man with tight-curling black hair and a proud face sits in a chair. He wears a black jacket with a high starched collar to his white shirt, and a pressed silk cravat. He has no arms nor legs. His feet come out directly from the short trousers he is wearing. The webs between each toe stretch as far as the toenails, so that they look more like flippers than they do feet. A young woman crouches beside him and wipes spittle from the corner of his mouth. He stares off into the air, unmoving, seeming not to take account of anything about him.

Glass jars are laid out on a table. Inside, the fetuses of animals float in yellow liquid, but they are twisted in deformity—heads tilted hopelessly sidewards, limbs folding one into another, spines bent almost double. I make to tap one of the jars.

"Don't be touching the hexi-bid-it-ets! They's precious, see you." I look down and there beside the table is a boy, not two feet high, dressed in tie and jacket, standing with his hands at his waist and glaring black blades up at me.

On the stage behind him, a Chinese goliath raises his arms wide, his thick robes billowing out like great curtains in a gust from an open window. He sings in his own tongue, but his voice is like a child's, like a bird's. The long, oiled corners of his moustache twitch and shiver.

The sign beside the next platform reads *Tree Man*. The backdrop is of a thick forest, and a form what seems human leans against it, in shadow. I see two legs, but they are thick and malformed. A hand reaches out to pick something from a small table. The arm is festooned in half-formed branchlets, with clusters of seedpods dangling beneath. A match flares in front of its face. The end of a cigarette burns. For an instant I see the body has, all across it, bulbous growths from which the skin hangs in globs and corms, pink and black and pustulous. Eyes, as I see them reflecting the glowing cigarette, stare straight into my own. They are filled with loathing.

I turn swiftly away as a hand touches my arm. "But here," Boas says, whispering in my ear, as if we walk in some holy space. "Come and see." We move towards a small pen.

The floor is covered in straw. Fronds stand in small pots, and there are two heavy, warped logs. Powerful coils twine about the logs and through the straw. They are coloured a deep emerald green, and black lines criss-cross along their length.

Boas whispers, "See!" He points.

The snake's broad, flat face and jaws, near a foot wide, rest upon one loop of its body. Its eyes are twin black mirrors with a million stars in them what are the lantern lights reflected. At that place where its tail should be, another head faces the first, exactly matching, mottled green and with black arrow marks upon it. It is entirely still, except where both mouths flick split tongues towards each other.

"We walk upon its back," Boas whispers in my ear. "May our feet tread lightly."

I stumble away between the exhibits, my hands at my face. I wrench up my eye patch and now before me is the final exhibit. *Wild Man* reads the sign. Some thing squats low on its haunches, its hair long and so thickly matted it spears up in high, dense clumps like reeds by water. It wears only a cloth across its private parts. It leaps and tugs at the strong leather belt about its waist and the chain attached to it what runs down to a rivet on the platform. It rages, cries out in grunts that have no language. Its nails are long enough to be talons. It glares down directly at me. Its eyes are black. It lunges forward and, when it pulls back its lips into a snarl, scarce a foot from my face, its teeth are filed to sharp-pointed fangs.

I see black eyes in the wilderness. Whirl and bite and shroud of leaves. It is not tamed. It must be fought. Fought with hands and teeth. In the dank gloom of the forest. The buildings of New York are the trunks of great trees. They soar upwards till they are lost in cloud. All of it—forest, city, the world entire—rears high above me now.

I see my son, David, alive, dancing his first hamatsa ceremony, panting after, his thick hair flat with sweat across his forehead where the mask was placed, his hands on his knees, gasping, exhausted, laughing, men around him, pounding his shoulders, laughing with him.

Harry lies by the flames, white face, unconscious, the great hole in his shoulder, the well of blood inside. I sing the sacred song. I know the plants what are the antiseptics of the forest. I understand the cleaning of wounds.

293

And I know his dark thoughts, his despair, even as I clutch hold of his belief. I draw out the corruption from him.

My eyes boil. The tears come to me at last and I weep. My rage is my grief. I hear myself like a dying animal.

I am in the forest, the place I know. But the huge trunks of cedar are the pillars of granite outside the museum. They rear up around me, shaggy, draped in moss, old, hoary men who mutter and grumble and are ponderous, but carry slow murder in their hearts. Moonlight slits through the canopy. Everywhere, the shadows twist and wander. Salal fronds wind up around my thighs, till I must wade through them like a churning tide. I smell the mould-reek of the forest floor, taste the sweet dust of the multitude of spores what ride the air. The Chinese giant's childlike song coils among the trees. There are masks hanging on all the granite pillar tree trunks. There are bear and wolf and killer whale, Hoxhok and thunderbird, sparrow and raven. The wood from which they are carved is become supple. Their black- and red- and white-painted features squirm. Their mouths open and close as if they are just now learning that such actions may be possible. On the ground, I see the fetuses of animals. I see smashed glass. A seal flashes past, so close I must duck to avoid it, though it is already gone, just its flipper, looking almost like a foot, brushes my cheek.

Now I notice how the light is not the weak light of lanterns swinging overhead, nor the glow of the city night. Instead, it is a flaming sunlight. I look out. A killer whale sounds on the waters of the Pacific. The jewelled surface of the sunlit ocean stretches away and I am floating on it, the cool ripples at my skin. There is no land in any direction. The whale's spume flies up, those great lungs exploding like the retort in a cannery. Its dorsal fin quivers. Its flukes climb over me, before it slides back under the water, making not a sound as it goes away into the deeps. I could follow it down till I am again between the high fronds of kelp that dance in the shadows of the ocean. There is peace in the dark places. There is an ending to things. So I might believe it.

Instead, I close my eyes. At last, the light through my lids grows darker, my grief grows less, and, when I open my eyes again, I am standing just inside the exit from the marquee, where a corner of the tent is lifted up and tied off. New York burns amber in the street lamps.

.

In 1900 a man was committed for trial at the Vancouver assizes for cannibalism, and although there was no doubt of his guilt, the jury acquitted him on the ground that they thought it was impossible for the evidence to be true.

William Halliday, *Potlatch and Totem: The Recollections of an Indian Agent* (1935)

ACKNOWLEDGMENTS

My first acknowledgment is to George Hunt, whose life and writings have impelled me forward these many years. That said, I have nonetheless chosen to play merry havoc with the facts of his life, in order to come at the truth of this fiction of mine. I have conflated certain elements of his biography, separated by many years, into one short period. I have manipulated his family tree to suit my own ends, and been more reckless still with others who appear in the novel—Harry Cadwallader in particular. *The Cannibal Spirit* is a work of fiction and must be considered so.

After many years of research, I am indebted to numerous writers for their work on Hunt and on the Northwest Coast (though they must bear no responsibility for my errors). They include Franz Boas (of course), Douglas Cole, Ira Chaiken, Alda Jonaitis, Ira Jacknis, George Quimby, Bill Holm, Robert Galois, Jeanne Cannizzo, Edward Curtis, Marius Barbeau, Gloria Cranmer Webster, and, especially, Judith Berman.

Many people have helped me. Roland Littlewood and Murray Last encouraged me at the beginning. University College London and the Wingate Scholarship funded aspects of my research. The American Philosophical Society, the American Museum of Natural History, the Royal British Columbia Museum, the University of British Columbia, and the British Library were all of great assistance, allowing me access to archives and other primary source materials. Julia Bell, Nii Ayikwei Parkes, Fran Merivale, Mariko Iwasaki, Katie Morris, and Niki Aguirre helped me learn to write (with similar caveats to those above). Later, Jo Baker, Graham Mort, and Alison Macleod read my manuscript and made important suggestions. Dr. Jeremy Pfeffer said, "It's the trial—aha!" Tom Geens had several inspired insights, and the story would be much diminished without them. Lee Horsley has been a constant support; she possesses the coolest eye. Jane Haynes has kept me alive these past years, and I owe her a great debt.

Shaun Oakey is a copyeditor without equal. At Penguin, Nick Garrison saw what others didn't and played a faultless hand from start to finish. Lapidary indeed …

My agent, Isobel Dixon, put her name and her ceaseless enthusiasm behind me, and I won't forget it.

George Green made me believe I could begin, and then guided me through all the long years to this novel's conclusion. The best friend and mentor I could imagine.

Finally, Anita Sivakumaran has harassed, poked, sighed, tapped sharp nails on desktops, remorselessly bullied me from beginning to end. She is the reason I plunged in, the reason I soldiered on, and the reason I had the daring to write those awful, arrogant words *The End*. Magnificent muse, fearsome editor—this book is for her.